Sarah Dunant is the ....
winner of the Silv..................................
commentator, she wa...
the BBC's *The Late S*..
the Words and, with Roy Porter, *The Age of Anxiety*.
Virago also publish Sarah Dunant's first novel, *Snow
Storms in a Hot Climate*.

Titles by Sarah Dunant

Novels
Snow Storms in a Hot Climate
Birth Marks
Fatlands
Under My Skin

Non-Fiction
The War of the Words: The Political Correctness
Debate (edited)
Age of Anxiety (co-edited with Roy Porter)

Transgressions

Sarah Dunant

A *Warner* Book

First published in Great Britain by
Virago Press 1997
This edition published by Warner Books in 1998

Copyright © Sarah Dunant 1997

Acknowledgements on p.377 constitute an extension of this
copyright page

The moral right of the author has been asserted.

All rights reserved.
No part of this publication may be reproduced,
stored in a retrieval system, or transmitted in any form
or by any means, without the prior permission in writing
of the publisher, nor be otherwise circulated in any form
of binding or cover other than that in which it is published and
without a similar condition including this condition being
imposed on the subsequent purchaser.

A CIP catalogue record for this book
is available from the British Library.

ISBN 0 7515 2283 X

Typeset by Solidus (Bristol) Ltd
Printed and bound in Great Britain by
Clays Ltd, St Ives plc

Warner
A Division of
Little, Brown and Company (UK)
Brettenham House
Lancaster Place
London WC2E 7EN

Transgressions

one

It first started four months after she had separated from Tom, although at the time, of course, she didn't think of it as 'It'. At the time, it was simply the morning when she walked into the kitchen and couldn't find the Van Morrison CD. She hadn't given it much thought then, just flicked her way through the rack and chosen something else.

But over the coming weeks she had missed the album. Called 'Enlightenment', it was recorded at the turn of the Nineties (years that seemed to have passed her by musically) and had a great opening track that roared out of the speakers, high and sassy, suggesting that there might indeed be life after the end of a failed relationship. In those scorching high-summer days when there was so much sun that even the plants were calling for mercy, it had become a kind of anthem for her, offering a vision of a future which she couldn't quite let herself believe in.

It had been her custom to play it first thing in the morning, as she opened up the French windows onto the garden and laid breakfast for herself on the slowly yellowing lawn. The day after Tom had moved out, taking his half of the kitchen with him, she had gone to the local department store and bought a whole set of absurd, brightly coloured plates and breakfast cups and a shiny black cappuccino maker, stylish, very Italian. It had taken her a while to fathom the instructions – she was one of those independent women who nevertheless left the electronic part of her life to whichever man was in it at the time – but once she had mastered it she was able to conjure up fabulous cupfuls of frothy coffee which she sat on the lawn sipping luxuriously, and which left thick white moustaches on her upper lip. There was, of course, no one to lick them off. Not that she minded that. On the contrary. After so long living in the shadow of a slow death, she felt a quiet, almost triumphant sense of release.

Still, she missed the Van Morrison. There were other albums of his she could have played, but they all came from different parts of her life, fragments of a musical autobiography that pre-dated Tom, and were therefore so long ago now that it was hard to remember they had happened to the same person. The pleasure of this album was that it felt new to who she was now. It had come the same week as the breakfast set, along with a brooding, melancholic version of Leonard Cohen songs sung by an American singer called Jennifer Warnes with a voice like raw silk, flaws and all.

This new music became a kind of benchmark of her progress. One day when she was in the car, 'The Famous Blue Raincoat' turned up to top volume, she imagined herself hearing it again in a couple of years' time, when the emotional landscape was different, and saying to herself 'Ah yes, that was one of the records I split up with Tom to', as if the act had been just another event in a life unfolding and not the end of it, as it so often felt now.

So much did she miss the Van Morrison that after a week or so she began a systematic search, taking down every CD from the shelf and checking it, to see if Van had somehow bedded himself down with Morrissey or Bryan Ferry by mistake. But the shiny little disc was nowhere to be found. It puzzled rather than worried her. She wondered briefly about Tom. Maybe he had appropriated it during one of his lightning raids on the house.

The atmosphere around the split-up had been so acrimonious that for a while it had seemed impossible for them to be in the same place together at the same time. It was agreed that anything he needed he would take while she was out. He sent her notes: painful, formal little lists decorated by unpleasant remarks, detailing what and when. The 'when' he honoured, the 'what' proved more problematic. In those first months she would often find herself looking for a certain plate or book, only to find that it had gone walkabout. Of course, some of these things were genuinely theirs, rather than his or hers; seven years of shared life made it hard even for her to remember what exactly belonged to whom. But that album, she knew, was hers. He didn't even like Van Morrison, for God's sake. She had thought about contacting him to check, but four months on it still felt too soon to hear his voice again. He might be tempted to read it as her finding an excuse to get in touch, and she couldn't bear the idea of feeling vulnerable to his arrogance. Not yet. Not any more. After a while she assumed she had simply mislaid the disc somewhere. She got used to not hearing the music and forgot all about it.

Towards the end of the summer, she went to New York for a couple of days' work, staying at a hotel on the edge of Central Park. She had been looking forward to the trip, her first as a single woman again, had even extended it by a few days to include the weekend. But when the time came she found herself inexplicably depressed by it. The city was rank, exhausted by the summer's heat, and the work dull. On the second evening she left the hotel for a stroll down Broadway, but the swelter left her dripping by the fourth block and she escaped instead into Tower Records, where the air was second-hand but bearable and the music, by chance, Van Morrison.

It was a live double album recorded in San Francisco in 1993, proof that he had not only survived the Eighties intact, but had managed to draw some creativity from the decade. She bought it instantly, along with another earlier concert album – 'Live at Belfast City Hall' – and a replacement for the one she had lost earlier. Once she'd started riffling through the racks, she found she couldn't stop. The Czech publishing company that had sent her to help run its trade fair had given her three days' expenses in hand. She spent it all in the next twenty minutes, exploring the back-lists, buying up bands she had once danced or sung along to, but could never be bothered to replace with CDs because they were too expensive and she would only ever be able to play them when Tom was out. In retrospect she wondered if their musical incompatibility hadn't been the source of all evil: what hope could there ever be for a rock'n'roll girl and a classical lover? The thought returned to her now as she defiantly picked out half a dozen new bands she had barely heard of, let alone listened to. New music for a new life. On her way back to the hotel she stopped by an electrical store and bought a portable CD player on her Barclaycard just for the hell of it.

She spent the rest of her trip curled up in bed, channel flicking on the TV with the sound down and the headphones on, the music feeling more real than the place.

When she got home, the summer was on the wane, and it wasn't long before she had to wear a sweater for her breakfasts outside. Still she persisted. The music went with her, pounding out from the French windows, louder now, less melancholic. Luckily, thanks to the capriciousness of Victorian suburban planning, hers and the gardens around hers were large, offering a version of urban privacy, the neighbours either too far away or too lazy to complain. Maybe after so many serious symphonies they enjoyed the change of music.

The sounds moved her feet as well as her mind. She bopped to Bruce Springsteen and Bob Seger as she deadheaded the roses and weeded the ground elder from between the dahlias, while inside she cleaned the kitchen to the beat of Counting Crows, Radiohead and a handful of other new bands whose songs were becoming familiar enough for her to sing the words to. It was, she realised, a long time since she had heard so much of her own voice. It still surprised her that such a confident sound should emerge out of such an otherwise shy personality.

It struck her that all this singing might mean, perhaps, that she was happy, but the word didn't seem to carry any meaning, and despite the music she would still have days where she would wake at four a.m. feeling as if the world had ended during the night and she was the only one left alive to mourn it.

Seven and a half years. Too long for an affair, too short for a lifetime. The question of who she was now remained unanswered.

Maybe it would have been easier if she *had* seen Tom again, to remind herself of what she had escaped from. But although she had a number for him (he had fallen on his feet – a work colleague had got a post in Saudi and left a bachelor apartment in the Barbican needing a new tenant) she never rang it. And he never called her. Friends of friends told her he was doing fine; busy, looking good. Did that mean he never thought of her, never missed her at all? Did she miss him? Yes, was the honest answer to that, sometimes, even though the last eighteen months with him had been increasingly unbearable; the rows moving from voice into violence with long frozen truces in between.

The corroding of emotion had already infected the sex, or what remained of it. For a while it had made it almost exciting; angrier, more selfish on both sides, providing a sense of novelty in an otherwise tired formula. But it also held seeds of a contempt which in the end would have poisoned them both. They both understood that, but it was she who had rebelled first, putting a stop to their mutual destruction. His withdrawal was so immediate, so complete, that it made her wonder if he had ever been there at all. Abstinence brought its own tension, which neither of them chose to talk about. Add it to the list of unfinished business. Maybe without her he would fuck differently; playful, creative, curious, the way they used to be a million years ago. Maybe she would too.

Not that she could imagine it. She didn't miss the sex. On the contrary, she rather relished her celibacy. She enjoyed the new expanse of the bed and its cool empty spaces. It was part of a deeper enjoyment of the intimacy of being alone. She would spend long hours in the bathroom, a woman at her toilet; crimping, waxing, creaming and pampering a body which was not to be seen by anyone but her. It was like being a teenager again, the pleasure being in the indulgence, cut off from any threat of disillusionment by reality.

Only very occasionally did her body betray her. One night, a few weeks before her trip to New York, she had the fiercest, most unexpected of erotic dreams: an old lover in a motel room on the edge of a desert, taunting, denying her, then finally giving. She woke in a sweat of desire, scared half to death by the power of the feeling; the power and the vulnerability that it exposed.

She had missed the Van Morrison album more than ever that morning. My, how that man could make love with his voice; the long, slow sensuous kind, rather than the wham-bam pelvic thrust she had become used to in the last days of the destructive rutting match with Tom.

She had opened the windows and stood on the grass, cradling her mug of frothy coffee against her body, enjoying the solitude and, for once, the quiet. Across the long expanse of gardens was a jigsaw puzzle of high Victorian windows and rooftops. The city was full of people she didn't know and would probably never meet. The anonymity of it all, of herself within it, was surprisingly exciting. It gave an edge to her loneliness. For a few days she even found herself looking at men again, wondering what they would be like in bed, if they in turn might fancy her. But it took a lot of energy, pushing her thoughts outwards, and by the time she got on the plane to New York her interest had faded.

Back home she made a last stab at conviviality. She threw a dinner party, going through her address book and inviting seven people including a spare man – a friend of a friend – to even the numbers. She cooked all day and laid a *Good Housekeeping* table. They came, ate, talked and left. Two of them wrote notes saying how lovely an evening it had been. She was depressed for days afterwards.

Towards the end of October it became, finally, too cold to breakfast outside. The French windows were closed up and it was only the squirrels and the cat who did any gardening, Millie scratching up the bulbs with her claws or standing in the middle of the lawn in endless stand-off with a sleek black tom that had taken to stalking her territory, green-eyed and taunting.

She stood behind the glass watching it all from inside. She didn't mind. She still played the music, staring out as the rain rolled in, but she had other concerns now. One of the publishing houses that she translated for had just arrived back from the Frankfurt Book Fair with a hard-boiled thriller by a new Czech writer, and they were in a panic to get it translated because there was movie interest in the synopsis, with names like Brad Pitt and Irene Jacobs being bandied about. She had read it some months before – the tale of a New York cop brought in to bust a Mafia drugs ring in the East – and though she had reservations about its originality she'd decided to take it on anyway, partly because they made her an offer she couldn't refuse and partly because living in another language would force her to live less in herself, or at least the self that she associated with Tom.

She upgraded her hard disk and bought a slang dictionary to mark the occasion. The novel was long, an Eastern European attempt at a blockbuster, and its translation would take her the rest of the year and into the new one. Why not? She had nothing better to do with her life. When this is finished, she told herself, I'll be ready; I'll emerge like a butterfly from a cocoon, transformed, reborn, ready to take on the world.

She bought a bottle of champagne to mark the beginning of her confinement. At 6.30 on the first evening, with the light already fading in readiness for winter, she went down to the kitchen to open it. She had been playing the Morrison San Francisco double album almost constantly that week; a good way to prepare her for translation, appreciating how some-one else could make words dance. But when she pushed the button to start the music, nothing happened. She pushed it again, then opened up the machine only to discover that the CD wasn't in it. Surely she had had it in the machine that morning? She certainly hadn't played anything else, and the case was still sitting there by the side. She checked inside. The second disc was in its place safely at the back, but the other one, the one she'd been playing, was not. Neither was it anywhere on the work top nor on the rack above.

As she searched further, the cat-flap snapped open

and Millie streaked in like a bat out of hell, trying, too late, to look dignified and victorious. On the lawn, twenty yards away from the doors, the big black tom-cat was poised, stock-still, staring in silent triumph. She went up and hammered on the French windows. It stood its ground, then drew back its ears, turned and sauntered lazily away. Millie curled herself round her owner's legs, yowling, eager for affection. 'Come on, girl,' she muttered. 'It's your garden. Don't let some man get the upper hand.'

She went back to her search. But the longer she looked the more obvious it became that the disc wasn't there. It didn't make sense. It had been in the machine, now it was gone. If she hadn't taken it out, then who had? With the exception of an hour or so in the middle of the day when she'd gone out for a swim and to buy the champagne, she had been in the house all the time.

It was then, for the first time in months, that she remembered the other Van Morrison album and its equally sudden disappearance. And it was then also that she began to wonder seriously about her ex-lover.

'But why? What could he possibly gain from it? Anyway, I thought he only liked classical stuff.'

'He does.'

'So?'

'So, the answer is, I don't know.'

'But you think it's him?'

'I don't know. What do you think?'

'I think you probably mislaid it somewhere.'

'Not "it". Them. And I've looked, and I didn't.'

'So was anything else missing? Anything valuable?'

'No, nothing. I checked.'

'Well, if it *is* him, it's a rather subtle way to go about getting to you. I would have expected something more direct from Tom, mean bastard.'

'Is he?' she said, surprised.

Sally laughed. 'Sweetheart, you know he is. God, when you two were together you couldn't get through an evening without him bitching at you, undermining you in a dozen different ways. He didn't want a lover, he wanted an acolyte. It was OK while you fitted the role, but as soon as you didn't ... Patrick and I would talk about it afterwards.'

How strange, she thought. All those years we were together nobody thought to mention how ill-suited we were. Now people can't stop telling me. She sat across the table, watching Sally dissect a lettuce leaf as if it were a cadaver. But then, of course, she had never told Sally what she really thought of Patrick. Better not to on balance. 'What? ... Sorry?'

'I said, does he still have a key?'

'Er ... yes. He was moving stuff out and then I never bothered to ask for it back.'

'Hmmmn.'

'Hmmmn, nothing, Sally. I just forgot, that's all.'

'Yes, well, if I were you I'd ask for it now.'

'I will.' She buried her impatience and called to the waitress, making signs for the bill. When she turned back Sally's face was a study in concern.

'It's a big house, you know, sweetie, easy to get spooked in. I wouldn't want to live there alone. Patrick thinks you should sell it. You could do it, even in this market. He knows someone who could get you a good price.'

'I'm sure he does. But I don't want to sell.'

'No, well, we won't talk about it ... How's the book?'

'Long.' She left a pause. Then took pity on her. 'But good.'

'Hmmn. Can I say something to you?'

She smiled mildly. 'I think you already are.'

'It's just I don't think you're helping yourself, that's all.'

'Why? How?'

'Burying yourself away in that mansion with just a computer and a cat for company. You'll go stale. Lose all the juice in you, or whatever Tom left after he did his own bit of squeezing. I think you should make an effort to get back into the real world, get out more, meet people, give yourself a chance.'

She nodded. 'I know you do, Sal. But I'm not you. This is my way and it works for me.'

'Yes, well ...' She lifted up her hand to acknowledge failure, then turned it into an extravagant gesture to attract the waitress. This time the bill came. To make Sally feel better she let her buy the lunch. Poor Sal. Always needing people to need her. Presumably that had something to do with the fact that Patrick didn't. 'So I expect this means you're saying no to Saturday night? I have it on good authority that this guy is very nice.'

'I'm sure he is, but I'm just getting into the flow.'

'What, weekends as well?'

'You know me.'

'Yes, unfortunately I do. How about next month?'

'Maybe.'

'All right, all right. I've said my bit. But you be

careful. Remember, the further you burrow in, the
further there is to crawl back out from again.'

'I'll keep it in mind. Thanks.'

Back home she unpacked the chocolate cake that
Sally had insisted on buying her at the counter ('If you
can't have fun with someone else, then have some fun
with yourself. God knows you could do with a few
calories') and cut herself a slice to go with her
cappuccino. Interesting, what other people think of
you. So, according to the rest of the world, it was Tom
who was the aggressor and she who was the victim.
Presumably that was how it had looked from the outside. Except it didn't square with her vision of herself.
Sure, he made more of a show of himself, talked longer
and louder, expressed more opinions. But half the time
they hadn't been worth listening to. Certainly not
worth competing with. The thought shocked her. Had
she really thought that about the man she'd lived with
for nearly eight years?

Apparently, yes. She went up to the CD rack and
flicked through the shiny line of titles, looking for
something to make her feel better. In the end she went
for comfort music and the camp eroticism of early Lou
Reed schmoozed its way into the room. 'Walk on the
Wild Side'. If only she could.

She thought, not for the first time in her life, how
wonderful it must be to be a musician, to be able to say
it all without having to say it to anyone in particular.
Alas, she couldn't do it. Being able to sing was only the
beginning. When she was younger her voice had been
good enough for people to suggest she do it profes-
sionally. But her talent had always been with others'

songs. She herself had had nothing to say. Or nothing she thought anyone would be interested in. Now, as a translator, she had the confidence to play with other people's words, but was still too often wrong-footed when it came to finding her own. Like literature, like life. Maybe that was what had gone wrong between her and Tom; he only talked more because she had talked less. Or maybe Sally was right. Maybe she just didn't have enough juice.

She went back to the CD problem. It was three days since the loss of the second Van Morrison and nothing further had happened to add to her suspicions. That meant two albums missing in three months. It didn't make sense. If it was Tom, then it certainly wasn't his style. Sally was right about that. Not only too subtle, but too long-winded. On the other hand, whoever had taken them (and she was certain now that they had gone) obviously hadn't broken in, and Tom was the only person who had the key. Maybe she should change the locks.

She tried to imagine him being in the house when she was out of it: standing in the kitchen, going through the CD collection deciding which one to pick, which one he thought she would miss most, then slipping the silver disc neatly into his pocket. He must have known how she would react; confused at the least if not frightened. Was he capable of that? What would be the point, except spite? Or a way of getting her to feel uneasy about the house now she was alone in it? Such was the level of blood-letting towards the end that she couldn't categorically swear it wasn't him. Well, damn him if it was. This was her home and she wasn't going anywhere, whatever the provocation.

She turned down the stereo and picked up the phone. She knew the number off by heart even though she had never called it. He had written it under the Dali Calendar picture for March and she had faithfully transferred it every month to the next page, not wanting to lose it but not wanting to accept it as important enough to put into her address book.

The phone rang once, twice, three times, then a machine picked up. His voice on the message was confident, cocky almost. I'm OK, it said, in case you might have any doubts about it. She expected to feel something when she heard it, a little scissor cut in the gut, if only from memory, but there was nothing.

'Hello,' she said firmly. 'It's me.' Then, 'I need to talk to you about something. Could you call me? I'll be in tonight.' She went to put down the receiver, then got suddenly flustered. 'That's Tuesday, Tuesday the twenty-fifth that I called.' Then, 'Thanks', as an abrupt after-thought.

She slammed the receiver down. Now, despite herself, she could feel her heart thumping louder. Come on, girl, she thought, you did just fine.

She made herself another cup of coffee and went upstairs to work.

two

The saucepan boiled over, filling the room with hissing smoke. Jake swore as he flung down the magazine and made a dash for the stove. As the pages fell, the centrefold of the woman's body spread itself out on the table, her perfect navel punctured by a couple of staples: lovely Lola, the fistful from Phoenix.

The pot was so hot he had to let it down on the edge of the table on his way to the sink. The boiling water splashed over the page and Lola's breasts wrinkled up in instant scalding. He rescued her, then, after a quick glance, tossed her into the bin. She'd never smooth out properly and anyway there was too much airbrush for his liking. He liked his women with body hair, something you could get your fingers into. He was lucky Customs hadn't opened his suitcase. What a way to start the job: American cop arrives to clean up the foreign city and gets caught carrying girlie pictures. He should have guessed. What other kind of leaving present would the boys have wrapped in brown paper?

He hooked out a strand of noodles and lifted it to his lips, then dropped it again as he realised how hot it was.

Hot and slimy. 'Fuck.' He pulled the arm of his sweat-shirt over his hand, picked up the pan and drained it into the sink, then dumped the remains on top of the girl in the bin. What a great way to spend your first night abroad: a bad porn mag and overcooked Pot Noodles in some poxy bureaucrat's apartment. Jeez, this was meant to be privileged housing. People had joined the fucking Party to get this much space. It was enough to make a guy feel sorry for himself, especially one who could still remember the taste of someone else's cooking. And the feel of her body as he reached for her in bed. Not now. Don't think of Mirka now. It was finished, shot to hell. And this was supposed to be the break: a new job, a new challenge, a blank sheet in the emotional typewriter. Just a shame it had to be her city. At least she wasn't in it.

He looked at his watch. Nine-thirty. Damn the noodles. With luck that restaurant down the road would still be serving. What the hell, if he didn't under-stand the menu he could always point at what other people were eating. A bottle of wine, some native cuisine, followed by a little night-life. He might stop in at one of the city's fancier hotel bars on the way home. Rumour was the Russian girls were on the move now, a whole new continent of talent hungry for hard currency. That's what you call free enterprise: when you can't sell your tanks you can always sell your women. If not to the natives then to the wealthy tourists.

Must have been like this after the war: Americans with their fat food parcels and GI-pay trading favours for silk stockings and bars of chocolate. Well, why not? When was the last time he'd got laid? That ditz-head dress designer he'd met at a bar on the Upper West Side. Christ, he couldn't wait to get out of that apartment, all dangling crystals and pan-pipe music. Still, it was proof that he could do it, that there were some women who still wanted him. Jake Biderman: thirty-six years old, firm butt, no paunch, a good head of hair and a cute smile when he wasn't thinking about it (or so Mirka used to say). The only damage done was the stuff on the inside. But they couldn't see that. Given the schmucks the world is full of, a lot of women would be grateful for his attentions, might even give it to him for free. Who was he fooling?

He grabbed his jacket and headed out into a warm Prague evening. Lola from Phoenix stayed sprawled out in the bin, her neatly airbrushed pubes decorated with a lattice work of Pot Noodles.

The phone rang in the darkness.

'God.' She switched on the light by the bed and screwed up her eyes to check the clock. 1.18 a.m. As soon as she picked it up she knew that it was him. Who else could it be? Bastard.

'Hi, Lizzie.'

'Hello, Tom.' The sound of his voice had her instantly on guard.

'Did I wake you?'

'No. I was cleaning the bathroom floor.' Like you never did.

'Good girl. Keeping the bugs away. So, how you doing?'

'I'm – I'm fine.'

'Good. Busy? I hear you're doing some writer a big favour, making his words sing.'

'Who told you?'

'Oh, you know, mutual friends, pretending to be nice, eager to keep me informed. No doubt you have the same problem.'

No, she thought, I don't. But then I don't ask. 'How are things with you?'

The words sounded absurd. Both of them being so polite; like talking to a stranger or an acquaintance, someone you don't know well enough yet to be familiar with. Maybe that's what they were now. Acquaintances. Intimacy dissolving back into distance, the story of a relationship gone full circle.

'Fine. I'm good. I've applied for a post in British Columbia. Going out in a couple of weeks' time for an interview. Associate professor, no less.'

'That's great. I hope you get it.'

'Yeah, well, it's all politics. As you remember.'

'Yes.'

'So, how's the house?'

'Fine.'

'I'm surprised you're still there. Must be big with just you rattling around in it.'

Me and whoever else cares to call round, she thought. There was a pause.

'Anyway,' he said. 'You phoned me?'

'Er, yes. I – I wanted to ask if I could have the key back.'

'The key?'

'Yes, Tom, the key. To the house. You've still got it.'

'Have I?' he said, in a voice that made it clear they both knew full well that he had. 'I don't remember. But if you say so I'll have a look. And if I find it I'll drop it round.'

'Don't bother, you can just post it.'

'Well, if that would make you feel better.' He paused and in the silence she could almost feel the politeness cracking under the weight of its own effort. 'You don't have to be there to receive it, you know. I could always just shove it through the letter-box.' And the word shove had a shaft of familiar anger in it.

'Whatever,' she said evenly, determined not to respond. 'Listen, have you . . . have you by any chance been here over these last few weeks?'

'What do you mean?'

'To the house. Have you come back to collect anything?'

'Why? What could you have there that I could possibly want?' he said quietly.

'I just—'

'Yes?'

'I just wondered if you had taken any of my CDs by mistake.'

'Your CDs? Which ones?'

You know which ones, you bastard, she thought. 'Van Morrison.'

'Van Morrison,' he said, treating the name as if it referred to the Pope, or someone as hallowed (or despised). I know what it is, she thought. You've been drinking. You're pissed, damn you. 'And what would I want with Van Morrison? As far as I remember he's got a voice like a cistern overflowing.'

'All right, Tom. You don't have to rise to the occasion. Just a yes or no will do.'

He was silent for a moment. 'Then the answer is no, I haven't taken your Van Morrison albums, or any other for that matter. Why? Has somebody else?'

'I don't know.' She paused.

'You mean you think you've had a burglary?'

'Er, no. I – I don't know.'

'You know you should really think of getting the police round to check the security on that house. I always said those back windows were vulnerable. Did you report it?' And the shift in mood was palpable. His voice had lost the edge. No aggression now, just a sudden concentrated concern that made you feel like you were the most important person in the world. Damn him, he could be so nice when he wanted to be. When he wanted to be . . .

'No, no, I didn't. It's nothing, only a couple of albums.'

'And you're sure you didn't just drop them in your handbag somewhere?'

'No,' she said firmly. The handbag, its size and miraculous capacity to lose everything and anything inside it, had been a long-standing joke between them, before it became a jibe. It was not meant unkindly now, though. Which made it hurt more than if it had been. Don't get into this, she thought. Don't, whatever you do, let him charm you. And don't start telling him your troubles. 'Listen, Tom, I have to go, it's late. I just wanted to check that—'

'—that I wasn't coming round prowling, just to make you feel bad, is that it?' Here it came again, the milk turning sour in his mouth. 'Well, sorry to disappoint you, but as it so happens I've got better things to do with my life than make you feel sorry for leaving it, all right?'

'All right.' She spat it back. Whoomph. You could always depend on Tom. As consistent as English weather. Take off your coat in the warmth and get hit by a hail-storm.

'Well, if you want my advice you'll put bars on the windows and change your music habits. Could be it's someone who can't stand the sound of his voice.'

'Yes, yes, and yes, Tom,' she said, this time letting herself rise to the bait. 'Thanks for nothing, OK? And send back the key.'

'I'll think about it.'

The receiver went dead in her ear. She held it like that for a moment, waiting for the pounding in her head to subside. The perfect phone call, Tom at his best: from caring to loathing so fast it made your eyes water. Once upon a time she had known how to handle it, could have given as good as she got, better even. But these last months had slowed down her reactions. Made her lazy, too secure. Bastard.

Bastard, yes. But liar? That too she had once been able to tell. Now she was not so sure. She put the phone down on its cradle. It rang again immediately. It had to be him. She let it carry on. But he was persistent. In the end she picked it up and said firmly, 'Good night, Tom.' The silence at the other end was alive in her ear. 'I hope Canada proves big enough for you.'

She pressed the disconnect button, then left the receiver off the hook. He was good with phone calls. Once, when they had been courting and his world still revolved around winning her, he had phoned her thirty-three times in a hotel room in Spain until she had agreed to fly to Paris to meet him for the weekend. It had been so intoxicating being wanted that much, putting down the phone only to pick it up again and hear his voice, laughing, rich with desire, refusing to take no for an answer. They had flirted their way through a small fortune in phone bills that trip. Who cared? It was like making love long-distance, the kind of thing that makes a man irresistible. But not now. Now, at last, she had turned her back on him. Which was no doubt what made him so mad. But did it also make him vindictive?

She turned off the light and closed her eyes, but the call had churned her up too much and it was impossible to sleep. She lay and listened to the night silence. Her bedroom was at the back of the house, overlooking the garden. It was hard to believe there was a main arterial road just a few hundred yards away. Sometimes in summer, with the windows open, you could hear an owl. Tonight's orchestration was less mellifluous, though. A high-pitched yowl cut through the silence, followed by another, shriller cry, almost like a baby crying. It turned her stomach for a second until she recognised it as cats. Then came a fierce, fast clash of voices. Fucking or fighting? Sometimes it was hard to tell. The screeches continued, angry yelps, hissing war cries, cold shrill little screams. Fighting. Amazing the number of words you could use to describe the sound of a cat's voice. She tried to think of all their equivalents in Czech. It was not like counting sheep. By the time the fight had stopped, she was wide awake.

She was suddenly thirsty and in need of a glass of water, fridge-cold rather than tap. She pulled on a robe and went downstairs. As she turned the corner down the last flight she heard a noise from below, a slamming or falling.

The door to the kitchen was locked, a security device which she sometimes used when she was out or at night when she wanted to keep the cat from roaming around the rest of the house. (She had, almost without thinking, kept it locked most nights since Tom had gone.) She turned the key and flicked on the light at the same time. She was not, as far as she could make out, unduly frightened – certainly no more than one would expect after hearing a stray noise in the middle of the night. The kitchen was empty, but not untouched. In the middle of the table the vase of flowers had been knocked over, scattering carnations and sprays of white mist all over the tablecloth, a small river of greenish water trickling down over the side and onto the floor. She stood for a second looking around.

'Millie?' she called softly. The animal responded with a sorrowful half-yowl from somewhere underneath the table. She squatted down and lifted the cloth. The cat was crouched at the centre of the darkness, trying to make itself smaller than it was. She put out a hand to reach it but it withdrew, hissing slightly. For some reason its fear seemed more frightening than her own and she turned quickly, checking around her, but there was nothing there.

'Come on, girl,' she said gently, coaxing again with her fingers, and eventually the cat came, bedraggled and war-wounded, a piece of left ear cut and bleeding, one paw held slightly off the ground.

'Oh girl, no prizes for guessing who you've been in battle with,' she said softly as she picked it up and held it to her chest.

The fur was wet and clammy where the vase water had splattered it. To have been so clumsy it must have come in still in flight, going for the high ground of the table without thinking. But the black tom hadn't followed. Unless, of course, that had been the slam she had heard – the cat-door snapping shut again after an intruder. She looked in the direction of the French windows, but the light only allowed her to see herself reflected in the glass – beyond that, the darkness was total. She put on the outside lamp and the patio and first half of the garden jumped into weak focus, empty, no sign of life.

She held the cat in her arms while she bathed the wound, then let it sit for a while on her lap licking catnip paste off her fingers. She talked to it softly, not paying much attention to what she said, sweet nothings: 'Silly animal. Your trouble is you never learnt to fight when you were growing up. And now it's too late to teach an old cat new tricks.' The fingers of her free hand stroked and tickled the little body, working through the fur, loosening a fur ball here and there, her nails snagging on the edge of the odd, infected flea bite. Poor Millie. She had been rather neglected of late. Born and brought up in a flat where the only taste of life on the ground was the view from a third-floor window, she had never really taken to freedom. Like others less feline, she seemed to have found the new house too big and too daunting; preferring the cosy darkness between the sofa and radiator to the wild seclusion of the garden borders or the great expanse of lawn. 'There's nothing to be scared of. You're supposed to like the dark, you know. He's just a fat tom with an inflated sense of himself. If you can't win by brawn you should use cunning. That's all we girls have got.'

The animal stretched its body lazily under her touch, the pleasure clearly now outweighing the pain,

and began to purr, a great motor of a sound, filling the
night silence, rich and deep. See. All anybody needs is a
little affection. She put her head back against the chair
and allowed the cat's sense of well-being to become her
own. She thought about Tom and how easily his love
had always connected into cruelty. She remembered
how hard it had been when they first split up, how each
day had been about reinventing herself without him,
and how long it had taken her to feel anywhere near
normal again. She had done it, though. And whatever
happened there was no going back.

She thought about work and the book. A year ago
they wouldn't even have offered it to her. But part of
the fall-out of these last months had been learning how
to put herself forward more. She had always been good
at her job, though until recently she'd tended to keep
that news to herself. Not any more. Six months ago,
after Tom moved out, she had redone her CV and
started ringing people rather than waiting for them to
ring her. The pushiness had paid off. From trade
conferences and the odd literary novella to best-selling
crime and punishment.

It hadn't been that hard. Her Czech connections
were good enough to ensure her advance warning of
this particular novel (for someone who had stopped
using the phone, she could at least still write letters:
always easier to say nothing to people you don't know
that well) and her contacts had paved the way for
Charles at the book fair. But it was more than that. She
also knew her thrillers. Over the years she had read a
lot of them. There was something about their coldness
that she liked, the way that the characters were so
often alienated from themselves and the world around

them. She understood that feeling; as a child she had seen it in her father, a man wrenched out of one country and never entirely able to root himself in another.

What would he have thought about this book? Czech words with American sensibilities. He would have seen it as evidence of a culture twice destroyed, first by socialism, then by capitalism. Certainly the book was unashamed in its homage to the West and in particular that hard-boiled tradition that America exported so well, junk fiction to go with the junk food. Despite its familiarity it was not so easy to copy, though in this case the writer had made an effort, chronicling the devastation of a post-Soviet economy, drugs and prostitution against the Pinocchio charm of the Charles Bridge and the grandeur of Wenceslas Square. Even the story had a certain swing: good cop, bad karma, a man wading through violence and driven by the memory of lost love.

For a translator its deliberate street slang was its own challenge. She was lucky, of course. For as far back as she remembered she had spoken Czech. Her father had never used any other language with her. Moving between the two tongues had been as normal as breathing. Until he took her to Prague when she was six, she thought they were the only two people in the world who spoke it, a secret language between father and daughter. It was only later she understood how this was a way of confirming his identity. Teaching her was reassuring himself. Their visit back was his first since the Forties. He had left a brash young man determined to win the war and get back his country. He returned prematurely old and disillusioned. Ten

months later the Russian tanks moved in on the Prague
spring and his exile became permanent. Later, after he
had his heart attack, while she was in her first year at
university studying – what else but Czech? – it was she
who had written the letter to the few remaining
relatives, a letter which turned into an elegy in his
native tongue. It was fitting. Towards the end all he had
had was memories and a language which his daughter
had helped keep alive for him. Sometimes, when she
was at her worst, she wondered whether that was
what she was still doing now, helping to keep it alive as
some kind of memorial to him.

She imagined him sitting at her shoulder reading the
book with all its crude images of violence and decay.
She didn't need his disapproval to have her own. As a
story the whole thing was shot through with a careless
misogyny. All acceptable within the genre, but none
the less distasteful for that. How will I feel, she had
thought when she decided to take it on, sitting at night
in an empty house translating scenes of women being
threatened and abused by men who enjoy their pain
rather than their sexuality? Rape, fear, torture – it was
so common nowadays that it was almost a form of
punctuation for a certain kind of novel. Some of it
would have to be cleaned up to make it to the screen.
You can't do those sorts of things to Irene Jacob and get
away with it, even if it is Brad Pitt who gets to lick her
wounds. As a translator she could take a decision not
to wallow in it, but it still had to be made flesh in
English. Well, she knew what she was doing. And if the
images got too rough, she'd make sure she worked on
certain scenes only under the cover of daylight.

Not that darkness scared her. At least not the

darkness of this house. That was what was so extraordinary about everybody else's sudden concern for
her. There was nothing in this house to make one feel
bad. There never had been. She had known that from
the moment she walked in off the street.

It had been the first property she had seen after her
mother's money had come through probate, and had
only been on the market for ten days. She had been so
certain that she asked the owners if she could phone
Tom from there and persuade him to come straight
over on his way back from work. They offered the
asking price that very evening. The couple who owned
it had lived there for twenty-five years and were
selling only because it was too big for them now that
the family had grown up and gone. They liked her, she
could tell, saw a future rolling out before her like a
carbon copy of their own: finding the right house,
having the children, fussing and fighting as they
watched them grow up and then, suddenly, having to
readjust as they found themselves alone again. She
had been charmed by the image then, could almost
share their vision of herself.

And it would have been the perfect house for it. It
was one of those mid-Victorian properties at the end of
a terrace, financed by the speculative proceeds of the
ones that came before and much grander than its
neighbours, the builder showing off his success in
bricks and mortar. It was built around a glorious staircase that spiralled up into the darkness from a wider
than average hall, a house where all the rooms were
generous ones, even up to the attic space under the
eaves where, it seemed to her, a translator might work,
happy and undisturbed, as the baby went down for its

morning nap, content in the proximity of its mother.

But it was not to be. Maybe it was the very perfection of the image that had turned it barren. Although the house itself had not been to blame, she was sure of that. In fact as the relationship had started to deconstruct itself and the thought of children receded, so the house had become a kind of surrogate dependant, wanting them, needing things, growing, responding to love and affection. And money. Like a child it had proved expensive. Redoing the roof, decorating the attic, building a new kitchen with warm wooden floors and wide work tops had gobbled up the remainder of her mother's money within the first two years. The final alterations had cost so much it had caused them to take out a joint mortgage, a statement of alternative commitment that came too late to save either of them. Without him she now paid it all herself. But still she never thought about selling. The house was her home, and she loved it. If money got tight later she'd get herself a lodger, some French or Spanish student who would appreciate the house's specialness and remember it in years to come. No. This was where she was staying. And it would take more than a few mislaid CDs, even if they had been spirited away by malice, to turn her against it.

Gently she eased Millie off her lap. She put her back down on the chair and turned off the light in readiness for going upstairs. But before she could close the door the cat curled its way between her legs and up to the landing above, looking down at her. Clearly tonight they were going to sleep together.

'Oh well,' she muttered. 'As of now I haven't had a better offer.'

Together they mounted the sweeping staircase into her room. It was 2.10 a.m. by the clock. On the bedside table the receiver was buzzing angrily, British Telecom's way of telling you you're out of contact. She replaced it and this time it stayed silent. She went over to the window. The world outside was silent also. The cold light of a half moon had opened up the garden to a series of shadows. On the back wall something was moving, but it was too dark to see what it was. Black against black. Poor Millie. She was either going to have to find the will to fight back or admit defeat. The cat had curled herself up at the end of the bed. It seemed she had already made her choice.

three

When the state stops paying the garbage collectors, the garbage stops being collected.

The street was awash with litter. Some of it would be recycled by the locals. Most of it you wouldn't want to use again. Like the condoms and the needles. The decay suited the surroundings. Veer off any tourist track in this city and it isn't long before old style turns to new shit and you hit the Gulags; suburban wastelands of Soviet architecture – the result of Stalin's steel mills pumping out industrial crap for the satellite states to buy – modern housing for modern workers. Poor fuckers, thought Jake, seven years into capitalism and there wasn't much gain for their pain. At least in America if you were born into shit it didn't mean you had to die there too.

Still, they had done their best. Most windows had managed their own touch of pathetic individuality: the lace curtain, a vase of scrubby flowers, the odd figurine. Nobody gave much of a fuck about second from the left on the top floor, though. This window was so filthy you wouldn't need to draw the curtains at all. Junkie town. Jake had seen it all before.

Inside, the room was so dark they had the light on, a single bulb hanging from the ceiling. Its glare did the woman no favours. She was sitting on a kitchen chair, her legs slightly apart, hands on her knees, not quite relaxed. She was probably in her late thirties, attractive, with shoulder-length blond hair and an English rose complexion on the edge of losing its bloom. She was wearing a T-shirt, expensively casual, tight, accentuating the heavy pull of her breasts, over a short black skirt. On someone less good-looking it would be the outfit of a hooker. On her it still had the gloss of Western style. On the floor beside her lay a pair of tights.

She slid both hands up her legs and under her skirt, shimmying her ass down to help her reach the top of her panties. She teased them loose, let them slip down onto the floor, then stepped carefully out of them. She stood up and pushing a lock of hair from her face, lifted her foot onto the chair, the skirt riding up high over her thighs to reveal a line of naked leg up to the curve of her buttocks. Then, slowly, she slid the fingers of her right hand up into her crotch.

She pushed her way inside for a moment, probing, playing, her body moving to the rhythm of her touch. Her face showed no signs of pleasure, no emotion at all, just a cool expressionless stare, her eyes fixed on the man who was sitting opposite.

He kept on looking. He was thin and sallow-skinned, a creature who hadn't seen the sun for so long he had started to feed on darkness. His eyes flicked between her face and her fingers, lips parted in a half smile, his breath an echo of sound.

After she had played for a little longer she deftly removed her fingers. Between them she held up a thick plastic tube, six or eight centimetres long, glistening, its covering slightly wet. She tossed it across the room. The man caught it neatly, lifting it briefly to his nose before peeling off the wrapping. Released from its covering, a heavy little bag unfolded, packed with white stuff. He held it up, weighing it casually in his palm.

'Ninety per cent pure,' she said softly, as if amused at the ritual, both his and hers. 'A thank-you from Jerome. He says to remember who it came from.'

'I already have,' he said quietly. 'I also remember from where.'

She nodded, then sat back down and reached for her panties; the gesture this time more ordinary, more self-absorbed; a women getting dressed after the show, now regardless of who was watching her.

'Uh uh.'

She glanced up at him, as if she was surprised to still find him there.

'Open your legs again,' he said quietly.

She gave a shrug, her hand already under the chair, creamy white lace curled up in her fingers. 'Sorry. I'm not part of the free gift,' she said coolly.

'I said open your legs.' And now the voice was harsh. 'Or I'll open them for you.'

She sighed slightly, as if his threats bored her, but she did as she was told, moving her knees just far enough apart to show the pubic bush under her skirt.

He sat staring directly at her snatch. She let him stare. She almost seemed to like it. Slowly she shifted her buttocks forward on the chair, spreading her legs further apart, so the view was better and more insolent. He laughed, tossing the bag down onto the table and walking lazily over to her. With one hand he lifted her chin up and held it cupped in his palm, a little too high for comfort. Then he slipped his other hand up into her. 'Just checking that everything that's mine is out of there,' he said slyly, his fingers working over-time.

She sat absolutely still, apparently oblivious of his touch.

'Satisfied?' she said after a while, and this time the voice dripped with scorn.

He slammed a finger further in and up, savagely deep, and this time she cried out. 'Bastard,' she said between clenched teeth.

'And what other kind of men do you know?' he said as he used his other hand to unzip his flies. 'Let's get on with it, eh?'

'Yeah, well, you'd better get your finger out if you want to fit anything else in. Unless, of course, it's even smaller than I think.'

'Bitch,' he said, as he hit her hard across the face. 'That's not where I'm going to put it.' And he hit her again.

Her eyes glazed over, the look of a woman on automatic pilot. 'Shit,' she said under her breath as the skin around her right eye began to swell.

'You got it, sweetheart.'

Outside in the shabby bar/café across the road Jake looked up to check the top-floor window. Then he ordered another beer and dug out a magazine.

She pressed the Save button. The little numbers at the bottom of the screen danced upwards.

Now there was no chance of losing the text she scrolled back up the page, highlighting certain phrases with the cursor. '. . . she slid the fingers of her right hand up into her crotch . . .' Crotch? Or should it be snatch? Snatch was more insulting. But for that reason it fitted better later, when it was the man doing the feeling. Snatch. Certainly more a male word, in English at least. She sighed.

Not the same problem with 'panties'. Like rubbish versus garbage the choice of the word was cultural rather than linguistic. Her first instinct would have been to use 'knickers', but that was too British. Only English girls wore knickers. The word carried instant overtones of school uniforms and dirty old men. But these guys were meant to be dangerous rather than pathetic. And a book which had its eye so firmly on the American market had to give its women a more titillating kind of underwear. Panties rather than plain old pants. Decisions. Language and sex. Always a challenge for the translator.

She read the completed pages back again. If her father had still been alive she could have asked his opinion. The thought made her smile. He'd always been so proud of her proficiency. Would the pride have helped overcome his sense of shock at the material? It was a tacky little vignette, though not without its erotic power. I wonder if it presses the same buttons for men as well as women? she thought. For her the trick of it was the woman's confidence and contempt, the sense – at the beginning of the encounter at least – that her body was its own kind of weapon. In her imagination she would be a younger version of Catherine Deneuve, with echoes of her impenetrable middle-class *Belle de Jour* personality.

The image of the uncrossing of the legs was grossly derivative, of course. For zeitgeist read Hollywood. Whatever his literary pretensions, the writer had simply risen to the Basic Instincts of Sharon Stone working a room full of American policemen. Not so much a comment as a rip-off. But while that scene had at least given Stone some of the trump cards, this one, in contrast, refused to let the woman get away with anything.

The same theme echoed through the book; sassy women finding themselves punished rather than rewarded for their daring. Yet, it seemed to be the kind of thing people wanted to read, already translated into half a dozen languages over Europe and selling well in all of them. And you could multiply any figure by a hundred when the English version coincided with the movie.

She scrolled up further to the first description of the woman. Would anyone notice that the word 'still' was missing? In the original text the woman was described as 'in her late thirties, attractive still'. She had left out the qualifier. Hardly a subversive omission (though she knew from the publicity blurb that the writer had recently left his childhood sweetheart to shack up with a wafer-thin foreign model) but it gave her a sense of pleasure. The quiet hand of the translator.

She looked at her watch. 6.40 p.m. Outside it was already dark. She should call it a day if she was going to get showered and dressed and make it to Sal and Patrick's in time for the party. It would be her first time out in what? two – no maybe three – weeks. Good old Sally, persistent as ever. Most of the rest of her address book had given up on her long ago.

She went into close-down, checking – as she always did – how many words she had done that day. 2,500. Not bad. At this rate she should finish the first draft by the end of January, and deliver maybe two or three weeks later. A winter spent in the company of pimps, prostitutes and tough guys. Some girls get their kicks in different ways. At least she was being paid for it.

Under the hard rain of the shower she thought some more about the book. She was 130 pages in already. Jake had already screwed up his career in New York by taking his sorrow and fury with Mirka out onto the streets and had been shunted off out to Prague on the pretext of watching the bad boys, while they in turn were watching him. She'd made good progress. But then she'd been at it solidly, not stopping for weekends, and working most evenings till about eight or nine o'clock. It was a tried and true method, a way of submerging herself in a writer's style, infiltrating herself into their world until gradually it became hers, her choice of words mirroring theirs. There was a quiet pleasure to be had in this, like working in unison with an invisible partner at your shoulder, watching over you, whispering in your ear. It could have its drawbacks, though. Like with this one, when getting into the words meant getting into the sensibilities, and the undertow of threat and sexual sadism.

To begin with, it hadn't troubled her. She had managed to keep the meaning of the images at a critical distance; dissecting syntax, looking for ways to reproduce linguistic rhythms. But in the last few days the violence seemed to have burrowed its way further under her skin. She would lie in her bed at night, rerunning certain scenes from the book, substituting herself for the women. As with today's scene; imagining herself sitting in that sparse cold room, crossing then uncrossing her legs, enjoying the insolence and the power, even down to the moment of pain.

In the mornings she made light of such stuff, seeing her identification simply as a reflection of a job well done. But the images of dodgy eroticism had uncovered something else, a series of memories that she would prefer to have left buried, about a time in her relationship with Tom when a visit to Amsterdam had sparked off a joint interest in porn. They had bought a clutch of the more graphic magazines home with them, giggling together as they sauntered through the Green Channel with half a dozen obscene publications stuffed under Tom's shirt.

But he had not been as cool as he appeared. He had been sweating so much on the way through Customs that the imprint of one of the cover pictures had leaked onto his skin. That night they had lain in bed, her tracing the outline of the man's erect penis and a woman's arched buttocks, the two of them caught between hysteria and desire.

As the months passed she realised, to her surprise, that she was getting more into them than he was, relishing the way in which the sex was so anonymous, and how the women's passivity took on a power all its own. For a while they used them a lot, relying on them as a kind of - what was the marketing phrase? - 'sex aid'.

Then she started to find herself coming back to them when she was alone in the house working. She discovered that she liked the fantasy even more when she didn't have to incorporate a real lover into it. So what? she had thought at the time. It wasn't as if the sex in them was particularly violent or damaging, more that it was so, well ... so divorced from real life. The more she used them the easier she found it to have orgasms with them, to orchestrate and control the pace and flow of her pleasure. Until, in the end, she got a little scared of how good and how alone they were making her feel.

By a kind of mutual consent she and Tom had stopped using the magazines so much, and after a while she had packed them away in a box under the bed; like the classic suburban couple, she had thought at the time, imagining their children coming upon them one afternoon when they were out, trying to square these pictures of explicit, exploitative sex with the image of their cosy long-married parents. But neither the marriage nor the children was to be and when she had looked for the box during that brief reawakening of sexual interest a couple of months after Tom had moved out, she found to her annoyance that he had taken the magazines with him. Their absence angered her – specifically, of course, because she knew that she could never ask for them back.

She stood in the shower, feeling the water run down her body, wondering just how much she would really like to have them again. Enough to go into a shop in Soho and flick through the magazine shelves, then present her selection at the desk, a big grin on her face? No, maybe not. She was laughing at the thought of her embarrassment when she heard the doorbell ring two storeys below. Damn. Chances were that by the time she got out and made herself decent enough to open it whoever it was would already have gone. She decided to let them ring. The bell went again, longer this time – whoever it was holding their finger against the button. Eventually it stopped.

She finished the shower and got out, pulling a new towel from the airing cupboard and wrapping its fresh warmth around her. She dried her hair and headed towards the bedroom. From the vantage point on the stairs she could see right down into the hall to a large buff-coloured envelope lying on the mat.

She went down to retrieve it. When she picked it up it turned out to be bulky as well as big. She tore open the top and a key fell into her palm. She didn't need to open the front door to know which lock it fitted. At last Tom had come through. But the gifts didn't end there. She dug further in and pulled out a CD wrapped around with the scrawled note, held in place with a rubber band.

'Only just found it after I got back from Canada,' it said. 'Sorry. No hard feelings. Will this make up for the delay?'

She slipped the paper off the plastic case. The CD with its image of an American city skyline at night was still in its record shop wrapping. Above the picture was the name, Van Morrison, and below, the title: recorded live 'A Night in San Francisco'.

She stared at it for a moment, not quite taking it in. So it had been him after all. And this was what? His way of making a joke out of it? 'No hard feelings.' It was incredible.

Or maybe not. Maybe the 'no hard feelings' wasn't a reference to the CD at all, but only to the key and how long she'd had to wait. Could that be it? Could the music be just a present? Except Tom didn't know one end of Van Morrison's work from another. To pick this one from the ten or fifteen CDs available couldn't possibly be coincidence. It had to be a statement. But if he had taken it, then why bother to buy it new? Presumably in order to keep the message ambiguous. So when would she get the other one back? Or did he already know that she didn't need it any more? After all, if it was him then his last visit would have revealed the fact that she'd already replaced the first CD. It was unbelievable. But it was, she realised, just like Tom to do something like this; admit everything and nothing at the same time with a gesture that was both cruel and generous.

Her sense of outrage moved into fury. How dare he? She pulled the front door open, hoping ... hoping what? To catch him still hovering behind it? But there was no one there and when she went out onto the street it was empty. From behind her a set of post-Guy Fawkes firecrackers went off alarmingly close. She jumped round, half expecting to see him, flinging up his hands in a gesture of surrender. 'Sorry, Lizzie. Just a joke.' But instead two teenage boys jumped out from behind a car where they had been crouching.

'Police,' shouted one of them in a howl of laughter. 'It's a raid.'

She slammed the door and went inside. From the hall phone she dialled his number. He wouldn't, of course, be home yet. The Barbican from here? How long would it take? Twenty minutes? More in traffic. His answering machine had a different message, a little less jaunty, she thought. She waited till the beep, but when it came she couldn't trust herself to speak, wasn't sure she would find the right words to register her contempt as well as her fury. It would be braver but better to do it face to face. Or at least person to person.

She thought about driving straight to his flat, confronting him then and there, but by the time she got herself ready the kitchen clock was showing eight-twenty and she was already late. Having refused the last three invitations, it wouldn't do to completely blow out this one. Sally might act casual about such things but she didn't easily forgive people who forgot Patrick's birthday.

She slammed the CD down on the work top. The cover of the old one was still on the rack above. She brought it down and sat them side by side. She was tempted to fling the new one straight into the bin, to not allow herself to be contaminated by it. But why punish Van Morrison for someone else's transgression? In the end she pulled off the cellophane and slipped it into the machine. She played the first three tracks before turning it off and heading out of the door, grabbing a bottle of wine on her way.

four

I f it wasn't the best of evenings, then neither was it
the worst. Patrick displayed a certain anal
retentiveness when it came to social events, which
made him death to anything as small as a dinner party
but at least assured a good level of organisation with a
gathering as potentially chaotic as a birthday celebration, especially one that was traditionally celebrated
with fireworks. With Sally's encouragement he had
gone for a combination of work and pleasure in the
guest list. There were a few faces she recognised, but
otherwise the place was full of men who usually wore
suits slumming it in expensive jeans and sweaters and
shoes that had probably never seen a garden, let alone
mud. Most of them had women with them, most of
whom were their wives, but there were the odd few
loners, all of whom she met during the course of the
evening, aided and abetted by Sally's solicitous
introductions.

It struck her that had she arrived less freaked out,
still fresh from the imaginative mischief of the day's
work, she might have psyched herself up to find one or
two of them attractive. Or at least bearable. She had

even gone to the social precaution of leaving the car at home, so that by halfway through the evening she was more than a little pissed. It didn't make her any more available, but it did at least serve to blunt her obsessive thinking about Tom.

When the fireworks had given way to the food she found herself sitting on a bench at the back of the kitchen with a guy whose name she couldn't remember. No one to set the world alight, but a little less clean-cut than the others, with a slightly fleshy face and the kind of eyes that didn't jump around when they looked at you. They were talking and eating, balancing kebabs and glasses on their laps. He was expressing reservations about the cinematic talents of Tarantino, in a manner that suggested intelligence as well as just perverse fashionability. She looked across at him. What would you do if I bent down now and slipped off my knickers? she thought. Would it bring us closer together? His finger tips were greasy with sausage fat. She imagined herself licking them. Afterwards. The thought was absurd. Outrageous. She had another drink, and found herself choking a laugh into it.

'—that kind of violence—What is it?'

It took her a while to recover. 'Nothing. Just an idea.'

'If it's that funny I'd like to hear it.'

'I doubt you would,' she said.

'You sure about that?' He smiled the question, benign in his curiosity, but she couldn't rise to it. The moment had passed and she was already bored and embarrassed at the same time.

In the end he gave up. After a while he drifted away and she knew suddenly that it was time to go home. She made her way through the house to the front hall from where she called her local cab company who said it would be fifteen minutes at least. She was still deciding whether to wait for them when her hostess appeared.

'Eliza! You're not going home already, are you? It's just getting started.'

Sally, glass in hand, equally the worse for wear. 'Sal, hi. Yeah, I've got to go. I've – I've got an early morning.'

'In which case you're going to be tired. It's after one o'clock, you know.'

'Is it?'

'Mmmm. You must have been having fun. He's all right, isn't he?'

'Who?'

'Who? The man you were supposed to meet three weeks ago, that's who. Malcolm. Fuzzy hair, nice body, good eyes.' Malcolm. Of course. The name she couldn't wait to forget. 'Are you going to see him again?'

'No. Why, are you?'

Sally laughed. 'I do believe you're drunk. Tremendous. At least I feel I've accomplished something tonight. So, tell me, how have you been? God, I'm sick of talking to your answering machine. I was ready to give up on you. I tell you if you hadn't said yes to this Patrick was all for changing sides.'

'Changing sides?'

'Yes. He was going to invite Tom instead.'

'He didn't, did he?' she said, altogether too anxiously.

'No, of course not. Don't worry. I told him it was *verboten*. By the way, talking of which, have you got that key back yet?'

'Yes.'

'Good. And how about the business with Van Morrison?'

'Oh . . . er . . . I found them again.'

'Where?'

'In the house.'

'There, I told you. Too nasty even for our Tom. Still, you are in his thoughts, you know.'

'What?'

'Tom's thoughts.'

'How do you know?'

She looked sheepish. 'Because Patrick had lunch with him a couple of days ago. Don't worry. I promise no secrets. Since when did I tell Patrick anything, anyway? But he said Tom was a bit down.'

'Why?'

'He'd been for some interview or other. In Canada? Was sure he hadn't got the job. Politics, I gather.'

'Yes. It usually is.'

'So. Poor Tom, eh? Patrick said he misses you.'

'Did Tom say that?'

'Lord, no, that was Patrick's gloss on it. He said he seemed in a bit of state. He got quite drunk apparently, and a bit bitter about things.'

'Things?'

'Yes, well, you know. You and him. Life, all the old Tom-type stuff. Patrick felt sorry for him really. That's why he wanted to invite him.'

'Well, thank God he didn't.'

'Indeed. Sad, though, eh?' She paused. And when she realised she wasn't going to get anything more: 'How does it make you feel?'

Sally, up and running, gathering gossip for the local newsletter. It was hard to take when they were both sober, let alone now. 'Actually, Sal, to be honest I couldn't give a toss. And I do have to go.'

'How about the cab?'

'I'll get one off the street. I'm sure someone else will take mine.'

'OK. Well, just don't go underground again, right? It takes a friend to tell you this, but you're not looking that great.'

Thank you, Sally. Except right at that moment she wasn't feeling it either. The fresh air helped, the night temperatures rapidly plunging their way towards zero. She was absurdly glad to be out of the house and on the street. She walked the fifty yards or so to the main road and stood waiting for a cab. After a few minutes a car with three guys stopped at the traffic lights, the one at the back rolling down a window. 'Hey, darling? Need a lift?'

'No, thanks,' she said, her voice instantly a middle-class parody. 'I'm waiting for someone.'

'Yeah, me,' he said, laughing, starting to open his door. She felt herself go tense, checking for other people on the street. Across the road a couple were walking, almost out of earshot, but then at that moment the lights changed and the driver slammed into second gear, taking off at an unholy speed, leaving the passenger clinging on to the door for dear life. She heard their wild laughter echoing down the road.

When a cab finally came she gave her address and sat back against the seat, exhausted. Too much social life after too little. She wasn't up to it. Give me written words any day. Nobody answers you back.

Her address was at the end of a maze of one-way streets, so she had to direct the cab driver for the last couple of blocks. As they turned the corner into her road she saw a blue Mustang pull out from the kerb and head off in the other direction. Bad electrics, Mustangs, she thought, remembering the trouble that she and Tom had had with theirs. The Golf may have less prestige, but it also had more reliability.

She paid the driver and made her way, somewhat unsteadily, to the door where she fumbled with the lock. The cabbie stayed where he was, engine running. It took longer with him watching but she was grateful for the surveillance. When she finally succeeded in opening it she threw him a wave.

'All right then, love?'

'Fine. Thanks. Good night.' Sweet, she thought.

Inside the house loomed up above her, dark and silent. Have you missed me? she wondered.

She flung off her coat and dropped it on the floor, pleased to be home but a little unnerved by the quiet. Both her head and her stomach were demanding attention. Sleep. That was what she needed. But water first. Lots of it.

She moved along the corridor towards the kitchen stairs and it was then that she heard it, seeping out from under the door: the sound of a voice as mellow as any instrument, an audience behind it, showing their appreciation. Van Morrison singing his heart out in San Francisco, and her kitchen. Oh great, she thought for a second in her blurred state, I love this track. Then reality registered like a sharp kick to the stomach.

She stood rigid by the door, her hand on the handle. There was a strip of light underneath, but then she usually left one on, for security's sake. Just as she also locked the door. She quietly turned the key in the lock and pushed. Nothing happened. She pushed again. No. The door was locked now. Surely she'd hadn't left it unlocked when she went out? But then she'd been late and in a rush. She turned the key back again. She realised that she couldn't remember. She took a few deep breaths, opened the door and went in.

The room beyond was bright and empty, just as she'd left it. Nobody there. Nobody at all. She walked slowly across the floor to the shelf where the little green lights on the stereo system were dancing in tune to the range of Morrison's voice. But she *had* turned the system off. That much she remembered with absolute clarity; she could see herself doing it again in memory, her finger hitting the switch, watching the light go out.

As she reached the machine the track ended, leaving a sudden huge silence. Then the little illuminated number jumped from one to two and a fiddle came in loud and pure. On the console the digital clock which registered how long each track was jumped from four minutes twenty-seven seconds back to zero, then started moving steadily through the seconds again. Four minutes twenty-seven ... the first track.

She thought about what it meant: that four minutes and twenty-seven seconds ago someone must have been standing here pressing the start button. No. It wasn't possible. But even as she thought it she knew it was. She found it suddenly hard to swallow, hard to sort out the music from the pulsing noise between her ears. Four minutes twenty-seven seconds. Which meant that whoever had done it had to be nearby. Could even still be in the house.

The shock of the thought sluiced adrenaline through her so fast that it wiped out the fuzz of the booze, leaving her sharply, completely alert.

She moved to the French doors and tested the

handle. The lock was firmly in place. She tried the
window. Same thing. No one had come in this way. She
thought about the downstairs loo and that little port-
hole window that she'd never got around to having
bars put on. She went out quickly, while she still had the
courage, but the room was empty, the window intact,
lock on, no sign of disturbance. You'd need to be a
midget to get through there anyway. Four minutes
twenty-seven seconds ... She wound back the thread
of her life. She would have been in the cab, coming to
the one-way system, turning into the street with the
blue Mustang taking off in the other direction. The
Mustang. It must have been parked opposite the house.
Of course. The Mustang. Why hadn't she realised it
before? Parked, waiting, the clock on the dashboard,
no doubt, keeping track of how long the album had
been playing.

It was so simple. If it wasn't for the car she would
never have suspected him. After all, he'd brought the
key back only that very day. The key? But it was an
Ingersol. You couldn't copy an Ingersol, could you?
Wasn't that what the security people said? She already
knew the answer. Tom could do it. Tom could do
anything when he set his mind to it. Bastard.

So how did he know that she wouldn't be there?
That tonight of all nights she'd be out? Easy. He had
knocked earlier and there had been no response. But if
he'd been waiting, wouldn't she have seen the car on
the street? It hadn't been there when she went out
looking for him, had it? She would have noticed it.

No, better than that. He didn't have to stay because
he *knew* she'd be out later. He knew about the birthday
party. Patrick had told him when they'd had lunch

together. Of course. He knew that it was she and not he who'd been invited.

So, he went away, waited a while then, what? Drove here, came in, switched on the machine and sat outside waiting, just slipping in to start it again every fifty minutes until . . .

But why would he possibly want to do such a thing? It was so cruel it was almost surreal. He must have known how much it would freak her. How much could you hate someone for ending something that was already ended, something that you yourself had helped to destroy? Then she remembered something. An incident from a holiday they had taken during the first winter they were together: stupid but telling.

They'd gone to Corfu, too early for the tourists and too cold for the beach, and to keep themselves amused had visited a set of caves in the north of the island. They and a German couple had had the guide to themselves, but his commentary had been so lousy that they contrived to lose him halfway through, negotiating their own route through the primeval landscape and the dense silence.

They had been underground for about half an hour, wandering through the deepest part of the caves where the surface was pitted by potholes and underground lakes, when suddenly the lights had gone off. The blackness had been instant, total, like death. He'd been right beside her when it happened but as she reached out to touch him he was gone. She'd found it funny at first, whispering to him in the black, until she had heard the most dreadful screech somewhere to her right, as if someone had stumbled and fallen into one of the chasms. She had been groping her way blindly towards the sound, screaming his name, when an icy hand had slid around her neck. Her fear had lifted her an inch off the ground.

'Oh, come on, Lizzie. It was just a joke,' he had said later as he held her to his chest, trying to stem her hiccupping sobs. 'Anyway, at least now I know how much you'd miss me.' The remark had turned her tears into fury. The row that followed had gone on for days, until eventually the early spring sun and his little-boy contriteness had forced her into forgiving him. But not forgetting.

She grabbed a bottle of water from the fridge and gulped down half of it. On the console Van was now into track five. She gave it another two minutes then picked up the portable phone.

The number rang six times, then connected.

'Hello?'

She slid the receiver away from her ear and held it up to the speakers as she flicked up the volume. For a man who didn't like Van Morrison it would have been a painful experience. Not painful enough. She pulled it down again. 'Hello, Tom,' she said steadily.

'Lizzie? Is that you? God, you took the top of my head off. I – er – was that the album?' He sounded distinctly shaky.

'Yeah. Van the Man. Your choice.'

He gave a little laugh. 'Well, you know what I think of him. But the guy at the record store in Vancouver thought it was a good one. A collector's item, he said. I rang the doorbell but you weren't in.'

'Oh, and which time was that?'

'What?'

'The first visit or the second?'

'Uh ... I don't know. I dropped it by after work. It must have been—'

'Don't lie to me, Tom.' And the explosion of her voice took even her by surprise. 'Just don't do it, OK? You creep. What do you think it feels like, being so scared that your gut seizes up? What is it with you that you can't leave it alone? You wanted out too, you know. It was mutual, remember. Or was that just more of your bullshit?'

'Hey, hey, what is this?' he said, his anger rising up to meet hers. 'I bring you back your key. As a way of apologising I buy you an album, and now you blow my head off. You know, I think—'

'I don't give a fuck what you think. I want you to stop it, right now, do you hear? I want you to stop it, or ... or I'll call the police.' And she heard the crack in her voice.

'Wait a minute,' he said, quietly now, more carefully. 'Stop what exactly? What are you talking about?'

'I'm talking about you coming round here tonight and putting on the stereo, so that I'd come in to find it still playing. This is my house and nobody, *nobody* is going to make me feel scared about living in it. D'you hear me?'

'But—'

'And don't bother to deny it. I know it was you, OK? I saw you. I saw your car. It was outside the house.'

'What car?'

'The bloody Mustang.'

At the other end of the line there was a slight pause. Someone or something made a noise in the background. He said something in reply then came back to the phone. 'Listen to me, Lizzie, I have absolutely no idea what you're talking about. I don't have the Mustang any more. I sold it two months ago to a guy in Stoke Newington. I can give you his phone number if you don't believe me. I drive a red Ford Capri now and I've been in all evening.'

'Yeah, and I'm sure you can prove it.'

'Yes, as matter of fact I can.'

And there was now something in his voice that made her pause. He sighed. The voice in the background muttered something else. He put his hand over the receiver. Then he came back on the line. 'Sorry. You still there?'

'Yes,' she said and her voice sounded suddenly very small to her.

'Listen, I haven't been there, all right? But maybe you should tell me what's happened.'

'It wasn't you,' she said flatly. 'You didn't take a duplicate of the key and come back here while I was out.'

'No. Why would I do a thing like that? Christ, Lizzie, what do you take me for?'

A bitter lover, she thought, but even as she did so she knew with utter certainty that he was telling the truth. So the car outside had had nothing to do with it. In which case who . . . ? Four minutes and twenty-seven seconds. And where . . . ? She had been standing with her back to the open kitchen door. Now she turned. Out of the door the house rose up three floors into the night. Three floors and a lot of places to hide.

'Are you saying you think somebody has been there? Has broken in?'

'I . . . er . . . I don't know. I came back to find the stereo on. It had been playing for four and a half minutes.'

'So, maybe you left it on repeat?'

'No,' she almost shouted in the receiver. 'No, there's no repeat button. And I turned it off. I know that.'

'Well, there must be some explanation. Maybe Millie hit the switch by mistake.'

Millie? Yes? No, it wasn't possible. She had left her upstairs asleep on the bed, with the kitchen door closed. Unless she had found another way out and come back in through the cat-flap. 'I'm sorry, I ...'

He sighed. 'It's all right. Really. Look, I know you think I'm a shit, and I know those early notes I sent were probably out of line. But it doesn't make me the enemy. Not any more. So if you're in trouble ...' And just for that second she didn't know what to say. His concern suddenly made her want to cry. But then she was scared, not at all herself. 'I mean you're sure about the switch, about turning it off? I don't want to risk your wrath, but you sound a little drunk.'

'I was, but I'm not now. And yes. I'm sure. I'm sure, Tom. I turned it off.'

There was a pause. 'You still scared?'

'No,' she said, but it was obvious to both of them she was lying.

'Do you want me to come round?'

'No. Thanks, I'm fine.'

'Well, you sure as hell don't sound fine. Have you checked the rest of the house, just in case?'

'No,' she said quietly.

'Then how about if I stay on the line while you do that?'

Yes, she thought. Oh, yes, please. What is it they say about the devil you know? 'What about ... I mean what about your guest?'

'It's all right. It's a friend. They can wait.' And despite herself a little something nipped inside the gut, something that wasn't fear. 'OK. So why don't we start with the cellar? Get the worst over first.'

And so together they made a slow pilgrimage through the house. In every room she checked the windows, beneath the beds, behind the doors, even – though she didn't tell him – inside the wardrobes. There was no one there. Not even Millie. The only thing she found that could cause any worry was in the top little bedroom, where the catch was off the window. But it was so far up from the ground that you would have needed a decorator's ladder to get in that way. She locked it now, screwing it down so tightly that it hurt her fingers.

He stayed close in her ear, not intrusive, but always there. The tour and his presence quietened her. When they got to the attic, he said, 'And how about through the little door? Into that big storage cupboard?'

'I don't think—'

'Might as well be thorough.' And she knew he was laughing at her, just a little. But it didn't really bother her. She opened the door and put on the light. A jumble of black bags and boxes met her gaze, the detritus of a lifetime. And a relationship. 'Nothing,' she said. 'Except seven years of *Classical Music* and *The London Review of Books*. I thought you said you'd cleared everything out.'

'See? Now you know why I broke in.' And this time they both found it funny. 'I'll come round and pick them up sometime. But you'll have to agree to let me in.'

'OK.'

By the time they arrived back down in the kitchen all

the fear and panic had gone, washed away. Somehow
she had known they wouldn't find anything. In fact,
even as she'd been looking, heart thumping with each
light going on, the house itself still hadn't frightened her.
Not really. Strange.

'So, that's it. It must have been the cat after all,' she
said. 'Thanks.'

'*Por nada*. But listen, you do what I said, OK?
Tomorrow you call the cops in to look at the place, give
you some security tips. Then the next time this
happens you can phone them. Get some hunk from the
Bill round to hold your hand in the middle of the night.'

'Will do.'

'And Lizzie?'

'Yeah?'

'Maybe . . . I mean, maybe you should get out a bit
more. Get used to coming home to the house empty.'

'How do you know I don't?' she said quietly, not
wanting to get angry again, but feeling it rise up
despite herself.

'OK. OK. Don't bite my head off. Patrick just mentioned something about your reclusive tendencies,
that's all. I . . . er . . . Anyway, you're all right, I take it.'

'Yes,' she said firmly. 'I'm fine. I'm in the middle of a
book and I don't want to be disturbed.'

'OK. Well, I – I just thought I'd check.'

'And you have. It's late. I'd better go,' she said, then
immediately felt like a shit for being so brutal. 'Listen,
I'm sorry I went for you. I'm tired. I've been working too
hard. Also . . . well, I wanted to say I'm sorry about the
job.'

'What job?'

'The one in Canada. Sal said you didn't get it.'

'Ah, well, see – that just goes to show how much the queen of gossip knows about anything. On the contrary, right at this moment you're talking to the new Associate Professor of European History at Simon Fraser University. Signed, sealed and delivered.'

'Oh, but that's great.' And she realised as she said it that she was, indeed, genuinely pleased. 'Congratulations.' Maybe that explained the change in him since last time. The good humour and the easiness. 'When do you go?'

'Next semester. Just imagine: me and five hundred nubile West Coast girls all eager for my teaching.'

She laughed. So did someone else down the other end of the phone. The laugh sounded light and female. Tom was playing to an audience now. It was time to go. 'Yes, well you should remember they're all politically correct these days.'

'Ah, but that's only because they haven't met me yet.'

What had her mother said about him the first time they met? 'Charm the birds right out of the trees.' God help the birds, whoever they were. 'Yes, well, when you get chucked out for sexual harassment don't call me as a character witness.'

'Oh, I don't know, I could always cite the night I saved you from the CD maniac.' And despite herself she laughed. 'So what do you think, Lizzie? Maybe we could have a drink before I go. For old times' sake,' he said, making it sound very casual.

'Yes. Maybe.'

'I'll call you. And remember. Ring the cops.'

She put the phone down and sat digesting the last interchange. Between the CD panic and all their sparring she and Tom had managed to make a kind of peace. After all this time she couldn't quite believe it. Maybe he'd take his friend with him to Vancouver. Nice place, Vancouver. Big horizons, warm currents, the chance to start it all again ... perfect for a man like Tom.

Here, though, she still had unfinished business. On the stereo Van Morrison was taking his last applause. The album clicked off, the CD button still blinking quietly in the corner. She sat for a while staring at it, then got up and went over to the console.

She moved the back of her hand across the control panel, pushing slightly against the start button. Nothing happened. She pushed harder, rubbing against the switch. Harder still. The light leapt up and the album clicked into place. Possible.

Then she switched the system off at the console power button. Once again she played the cat, using her hand like the flank of the animal's side. But this time the button was too close to the wall. To have activated it Millie would have needed to use her paw like a finger. Absolutely not possible. But could she really swear that she had turned it off?

She did so now, making double sure by flicking the switch at the plug. It would mean reprogramming the tuner tomorrow, but it was worth a good night's sleep. She checked the windows and doors one more time. There was still no sign of the cat. She took a box of cat biscuits out from the cupboard and rattled it noisily next to the window. Millie's ears had the range of a nuclear submarine when it came to food. She waited, but the cat didn't come. She dumped a handful into the bowl anyway and, taking the portable phone off its hook, went upstairs, locking the door behind her.

She had only been gone a few moments when the cat-flap snapped open, then shut again. But she was already too far away to hear it.

five

To her surprise she slept almost immediately. When she woke the sun was out and the sky was a perfect washed blue, a line of condensation on the window testifying to an early frost outside.

She lay in bed, feeling heavy with sleep. The clock read 10.15 a.m. She must have slept through the alarm. Downstairs she heard the thud of the post on the mat. What the hell? It was Saturday and at least nobody had murdered her in her bed. She replayed the last hours of the night before, fingering the fear like a new bruise, seeing if she could make it hurt again. But the daylight had obliterated all manner of shadows and she couldn't be bothered to try and find them again.

She stretched, half expecting her feet to dislodge Millie off the end of the bed. Then she remembered that the cat had still been out, and the kitchen door would have kept it locked up. She thought about getting up and dressed, then decided not to bother. Instead she'd have breakfast in bed with the papers, take it easy. So today she'd only do 500 words. Or maybe none at all. After the drama of last night she could, perhaps, allow herself a little time off from the Prague underworld. Even her American cop let himself do some sightseeing in between the bodies.

She lay for a moment thinking about Saturdays, how they used to be when she and Tom were first together. How sometimes they would sleep till noon then wander down to Camden Lock and have a late lunch at the Moroccan restaurant on the canal. It had been great to be so lazy and so comfortable with someone. Not to care what you looked like or what you did, just to hang out as if it could all go on for ever. Is that how real marriages work? she wondered. People just keeping on keeping on, growing older and slower till they got to look like those happy/sad ads for pension plans. One thing you could say about her and Tom. They would always be young together, no paunches or liver spots, no hardening of the arteries.

It was, she realised, a long time since she had thought of their relationship as something to be celebrated rather than regretted. What had the feckless Sally once said to her? 'It's like death, darling. You can't hurry the grieving, it has to take its own course.' Eight and a half months. At least now something was shifting. Vancouver, eh? He wouldn't come back, she knew that. He'd meet some woman – if he hadn't met her already – and end up buying a house near the university and siring a pack of little Canadians with funny accents and a love of the great outdoors. And with any luck they wouldn't notice the ways in which he became dissatisfied – as he most certainly would do; either that or he'd grow up a bit and find a way not to take it out on them.

Interesting how clearly one can see someone else's

future, at the same time as not understanding one's own.

She thought back for a moment to Tom's comments of last night. Had she really became so reclusive? What others saw as a symptom of pain she thought of as a part of her recovery. She tried to imagine waking to another lover beside her, turning to them in sleepy lust, the world and the morning spread out endlessly before them. But her imagination was stubborn and the bed remained large and empty beside her.

She pulled on her dressing gown and went down to the kitchen. Before she entered she gave the door a little tug to make sure it had stayed locked, then opened it and swiftly walked in.

It was exactly as she had left it eight hours before, the Van Morrisons all in their little plastic boxes on the shelf, the stereo turned off at the mains, the overhead light still on, eclipsed now by the morning sunshine. The only thing that was different was the cat's bowl, which was empty. Millie had obviously come and gone in the night. She went to the French windows to see if she could spot her, but could see no sign. On the edge of the patio where the paving stones met the grass a small brown lump caught her attention. A plump clod of earth? A wet cloth?

She turned the key to the French doors and went out, her feet cold on the stones. It turned out to be a bird, not one of the little ones that Millie sometimes proudly pulled in through the cat-flap in spring, but a fully grown thrush. The pattern on its breast was startling, perfect little nut-brown marks against downy cream feathers. It was well and truly dead, its eyes staring and glassy, its neck lying at an awkward angle. It didn't look so much mauled as broken. She put out a finger and touched the breast feathers. Cold. A long time gone. She looked around the garden, but Millie was nowhere to be seen. She picked up the little body and carried it across the lawn to the nearest flowerbed. The grass was wet and slimy beneath her toes, like walking on snail trails. She slid the bird under a bush. It was neither the time nor the climate for burials, and anyway, Millie would just have it up again. She wondered where it had come from, or more importantly where it would not go back to. Would anyone miss it? Come looking for it? No such thing as a formal identification for these little fellows. She smiled. So much for her day off. The smells of the Prague city morgue were already curling their way back into her nostrils. She made herself an industrial-size cappuccino and gave in to the inevitable.

The head had been savagely beaten. The flesh of the face was unrecognisable, a mash of blood and bone, the jaw crushed so badly that even the dental work might not be salvageable. The only thing that remained was the hair, soaked and matted but still intact. Blond. Long. Fine. Woman's hair. With any luck the torso would be in better condition, depending, of course, on how long it took them to find it.

Jake swallowed the saliva that had gathered in the bottom of his mouth. Ten years a cop and he thought he'd seen everything. But there was always something more, always another one worse than the one before. No point in throwing up though. This early on in the job he had his reputation to think of.

'If you can keep your head while all around are losing theirs, eh?' he said, half under his breath.

'What?'

'Nothin'. Just an English poem.'

' "A thing of beauty is a joy for ever",' the officer said, his accent curling the words in on themselves. 'In this case, I think not.'

Christ, these European cops. They certainly had themselves an education. Some of them even knew American movies better than he did. Had studied them like some kind of life-style correspondence course. 'So, Jake, who do you think she is?'

He shook his head. But the fact was he already knew. The hair had given her away.

She had left the flat at four-fifteen the previous afternoon, the same short black skirt, the same leather jacket, only this time she was wearing sunglasses; sunglasses and no sun. First he thought it was affectation, until she had crossed the street and shimmied straight past him into the cafe. Then he had seen the bruise, a great fat strawberry of a thing, already puffing up under the left lens. She wore it well though, head up, a kind of fuck-you quality to the walk. Good body, he noted, lean, well kept, curved in all the right places, her breasts high and heavy like ripe apples. A little like Mirka's. Jesus, how long would it take before he could look at a woman and not compare? Longer than the six months it had been.

Anyway, this woman wasn't worth the comparison. Within the scheme of things she was just blond trash, a carrier of other people's messages and possessions, a gift to be used – or abused – as part of a larger seduction plan. What she would have brought him would have been the sample, a token of goodwill to show the purity and the quality, quality which could be guaranteed if he and his bosses decided to move their order. And if the Americans were going to sew up the old Soviet market they needed to get those orders.

They. He knew them so well he could taste the salt in their sweat. Not that the big guys sweat much. They pay others to do that for them. Theirs was the brain-work, the strategy, the boardroom tangos. Except it didn't take a genius to sort this one out. With the Western market at saturation point, this was where the action was now. Their Nineties' business plan had them carving up the post-Soviet block within the next three to four years, bribing the small guys, buying out the big, and neutralising those who couldn't be bought. Then they slam down the price, create the appetite and hey presto, new markets, big profits. Proof that capitalism works.

Czechoslovakia was the perfect place to do it all from. Germany to the left, Russia to the right, Hungary and Poland on either side, an economy moving fast enough to have money, and the kind of foreign invest-ment that meant they could launder the profits with-out anybody asking. All this in a cute little Pinocchio city which was fast gaining the comforts of home but where American law couldn't touch them.

But the same didn't go for American law enforce-ment officers. This job had had Jake's name on it from the beginning. He'd already run a couple of successful operations against these guys in the States, so when the Czech government decided to come clean and admit they had a problem, Jake's name was high on the files. Everyone in the department knew he needed a reason to get the fuck out for a while, and what other American narcotics cop could negotiate his way through the Prague old town without a tourist map to help him? That's what eighteen months married to a Czech beauty did for you. Visiting the family. They'd only come here twice, once before the wedding, once after, but it still made him more of an expert than the rest of the division. Not to mention the seventy words of Czech he'd picked up with which to charm the in-laws. She had laughed at his accent, but you could tell she liked it. Fuck it, if they'd been together she could have been with him now, back in her beloved city, away from the madness of New York. She'd end up back here anyway. She never had the stamina for America. If she had she would have stuck by him. What fucking cop's wife walks out the first time the going gets rough?

Let it go, Jake, let it go.

He glanced back up at the apartment window. Not his pitch. The guy in the car down below would check out the man. His job was the woman. She ordered a brandy, then left it on the bar while she went to the john. She was there a long time. As she walked back in she looked around her to check no one was watching. She took a sharp hit of the drink, then sniffed loudly, tossing her fair hair across her shoulders, as if getting something off her back. Yep, she was good-looking. But it wouldn't take long now. Just like home. For all its fancy history and high hopes, once you started really looking this damn city was as dirty as New York. But then a junkie is a junkie the world over.

The night before he'd left home he'd stayed in Manhattan, gone down to the Village and caught a

French movie in some art-house cinema; a street thriller it was supposed to be. The girl in that was a druggie too, but far too pretty for the part, too much of a pout on her well-shaped cheeks. Jeez, hadn't any casting director ever really looked at one of these girls, for Christ's sake? Looked at what smack does to a body if you take it for long enough: how it digs out all the fat of the face, turns the skin yellow, wrecks the joints? Not exactly what you'd call value for money. But then it isn't long before the brain stops counting costs.

The woman at the bar had a way to go, but it was only a matter of time. She finished the brandy and ordered another slivovitz. So much the national drink that the bartender didn't bother to measure it. The liquid slopped over the edge of the glass onto the counter. He imagined her licking it up. For a plum brandy, it was a hell of a lot more brandy than plum. He'd got legless on it his first night at the hotel. And paid for it all the next day. But she looked like she'd been drinking it all her life. She pulled a small compact mirror from her purse, slid the glasses up and looked at herself, assessing the damage, running a tentative finger over the line of the ripening bruise. It must be hurting now, he thought; a throb like a hammer-blow to the centre of the eyeball. The brandy would do nothing to smooth that away. She slid the glasses back down. He watched her carefully over the top of his newspaper, working out how to begin the conversation. Strictly speaking, it was against the rules; his role was to watch, not talk, but two weeks into this job and they were getting nowhere fast. And everyone knew Jake Biderman wasn't a man to stick to the rules.

He put down the paper, got up and walked her way,

sliding himself onto a stool a couple down from her. She threw him a derisory glance, dismissing him instantly. He smiled. 'Hi.'

She ignored him.

'Is bad?' he said, in Czech, doing damage to the words. He tapped his eye to make sure she'd got the point.

Again she didn't seem to hear, putting up a hand to her chin and letting her hair fall over the cheek and her eye.

He waited. Then said, 'You know him?'

She shook her head as if she couldn't quite believe his tenacity. 'Fuck off,' she said sweetly, in English.

The guy cleaning glasses at the end of the bar laughed.

She had style. He had to hand it to her. 'Can I buy you a brandy first?' he said, grinning.

She looked up and into the mirror behind the bar, her attention momentarily distracted. He followed her glance. A man was walking past, then he was gone.

She got off the stool slowly, her ass sliding its way down. Nicely done. Practised, almost. Standing closer he could smell her, something rank and sweet at the same time. It didn't put him off. 'What are you, eh?' she said quietly. 'American?'

'Right first time. That's very good.'

'It was hard,' she said dryly. 'So, Mr American, you like foreign women?'

'I like,' he said. 'Yes, I do.'

'Good. I like you too. Your country gives us money now we're on your side. Money and other things.' She laughed. 'So how about I get *you* a drink instead?'

Her accent was crisp and clean, but then it would

need to be given her job. English was still the language of commerce, legal or illegal. He leaned back in his chair. 'Fine by me.'

She slid her hand back towards her glass, and lifted it to her lips, dragging her tongue along the surface of the liquid like a tiny spoon, scooping up a little mouthful: a deliberately provocative gesture. He nodded in approval. Then she put down the glass in front of him. 'There you go, Yankee. This one's on me.' And she turned on her heel and walked out of the cafe.

The bartender was pretending not to watch. Jake waited till she was out of the door, then got up to follow. He was halfway to the exit when the man's voice reached him. 'Hey, Mr America?'

He turned back.

'The lady get you the drink, she not pay for it.'

By the time he got onto the street she was nowhere to be seen. Shit. He moved swiftly to one corner, then back along to the other. As he turned into the main road he saw it happen as if in slow motion. Across the other side of the street a beat-up black saloon glided to a halt, the back door opening as it did so. They seemed to scoop her off the sidewalk, like a well-practised move in an ice-skating programme. She didn't even have time to struggle. Before the door was closed the car had accelerated and was moving away. He stood, the registration going round and round in his head like a mantra, until he had ripped out a pen and a matchbox to scribble it down on.

That was the last he had seen of her. Until now. When he had got back to base the second watch told him the man had left the apartment ten minutes after the girl, en route to a hotel. He had looked just fine.

Twenty-four hours later a ticket to a left luggage compartment at the Central Station had been delivered to the office he was working in, his name on the envelope. The luggage attendant told them the metal box they found there had been left some time that morning. He couldn't remember who had done the leaving. But then, as Jake knew, give enough money to a man who doesn't earn much and you can wipe out whole layers of memory.

He took one last look at the mess, then turned away.

'Detective Biderman?'

He turned. The pathologist was standing in the doorway, grey hair, glasses, running to fat. He'd seen him before at half a million other murders. Bodies and their dissectors; they were the same in any culture.

'Yeah, that's me.'

'I have something for you. It was found in the lining of the box.'

'For me?'

'Yes.'

Jake followed him into a little cubicle off the main lab. Above the bench, against a light and held up at the corner by a tiny pair of tweezers, a sheet of lined paper was hanging. The words on it were big and scrawled, capital letters in English.

YOU'RE A LONG WAY FROM HOME, BIDERMAN. KEEP YOUR NOSE OUT OF OTHER PEOPLE'S BUSINESS. OR WE'LL CUT IT OFF. JUST LIKE HERS.

She took a swig of her coffee. The cappuccino froth was cold in the bottom of the cup. Not so much a translator gripped by her story as one tired of trying to make it less absurd. On first reading she hadn't given it much thought, but now, playing with each word, she found Biderman's behaviour ridiculous. If he were half as good a cop as this story was trying to make him out to be he would never do such a stupid thing as approach the girl in the first place.

But if he hadn't approached her he wouldn't now be plagued with guilt that he might have contributed to her death. And guilt, of course, can be a powerful motivating force when it comes to getting the hero to slay the minotaur. Especially the kind of minotaur that eats blondes for breakfast.

As for the blonde herself, well, she was expendable. That had been clear from the moment she opened her legs to a stranger. For women like her the range of male emotions was limited anyway. Guilt was probably the best of them, with contempt and lust mixed too close to call. The Madonna and the Whore. With the whore down, there was still the Madonna to go. Mirka better make her appearance soon. You can't keep Irene Jacobs in the wings for too long.

She pressed the Save button. She might as well admit it, she wasn't doing so well today. Like keeping Tinkerbell alive, you need to believe in some kinds of fiction to make it work. Cynicism breeds bad translation.

She got up and arched her spine, using her hands to massage the small of her back. The computer table was too low for her chair and with every page her body curled further over. She looked out of her window. Her study was at the very top of the house. From where she sat she had a bird's eye view of other people's gardens, though not, unless she stood up, her own. In summer it made her the perfect peeping tom on an outside world; children playing, families barbecuing, old men tending their rhubarb patches, and the gay couple with the fenced-in roof terrace who sunbathed nude, believing themselves to be private behind a forest of greenery.

Not now though. Now it was winter and the leaves had fallen from the vine. A woman to the far left of her view was taking in a line of washing, some of it standing up on its own accord with the cold, while three houses further along a man in a hat and coat was doing something to the fence at the bottom of his garden. He'd have to hurry. It was only mid-afternoon, but the natural light had all but drained away. It would be dark soon. Earlier today than yesterday. Earlier still tomorrow. From the middle of November you could almost count the minutes lost from each day.

Tom had left in March when the light was growing stronger. The best time to start again. This would be her first winter alone in the house. She had thought of going away for Christmas. When she had planned the translation schedule she had set herself a theoretical deadline of 300 pages, followed by a week in the sun. But the brochures with their cover photos of Nile sunsets and rose-red desert ruins had lain untouched on her desk. There was no sun in this book. And somehow, already, she knew she wasn't going anywhere either.

Her back still hurt. She lay down on the floor and uncurled her spine, trying to make the bottom of her backbone touch the floor. She lifted her legs slowly off the ground, keeping them straight until she could feel the ache singing up through the back tendons. Then slowly she lowered them to the floor. She did it again.

Her stomach muscles joined the chorus of complaint. She decided not to listen to them. Maybe Sally was right after all. Maybe she had been spending too much time on her own.

Could it be that that was what this whole thing with the CDs had been about? Solitude inducing a form of paranoia, turning the normal into the weird? She could almost hear Patrick and Sally over the dinner table: 'And then apparently she rang him at two o'clock in the morning and screamed down the phone. Accused him of trying to persecute her. Something about a stereo being on when she got home. She was drunk, of course. But still, I mean it's hardly normal behaviour . . .'

What if she *had* simply left the machine switched on and Millie *had* brushed against it? What if the two Van Morrison CDs had genuinely got mislaid, slipped behind a kitchen cabinet or something and she had let an over-active imagination fill in the rest? You hear such stories of women living alone; a culture of threat and fear manufacturing shadows where there are none. In a house full of people a lost CD would simply be someone else's untidiness. Had Tom's leaving turned her into some kind of lonely neurotic? She heard his voice again, concern taking over from anger. Maybe it was she who really needed the revenge? And this had been a way of allowing herself to get angry enough with him to take it?

Except I don't feel like that, she thought. I feel OK. Better. More myself without him. Of course there were other times, times when it hurt still, when the sense of loneliness made you want to scream. But that was inevitable, a part of the process of separating; another step on the long night's journey into day. Underneath she was fine. Wasn't she?

Yeah, and how do mad people really know that they're mad?

She found herself amused rather than disturbed by the idea. In her case maybe the trouble had been sanity rather than madness. Being too nice and too normal for too long; fitting in, making allowances, behaving as she ought rather than as she wanted. Well, not any more. So God help any burglar who saw her as an easy touch.

She got up and went back to close down the computer, but as she did so her eye was caught by a lazy sentence construction, made lazier by her loss of interest, and by the time she'd sorted it out her appetite for the words had returned. She ploughed on for another couple of pages.

The day ended and the street-lights came on. Jake spent hours in his office waiting for a body that never arrived. But then everything took longer in this damn country. Why use computers when you can just employ more people to fill more filing cabinets? Bill Gates was going to clean up around here. And with Gates would come the pirates. Give it a couple of years and there'd be as much profit in illegal software as in drugs. But where's the buzz in chasing computer nerds? Who wants to be that kind of cop? Not Jake Biderman, that's for sure.

Eventually at around ten o'clock they tracked down the kidnap car to a stolen vehicle taken from the suburbs. Except it wasn't that easy. Right number-plate, but wrong car. Simple enough trick in any language to turn the plates around. He kept thinking back to the snatch; the smooth, apparently planned way it had unfolded, how little she had fought back. He saw her glance up into the bar mirror in the cafe, the figure moving out of sight. Maybe it hadn't been such an unwelcome pick-up after all. Maybe they had spotted him as well as her. It wouldn't be the first time an organisation had killed their own carrier. Especially if they thought she'd been talking to the wrong people.

In the end he gave up for the night and went back to his makeshift apartment where the TV was playing American reruns with Peter Falk's mouth moving out of time to the dubbed dialogue and where he felt suddenly homesick for the real thing.

She left him there, eating stale bread and sausages, worrying at the scar tissue of his dead marriage, and thinking, always thinking, of Mirka, her voice, her hair and the way her breasts rode high, like the woman with a clever tongue and no eyes left under her sunglasses.

Suddenly she was hungry too, but like Jake had no appetite for cooking. Or TV. She picked up the phone from her desk and dialled a pizza takeaway, arranging to collect it in half an hour after a visit to the local video store. She grabbed a bag from the hall table and went.

At the local newsagent's she flicked through the racks, rejecting dozens of movies about police corruption and terminator cops, and settling, instead, for one where Jeff Bridges escapes from a burning plane only to find himself unable to connect with the world afterwards. Sally would no doubt see it as a metaphor.

The smell of the freshly baked pizza was exquisite.

She sat in the car feeling its greasy warmth seeping through the bottom of the box onto her lap, and watching while a group of teenage girls lounged on the street corner, talking, laughing, self-consciously confident, as if the world owed them a living which they might or might not be bothered to collect. I was never like that, she thought. Never so sure or so flamboyant. Was it just me, or is there something about this generation that really couldn't give a toss?

Across the street a young man walked past, slicked hair and Doc Martens. One of the girls wolf-whistled, while the rest of them shrieked, doubling up with that uncontrollable giggling that seems to be the preserve of pubescent hormone levels. The guy smirked, even blushed slightly. Sexual harassment: you couldn't really do it to men, they liked it too much. She left them to it.

When she arrived home the pizza was already turning cool on her lap. She decided she would put it in the oven for ten minutes while she made a salad and opened some wine. She noted with relief as she made her way downstairs to the kitchen door that there was no sound of Van Morrison to welcome her.

There was, however, something else.

She saw it immediately she walked in, right in front of her, slap bang in the middle of the kitchen table like some bizarre art exhibit: a neat shimmering stack of CDs, built with such precision that it reached like a miniature plastic towerblock halfway up to the light-fitting above. There must have been twenty or thirty of them, her whole collection, and they had all come from the same place, the same empty kitchen shelf by the stereo. A perfect musical migration.

'Oh, my,' she murmured, for one second as much in wonder as in fear.

Then, as she put down the pizza and reached for the phone, 'Well, at least this means I'm not crazy.'

six

She waited in the kitchen, standing watch over the obelisk, as if without her vigil it might somehow disappear as fast as it had come, leaving nothing for them to see. They had promised to get there quickly and they did.

'They' turned out to be him. He was a young officer, a big man already going to flab though the uniform helped, made him appear older, more solid. He studied the tower, asked a few questions, then checked the house, moving systematically from room to room, testing all the windows and the locks. He found nothing. She was, she realised as he told her, not entirely surprised.

'Though I should tell you you're not particularly well protected here,' he said, rattling the French doors in the kitchen. 'A committed burglar could get through these without much trouble. To be really safe, you need bars. And I've seen more effective locks...' He tested it again, lifting up the internal catch until it clicked, then turning the handle. The door opened. He looked out into the garden then closed it again. 'You're sure you didn't—'

'Leave it open when I went out? Yes, I'm sure.'

'And nothing else has been taken or removed?'

'Nothing.'

He came and sat down opposite her, the exquisitely constructed little tower between them. He stared at it and at her for a moment, then flicked open his notebook and jotted something down. He looked up. Just for the record ... 'How long did you say you'd been living here, Miss, er ... Skvorecky?'

As pronunciations go it wasn't worth correcting. 'Three years.'

'And nothing like this has ever happened before?'

'No. Nothing. Not until the first incident with the CD.'

'And that was?'

'Late July. I think.'

'Right. And this boyfriend you mentioned. He moved out when?'

'Nine months ago.'

'And he no longer has a key.'

'No. Not now.'

'How did it ... er ... end?'

You're too young to want to know, she thought. 'Um ... well, we didn't get on for a while. But it's better now. I mean I really don't think he has anything to do with this.'

'With this,' he repeated. 'So let me get this straight. What we're looking at here is two missing CDs, a stereo that was playing one night when you came in late and these boxes, which have been what? – moved from the work top onto the dining table, yes?'

'Yes,' she said, well aware of how absurd it sounded. 'I don't know about the first incident, but I'm pretty certain the second and third happened while I was out.'

'Right. But there was no evidence of forced entry at those times either?'

'No.'

'So, if no one's breaking in then we're looking for someone with a key. Have you ever lost one? Had your bag stolen, or mislaid it somewhere and not had the locks changed?'

She thought about it. 'No. No, I don't think so. When we bought the house the couple gave us all their keys. There were three sets. I've still got them.'

'Yes, well, we do recommend that people change the locks anyway when they move. And I'd certainly suggest you do that now. Even if it's just to set your mind at rest. Is there anything else?'

'Like what?'

'Oh, doorbells ringing at strange times, phone calls, that kind of thing. Any sort of suspicious behaviour.'

Should you count dead birds on the lawn and upturned flower vases in the middle of the night? 'No,' she said. 'Nothing.'

He rubbed his nose. Then looked up at her. 'And you are absolutely sure that you didn't move the discs yourself? I mean when you were cleaning or tidying up . . .'

They both looked at the skyscraper between them. Of course he had to ask. It was, after all, what he was thinking. Just as Sally and Tom had no doubt thought the same thing about the earlier incidents, but had been too polite to say it directly. Come to think of it, it was what she herself had been considering only a few hours before. But not now. Not any more. 'No,' she said firmly. 'On the contrary. I'm absolutely certain I didn't.'

He let out a breath. 'Well, I'm afraid there's not much

I can do right at this moment. There's no actual crime been committed – and, as I say, no evidence of any break-in. But I'll make a full report and if anything else happens, anything at all, you just call us and we'll be round pronto.'

He snapped his book shut and stood up. Yes, a big man. Did it make him safer on the street at nights, she thought? Would she feel less scared now if she had his bulk?

'I see. And is that it? I mean don't you want to take the boxes for fingerprinting or something?'

He pretended to give it some thought. 'I – I don't think so.' He paused. 'Would it – would it make you feel better if I took another look around the rest of the house? You know – just to check everything is ship-shape?'

'No.' She shook her head, suddenly sick of his conde-scension, sick of having to ask men to hold her hand. 'No. I'm sure it's fine.'

'Good, well then . . .'

She saw him to the door, eager to be rid of him and scared to let him go at the same time. He gave the house a last look, peering up into the spiralling dark-ness of the staircase. 'Big place for you to be in on your own, if you don't mind my saying. Maybe you should think of getting a lodger.'

'Yeah,' she said. 'Perhaps you've got some trainee policemen who need a place to stay?' Knowing as she said it that it could only make matters worse.

'Yes, well, I'll make a note to the station home-beat security officer. He does a lot of visiting women who live alone. He'll be able to suggest some nifty security devices. Make you feel more secure anyway. For now

I'd call your local locksmith. He'll sort you out.'

That's what I need, she thought, sorting out. Maybe I should call Jake Biderman. Get a cop who isn't afraid of weird women. And who knows how nasty the world can be.

As the door closed the silence rushed in to greet her. She turned and looked up into the stairwell. 'Hello!' She shouted angrily. 'Anybody up there?' She went up the stairs, marching into every room and turning on the lights, leaving all of them on behind her, until the house was ablaze like some ocean liner at night. Then she went through the Yellow Pages until she found a twenty-four-hour locksmith. 'All locks changed in under three hours. Guaranteed.' The charge would no doubt be astronomical, but she rang the number anyway.

Back in the kitchen the plastic tower was just as she had left it. She looked at it, calculating the distance between the shelf and the table, how many journeys it would take to move it, why the hell anyone should want to. Then, slowly, she started to dismantle it, keeping note of the order of the discs as she did so; rock'n'roll at the top, the few remaining classical albums Tom had left her at the bottom and the six Van Morrisons all together, just as they had been on the shelf. No message here. Or none that was obvious. But then there wouldn't have been a lot of time to arrange one. After all, she hadn't been out for more than forty minutes or so.

She picked them all up, balancing them one on top of the other again, and walked the stack slowly across the room back to its shelf. But the pile was too unstable and halfway across it disintegrated in the middle, boxes springing out on all sides, clattering to the floor, a couple of them smashing open on the wood, their shimmering little discs rolling like silver wheels into the dishwasher or under the table. She gave a loud cry as the explosion took place. Then one cry turned into another and soon she was standing in the middle of the room, gulping back the sobs.

Something is happening here, she thought frantically, something is happening that I don't understand, and if I'm not careful the fear will stop me thinking straight.

It took her a while to get herself back in control. She splashed water on her face from the kitchen tap and used a tea towel to wipe it away. Then taking deep breaths she gathered up the fallen CDs, taking great care and attention with every one, checking it for dust or damage, reuniting it with its box and putting them all back on the shelf. The last one was a two-disc set of Vivaldi string quartets that Tom had brought her back once from a working weekend in Milan – 'It's the acceptable edge of classical. Got tunes. You'll love it.' Despite the sarcasm he was right. She had. Because of its associations she hadn't played it since he left. Now suddenly she wanted to hear it again.

The music flowed in like a wave. She turned it up more loudly than its elegance could really bear, then louder still, treating it like rock'n'roll. She went over to the French windows and pulled up the catch which released the locks from the top and bottom of the frames and opened both doors out onto the garden.

Outside it was dark and near to freezing. She stood staring into the night, her breath making clouds of smoke, her body tensed against the cold. Somehow it made her feel better, the temperature giving her something real to shiver about. Across the long gardens a security light at the back of one of the houses beyond snapped on, fierce, penetrating, then just as suddenly switched off again. Night life. The place was full of it. The feeble glow of the kitchen light picked out a small dark shape slipping out from the undergrowth across the grass. A cat; not Millie, but her adversary, the ubiquitous black tom. Halfway across the garden it registered her presence, turning, staring straight at her, ears back, body ready to pounce. She held its stare. Then equally suddenly it relaxed and moved on and out of sight. Damn animal. It treated the place as if it owned it. Certainly these last few weeks, since the fight with Millie, it was always around, sleeping in the flowerbeds or dancing its way across the top of the wall. Millie, in contrast, had given up the battle, more often then not spending her days as well as nights inside. Poor Millie. Too young and too active to be confined to the house. Some would say just like her owner.

She closed and locked the French windows, checking the bolts as she did so. The doors had been put in at the same time as the kitchen extension eighteen months ago. The locks were new too, state of the art apparently, with the inside catch releasing two steel bolts into the top and the bottom of the frame. The glass was double-glazed and laminated; burglar-proof her builder had assured her, though evidently he and the police differed on the precise meaning of that phrase. On the other hand there was still no evidence that anyone had actually broken in through them. In which case how had they got in?

Not yet, she thought. Not yet. Not until I'm ready.

On the table the pizza was cold and congealed in its box. She put it on a baking tray in the oven. Then she got out a salad bowl and started to cut up peppers, lettuce and mushrooms. She turned off the Vivaldi and tuned in instead to the radio, where someone was talking about a breakthrough in bone-marrow transplants and how things that had seemed impossible only a few years ago would soon be commonplace. She liked that idea and listened carefully, deliberately not thinking of anything else. Gradually the kitchen became hers again, domestic, tamed.

When the salad was ready and dressed she took out the pizza and opened a bottle of wine. The sound of the cork sucking its way out of the bottle made her feel safe. She lit the candles on the table, but didn't turn the lights off. She had eaten one, maybe two mouthfuls when the doorbell rang. It took the top of her head off even though she was expecting it.

In the crack between the door and the chain a middle-aged man with a worn, moon-shaped face was standing holding a bag. 'Locks Today,' he said rather mournfully. 'You called.'

She pushed the door forward to release the chain and he walked in, putting his bag down in the corner. 'The front door, is it?'

'Yes.'

He fingered it, turning the handle, watching the lock snap out and back again. 'Hmmn.' Then he looked at her. 'You should have asked to see a card, you know.'

'What?'

'Anybody could turn up at your door and say they were from the locksmith's. You should ask to see some form of identification.'

Amazing, she thought. Now even the good guys are strange. 'But you're the only people who knew I called,' she said.

'Hmmn,' he said again. 'You'd be surprised.'

She made him a cup of tea and he set to work. It took him the best part of an hour and a half, replacing the Ingersol and adding a Chubb. She sat on the stairs watching him. For a recluse she was entertaining a lot of men tonight. It seemed important to keep them all in her sights.

If he found her presence strange he didn't remark on it. No doubt he was used to nervous women watching his every move. It must be a bit like being a doctor, she thought: always getting called out in times of emergency and distress.

After a while she got hungry and went back into the kitchen and resurrected the pizza. It wasn't at its best, but he accepted the slice she offered and it started them talking.

When he asked why she was changing the locks, she told him. He listened, eyes still on the wood, chiselling into the hole where the second box would go. She got the impression that the story didn't surprise him. But then presumably he'd heard worse.

'And it was the police who told you to change the locks?'

'Yes.'

He sniffed.

'Why?' she prompted. 'What do you think?'

He shrugged. 'Well, it can't hurt, can it? But it doesn't

sound to me like you've got anyone coming through your front door.'

'No?'

- 'Well, to start with, all this stuff happened in the kitchen, right?'

'Yes.'

'So why go in there and not in the living room or upstairs? You can scare someone a lot more by doing stuff up there, I can tell you.'

And it was clear that he could. She decided not to ask. She wondered how old he was. Late fifties? Maybe older. Her father would have been seventy-eight now, her mother nine years younger. When she was growing up she had got used to him being old, to being the only child of ageing parents. But she still wondered what she had missed, not having him around when she was an adult. Maybe she would have depended less on Tom. Made him more a lover and less a parent. Well, it was all academic now. To lose one parent prematurely is a misfortune, to lose two is what? Bad luck or bad karma? Do orphans have more trouble with long-term relationships? She offered him another slice. He shook his head. 'So what do *you* think?'

'About this?'

'Yeah.'

He stopped chiselling and tried the box. It slipped in neatly. He stood back and looked at his work. 'You'll think I'm daft.'

She gave a laugh. 'No dafter than everyone thinks I am, I can tell you.'

He looked at her. 'I think you might have some kind of poltergeist.'

And as he said it something turned over in her

stomach, something hot and cold at the same time, and she realised that she been waiting for someone to suggest, if not this, then something like it. 'Have you – I mean, have you come across things like this before?'

'There's not a lot I haven't come across doing this job. But yeah, I've seen houses that have had some kind of spirit in them. One lady in the East End had me change all the locks on the doors and windows six times in as many months. It didn't do any good. She'd still wake up in the morning to find them open again. Nothing taken, nothing harmed. Just wide open again. Back door mainly and the two upstairs skylights. Mischievous little tyke that was.'

'My God. What did she do?'

'Can't remember. All I know is I stopped doing her locks. Maybe she moved. It's usually either them or you. Unless you just get on with it and leave them to it.'

'And what makes you think that's what's happening here?' she asked almost in a whisper.

'Nothing, except it fits the facts, that's all. You've got stuff happening you can't explain. It's not – what's the word that the woman used to use to me? – not malevolent. Peculiar rather than serious. You say the house feels all right, that you don't feel scared in between times. And it always happens in the same place. The only funny thing is you've not had trouble before. From the couple I've come across they usually seem to make their presence felt as soon as they find the right person.'

I don't believe this, she thought. It's absolute nonsense, like watching some dreadful New Age documentary on television. I don't believe a word of it. But even as she thought it, she knew that she did. 'I . . . well, I haven't always been alone. I mean I lived with someone for the first two years. He's only recently moved out.'

'And all this has started since?' She nodded. He made a little noise with his tongue. 'Well, then, I'd say that's what you've got.'

He stood up and slipped the new key into the lock, then turned it to and fro. It clicked out and in smoothly. He handed it to her, along with a couple of spares.

'What should I do?' she asked, panic-stricken that now he was finished he might go and leave her.

He bent down and started packing up his tools. 'I suppose that depends on you. I mean how upset it makes you living with it. Sometimes I gather they just go away. Something about the energy around them. I can't say I understand that really. You could always see a priest. Come to think of it, that woman I told you about – with the open windows – I think that's what she did in the end. Got some kind of exorcism done on the place.'

'But I don't believe in God.'

He shrugged. 'I don't believe in luck but I still do the lottery every week. You could always give it a try. It'd be cheaper than fitting new locks, that's for sure.'

He was writing something on a pad. Maybe he carried certain addresses with him in his head. 'Still, you won't be bothered with burglars for a while.' He looked up. 'I can knock off the VAT if you've got cash. Otherwise the boss insists on a cheque with a banker's card number, though, course, you don't need to put your address on.'

It took her a while to realise the last bit was a joke. She stared at him as he handed her the bill. It hadn't all been a joke, had it?

She laughed. 'I'll, er – I'll get you a cheque. It's in my study.' She started to go up the stairs, then she turned. 'You're not . . . I mean you really think that's what this is?'

He looked up at her and shrugged. 'Listen, you asked me what I thought, and I told you. I said you'd find it daft. With VAT that'll be one hundred and seventy-nine pounds forty, including the call-out charge.'

seven

She lay awake for hours after he left, the kitchen door locked, the hall light on, Millie heavy in sleep at the end of the bed.

In the semi-darkness of the room the house felt as it always did: empty, quiet, nothing to get worked up about, unless of course, you chose to infect it with your own anxiety. Even as she lay there, theoretically scared witless by the prospect of some kind of presence around her, she felt OK. Despite whatever it was.

Whatever it was ... That was the point where it all came apart. How exactly do you think about forces you don't believe in? How does one visualise something that doesn't exist?

What had the locksmith said? That it/they usually made their presence felt as soon as they found the right person. Is that what had happened with her? She'd split up with Tom and in the spaces left in between she'd become a conduit for some kind of lost spirit that had been hovering around, searching for someone appropriate to latch on to. She remembered reading somewhere how poltergeists tended to favour young women, girls on the edge of puberty. Maybe hers was only a learner, had mistaken her fondness for Van Morrison for teenage rebellion.

She shook her head. It was crazy. All of it. There was nothing living in this house but her. Her and her unconscious. And since when had that been so demented as to be obsessed with the movement of CDs around kitchen surfaces? No. The only supernatural thing about this evening had been the size of the locksmith's bill.

But if that wasn't the answer then what was? How did one explain the movement of thirty-three CDs from one side of the kitchen to the other? The question played and replayed inside her head, like a swarm of flies, until it was hard to make out the sense for the buzzing. Someone or something was getting into her house and trying to scare her. That much was fact. If it wasn't supernatural (even the word sounded mildly ridiculous) and it wasn't Tom, then it had to be someone else. But who? What kind of intruder would go to such lengths just to play games? Disappearing CDs, manipulating stereos, moving stuff around the room? It hardly amounted to a sustained campaign of terror. On the contrary it was more like mischief than malice.

'Of course, that's what it is, darling.' Sally's voice wafted into mind, loud and clear. God help any poltergeist that ever tried to muscle in on Sally's territory. No room. No room.

She let her voice continue, if only to drown out anything else. 'I mean think about it. The police must come across this kind of thing all the time. You obviously just left your handbag somewhere – you know what a loony you were those first few weeks

after Tom moved out, you were always leaving something somewhere – someone picked it up, maybe even
took a duplicate and hey presto, decided to have a bit
of nasty fun at your expense. They probably live
nearby, on the same street or something so they can
see when you're not there. There's that squat three
doors down, isn't there? It's just the kind of thing someone there would do for a laugh. Freaking out the
bourgeoisie. Nice couple of CDs and then a bit of
intimidation. I mean look what it's done to you. Got you
listening to spook tales from some guru locksmith, for
God's sake. Poltergeists! You'll be a candidate for the
funny farm if you go on like this much longer, Eliza.
What you need is to get out more and have a bit of–'

In her head she faded down the volume. Good old
Sally. Always knowing the best way to undermine a
friend. Well, if she was correct, time would tell. From
now on it would be the right key, but the wrong lock.
She would have only to wait and see.

In the bedroom the central heating pipes groaned
softly under the floorboards, relaxing after a hard
day's work. Interesting how when you start to listen
there's no such thing as silence. She thought of all the
other nights since Tom had gone, nights when Millie
would start up from the end of the bed, instantly on the
alert, registering some bird wing over the rooftop or a
mouse scrabbling in the wainscot two houses away.
Or maybe it hadn't been the call of the wild after
all. Maybe she had been hearing something less
appetising.

Certainly Millie's behaviour had changed too. She
no longer spent time in the kitchen, despite the
proximity of the food bowl. Of course she had an

enemy of her own down there. One with claws and
teeth. What was it they used to say about black cats?
Witches' familiars? A cat-flap needs no key. Any little
body with a will and an appetite can squeeze its way
through there . . . But not even a smart cat can prise its
way into CD boxes, or carry a perfect stack of them
across the room.

The absurdity of the thought collided with the
terror and she tried to make herself think of something
else. But her world seemed to have shrunk and all
roads led back into the dark.

In the search for somewhere where she felt in
control she moved to fiction. Yet even there she found
scant comfort. Jake Biderman may be better at things
that go bump in the night, but he was about to enter his
own spiralling nightmare. A few pages on would see
the next delivery of post; a plastic rubbish bag left at
night in a warehouse, where he was on a stake-out,
with his name on a label tied around the top. His name
and a note:

NOW YOU'VE GOT THE COMPLETE SET, JAKE.
CONGRATULATIONS.

Even before he opened it and saw the mangled
remains the smell had made his stomach turn, as
had the knowledge that someone out there was
playing games with him, knowing more about what he
was doing than he did himself. And enjoying his
discomfort.

Poor old Biderman, she thought. Maybe you should
get the locks on your apartment changed too, just in
case. But then she knew more than he did, knew what

was in store for a man who still loved his wife but didn't know how to save her.

So much for the reassuring power of fiction. She curled herself up under the duvet, trying to shut out the image of the body in the bag, trying not to imagine the burn marks and the slashes. Mutilated female torsos. How was it that so many roads led to the same misogynist nightmare? When did it start, this obsession with sexual violence? Did the legends of the past all go for the vagina and the womb or was it a more modern twist of the imagination? Maybe you could date it back to Jack the Ripper and the curdling of gynaecology into terror. Was it coincidence that such violence took place around the same time that women started asking for more?

The feeble shot of feminism faded, neither triumphant nor fierce enough to cast out the demons. She lay in bed, listening to Millie's quiet breathing. And what else? A noise from downstairs, a click, or maybe a rumble. Real or imaginary?

It hardly mattered. Once heard there was no stopping her. What if it – whatever it/he was – was back, rattling the front door only to find it newly locked? What if, enraged by the rebuttal, they were even now chiselling their way in through the kitchen window?

Absurd. Don't even think about it.

But suddenly it was impossible not to. Her ears strained in the silence and located something else; a scraping noise from somewhere below. Her imagination made it flesh. She saw a figure moving across the kitchen floor, this time ignoring the CDs in search of bigger prey, going for the door, picking the lock, then climbing silently upwards to the floors above. She could make him out more clearly now: a figure darker than the darkness, the features of his face mashed flat by the savage pull of a stocking, no character, no feeling, just a cold madness intent on violence. He was so familiar he hardly needed imagining. The psycho-path and his pathology; sexual pleasure rising and exploding with the blood and terror of the victim. The image was so exploited, so grotesque, that you might almost expect it to be easier to handle, easier to mock. Only it wasn't. Fear spread like an inkstain across her mind. The more she tried to control it, the more certain she was that it was actually happening, the more precisely she could distinguish the individual choreog-raphy of sounds: the click of the lock, the scraping open of the door, the tell-tale creak of his tread on the wooden stairs. The panic wrapped itself around her, making it hard to breathe. By the time he got as far as the landing she was drowning in the echo of her heart-beat as it pumped the blood around inside her head.

But at the same time as she went under, something flew free. A part of her sat above on the bedstead looking down, impatient, scornful. 'Just look at you,' it said fiercely. 'Scaring yourself stupid. There's abso-lutely nothing there. You know that. You're just making it up. Making yourself sick with fear. Stop. If you stop, so will it.'

Against the odds the voice got through. With what seemed like a superhuman effort of will she pulled off the covers, got up from the bed, walked over to the door and pulled it open.

The lights from the hall flooded in.

Nothing. The staircase both above and below was

empty. There was no one there. No madman, no steps, no sound. She pushed herself further, willing herself down the stairs towards the front door, then, when she found it locked, down again towards the kitchen. She waited by the door, listening. Then she turned the key and went in, snapping on the light-switch as she did so. The place was empty, the night at the windows silent. No intruders inside or out.

'Whoever or whatever you are I'm not afraid of you, do you hear?' She waited for an answer, a flying CD or a scrape of furniture, but there was nothing. That's because there's nothing here, she thought. If there was I would feel it.

She stood for a moment longer, then went back upstairs. Millie stirred, lifting her head to check what all the fuss was about. She picked up the warm little body and moved it further up the bed, offering it usually for-bidden territory. The cat nestled in against the warmth of her body and almost instantly fell back asleep.

She lay there feeling the rhythm of its breathing against her chest. She felt calmer. Drowsy. After a while she too fell asleep.

Once again she slept soundly and long. And when she woke to a bright early morning and the sound of a milk float halfway down the road, she felt as if she had won a battle, had proved herself in some quiet way that she didn't completely understand.

Millie was already up and hungry. They went downstairs together, the cat weaving its way in and out of her ankles, eager for breakfast.

It had already been prepared.

As she opened up the locked room, the sight that

met her eyes was extraordinary in its ordinariness. The table was laid for two with plates, cups and saucers, a jar of marmalade and box of cornflakes. While in the kitchen area in the middle of the floor sat half a dozen saucepans, a handful of cat pellets in each of them.

It was then she remembered the locksmith's words and decided that what she really needed was a priest.

eight

It wasn't exactly the kind of service you found in the Yellow Pages. She didn't even know for sure where her nearest church was. There was a Victorian mausoleum a few streets away but from what she remembered God had vacated it some time ago, leaving it to the tender mercies of property speculators. Yet there had to be a working priest or vicar somewhere in the area. She had a vague memory of a circular being pushed through the door last Christmas with details of family services. At the time she had already been in the process of losing what little family she had and the exhortations to joy and celebration had left a bitter taste in the mouth, ensuring that the pamphlet went swiftly into the bin.

Even now the thought of cloying sympathy and understanding sent another kind of shiver down her spine. As she dressed hurriedly she toyed with the alternatives. Like going back to the police. But you could see how, from their point of view, breaking and entering a set of kitchen cupboards would be no more criminal than the transportation of CDs across a kitchen – or any less crazy. For them she was already a woman in pain after the end of a long love affair, and, as such, could be relied upon to find all manner of strange ways to draw attention to herself. She could almost read the police report.

That left Tom or Sally. But ex-lovers are not the people to ask for help when you're trying to stand on your own two feet and the price of Sally's friendship, fulsome though it might be, would be the news of her advanced looniness all round the bush telegraph by nightfall.

There were, of course, other numbers she could have called, just as there had once been other friends. But looking down the list in her address book made her realise how far into retreat the last nine months had taken her. Some of these people she hadn't even spoken to since the separation, while others who had tried to keep in touch had more or less given up trying. This was neither the way nor the time to reconnect.

Her isolation drove her into the arms of the church. Once on the streets it wasn't hard to find. It had been built in the grounds behind the old one, its modern façade facing onto another street. Thirty years ago its glass and concrete had probably been seen as daring, but now, like most Sixties buildings, it carried its architectural origins as stigma rather than triumph. Was God more of a Gothic man, she wondered, then slapped down the thought sharply. This wasn't going to work unless she took it seriously.

The front doors of the church were locked. Through a long, coloured window in the side she made out a large open space with a flat altar at the front and a gaunt wooden figure suspended on a crucifix above it, the light catching the flank of the body, the criss-cross of ribs running along the grain of the wood.

Next door there was a house, modern, fake Georgian, with a winter climbing rose round the front door. Altogether too twee for London. She looked at her watch. It was just after nine o'clock. Ah, well, servants of God must be like doctors; ready at all times. She rang the bell. It took a while, then a slim woman with short greying hair and a strong-cut face answered. She was wearing trousers and a sweat shirt, the clothes reading somewhat younger than her years.

'Hello, I need to see the priest – er – I mean the vicar.'

The woman nodded, then gave a little smile. 'Well, you'd better come in.'

She showed her into a small room, halfway between someone's study and a dentist's waiting room. 'If you could wait one minute.'

Who'd be a cleric's wife, she thought? Always cutting up those loaves and fishes for someone else to perform the miracles. She looked around. On the table was a set of pamphlets showing pictures of Jesus surrounded by a rainbow-coloured collection of little children, and to the side in the corner there was a big box of well-used toys. Maybe pastoral duties had now taken over from Social Services. What am I doing here? she thought, suddenly panicky. I must be out of my mind. Well, yes, that was one suggestion.

The woman came back in, closing the door behind her and sitting down on the chair opposite. She had changed her clothes; a skirt and sweater with a quiet but distinct sense of style. The subtlety of the outfit was somewhat undermined by the dog collar, which stood out like a neck brace.

The sight of it took her completely aback. But then

its wearer was obviously used to that. She smiled broadly and put out her hand. 'I'm sorry. I should have made it clear earlier. I *am* the vicar. Rev Catherine Baker. And you are . . .?'

'Er . . . Elizabeth. Elizabeth Skvorecky. I'm sorry. I had—'

'Don't be. It happens all the time. And in my experience the women always feel worse about it than the men. A doctor friend of mine tells me it still happens to her, even after twenty years. So I have a long way to go. Anyway, I can assure you I am fully qualified and ordained. So, how can I help you?'

It was possible, she thought later, that being so thrown off-guard was no bad thing. In her head she had rehearsed the story as she walked the streets, making it more manageable, less disturbed. But here in the heat of her confusion it came out differently, more like it felt.

The woman listened in silence, her face giving away nothing, not even the expected softening of sympathy.

'Well,' she said at last after it was over. 'What a remarkable story. I'm surprised you're not scared out of your wits.'

'You should have seen me an hour ago.' She laughed sourly. 'I'm not sure I've got any wits left to be scared out of.'

'I find that hard to believe,' the woman said quietly, then, after a pause, 'But you say that despite all this the house doesn't feel bad?'

'Er . . . no. I mean not unless I let it.'

'Of course.' She nodded understandingly, as if remembering some similar moment of panic in her own life. Surely not, thought Elizabeth. Surely nothing has ever happened to you? Doesn't God protect his own from fear of the Devil? Or is the real comfort to be had from surviving the test of temptation? 'So tell me, had anything like this ever happened to you before? In another house, when you were younger perhaps?'

'No. No, never.'

She nodded, silent for a moment. Then: 'Well, I'm not sure I know what to say. Certainly on the evidence of what you've told me, it might seem that your locksmith is right. And that you probably do have some sort of psychic disturbance going on.'

'Psychic? You mean a spirit?'

'No, not entirely,' she said slowly, a woman clearly concerned to pick the right words. 'And before we go any further there's one thing you should be absolutely clear about. Whatever is happening in your house – and clearly some very strange things are – we're not talking about any kind of evil. This has nothing to do with . . . I don't know, the Devil or Satan or anything like that.'

'Just as well, really, because I don't believe in him,' she replied, aware of just how tartly the remark came out.

The woman smiled slightly, taking in what she had been told. 'So though I'm sure you do feel scared, it's very important for you to understand that there is nothing to be scared *of*. The Church deals with a number of these kind of disturbances. They're more common than you might think. And in most cases they can be sorted out.'

There was a moment's silence. The two women sat eyeing each other up. She doesn't know what she's doing, thought Elizabeth. Despite what she says she's obviously never come across anything like this before and she's playing for time, trying to work out how disturbed I am.

She suddenly wanted to be out of there, to get up and leave. Except where would she go but back to the house? And now she was away from it, it was, she realised, the last place on earth she wanted to be.

'Are you saying you think it's me? That I'm causing it?'

The woman frowned, opening a comfortable furrow across her brow. 'To be honest, at this moment I have no idea what's causing it. What I *do* know is that in some cases these poltergeist-type phenomena can be related to the emotional condition of someone in the house; their anger, their pain, not necessarily negative emotions, just things that haven't been resolved. And that understanding or acknowledging that connection can help it to go away. But that's only an observation. To get any further I'd need to come round and look at the place, talk some more. But that, of course, would be up to you.'

It had been at least two decades since she had given any serious consideration to God, an early teenage flirtation with religion driven out by a local charismatic vicar without charisma. On the odd occasion since, when she had met believers she had found them almost offensive, their certainty exhibiting itself as a form of complacency, like membership to a club she didn't want to join. But this woman didn't feel like that. Maybe that had something to do with being kept out of the club so long herself.

Oh well, she thought. What do I have to lose?

'When would you like to come?'

*

They decided on five o'clock that afternoon. A clever time: the hour of long shadows and the collapsing of the day into dark, a perfect invitation to ghosts and ghouls, not to mention those with over-vivid imaginations.

The question was, what should she do till then? She left the vicarage and walked the streets for a while, but the wind was too cold to make it comfortable. She made her way to the High Street where a fancy new coffee shop had opened up since she was last there, a blackboard outside chalked with special offers. She went in and ordered a cappuccino and a sweet croissant and sat in the window seat watching the world go by.

The shop across the road was putting up its Christmas decorations, a young shop assistant perched inside the main window with a spray can, desperately trying to work out how to write 'Happy Xmas to All Our Customers' backwards. They were late. The rest of the street was already decked out, the usual collection of chemical snow on fake mullion windows and reused plastic Santas with bulging bellies and sacks. Christmas. She had been so busy she hadn't noticed how close it was. Who would she spend it with this year? No doubt Sally and Patrick would feel they had to offer, unless of course they'd already invited Tom. Either way she could do without it. Maybe she should stay at home and have it with the poltergeist. If she could train it, perhaps it would do the washing up as well as laying the table.

What words had the vicar used? 'It's usually related to the emotional condition of someone in the house'.

Who else if not her? Unless it was Millie that was causing it, her fury at having her space usurped. That would at least explain the cat pellets.

But that wasn't what the vicar thought. The vicar thought it was *her*, acting like some overgrown teenager, burying an excess of emotion in an orgy of kinetic tricks. If this was all some manifestation of her psyche then what a miserably tame affair it must be; all it could rise to was laying the table and rattling a few pots and pans. If she was really repressing that much pain wouldn't there at least be a few cracked windows or exploding electrical gadgets to reflect the depth of her despair?

Despite all of the sarcasm she knew she was scared. And that was why she didn't want to go back to the house.

The supermarket had more people in it than she had seen for months. She had, she now realised, been keeping away from crowds, shopping in smaller places close to home, rushed little expeditions at the end of the day for only the most vital of supplies. The choice seemed overwhelming. She went through the aisles plucking out anything that caught her fancy; ingredients for exotic meals she'd never cook, an expensive bottle of brandy, useless luxuries like cans of grossly scented air freshener, the consumers' way of driving out unwanted household presences. As she unpacked them at the till she almost told the cashier, 'These? Oh, these are my ghostbusters. Would you recommend meadow fresh or something a little more evergreen?' How absolutely absurd, she thought. For life to be so normal and so strange.

She bought so much she had to get a taxi home. She

waited till she had unloaded the bags and got the door open before paying him, just in case the spirits had multiplied and were waiting behind the front door to spook her. But there was nothing there except the post and a special offer coupon from the local Indian take-away.

In the kitchen the landscape had altered slightly. The saucepans were as she had left them, but the cat pellets had gone. Her heart started an instant acceler-ation till she spotted Millie curled on a chair looking like she'd died and gone to cat heaven. She tipped up the chair and the cat fell off, yowling in overfed protest.

'You're not supposed to eat the evidence,' she muttered as she kicked her out of the room.

Outside, a watery sun was throwing pale shadows across the lawn and the few remaining geraniums were curling under the onslaught of the cold. She sighed. Her kitchen. Her garden. She remembered back to the summer when the place had been vibrating with her sense of release. She saw herself dancing across the floor, the stereo blasting, a new contract on her desk and a whole life stretched out in front of her. Where had that extraordinary optimism gone? Shrivelled up by a frost of paranoia and fear. Even the cappuccino machine and her bright new mugs no longer seemed so inviting. How quickly it can all fall apart.

On the wall bracket the phone rang. She had to stop herself jumping at the sound of it. She listened while the answering machine took the call.

'Hi, there. It's Charles. Listen, I just looked at my diary and saw it was already the beginning of December and I was wondering how it was going with you and the words.

'I've got more news on the movie deal by the way. It's all systems go, apparently. They're going for a script based on the idea rather than the translation – well, they're never anything like each other anyway. But it's absolutely brilliant for us, of course, because it means not only all that free publicity but if we're lucky we might even get a photo on the paperback cover. The divine Irene Jacobs eating a bratwurst or whatever you call them. Or should we go for something darker? Bit more grisly – her disembowelled with Brad scooping her innards back in. Yum yum. Course, it also means we have to get our skates on. Limited hardback summer release with mass-market paperback tied to the film release a year later. Which, my dearest, I'm sure you're more than capable of, fast little wordsmith that you are. You wouldn't have a fit if I pulled the delivery date forward by six weeks or so, would you? Eh? So easy to ask favours from a machine, isn't it? They never answer back. No doubt I'll get to talk to the real person soon enough. Anyway, call and let me know what you think. And keep these bloody words flowing. Love and thoughts.'

'To you too, Charles,' she said as she held her finger down on the button to erase the message. 'But don't hold your breath.'

In homage to the spirit of happier times she let the cappuccino machine do its work. As the water snarled its way into steam she thought of all the records she could play to drown it out, but somehow even the music had lost its attraction. The Reverend's visit – in her mind she couldn't bring herself to call her Catherine – was still hours away. She could either sit and watch the clock go round to check someone wasn't moving the hands, or she could get on with work.

Work. If Charles was serious about pulling the deadline forward it didn't leave her much time to have a nervous breakdown about the current spiritual activity in her house. She needed to get Jake and Mirka into crisis and violence, then out of it again. The schedule wasn't impossible, only a little more intense than she would have preferred. Especially now. Biderman and his tortured soul. Not to mention the tortured bodies. Maybe the problem was that she'd been close to it for so long it was beginning to feel like real life. Could it be that her isolation had given it too much prominence, had even encouraged his nightmares to leak into hers?

Stupid. Once she thought about it, it seemed so simple. A matter of attitude. If that was the problem she should simply stop trying so hard, start treating it as work, rather than feelings. More matter, less art. No one was going to read it that carefully anyway.

She looked at her watch. One forty-five. She locked the kitchen door and made her way up. Inside the privacy of the word processor Jake was about to be frightened. But not me, she thought, as she climbed the stairs. Not me.

He left the black plastic bag in the hands of the forensic boys and made his way back to the office, picking up breakfast en route. But when it came to it he couldn't face the food. Instead he went for the liquid. The caffeine punched him in the gut, Jesus, in America this concentration of any drug would be illegal. Here they drank it like water. Still, he needed to wake up. He poked his fingers hard into his eye sockets. Even after a shower her rotting was still all over him, resting in the pores of his skin, sliding up into his nostrils, the smell more animal than human now. At least dead flesh felt no pain. The best you could hope for her was that she had died halfway through. Fuck 'em. He remembered the sweet-sour perfume of her body alive, standing close to him in the coffee bar. It doesn't take much to turn a person into manure. Poor little slag. Nobody deserved that...

Christ, even with the coffee he was tired. Not so much to do with fighting sleep as fighting fear. Fear. That was something they didn't teach you about in police academy. Or not enough. They never told you how much of a disease it was, how it attacked your mind as much as your body, filing down your nerve ends till they screamed. If you let it get the better of you it could drive you half mad

The secret was controlling the memory. It was the kind of advice you'd give to a kid. If the book scares you, don't read it. If the memory scares you, man, forget it. Easier said than done. Like wiping out the sight of broom handle stuck up a vagina. Or worse, the look in a girl's eyes.

He'd only been a cop for eighteen months, out on the street for less than a year, still wet behind the ears. And other places. It wasn't even a dangerous job. He was one of a couple of dozen extra men brought in to make house-to-house calls in the sleepy Westchester suburb. Jesus, it was so respectable up there you'd think they'd abolished crime. Still, according to the bosses, the guy they were looking for was maybe somewhere in the area.

The girl had been kidnapped three weeks before, lifted off the street on her way from her job at the office. Just an ordinary worker for an ordinary multinational. Except for the fact that daddy damn near owned the company. The first couple of ransom notes had come along with a video, her half-naked in some kind of cage, eyes like a rabbit in the headlights, babbling some script about used bills and drop-off points that he'd written for her. Except when they gave him what he wanted he didn't come for it. Just sent back another film to add to the police porn library. It was the worst kind of case, the bosses said, one where he was more interested in the girl than the money. What they didn't say was they'd had a carbon copy of this one ten months before. But then nobody likes to admit they got a serial on their hands. Sickos with a habit. The world was full of them, clever bastards.

This time though they did have something. When they circulated the details of a suspicious-looking van parked behind the office, someone reported a sighting of it turning off a highway upstate two days later. It was pure luck really. It could have been going anywhere. To any one of five thousand houses. Or none of them. It was a long shot. But Jake sort of knew the minute he knocked on the door. Funny how some houses just smell of the shit that's going on inside them.

The guy had been shifty right from the start. Had a good story. He was some kind of writer working on a book. He had a studio all set up in there – bookshelves, word processor, printer, the lot. But even though he didn't put a foot wrong there was something about him that was messed up. Jake could feel it as he stood in the bedroom door looking round, could feel the guy's body behind him, humming with tension. If they'd plugged him into an electricity socket he would have lit up the whole damn street. But there was nothing to incriminate him. Nothing in any of the rooms. Upstairs or down.

It wasn't till he got back out on the street again and looked along the roofs that Jake realised he hadn't checked the attic. There must be one. The guy two doors along had had his converted and the houses were pretty similar. Yet he couldn't remember seeing a trap door anywhere, though in one bedroom there had been a couple of big cupboards right up to the ceiling. Heavy mother fuckers, probably. Unless they were empty.

If he'd been more experienced he would have radioed for help. But if he'd been more experienced he would have known to trust his gut. He drove the car into the next street and walked back. When there was no answer he went in through the back.

The guy was already halfway up into the attic when he caught him, the cupboards pushed back against another wall. He told him to freeze, but when the man turned he had a gun in his hand and the shots missed Jake by inches. His own found a home. He got him in the upper leg, and then when he still didn't stop firing, Jake got him in the stomach. The guy fell like a lump of bird shit, straight down, thud, then lay doubled up groaning and moaning like an animal. He kicked the gun away from him and radioed for help. It was then that he heard her.

She was still screaming when he got up to her. She was in this metal cage, half naked, filthy, shaking, a chain round her ankle connecting her to the bars.

There was a dog bowl near by with scraps in it and a pot a few feet away. The smell of urine was everywhere. But nothing shook him as much as the look in her eyes. You couldn't even call it fear. More like stupor. He even wondered if she'd been drugged, except nobody drugged could scream that much. He hadn't dared touch her. All he could do was stand there, talking, telling her she was OK now, that she was safe, while yelling to them back at base to get a woman out here, and fast.

Later he would hear that she'd had a series of breakdowns, spent the next year in and out of institutions. For a long time after she became his recurring nightmare – the eyes and the scream. His partner Ernie said it was only natural. That even the best cops sometimes discover that the filth doesn't wash away. Her distress became such an obsession that in the end he even asked permission to visit her, see how she was. Not surprisingly the request was refused. Last he heard, three or four years back, she was still in trouble, running up Daddy's bills with a score of shrinks who couldn't even get her to go out of the house on her own.

For him it had got easier. Mirka had walked into his life, lovely and unscarred, and the warmth of her body had dispelled his nightmares and kept the cage at bay. She had loved him and he was healed. Simple as that. Except nothing lasts for ever. How it got lost he still couldn't quite remember. Somehow the grind and the dirt of other cases and other pain started to wear away at her optimism and patience. She got scared for him. And then when she couldn't do anything about that she got scared for herself. He said she was the one who had changed. She said it was him. By the end it didn't matter.

By the end their rows were so loud and vicious it was clear they both had. But he was the one who got the nightmares back. The day after he moved out, sleeping on Ernie's couch, the cage and the screams came back. And kept on coming. He had lost his talisman against fear. For a while that spring he thought that he, like the girl in the attic, might die of it. But he hadn't. Instead he'd thrown himself into work. He was still alive.

He drained the coffee cup and picked up the phone to New York. It was time to put the screws on the bad guys, made them hurt too. Half an hour later he'd got what he needed. Back on their home ground the big boys were going to find somebody putting salt on their tails. After all, international businesses have to keep the profits up in all their markets, not only the expanding ones. And this time he'd make sure they knew where the salt was coming from.

She had worked fast, letting the word count mean more than the words. She read it back for typos then put it through the spell check. Maybe she should print out a copy of it for Reverend Baker as proof that the higher you go the harder it is to find God. Attics. Always the places where the secrets are kept, like the dark bits of the mind. Except the contents of this particular attic would surprise no one, she thought scornfully. Women chained up as dogs; they were a dime a dozen these days. What else should any modern self-respecting psychopath do with a kidnap victim? Sadistic chic. Maybe that was what angered her so much about the scene; its fashionable conformity, its predictability, right down to the abused turning into the mad.

If before she had been afraid of her cynicism, worried that it might somehow undermine the text, now she felt emboldened by it. How much more challenging if the writer had seen fit to give the caged girl a different future: six months of therapy which blew away her fear and turned her into a lawyer or a painter with a husband and children of her own, and a house where she had no problem converting the attic into a well-lit playroom.

The least he could have done was to fight fantasy with fantasy. 'Jake later heard that Mary Louise Brown had joined the police force, where she became known as a kind of avenging angel for women in trouble, swooping down on violent men and snapping their bodies between her dog-like teeth until they screamed for mercy, then leaving them for dead, taking their young women victims home and tending their wounds both mental and physical till they were strong enough to go back out on the streets and break a few balls of their own.'

Maybe she should just stick it in. One paragraph in 500 pages. They probably wouldn't even notice. Charles was a notoriously sloppy reader, and with the deadline snapping at his heels he wouldn't bother that much. Just her own small notation: like the Renaissance biblical copyists leaving their individual mark on the page.

Her fingers were hovering over the keyboard when, three flights down, the doorbell rang. The sound brought back the present and the kitchen and the fear that wasn't in the words. She rose up to greet it.

nine

The Reverend was waiting on the step with a pot of what looked like early daffodils in her hand. She was wearing a long flowing coat, rather splendid, and her hair, caught in the wind, was a halo of salt and pepper grey. She looked, well – unlike a vicar.

'Hello. Any further developments?' she said as she held out the plant. 'Oh, these are for you, by the way. I'm afraid it's early days, but they always come through in the end.'

'Thanks. Er . . . no. Though while I was out something ate the cat pellets.'

'You don't think it could have been the cat?' she said with such a straight face it took a while for the humour to register.

She led her downstairs. As she unlocked the door she thought, what if it's all gone away? What if I did just imagine it all?

But there it was, the table laid and untouched, the pans on the floor with a few errant pellets still scattered in between.

The woman stood in the doorway, then came in slowly, looking around, obviously trying to get a sense of the place. What was she after? Signs of fraud or distress? Apart from her plump policeman it was so long since anyone had been here. When was the last time? It must have been the dinner party after she got back from New York, two, two and half months ago now. No wonder this spirit had got so cheeky. It must have assumed it had the place to itself.

The Reverend walked over to the windows and looked out. 'What a lovely garden. You've done some work out there.'

'Yes. Would you . . . would you like a cup of tea?'

'Thank you, I would.' She flicked up the handle on the kitchen door. It was locked. 'How do you open this?'

'You have to pull up the catch above. It releases the lock.'

'Ah. Yes. I see. Sad, isn't it?' she said, locking the doors back up again. 'The way winter cuts it all off. Makes you feel like a prisoner in your own house.'

'Yes, I suppose so.'

Is that what I'm supposed to be feeling? she thought. Would a sense of climatic siege have been enough to give birth to this psychic mischief-maker?

She got on with making the tea while Catherine squatted down by the saucepans, picking up the odd cat pellet, then moving to the table, running her hands over the crockery, holding up the cornflakes packet, apparently reading the back panel for clues. What was she doing? Listening for the call of the wild, the echo of a paranoid soul trying to get out? This isn't going to work, Elizabeth thought. She can't help me. I should never have let her come.

'You said you were a translator?' the woman asked as they sat together at the other end of the table from the breakfast things, cradling their mugs of tea in their hands.

'Yes. Czech into English.'

'Ah, that would explain your surname. Your father's Czech?'

'Yes.'

'What do you translate?'

'Oh, different things. Some business stuff, books, short stories. I'm working on a novel at the moment.'

'Really? Anybody I'd know?'

'I doubt it.'

'So not Milan Kundera.'

She smiled. 'No. Rather more pulp, I'm afraid. It's a thriller.'

'Is it good?'

'It's popular,' she said. 'Got its eyes on the American market.'

'Aaah. And you work from home?'

'Yes. I have an office at the top of the house.'

'So when you're up there you presumably wouldn't be able to hear anything going on down here.'

'That depends what it is. I suspect if it started throwing plates I would.'

'Do you think it will?'

She shrugged. 'What do I know? Apparently I'm just controlling it.'

The woman smiled. She opened the sugar pot and scooped out a hefty spoonful. There was a silence. It didn't seem to bother her. 'I rang a couple of people this afternoon,' she said at last. 'To get some advice. I've not come across many poltergeists before. They said that sometimes though it can be a manifestation of distress, it may well be distress that the person themselves doesn't even know that they're feeling.' She paused. 'You mentioned this morning that you'd split up from your partner.'

'Yes.'

'How long were you together?'

'Seven and half years.'

She nodded. 'Do you think you're perhaps still mourning that?'

Here it comes, the pseudo therapy. I don't want to talk about this, she thought, suddenly extremely angry. She took a deep breath and sat waiting for her fury to activate a few bits of crockery, start some thrashing and smashing around the room. Everything remained stubbornly in its place.

'We did the right thing,' she said in the end, through half-clenched teeth. 'And I've been more happy than sad.'

'But sometimes lonely?'

And what would you know about it; shacking up with God every night, telling him your deepest thoughts, getting the hotline version of things then going out and dispensing divine love like breakfast wafers to anyone who sticks their tongue out. She shrugged. 'Maybe . . . sometimes.'

But it was clear that more was expected of her. The silence grew. She ignored it angrily. Many years before, after her father died and she had found herself in a vice-grip of pain which seemed altogether too vicious to be just grief, someone had advised her to see a psychotherapist about it. She had even gone as far as having – what did they call it? – an assessment session. That person had been a woman too, very quiet, very calm. She had asked a few questions and then left her to talk. They had spent forty-five minutes in total silence, at the end of which time Elizabeth was absolutely clear that whatever the pain, it was hers and hers alone and could not or would not be shared.

Eventually, over time, the crippling grief had eased itself and become manageable, more soaked into the fabric of life. Now, as she sat here, this silence seemed to put something of the same weight of expectation on her shoulders.

'You know one of my colleagues this afternoon told me this story about a parishioner he'd seen a couple of years ago,' the woman said, helping herself to more tea as if nothing had happened. 'She lived alone, this woman, not a member of the congregation or anything, just someone who turned up one day rather like you did. She was older than you – in her early fifties, I think he said – very creative apparently, an artist. She had been diagnosed with breast cancer and had to have one breast removed. She was so traumatised by the operation that she couldn't work. They'd offered her reconstructive surgery but she'd refused.

'Anyway, then these things started happening in her home. She had some very beautiful objects – she'd travelled a lot, all over the world. And some of them started to go missing. Statues, ornaments, that kind of thing. But only when there were two of them. One would suddenly go. It affected even quite mundane things, apparently. Once she had two milk bottles sitting on the kitchen table. One of them disappeared. Each incident was the same destruction of symmetry. He said that she hadn't even noticed this pattern until he pointed it out to her. And that when he did she got very upset. She was upset for quite a while. But after that it stopped. Somehow the release of the pain, no longer denying it, helped her to come to terms with it.

'She went on to do a rather wonderful set of sculptures about women's bodies. There was an exhibition of them in a gallery about a year ago. I'd just got the post at St Mary's. I went with my colleague to see it. Although he didn't tell me the whole story until later, when I spoke to him today, in fact. It's amazing, don't you think?'

'Yes,' she said, because it was. 'Did they come back later?'

'The objects, you mean?'

'Yes.'

The woman laughed. 'You know I asked him the same question. He said he couldn't remember. Men. They sometimes miss the obvious.'

'Is that a theological observation?' she asked because she couldn't resist it.

The woman laughed again. 'I don't know. Probably. Probably mildly heretical too.'

I like you, Elizabeth thought. I like you very much. But I still don't see how you can help me. How anybody can. 'It's not that I miss him,' she said, after a while. 'I don't think we were very good for each other. It's more than I don't quite know what to do now. Or if I want to do anything. Sometimes I don't know how people get close to each other. Why they bother.'

'Are your parents still alive?'

'No, no. My father died before I met Tom, my mother three – no – four years ago.'

'I see. How about friends?'

'Loads,' she said. Then, quietly, 'I don't see them much these days.'

'Which means you don't go out a lot?'

'Hardly at all.'

She left a silence. 'Do you mind?'

'Mind what?'

'Being so alone. I don't mean lonely necessarily, just alone.'

'Er . . . do I mind? I don't know. I don't seem to be able to do anything different at the moment.' This is the longest conversation I've had in months, she thought, maybe the longest since Tom left. Weird.

'You don't think these things happening . . . well, you don't think they might be a way of keeping yourself company?'

The very idea of it made her laugh out loud. 'What? Somebody putting on the stereo before I get home, or laying the table and feeding the cat for me?' But she thought about it anyway. Once again it made no sense. How could she have done these things to herself? It was not only absurd, it was, surely, impossible. 'I'm not mad,' she said angrily.

'No, you're most certainly not.'

'But then, how? I mean do you really believe that I did all of this without knowing it?' and she gestured to the cups and saucers on the table in front of them.

'Not consciously, no, of course not. Any more than the woman with the mastectomy consciously moved her own objects. But the unconscious is an extra-ordinarily powerful force. In terms of the psychic energy it can release . . . well, I don't think it's inconceivable. Do you?'

'I don't know. Sometimes I think it's nothing to do

with me. Sometimes I think that someone's just trying to scare the shit out of me. See how strong I am.'

'And how about if you were doing that to yourself? Testing yourself now that you're alone.'

She shook her head. 'If I am, then I don't need a priest, I need a shrink.'

If the woman was offended by the remark she didn't show it. Maybe the two professions saw themselves going hand in hand now. Soul doctors for a soulless world. 'Perhaps what you need is to decide that you've passed the test.'

'What d'you mean?'

'I mean that you're coping so well it's obviously important to you to do so. It could be that it's time to let yourself off the hook. Accept that you can sometimes be lonely without being destroyed by it.'

'I don't know.' God, how many times can you say that phrase? she thought. At one level everything the woman said made some kind of sense. But then in the land of the blind the one-eyed man is king. Maybe that was the problem. 'I really don't know what to think,' she said carefully. 'What do your colleagues suggest?'

'About you?'

'Yes.'

'Not anything specific. Each case is unique to itself. Although they do say that prayer is effective.'

'Yes, well, that's hardly an option for me at the moment.'

She smiled. 'I think they meant me rather than you.'

'What, you praying for me?'

'Yes. Does that upset you?'

She laughed. 'Not at all. It's just it's the first time

you've mentioned God. I did wonder why you hadn't brought him up earlier.'

'Why? Would you like me to have?'

'I don't know. I thought it was, er . . . well . . .'

'Compulsory?'

'Something like that.'

The Reverend sat quietly for a moment. 'You know there are times when I think they only let women into the Church because they didn't know what else to do. Then at least if things got worse, they could blame us.'

She stopped, playing with the rim of her cup, deciding where to step next. 'I think that people's lives are very hard at the moment. There no longer seems to be any sense of a future, no vision of utopia to work towards. At least not any social or political one.'

She paused. 'But the fact is I do think God can help. I think that realising that you're loved, that you're cared for, is the most powerful gift a person can be given. It's like opening a door that's been locked for too long. Once you've seen outside, everything, even the room behind you, looks different. It gives you such strength, such freedom. And nothing can ever be so frightening again. Or quite so painful.' She stopped, then smiled slightly. 'Or that's how it was for me. And still is.'

She had done it as well as it could be done. They both knew that. It wasn't that the idea wasn't tempting. Who in their right mind wouldn't want things made easier? Or less painful. But wanting wasn't the same as getting. Or believing. She shook her head, almost more embarrassed for the woman than for herself. 'I'm sorry but I don't think we're fighting the same demons,' she said quietly.

The Reverend smiled, pushing her tea cup away from her across the table. 'I'm not entirely sure about that. But don't worry. It's not like Avon calling. You're not expected to buy the product.' Despite herself Elizabeth laughed. 'I might just pray for you anyway. If you don't mind.'

'Be my guest.'

'Good.' She got up. 'I'm afraid I'm due back at the vicarage at seven o'clock,' she said. 'Will you be all right on your own?'

'Yes. Fine. Thank you.'

She saw her to the door. Despite the awkwardness of God's name between them the atmosphere was not hostile.

'Can I make a suggestion?' the woman said as she picked up her coat. 'I think you should start seeing people again. Make a deliberate effort. Get yourself out of the house. Perhaps you should think about trying to find another boyfriend.'

'Boyfriend?' How coy the word was, full of teen romance and sucky, smooching kisses. Church magazine stuff. 'Don't tell me you think all this is really some weird manifestation of frustrated sexual energy?'

The laugh was almost a guffaw. 'No, I most certainly don't think that. However, I do think that *it* – whatever it is – could well be exaggerated by you spending so much time on your own. I can't see that it would hurt to relax for a while. Be kind to yourself, have a good time. Maybe use that breakfast table laid for two.'

The suggestion, coming as it did from her, seemed so outrageous that it made Elizabeth laugh out loud. 'I'll bear it in mind,' she said as she held out her hand. 'I must say this is one conversation I certainly couldn't imagine having if you'd been a man.'

'I'm delighted to hear it. Can I quote you in my newsletter?' She took the outstretched hand and shook it. The grip between the two women was warm and firm. Physical contact, thought Elizabeth – maybe I have missed it more than I realised.

'You do know that I'd be happy to come again if and when you need me?' said the Reverend, closing her coat over the dog collar.

'Yes. I know that.'

'Alternatively you could always call me.'

'You sure? Some of this stuff happens late at night,' she said, smiling.

'Any time. I'm sure. Goodbye, Elizabeth. And good luck.'

Back in the kitchen she cleared up the tea things, and unlaid the breakfast table. Spoons, forks and knives. Clearly her unconscious was in need of a full cooked breakfast. Not her usual style at all. She turned her attention to the floor, washing up the saucepans and putting them in the cupboards. The place returned to normal. She sat and looked at it. Her kitchen. Was it also really her soul? 'No more, all right?' she said quietly, looking around. 'It's time to move on.' Then she called Sally.

'Darling, a voice from the grave. You don't even have the answering machine on any more.'

'No, I've been busy. Wrestling with the Devil.'

'Mmmmm. Nice. How was he?'

'You wouldn't want to know. Listen, Sal—'

'No, you listen. I've been trying to get in touch with

you because – guess what? A certain desirable man we know has been pestering Patrick for your phone number.'

'Is he scared of the dark?'

'What?'

'Nothing. Tall, floppy hair?'

'That's the one. You must have scored a hit. So, shall I invite him round again?'

'No.'

'Now listen, Eliza—'

'Just give me his number instead.'

ten

Given the shit up till now, it had been a good week for Jake. The crackdown at home had been sharp enough to get a few of the middle guys squealing about the unfairness of New York police protection no longer buying what it used to, and by the time they'd finished complaining, they had a good idea who was to blame. And why.

At the same time Jake's end was starting to pay off too. These Eastern European cops may have been living in the Dark Ages, but at least it meant that they knew how to squeeze balls. Put it all together and pretty soon they had themselves the name of a fancy antiques merchant operating off Wenceslas Square: a guy who specialised in selling illegal religious artefacts to tourists who then found themselves having to pay him even more to swing a licence to get them out of the country. So far, so acceptable. But he had got greedy and in the last twelve months he'd also started importing stuff from further east, shipping it overland through routes that were growing white with the powder they were leaving behind. Of course they could have just stopped every truck at the border, but that wasn't the message Jake wanted to give. He was looking for something more subtle. And anyway it was always easier to deal than bust.

It was what Jake was good at. The guy turned out to be Mr Urbane; good English, good breeding, good lies. A shrewd man, though. Somebody who could see the attraction of a deal where he got to keep one illegal trade rather than losing both. 'Don't worry,' Jake had said to him as he let himself out the back way. 'They'll never know it was you who told us. You have our word.'

But if I were you, buddy, I'd look after my family now, he thought. Don't wait until death duties take their toll.

Yep. He was feeling pleased with himself. Three weeks down the line and they were going to wonder why they'd messed with him. If he were them he'd make himself an offer he couldn't refuse soon, just to get him off their backs. Then he could have the pleasure of telling them to go fuck themselves. He was lucky really. His honesty had less to do with scruples than with temperament. Money had never been the high for him, he got off more on the pleasure of the fight, though there were times when he was at his most sour when he wondered if Mirka's pain might have been relieved by a bigger bank account. He knew enough cops' wives where it had been. But then who'd want to live with them anyway, smart bitches with faces and butts reconstructed by the surgeon and not enough intelligence or curiosity to ask where all the bonuses came from? That was never Mirka. Not the body work nor the lack of brains. If anything she had too much of both. Christ how he missed her; her wit, her style, the way her foreign accent caressed New York slang, the shine of her smile, the tight curls of her pubes and those few straggling dark hairs that led up to her navel. There had been times these last six months when the need for her had driven him half crazy with pain. He must have picked up the phone and dialled her number a dozen times before he could stop himself. But he had always put it down again before she answered. He wouldn't go crawling to anyone. If she wanted him she knew where to find him. Yes, Jake was a man for whom the fight was often sweeter than the victory. But then she knew that about him too.

After the meeting he took the rest of the day off to celebrate, wandering through the old city, sitting out in the squares, enjoying the way the first heat of spring encouraged the women to take off their coats. But his heart wasn't in it. All the body curves led back to the one he couldn't have and he ended up in his local hotel bar drinking more than he should and paying in dollars to smooth his drunken path.

By nine o'clock he could barely get off his chair. When he got back there was a message on the answering machine. The sound of her voice sobered him up faster than a bucket of cold water. The worst thing about it was she didn't even sound mad any more.

'Listen, Jake, I had better tell you, just in case you find out from someone else. I am on my way to Prague. I just got a phone call from the woman who looks after my grandfather. He's had a stroke. I am catching an early flight to Paris, then a connection on. I get in late tonight. I'll stay at a hotel then go south in the morning. I'll call you when I get there. I - I hope things are well with you. I - I think of you even though I don't want to. I'll talk to you soon.'

Mirka in Prague. Jesus Christ. Mirka, here, tonight. He looked at his watch. Nine forty-four. New York was seven hours behind. The flight would be – what? eight, eight and half hours depending on the connection. He called the airport while he changed his shirt. They didn't answer. In the end he cut his losses and grabbed a cab, applying the aftershave as he went. She would have seen him better. But then she would also have seen him worse, and at least this way he would see her at all.

He calculated without the roadworks on the airport route. Jeez, why did they bother? Even when they'd mended the roads they weren't drivable. Fuck it, he should have commandeered a cop car. Then he could have put on the siren.

It was almost quarter to eleven when he finally got there and the last Paris flight had been in for forty minutes. He rushed into the Arrivals hall. There was a trickle of businessmen coming out with duty-free bags. No, they hadn't seen the woman he described. He thought of having her paged through the tannoy but the queue was enormous. He ran around the airport, then went outside.

He spotted her immediately. She was down the other end of the concourse, where the taxis were parked, a man in a chauffeur's hat by her side. He knew it was her, would recognize that mane of chestnut hair and the long clean line of those beautiful legs anywhere. He called her name, but she was too far away to hear. He started pushing his way towards her but she was already halfway into a black saloon, the driver shutting the door.

'Hey, you!' he shouted. The driver turned towards the sound of the voice and seemed to see him, but instead walked quickly to the other side of the car and got in. The engine started immediately. He was within twenty feet of the car as it pulled out. He screamed her name, and she must have heard something because he saw her turn in the frame of the back window. He waved frantically and saw in her face that she had recognised him, because she looked suddenly startled, then lifted a hand and leaned over to say something to the driver. Instead of stopping, the car moved smoothly away. He ran out into the road to follow, only to be blasted from behind by a car horn. He jumped out of the way in time to watch the saloon glide down the slip road, out into the central lane, accelerating all the time.

Catching his breath he watched it go, and, as he did so, something cold gripped at his bowels. He had seen the car before. Not the same number-plate, of course. That one he would remember anywhere and anyway, he already knew it had been stolen. But the car he *had* seen, with its door half open, offering another woman a lift, one from which she didn't come back.

A phone call about an old man with a heart condition. It could have come from anyone. If he hadn't been drunk he would have seen it from the start. But he still wouldn't have got to the plane in time. Jesus, not Mirka. Please God, no, not Mirka.

Finishing the chapter made her late for the film but at least it kept her mind off the date and the kitchen. She ran all the way from the Underground. He was waiting outside the cinema, tickets in hand, clearly a little pissed off. She was still apologising as the credits rolled, the lateness helping to overcome her shyness.

The movie had a smaller body-count than her novel,

and none of its corpses was female. In fact, it turned out to be quite a good idea: a swanky little thriller with a plot that snaked its way through sex into murder and a large bank account. In the end the villains won, but their triumph was a good-humoured affair, more a victory for charm than a defeat for morality and therefore not to be taken seriously. He had chosen well. It was, she thought later, the perfect film for a first date.

Afterwards they went to a Thai restaurant in Frith Street where the food was great, but the spice warnings not entirely accurate and one of the chilli dishes took the roof of her mouth off. At least it gave them something to laugh about as she gulped down the water. He had a good laugh, unselfconscious. It was, she thought at the time, the kind of laugh you could imagine going to bed with, should your imagination that way incline. By the end of the second bottle of wine she was beginning to see how it could.

They haggled over the bill, then agreed to split it. They lived near enough to one another to share a cab home. At the door she invited him in for coffee. He accepted and paid the fare. She let him.

She had trouble with the Chubb. It was, she realised as she fumbled in the dark, only the second or third time she had opened it, and never in the dark. He offered to help and in the end she let him. 'You're well protected,' he said, as one lock led to another. Neither of them took it any further.

Inside, the house was quiet and well behaved, as it had been for the two days since she had made the date. Maybe it was biding its time, waiting to see how far she would go. She ushered him down to the kitchen. As she unlocked the door she wondered if she shouldn't make

some casual comment about a crazy cat, just in case
the floor was littered with dessert spoons and potato
peelings, but she couldn't think of a way to bring it up,
and by then the lights were on and the room was
revealed as tidy and benign.

'Nice kitchen,' he said, and appeared to mean it.

He flicked through the CD shelf as she made the
coffee. 'How do you put this thing on?' he asked,
fiddling with the switch.

'It's off at the mains.'

'Doesn't that mean you have to re-tune every time?'

'Yes.'

'Why don't you just use the switch?'

'It's a long story.'

He slid in a disc. By their music so may they be
judged, she thought. It was as good a method as any
other.

kd lang's voice cruised its way into the room, its
mind on women's bodies. Well, that has to count for
something, she thought.

He stood against the side and watched her as she
fiddled with the coffee percolator. As she turned to say
something she suddenly saw Tom in his place. He must
have stood there a thousand times, leaning his back
against the work top, hands in his pockets, head on one
side, pontificating about something or another. Except
now she could no longer make out his face, no longer
read every contour and feature from memory. Was he
already so physically forgotten or was this more of a
temporary eclipse?

'Sally tells me you have a really good voice,' he said.

'Does she?' Trust Sally.

'Yes, she says you used to be in a band.'

'Yes, well, Sally is tone-deaf and has an active imagination.'

He laughed. 'I must remember that. But you did sing.'

'Usually only at parties when I was drunk. It was never a serious proposition.'

God, you make it sound so boring, she thought. That's what seven years with Tom did for a girl; scrubbed out the glamorous bits and replaced them with tales of under-achievement and failure. But then you couldn't have two high-fliers in the house. Especially when one of them was never that sure about the power of his wings. Next time I have this conversation I'll make it sound better, she thought. More about possibilities.

She walked over to the other side of the room to get another pack of coffee from the cupboard, near to where he was standing. He watched her come, then moved to let her in, but not very far. She could feel the heat of his body. And the sound of her own breathing. You can bring a horse to water, she thought . . . How do you do it? It was so long since she had contemplated the dance of courtship that she was suddenly petrified lest she couldn't remember the steps. Or that even if she could they would somehow have changed by now.

She moved out of his reach again. On the stereo kd was trying to help. '*Where is your head, Katherine? Where is your head?*'

'There's a bottle of brandy in the cupboard to your left, if you want,' she said, anxious to gain some independence from the song.

'No. I think I've had enough. How about you?'

She nodded her head. They talked small talk while she made the coffee, their minds both distracted. He doesn't find me interesting enough, she thought. But then that's hardly surprising. Neither do I.

When the coffee was ready she poured it out and brought his over to where he was standing. Their fingers touched as he took it. 'Thanks,' he said. She grinned, he grinned back. Your move, she thought. Please.

'*Surely help will arrive, to cure these self-induced wounds. Why hurt yourself, Katherine, why hurt yourself?*' This time they both listened. I'm blushing, she thought. What now?

He put down the cup and leant his body slowly towards her. She didn't move. He kissed her gently on the lips, more a caress than a real kiss. She waited for the saucepans to catapult themselves out of the cupboards and the light bulbs to flash on and off. The kitchen remained dormant. He smiled, then kissed her again, this time pulling her towards him and sliding his tongue in between her teeth. It was thick and pushy. She didn't know if she liked it or not. She found herself thinking of Jake Biderman, and the woman with no eyes. She broke off, suddenly panicky.

He laughed softly and released her. It would be easy to leave it there, a test drilling. No oil. My God, she thought. We can't stop now. It's either you or a full church exorcism. This time she reached out for him. And this time as she kissed him the need translated into something close to desire. How strange, she thought, this feeling in my stomach. It's almost like fear, the same sweet-sour turbulence. The kiss continued, hungry on both their parts now, both of them pushing for more. She stopped thinking, starting to feel through her body rather than her brain. The sweetness turned to heat. They broke apart for a second, then came back together. The coffee went cold on the side. The sense of release was so powerful it made her shake. He took this as a further invitation. He slid his hand under her skirt, teasing his way upwards. Each touch was like a minor electric shock. No time to stop now. They both knew it.

'Shall we go upstairs?' she said thickly.

He had moved his tongue from her mouth to her ear, darting it in and out. She could hear a slurping, slipping sound, almost like sex. 'I don't know,' he said eagerly, between licks. 'Do you think we can make it that far?'

She had an image of the kitchen table, him bent over her, bent over it. Not quite what the Reverend had had in mind for breakfast. But although it excited her she suddenly couldn't handle the idea of that room. Not here, she thought suddenly. Not where they could be seen. She didn't ask herself who exactly would be looking.

They broke apart to move upstairs. The abruptness of the separation was alarming, and she found herself suddenly unsure. As she led the way up out of the kitchen she felt him run a finger lightly down her spine. Her body shook beneath it.

By the time they reached the bedroom she was having trouble breathing, the adrenaline squeezing her lungs as well as her gut. It was becoming hard for her to distinguish excitement from fear.

She moved into the room, instinctively placing herself away from the bed, nearer to the window. It seemed so long since they'd touched each other that they felt like strangers again. She turned to face him and as she did so she knew she was in danger of losing it. God, what am I doing? she thought. I don't know this man. I probably don't even like him that much. For a terrible moment she thought she was going to cry. He took a step towards her. 'I'm sorry,' she said too loudly. 'I – I think I may have made a mistake.' Then she laughed awkwardly. 'I'm not sure I really want to do this.'

He looked at her with a slight smile playing on his lips. Good firm lips, almost pouty. She remembered them from the party. But where was the excitement of playing with fantasy now? 'Yes, you do,' he said quietly. 'It's just that it's been a long time and you think you've forgotten how. But you haven't. You know what they say about riding a bicycle. All you have to do is get on.'

The crudity of the remark sent a stab through her gut. But this time it hurt more than it exhilarated. What calculated little sob stories had Sally been pouring into his ear, selling him the notion of a bereaved woman who needed a little reawakening? 'Just relax,' he said. 'It'll be OK.'

He moved towards her and cupped her head in his hands. There had been a similar gesture in the movie they had just seen; the opening of a raunchy love scene. She understood the homage to be deliberate. He smiled at her. Though she had no idea who he was she knew it shouldn't matter. It was just sex, nothing personal. Once upon a time long long ago she had been good at this. Or if not good, then at least easy. He kissed her, the tongue back again, deeper this time, more insistent, more like a surrogate prick. What was so different about then and now? she thought frantically. Was it just that I was younger? Or did it matter less? Has the failure of Tom and me really made everything so hard? Oh God, give me a bit of time. Let me find my own space.

But he didn't hear her. She stayed semi-motionless in his arms, not responding, waiting for him to realise the depth of her ambivalence. But he had other things on his mind. His hand slid up her skirt again, this time in between her thighs. She thought of the woman in the dingy Prague apartment. The trick was to go with it, imagine yourself getting power from it. But again her body betrayed her, keeping her legs too tight together. In the end he had a choice. He could either force it or let it be. 'Please,' she murmured, but he wasn't listening and anyway it was hard to know if she had actually said it out loud. He pushed his hand further up, until it reached her crotch. She cried out, but he cut off the cry with his tongue. Their silhouette in the window must have looked like true romance. She gathered herself up and, with a single shove, using her body weight, she pushed him away.

He lost his balance as he moved and tipped sideways, half falling against the bed. As he picked himself up she saw the battle between embarrassment and fury in his face.

'I'm sorry,' she said frantically. 'I'm sorry . . .'

'Yeah, so am I.' And it was clear that the anger was winning. 'I mean I was under the impression I had been invited. You did ask me up here, didn't you?'

'I said I was sorry.' But the harder she strove to keep it in, the more she could feel the inexorable pull of tears. And, once started, she knew they wouldn't stop. 'I just . . . I didn't mean to . . . Oh, shit, shit . . .'

He watched her disintegrate, watched the sobbing take her by the shoulders and shake her back and forth, a series of breathless little yelps which she couldn't control.

'Hey, listen, it's all right,' he said a little too loudly, embarrassed into a kind of pity. 'You don't need to worry. It's over. I'm not going to force you.'

But this time it was she who wasn't listening. She put a hand up to her mouth and nose to try and somehow stem the tears, but to no avail. She wanted to tell him to go but the words wouldn't form.

He stood there like some overgrown schoolboy trying to assimilate what he'd done wrong, wanting to be out of there, but not knowing how, and with enough conscience to be worried about the emotional chaos he might leave behind. 'Look,' he said. 'It's all right. I'm not going to hurt you. Nothing happened. You're OK. If you want I'll go. Is that what you want? To leave you alone?'

She tried to nod her head, but the sobs prevented her. Then finally she took a huge, sudden breath and flung her head back, keeping her eyes tight shut, gulping it back down, holding it all in again. The heaving stopped and she swallowed hard. When she opened her eyes he was gone.

She let out a long silent breath, tasting the pain in with the relief. She sank onto the bed and put her head in her hands, moaning slightly to herself.

But when she looked up he was there again, standing in the doorway, a glass of water in his hand. He hesitated then approached carefully, holding it out at arm's length, as if he was feeding an animal that one knows might bite. 'Here,' he said. 'Have a drink.'

She took the glass and sipped it. Then she gave a large sniff. 'Thanks.' There was silence. She pushed back her hair. 'I'm fine now. You can go if you want. Thank you for . . . for – well, you know . . .' she trailed off.

He grunted. 'You're sure you're all right?'

'Oh, yeah, I'm tremendous. It's just my body that's causing the trouble.' And then she gave him a grin so he'd know it was meant to be a joke.

He smiled awkwardly back. 'Well, if you're sure . . .' He moved his weight from one foot to the other. Important to do this right. After all, reputations were at stake. 'Listen, if it's any consolation, er . . . well, we were probably rushing it a bit.'

'Were we?' she said, in spite of herself genuinely interested in the idea.

'Well, you know, first date and all that. These days people don't always . . .'

'Don't they? God, I used to,' she said. 'I mean when . . . but that was a while ago.'

He nodded. 'Actually, I was quite surprised that you rang me at all.'

'Why?' She gave another great sniff, like a child; it was a strangely satisfying sound.

He shrugged. 'I don't know . . . I just got the impression you weren't particularly interested . . . at that party, I mean.'

'And were you? Interested?'

'Ummm . . . yeah, well, you know how it is. I mean you're a good-looking woman. Bright, funny. A bit strange, but that's OK.'

'Strange?'

'Yeah, er . . . bit tied up in yourself. Well, so are most people in one way or another. Especially when you don't know them.'

'Yes,' she said, running both her fingers under the bottom of her eyes and watching them come up black. 'I suppose they are. But if you didn't think . . . I mean why did you ask Patrick for my number?'

He frowned. 'Your number? I didn't – I mean—'

'Oooh. Oh, it's OK,' she said hurriedly. 'Don't worry. I think I know what happened. Shit. Oh, well ... What exactly did Sally say to you?'

He gave a little shrug. 'Nothing much. Just that you needed taking out of yourself. That it was the end of a long affair.'

'Yeah, well, ain't that the truth,' she murmured as much to herself as to him. She smiled. 'Listen, thank you. You've ... er ... been very kind.'

He looked at her, then shook his head. 'No. I don't think that's quite the word. I'm sorry too.' He paused. 'I wouldn't want you to think that I ... er ... well, I mean if it makes you feel any better, I was really into it. I just couldn't believe that after downstairs – well, that you weren't, I suppose.'

'No,' she said. 'Neither could I.'

He smiled at her. There was a silence. What is this? she thought. A second chance? She felt the thrill of a low electric voltage in her stomach, but she was still too scared to let herself take note of it. 'It's all right. I understand. You can go. Honestly, I'm fine.'

But this time he deliberately held her gaze longer than was polite. Maybe he liked mad women. It takes all sorts. 'Well, I mean if you really want me to ...' Male ego: a terrible and wonderful thing.

She shook her head fiercely, as much in confusion as denial. 'I just don't want to screw it up again.'

He waited for a while, then moved a step towards her. 'You're a very attractive woman, you know.'

She laughed angrily.

'No, I mean it. I would never have stayed in the first

place if I didn't. Nobody needs to get laid that much.'

'That's true,' she said.

'You still are . . . attractive, I mean.'

'Funny. Right at this moment I thought I looked like a panda.'

'What?'

'The eyes.' She looked up at him. 'Mascara rings.'

'Oh, I always like it untidy. Looks kind of . . . I don't know . . . slutty.' He made a clicking sound with his tongue. 'Whoops, that's probably not the right word.'

'Oh, I'm not so sure.' She laughed. At this time there was a touch of delight in it. They both noticed it. He stood his ground. If she put out a hand she could touch him. The guilt had gone and suddenly he was no longer such a little boy. His new-found confidence was infectious. Or maybe it wasn't just his. 'Have you ever seen *The Big Easy*?' she said.

'What?'

'It's a film.'

He shook his head. 'I don't think so. Why?'

'It's got a good sex scene in it. A bit like this, only Ellen Barkin isn't quite so off her head.'

'Who's the bloke?'

'Dennis Quaid.'

'Well . . .' And you could see that despite himself he was flattered. 'What happens in the end?'

'You know, I can't remember. I think they try again and then the phone rings.'

He looked at her. Then they both looked at the phone by the bed. God help me, she thought, I hope I'm doing the right thing. She put out a hand and slid it off the hook.

eleven

Of course, life is not like the movies. Not only does the phone not always ring, but neither does the earth move. Though sometimes things do not need to register on the Richter scale to be memorable. Sometimes the quiet shudder can be as powerful as the crack of the tectonic plate.

He was, she thought, as she lay there underneath his sleeping body, not the world's greatest lover, but then neither was she. He had been right, though. She still knew how to ride a bicycle.

Truth be told it had moved a little too fast from the kissing to the fucking. She could have wished for more ceremony, more touching, playing, caressing. Her body felt so much like a foreign country that she needed its landscape to be charted and admired before letting the tourists take possession. But she was scared that if she articulated her own desire it might suddenly evaporate, and she would lose it again. At least this way, carried along in the current of his passion, she felt safe, inside the pleasure dome, rather than watching from without, trying to get in. And if the actual fucking lasted too long, was too much governed by his own need, and not enough of her own, then there were ways in which she could make it work for her, the very distance between them helping her to realign, find a place both in her body and her mind where she could regulate the pressure and use it to satisfy herself. In the end, she tried too hard and missed, falling off the wave when it was still gathering force. But to have been on the surf at all after so long seemed like an enormous achievement, so much so that as they both lay there afterwards, she felt all right about the white lie which she had offered when he asked. Some things, it seemed, hadn't changed within the dance. Still, it would be nice to have ridden the wave to the shore. In the post-coital warmth of the night even her greed seemed healthy.

She leant over and kissed him, but it was too soon for him to be really interested. His very reticence made her flirtatious. He smiled and yawned. 'I should go,' he murmured sleepily. 'I have to be up early.'

'I'll put on an alarm,' she said, suddenly needing him to stay very much, although how much that was to do with her body and how much to do with the likely behaviour of the kitchen she couldn't tell. He peered up at her in the darkness, a silent question on his lips. 'It's all right,' she added gaily. 'It's not an invitation to move in. I'd just like it if you stayed till morning. If that's OK?'

He smiled, and kissed her on the nose. 'Sure,' he said. 'Anything for you, sexy lady.' But it was more courtesy than lust, and within minutes he was asleep, half on top of her. Interesting how we all have to try to make it better than it is, she thought.

In sleep he grew heavier, his right leg thrown across

her thighs like a tree trunk pinning her to the bed. She tried to shift him, but it was impossible. She lay awake for a long time underneath him.

The house was quiet around them. So, was this it? she thought. Have my unconscious rebellious energies really been tamed by sexual release? She certainly felt different. More open, lighter, as if – despite his weight – a burden had indeed been lifted off her. How weird, this thing called sex. The way its energy ran like a current underneath one's normal life, vital, crucial, even when it didn't seem to be there, always ready to smash its way through the surface, consuming everything in its path. The image was so clumsy and Freudian that it made her laugh. But even that was OK too. She slid her hands down her body, over the soft flow of her breasts and her belly towards her vagina, her fingers searching their way to the tiny concealed nub of her clitoris. She rolled her forefinger over the mound, her breath catching in her throat as the touch found its mark. She was already halfway to orgasm in her head, but the weight of his body on hers left her no room to move herself properly and in some ways it felt almost discourteous, doing it without him. She lost the concentration and let the touch slip from arousal into erotic comfort, almost like an adult version of sucking your thumb. Maybe tomorrow morning, she thought, or later in the night. And she smiled to herself.

In a deliberate attempt to test her new-found sense of security she moved away from thoughts of sex into the kitchen. And it was then she remembered that she hadn't locked the door.

When they had left the room an hour or so before they had still been in the grips of that first stumbling passion. Not only had she not locked it, she couldn't even remember shutting it, which meant that even now it would be wide open. The realisation rekindled a stab of panic, such an instant distress that she even thought of shaking him awake so she could send him downstairs to close it. But post coitum all male animals sleep like the dead and try as she might she couldn't rouse him.

She lay back, tired from the effort. The sense of panic gradually subsided. So the door was open. What could it possibly do to them now? Suddenly the whole idea was ridiculous. As if it was only her definition of the space that had made it so threatening. Maybe this was exactly what she needed to do. Open the door and let it all flow out. Discover that, like sex, it simply needed to be freed, to be allowed to become playful rather than frightened, and then with the whole house at its disposal it would simply fade away, overwhelmed by space and possibility. After all, if her enlightened vicar was right and she was the cause of it, then surely her release would already have triggered its own.

I'll make a pact with myself, she thought. If there's nothing there tomorrow, I'll take it as a sign. She lay awake for longer, watching the digital clock blink its way into morning. 1.30 . . . 2.00 . . . 2.30. She thought of trying to wake him, to get him to touch her some more, but the edge of her desire had faded into sleepiness now and she decided to let it be. 2.45 on the clock. She never made 3.00.

The alarm went off what felt like minutes later. It was still dark and the air outside the duvet was freezing. She reached out and slammed the button down. The little green lights flashed 6.00. Beside her he groaned. She turned to meet him, interested by her own pleasure at finding him there. She ran a hand lightly down his chest, giving him the chance to take it further, once more surprised by her own appetite and ease. He half responded, then registered the time and moved gently away. It was a new day now, and they were both working people.

Luckily the feeling of night allowed them a continued semblance of intimacy. He touched her on the cheek, then pulled himself heavily out of bed. 'Ooooh, God. I don't want to do this.'

She made a move to join him.

'No. Relax. Go back to sleep,' he muttered. 'It's too early.'

'It's all right. I'll get you some coffee—'

'No. No, I'm fine. I'll go home and have a shower – I have to pick up some stuff there anyway. You sleep.'

And it was clear that he would prefer it this way, a clean exit, no last speeches, no having to pretend anything. She lay back and listened as he stumbled towards the bathroom.

'How will you get back?' she called as the water flushed.

'I'll phone a taxi. I have a number.'

Do you? she thought sleepily. And how often do you use it, I wonder? She lay listening to him making the call against the sound of the cistern flushing. A man with a portable phone; there had been some changes in the world since her last one-night stand. He came back into the room, quietly fumbling for his clothes around the bed. His clumsiness was rather endearing, she thought. When he was dressed he perched himself on the side of the bed and leant over to find her. Their lips met. His breath smelt bad. But then so, no doubt, did hers. 'Goodbye,' he said. 'Sleep well.'

'Bye. Take care.'

'Yeah, you too.' He touched her cheek again. 'I'll . . . I'll call and—'

In the half-dark she lifted up a hand and put it over his mouth. 'Don't worry,' she said softly. 'I'm sure we'll see each other around.'

Above her she heard him give a little sigh of relief. 'You're lovely,' he whispered. 'I mean that.'

'Yeah, I know.'

Then he was gone. She lay and listened to his footsteps on the stairs, the sound of the door opening and slamming shut behind him. Gone. Relief and regret in almost equal measures. When she was younger, and did this kind of thing more often, the end was always one of the sweetest parts, assuming you knew how to play it: a mutual sense of romance without the responsibility of a future. She was pleased with herself at having remembered so many of the moves.

She lay for a while tempted by the thought of sleep, intrigued by the faint smell of him on the bedclothes, and the way she didn't seem to mind it. But though she lay with eyes closed sleep didn't come. If she got up now she would be jet-lagged and slightly crazed for the rest of the day, but what the hell – that could be just what she needed . . . the freedom of a kind of emotional unravelling.

6.45 a.m. She pulled on a dressing gown and went downstairs. The kitchen door was half open, the beginnings of a charcoal dawn seeping in through the French windows. She pushed and it swung open all the way. I am healed, she said to herself under her breath as she went to switch on the light. I am healed and you are now just a kitchen . . .

And so it was: a kitchen as they had left it. The two coffee cups cold on the side, the kd lang CD case open by the stereo, the disc still in the machine. She put on the kettle and made herself a cup of tea, standing looking out onto the garden as the heating gurgled on and the morning came in, heavy and cold. Welcome to a new day, she thought. Then she took the mug of tea and went back upstairs to bed, just for a while. And it was so warm and comforting there that she put the cup down and settled herself deeper under the covers.

When she woke she felt dreadful, clotted by sleep and confused. Through the curtains she could make out a grainy light which could have been dawn but might also be the prelude to a winter twilight. The clock by the bed stood at 4.03 p.m. How extraordinary. She had slept the day away. The house was again quiet around her. She lay for a while savouring the exhaustion of too much sleep rather than too little and this anarchic new relationship with time, its very lack of control filled with possibilities. And then, suddenly, she was very hungry.

Downstairs the kitchen was ordinary, with even Millie consenting to be there, albeit equally ravenous and complaining. She fed the cat, then herself, going for a full breakfast of eggs, bacon and two chunky pieces of toast, all to the accompaniment of Morrison's 'Tupelo Honey', a love song from a time in his life when it seemed as if love came easily, and brought with it guaranteed redemption. Dusk came in as he sang and she felt happy.

Afterwards she lay long in a hot bath, then went in search of some clothes. In the bedroom she found last night's wardrobe storm-tossed around the room, the sweet evidence of someone's lust for her. Even the smell of the clothes was different. She picked them up and put them into the laundry basket, and went to the cupboard.

Getting dressed had assumed an unthinking monotony for her over the last months, always going for the same sort of garment, loose-fitting, enveloping, hiding rather than exposing or exploring. Now she found herself in search of something else, something tighter, something that she could feel, that showed her who she was.

She looked at herself in the mirror, and saw a woman with a body; with curves and plumpness and hidden places, and it brought back a sudden longing for him. Or if not him then his touch. She imagined him standing behind her, slipping one of his hands inside the top of her T-shirt, cupping his palm under her breast, feeling its weight, teasing the nipple, bringing it to obedient erection. In the mirror her eyes sparked with reawakened desire. She felt a sudden confidence, almost a sense of happiness. Thanks, Malcolm, she said, allowing the rush of feeling towards him precisely because she knew she would never see him again, and because they had absolutely nothing between them but a night that was already gone.

The feeling gave way to one of contentment. It sat more easily with her. She had never been someone who had counted on or even anticipated happiness, was never one of those radiant young women who assumed that life would deliver what they asked of it as long as they wore the right shoes and reapplied the mascara regularly enough. On the contrary, she had never really known what she wanted, had certainly never understood how to fit men into the landscape.

Instead she had simply treated them as sex. To her surprise she had found herself rather good at that, though some would have diagnosed it as a defence against feeling. She was adept at asking only for what they could give and she didn't feel diminished by what they couldn't. Rather she felt relieved. She had certainly never been interested in falling in love.

Tom had been the first one to call her bluff. He had needed to be adored and in order for that to happen he had to awaken that capacity in her. The trouble was once she'd been won, he wasn't that interested in adoring her back. By the time she realised the depths of his narcissism it was already too late. By then she was hooked, and the sex had become emotion, which, of course, meant that it no longer offered any defence at all.

In the end her loyalty could only be eroded gradually, death by a thousand careless moments and unthinking remarks, a steady trawl of missed opportunities. And so, gradually, she withdrew. Only by that time his ego had grown so monstrous with the feeding that he didn't even notice she was no longer there to nourish it. No wonder they took such an unconscionably long time to die.

But all of that was over now. And nine months down the line she was, finally, more like herself again. Last night, for all its traumas, had helped her realise that.

She ran her finger lightly along the line of her breast and returned to the mundane task of brushing her teeth. Then she made herself a cappuccino and went up to her study to work.

And because she was feeling so steadied and so sure it never occurred to her to wonder what she might find there as she pushed open the door and turned on the light.

twelve

If you counted the English version as well as the Czech there was probably something near to five hundred pages of manuscript scattered around the room. A snowstorm of huge white leaves, so wild it was almost beautiful, as if someone had held the sheaf under a fan and then let go. But white was not the only colour. There was also red: great dark trails of it, smeared down the walls, running over the desk, flowing down the computer screen onto the keys, thick and glutinous.

She let out a long moan, a physical pain in the sound, the coffee cup falling from her fingers, adding its own streaks of dark colour to the walls and floor. When, finally, she got her wits back she moved slowly across the room to the computer screen, her feet crunching on irregular verbs and images of violence. As she got closer she realised the machine was on, humming quietly, the screen so smeared with gunge that you could barely see what it showed. She put a finger out to touch the stuff. It was sticky. She pulled back and smelt it. There was a tangy, spicy quality to its scent. When she brought it to her lips the taste was unmistakable: ketchup – one of the world's great fake bloods.

She used the palm of her hand to wipe it off the screen, leaving a dirty smear but uncovering what was written below. It was an extract from the book, an early test draft with the letters big, blown up to three or four times their normal size. It read:

'THE DOOR OPENED AND THE MAN WALKED IN. HURRIEDLY MIRKA GOT UP FROM THE MAKESHIFT BED AND TURNED TO FACE HIM. "I WANT TO—"

"JUST SHUT THE FUCK UP," HE INTERRUPTED IN COARSE DIALECT. "NO ONE GIVES A FUCK WHAT YOU WANT, D'YOU UNDERSTAND?"

SHE STOPPED, BUT STILL SHE HELD HIS GAZE. THE MAN STOOD WATCHING HER FOR A MOMENT, THEN HIS FACE RELAXED AND HE GRINNED. "SO, NEW YORK LADY, WHAT DO YOU THINK WE SHOULD DO TO THAT LOVELY BODY OF YOURS, EH?"

AND HE MOVED TOWARDS HER.'

For a while she could do nothing. The sense of violation, the sheer magnitude of the intrusion was so great that she couldn't even think straight. She sat heavily on the computer chair staring at the screen and the keyboard, where droplets of ketchup had sunk in between the letters, already dried and flaky. Like old blood. The viciousness behind the intention shook her into action. She reached for the phone and dialled a number. A man answered.

'Hello. Is Catherine Baker there?'

'No. I'm sorry. She's away at a conference in

Southampton.' A man's voice, nice, husbandy. 'She won't be back until Friday. Can I take a message?'

She didn't bother to reply.

'Did you know that too?' she said out loud to the room around her. No one answered. She dialled another number. Three digits. But before the voice could reply 'Emergency, which service do you require?' she had pressed the disconnecting button, suddenly as scared of their scorn and disbelief as she was of the echo of violence around her.

And then, because there was nothing else that she could do, she started to think.

If Catherine Baker's analysis was correct and this latest act of vandalism was one more reflection of a psychic disturbance in her, then the only conclusion she could come to was that she was, in some way, clinically insane. There could surely be no other explanation for the chasm between her newly felt sense of calm and the room's anarchistic violence. Yet how could anyone be that mad and not know it?

But if that was not the explanation then there was only one other. That somewhere between six last night, when she had gone out to meet Malcolm, and an hour ago when she had woken up for the second time, some*body* rather than some*thing* had been in her house. Like all the other times presumably, they had somehow got in through the French windows, then this time having found the kitchen door open, they had climbed the stairs up to the attic and created havoc with a ketchup bottle.

A ketchup bottle? Theirs or hers? Suddenly the very absurdity of the question made it seem desperately important. She ran downstairs to the kitchen and wrenched open the fridge. Sure enough, the place in the door where the ketchup customarily sat alongside the lemon juice was now empty. She checked the bin for an empty bottle but there was nothing there.

She was still standing staring into the garbage as if it might deliver an answer when Millie smashed her way through the cat-flap and came yowling across the floor, all semblance of dignity lost in flight. The flap banged again; this time admitting the black tom in wild pursuit. She picked up the first thing she could find, a fork on the sideboard, and flung it at him. It missed, but he swerved and turned, ears back, hissing, a raw violence in his fury, before making a run for it, dodging past her, back out through the flap and across the garden and over the wall. She watched him go, her heart pounding against the side of her ribcage.

It's just a cat. It's just a cat, she said to herself. But the thought of its malevolence persisted. Ever since it had arrived in the garden both she and Millie had been living under a regime of terror. She stared down at the cat-flap. Maybe she should block it up. Keep out the outside world.

Block it up . . . Keep out the outside world . . . The two thoughts moved around in her brain. The outside world, the cat-flap.

She moved over to the French windows and stared down at the lock above the handle. Then she looked at the cat-flap. It was swinging slightly, still settling on its moorings. The distance between the two was about four or five feet. She put her hand on the catch of the lock and as she did her fingers encountered a kind of roughness at the base of the catch, a scarring on its smooth metal surface.

She played with it further, then squatted down to examine it more carefully. Yes, the steel underneath was definitely scored as if something had been scraping persistently at it. Once again she looked from it to the cat-flap. And this time slowly something began to make sense in her brain. She moved around the kitchen, intent suddenly, searching through the drawers. She found a skewer – the kind you used for barbecues, when she and Tom had been sociable enough to have them. She took it over to the door and slid the tip of it into the gap between the top of the handle and the catch of the lock. Then she wiggled it up and down, until the leverage of the skewer had enough force and it pushed the catch upwards. She turned the handle of the door. It opened, the lock released.

Her heart beating faster she went outside, closing the door behind her. She squatted down by the cat-flap and, holding the skewer at arm's length, pushed her arm through, until she could bend it at the elbow. With her forearm extended and the skewer at the end of it she could now reach almost to the handle of the door. Almost, but not quite.

She withdrew her hand and went inside, locking the door behind her. In the living room she found a poker, long and thick, tapering off at the end to a thinner tip of metal. She went back and repeated the exercise. This time the poker reached to the catch. It was hard to keep her hand steady enough, but she managed it. The tip of the poker slipped in and under the catch. Of course the door was already open. She could have tried locking it that way, but she was scared she might never get back in again. Someone else could have done it though. Because somebody already had. She now knew that with absolute certainty, knew that somebody had crouched where she was crouching now and teased and prodded the lock until it released itself and let them into her house.

And then, of course, everything was suddenly explained. How they had got in only to find themselves confined to the kitchen because the door kept them out of the rest of the house, but how, with a little imagination, there had been enough mischief to be done there; from the casual appropriation of a couple of CDs to more sinister play with music, moving on to the repositioning of furniture and the laying of the table. Each act a little bigger, taking a little longer, exhibiting a greater confidence in the intrusion, almost some kind of game-plan.

Until this last one, when fate had left the kitchen door open and given them the whole house to play in.

Them? But who? And where from?

The first two questions she still couldn't answer. But the last one she at least had some idea of. She looked out across the garden. She must have stood out here a hundred times since Tom left, on each occasion feeling utterly safe, the anonymity of all those blank, dark windows staring back at her. She remembered the mornings in the summer when she had breakfasted out here, comforted by the nearness of the world yet protected by her sense of privacy within it. And all the time somebody, somewhere had been watching her.

Night was coming in fast. She walked to the end of the garden and looked around at the semi-circle of houses which backed onto the end of hers. Her garden wall was high, almost as tall as she was, but it was hardly unscalable. Any one of the connecting gardens could have led to it, and in turn have connected back onto others. She counted the windows around her. There were dozens of them.

She turned and looked back at her house. The kitchen was lit up, the work tops, the hob, even the table clearly visible. She had no blinds, no curtains. She had never felt the need for them. Above the kitchen was a small loo window and then, to her right, her bedroom. It was just a dark shadow now, but with its light on, or even the light from the hall, the area around the window itself would also be seen. She sometimes stood there too. And last night it hadn't just been her. Last night she had been there with a man's arms around her, the two of them silhouetted in the frame in that parody of an act of love, which now, it seemed, had led directly to an act of violence.

It was the logic of that connection that scared her more than anything else. She walked quickly back into the house and locked the door behind her. Then she went into the cellar and found a large ball of garden twine. She used it to secure the lock to the handle, winding it round and round and round, until there was no room for manipulation, no sliver of space where a metal edge could get in and release the lock. Then she went out of the kitchen and locked the door, pushing a broom up against the handle and wedging it against the wall, so that even if the lock broke, the door would not open. From the hall she called the locksmith, then went upstairs to clean the study.

He arrived before she'd finished. When the doorbell rang she had gathered up the paper, relocating each sheet in its own order and language, scrubbed most of the ketchup stains from the walls and was at work on the computer, painstakingly scraping out dried globules of gunge from in between the keys.

This time she asked to see some kind of identification before she opened the door. He slid a card through the space left by the chain. It wasn't the same man; this one was younger, with a broken nose and a bony face. She spent a long time checking his credentials.

'I asked for the man I had before,' she said as she took the chain off the lock.

'He's out on another job,' he replied, with equal lack of charm. 'This is my night off. They had to call me in special.'

'I don't care. It was the other man I wanted.'

He shrugged. 'Look, if you want to complain call the gov'nor. You'll still have to pay the call-out charge. If you want it done tonight it's me or no one.'

She scowled and showed him down to the kitchen. It took her a while to unwedge the broom. He glanced at her strangely. 'You had a burglar?' he asked, sounding supremely uninterested.

'You could call him that.'

At the French windows he screwed his nose up at the twine. 'Is the lock broke?'

'No. It's extra protection. They're coming in through the cat-flap, pushing something in and manipulating the lock.'

He looked at her as if she was mad. She did nothing to reassure him. 'So, what d'you want me to do? Change the lock? Add another?'

'Both. And stick in some bolts at the top and bottom.'

He shrugged. 'I've got nothing but time and it's your money.'

As she sat and watched him the darkness thickened outside. He didn't like her sitting there. It made him nervous. Well, it's nice to have someone who's more jittery than I am, she thought, as she watched him sniffing, running a quick hand under his nose, apparently unembarrassed by his lack of a tissue.

If it was *him*, what would I do? she thought. If it was him in here now? I'd have to hit him with something. A plate, a saucepan. The kitchen knives were sitting in front of her in their block. Would I do that? she thought. Could I? Could I really pick up one of those and use it?

He glanced up and caught her eyes on the knife block. He gave her an edgy little smile. 'You know, if you're really worried about burglars, you could always call the police,' he muttered, as if it was something they had already been talking about.

'The police?' she said rather dreamily. 'Yes. They're such a help, aren't they?'

He went back to his work even faster. An hour later, the door was transformed into something out of a cartoon, locks and bolts everywhere. He ran her through them all. Then she got out the poker and tested the ones at the top and bottom. They were a long way from the cat-flap.

He was already gathering his tools and heading for the exit. He made out the bill with the door open, was even about to pocket the cheque before she'd given him her banker's card.

'You better write down the number,' she said. 'For all you know I could be a fraud.'

He glanced up at her. Not you, lady, she could hear

him thinking, you're too crazy for that. She liked the fact that he was scared of her. As he handed back her card she gave him a big wild grin. He couldn't get out of there fast enough.

With the front door locked up she now went back to the kitchen, once again tested all the locks. She pulled the bottle of brandy from the cupboard and poured herself a hefty slug. Then she took the portable phone from its bracket and stationed it next to her at the table. She would have liked to listen to some music, feel the sense of someone else's company around her, but the stereo could be heard in the garden and she didn't want to put him off. When she felt ready she closed the door out of the kitchen, came back to her seat and switched off the light.

The dark jumped in around her. She waited, breathing deeply and evenly. Eventually black became gloom and she began to make out the shapes; the bread bin, the shelves, the frame of the French windows and the intense live blackness beyond. She moved her chair back against the wall. From outside looking in you would not be able to make her out at all. After a while her pulse returned to its normal rate.

She had been sitting there for maybe an hour when the phone rang. It cut through the silence like a knife flash out of darkness. She grabbed so fast she missed and it fell to the floor where she had to scramble to find it, then peer and grope in the dark to get the right button.

'Hello,' said a man's voice when she finally connected. 'I thought you were out.'

'Who is this?' she asked harshly.

'It's me, Malcolm. Remember? From last—'

'Malcolm. God. Malcolm.'

'Yeah. How are you?'

'Fine. Fine.'

'You . . . er . . . sound strange. What are you doing?'

Sitting in the dark waiting for a man, she thought. 'Nothing. Just . . . just hanging out. How about you?'

'Oh, this and that. Listen – I – er . . . I'm sorry, but I left my watch there.'

'What?'

'My watch. I must have left it in your bedroom. I think on the bedside table.'

'Your watch?'

No doubt an analyst would have something to say about that particular memory lapse. But then that's what they're paid for. Given the embarrassed tone of his voice it seemed clear to her that it was only a watch. 'Yes.'

'Oh. So what d'you want me to do? Do you want me to post it to you?'

'Yeah. Or . . . or I could drop round and pick it up.'

'When?'

'I don't know . . . I mean I could come now. I've just finished at the office and, well, I – I kind of need it for tomorrow and—'

'No,' she said louder than she intended. 'No, not now. Not tonight. I'm – I'm busy.'

'I see. Well, then maybe you could stick it in the post.'

She scribbled down the address in the darkness. As she wrote the postcode she wondered if she might be misjudging the conversation, if he was really saying something else. What would she think if he was? Hard to know. Things had moved so far since last night. She didn't feel like the same person at all. 'I'll make sure I do it tomorrow.'

'Thanks.' Pause. 'Are you all right?'

'As well as can be expected under the circumstances,' she said, laughing, before she had had time to think about it.

This time the pause was a silence. He laughed back, but a little uncomfortably. 'Well, I'll see you around then.'

'Yes.'

The line clicked and she put the phone back on the table. She re-ran the conversation in her head. He would think she was weird. Add him to the list.

She looked at her watch in the gloom. Nine-thirty. She sat and waited some more. It was still too early. But she had all night and he would come. She was sure of it. Time passed. She thought of Jake sitting by the phone, his nerves eaten by fear, waiting. Waiting. His call would be different from hers. They wouldn't even want money. Just to flay him alive a little with the sound of her voice. And make sure the shipment that was on its way got a clean bill of health. He had already called off the tail on the men fingered by the antiques dealer. He knew he was defeated the minute the car had pulled away, knew he'd give them anything they wanted. Swallow the fury and hold it later for revenge. 'When do I get her back?'

'Don't worry. You'll see her tomorrow morning.'

The box with its bloody little contents wrapped in tissue was on his doorstep at six a.m. The blood had dried fast to the paper, he had to pull it off. It was stubby and cold to the touch. It looked absurd more than horrific, the flesh waxy and cold, almost like some kind of joke marzipan fruit. Why was it always fingers? Fingers or ears. Maybe they were the only amputations you could do without a doctor present. After all, you wouldn't want them to die from lack of blood.

Was that her talking or the book? She tossed her head to get rid of the thought and as she did so, across the darkened kitchen the cat-flap snapped open. She turned her head in time to see a dark shape padding its way across the floor. She let out the breath she didn't realise she'd been holding.

Millie took her time at the water bowl, the sound of her lick-lapping unnervingly loud in the stillness. Then when she had had enough she jumped up onto her mistress's lap, stretching herself out under one hand, nuzzling into it, demanding to be caressed.

She obliged, glad of the warmth and the company. They sat together as the night deepened. Come now, she thought. I'm ready for you now. Ready to watch from the shadows as your stretched coat hanger fails to gain you entrance and you realise too late that you've been rumbled. Then watch as you creep back across the gardens to a house where one particular window will light up and I will know what address to give to the police. Or maybe I wouldn't even bother. Maybe I would simply track you down myself, enact my own revenge like the avenging angel of my fantasies. What would she do? How would it feel? The thought excited and terrified at the same time. She let it go.

Time passed, and after a while she stopped thinking, and grew still in the rhythm of the night silence, waiting now as if she could wait for ever. Eleven, twelve, one, two. The French windows and the cat-flap stayed closed.

*

At two-thirty she began to feel suddenly sleepy, her body stiff from being in one place too long, her mind numb with the quiet.

She got up and walked to the window, peering out into the gloom. The garden was empty. There was nobody out there, she was sure. So she had been wrong. He would not come tonight. Of course in some ways it made more sense for him to wait. Let her stew in her own fear a little longer. There was no point in driving herself even madder through lack of sleep. She checked all the locks and bolts were in place and, locking the kitchen door behind her, she went up to bed.

thirteen

She never knew what woke her, never could work out if it was an actual sound or some subliminal reverberation of terror breaking in through the layers of dreams. All she knew was that suddenly she was out of sleep and wide awake, eyes open, mind alert, with no sense of the journey from the unconscious to the conscious, no residual grogginess at all.

She was lying curled to one side, her head facing the entrance to the room. The flickering digital clock told her it was 4.03 a.m. She lay still, her eyes acclimatising to the darkness until at last she could make out the shape of the bedroom door, half open. And as soon as she saw it she knew something was very wrong.

She was instantly rigid with fear, as if everything in her life that she had ever been afraid of was at this moment gathered together and tapping at the window of her brain. She lay exactly where she was, not moving a muscle, not even allowing herself to blink. She tried to breathe normally, but the action seemed to hurt her chest. What is it? she thought frantically. What is it you can feel?

The answer came from her ears rather than her

mind; somewhere in the room behind her she registered the sound of a long release of breath, so steady, so
controlled that there was almost a sweetness in the
sigh. Millie, she thought immediately, the fog of fear
lifting a fraction, giving her back her wits. Millie
sleeping too close. She waited for what felt like an age.
But when it came this time there was no mistaking it.
The sound was too loud, too nasal for Millie, the
exhalation too drawn out, as if the breath was being
released through the mouth rather than the nose. Not
animal but human, and coming from close by.

Her mind rejected what it couldn't handle. It wasn't
possible. How could anyone have broken in through
those locks? This was her imagination playing truant
from reason, scaring her as it had scared her that night
when she had followed him up the stairs only to find
the landing empty of everything but her fear. Learn
from then. Only confront it and it will, once again,
disperse like smoke.

She swallowed once, twice, then slowly, with a
languor that might have been read as sleep but was
more the semi-paralysis of terror, she shifted her body
over from the curled position until she was lying on her
back. And as her feet moved further down the bed they
encountered an obstacle at the bottom, too heavy and
too firm to ever be the body of a cat. And this time she
knew that the nightmare was real.

She froze, too late remembering to complete the
move naturally. Time stopped still. She opened her
eyes again and through the fringe of her lashes she
made out the shape of a figure sitting at the end of the
bed.

Oh, God, may my death be without pain, she

thought, the idea retching up from the epicentre of her soul, blocking out everything else. Without pain and without humiliation, please, oh, please. But even as she thought it she knew it was impossible. Because that is not how the world works, and because no one is allowed to make pacts with God so late in the day.

When you can't depend on mercy, what else is there to do but fight? But how? The phone was on the side table, the distance between it and her a hundred miles and nothing in between to help. I don't want to die, she thought again, the terror rising up like a wild wave and wiping out all thought. Not me. Not now. She closed her eyes and tried to steady her soul, concentrating on her breathing, making it as even, as relaxed as his. But even as she did so she knew he wasn't fooled. In the darkness he moved a little, she felt the bed tremble under the shift of weight. He knows I'm awake, she thought. He can feel it, just as I can feel him. And if I don't do something soon I will drown in my own fear, and then I might as well be dead.

Her voice, when it came, was splintered with tension, but stronger than she felt.

'Who are you?'

The words hung in the darkness. He gave a little snigger. 'You're awake.' And in contrast his voice was rather like his breath, unexpectedly soft, almost sibilant.

She kept swallowing back the fear. 'How did you get in?'

'You left the kitchen door open.'

No, I didn't, she thought. No, I didn't. But then she thought again. Of course she *had* left it open. But not tonight. Last night. It took a while for the meaning to sink in. Last night ... twenty-four hours ago. He had been somewhere in the house for a night and a day.

'Where ... Where have you been?'

Again that sniggering sound, half laugh, half noisy sigh. 'Wouldn't you like to know. Here, there. Everywhere.'

It was the way he spoke as much as the words; flat, emotionless. She made an involuntary move, her legs pulling up the bed to get away from the closeness of him.

'Don't move.' The voice exploded outwards, harsh and cracked. She noticed his left arm jerk swiftly from behind his back to his side. What's he holding? she thought. Jesus, what's he holding?

She froze, then swallowed again, the saliva and the fear. 'I have to sit up,' she said. 'I can't breathe lying down. I have to sit up.' And it was clear from her voice that she was telling the truth.

She waited. He said nothing. She waited some more, then took the silence as assent and pulled herself up fraction by fraction, until her head was resting against the propped pillows, her feet curled away from the weight of him.

'That's enough,' he barked.

She stopped instantly.

'You move any more, you touch anything, you do anything funny and I'll kill you, d'you hear?'

She nodded, her eyes back down on the hand. But you haven't yet, she thought, thirty seconds in and you haven't killed me yet. And as long as we're talking there's still space between us.

In the semi-darkness she could make out more of him now: he was smaller than she had first thought, wiry, with short stand-up hair above a narrow, rather squashed face. I'm going to throw up, she thought. No, you're not. There's no time for this now. She swallowed again. The silence grew. He seemed content to wait. Maybe he was enjoying her fear.

'Why me?' she said when she could be sure of her voice.

Again no answer.

'Was it the music?'

'What?'

'All those months ago? Was it the music?'

And this time he laughed. 'You used to dance in the garden.'

So I did. So I did, God help me. 'You must like Van Morrison.'

'Who?'

'Van Morrison. The CDs you took. They were both his.'

'Oh, I don't play them,' he said. 'I just keep them on my windowsill. To remind me of you.'

The remark sent a tremor through her. That first CD had gone missing in July. Nearly five months. Five months of a creeping obsession with no form of release. Don't even think about it. Just keep talking. Keep the words flowing. She made her voice light. Like conversation. 'So if I looked out could I see your window as well as you can see mine?'

'No more questions,' he said, the voice retreating suddenly back into fury. 'Just shut the fuck up, d'you understand?' And his words were an echo from something else, but she couldn't think what.

'Sorry.'

'Yeah. Sorry.' And the word was a sneer, a mockery

of her own politeness. By his side his hand twitched again. 'You ought to be. You ought to be.'

She had to freeze her own muscles to stop herself from shaking. Why isn't he doing something? she thought. He must know how terrified I am. Why isn't he making his move? She stared into the darkness, waiting. But this time she couldn't find anything to say. Still he stayed where he was. And then she remembered where she had heard those words before. They had been on the computer screen, Mirka's kidnapper moving towards her in the cell . . . The translation. How far had he read?

'You screwed him last night, didn't you?' And for the first time the voice had some animation in it. 'I heard you. Heard you doing it.'

Where had he been? Outside the door? In the bathroom? A million places. Try not to think about it. 'Mind you, I bet you've had some practice. Must get it from writing that stuff.'

'What stuff?' she said although she already knew.

'You know what stuff. The stuff in your book.'

'How much of it did you read?'

'Oh, I've got it all. Loads of it. Tons of it. Garbage.'

'How—?'

'I told you. Garbage. Rubbish bins. Your leftovers.'

Rubbish bins. He'd been going through her rubbish bins, must have collected all those pages of first drafts, corrected, scribbled on, then thrown away. It would have read even more crudely before she started to polish it up. No wonder he must have thought her weird enough to target.

'I didn't write it. It's not mine. It's just a book that I'm translating.'

'Yeah. I bet it is. Bet you're not like those women either.' And again he laughed.

His hand shifted near to his body and this time she saw what he was holding. A length of twine, from the same ball that she had used to secure the French window lock. She kept on thinking to keep feeling at bay. The garden twine. So he had been in the cellar. Was that where he had hidden? Had he slept there while she slept upstairs, or had he waited until the house was quiet and then started roaming, listening, watching, touching . . . ? Touching. Everything but her.

Why not? In the last twenty-four hours he would have had ample opportunity to catch her unawares, to attack her in her sleep, incapacitate her and drag her kicking and screaming into his fantasies. But instead he had waited until she woke of her own accord and now here they were still sitting with an ocean of bed-spread and fear between them, with him making suggestive remarks like some sniggering teenager.

She looked at him again, and as she did so she became aware of his tension as well as her own, aware of the way he was holding his body, rigid, hunched, his fists clasped tightly at his side. Maybe she wasn't the only one who was scared by what might happen.

She moved her body back against the pillow.

'Don't move,' he shouted. 'I told you not to move.' And as he said it he made a jerky move towards her, bringing up his other hand in a threatened blow, revealing as he did so a hammer clutched in his fist.

At the sight of it they both seemed to flinch at the same time. For a second she thought she was going to lose it, but through the wave of panic she thought, I was right, he *is* scared. He is scared. At some level he's as scared as I am. Except that when he gets frightened he gets violent.

'It's OK,' she said quickly. 'It's OK. I've stopped. See.'

She waited. So did he. Then gradually the hammer went down, so now both fists were close by his side, weapons tightly grabbed. She tried not to look at them.

'It's just that I'm cold, that's all,' she said gently. 'Do you understand? I'm scared and that makes me cold. I need to reach out and get that top that's on the bed near you. Is that OK? I'll get it and sit straight back here. I won't do anything else. I promise.'

Another live silence. He could have got it for her, picked it up and flung it at her, or told her once again to fuck off, but he didn't. Instead he just stared. Then he grunted.

Infinitely slowly and gently she leaned forward, until she was within touching distance of him, as if testing herself by getting closer than the fear allowed. He stayed rigid. She picked up the shirt that was lying on the duvet, and gathered it quickly to herself. She was about to move back when something made her stop. For that second they sat there, frozen in time. Then, instead of retreating, she turned her head towards him. He was near enough now for her to smell his breath. A hint of mint? Some kind of breath freshener, like some awful parody of a date. He gave a nervous snort, but stayed still.

She risked a look. In the half-light his skin was sallow, the face angular, the mouth, now she could see it, thin. How I hate thin lips, she thought, like a small soul, dried out, stretched too tight, only interested in taking, not giving. Not the kind of mouth any woman would want to kiss.

The thought repelled her, but she held on to it nevertheless. What advice was it that they always gave to rape victims? If you can't fight it, lie back and let it happen. Bullshit. But if she resisted he would hit her. He could do it now if he wanted; smash in the side of her head with his hammer, then fuck her in a pool of blood. But you won't do that, she thought. Not yet. Because you need me alive. If I'm dead there'd be no one to take notice of you. And you need that. You need my attention.

She was working on instinct now, moving to a place where reason couldn't reach. Survival versus fear. She made herself go back to the mouth, pinched, almost disapproving. She tried to imagine running her finger along the line of his lips, teasing them open, slipping inside. Sex. The longing and the fear of it can mess up a person so badly. She thought of all his long drawn-out games in the kitchen. How there had been almost a coyness to them, as if he couldn't bring himself to admit what he really wanted. Not until he had witnessed her doing it herself.

Except he couldn't get it like Malcolm. Which was why he needed the hammer. His violence, her fear – the one endlessly dictating the other. But why does it always have to end in blood and horror? Why can't there be another way? There has to be . . .

Do it, she thought. Stop thinking and do it. For once in your life just go for it.

And still they didn't move. Still they sat there frozen in the night.

'Why don't you put down the hammer?' she said at last and to her amazement her voice sounded almost loving. 'You don't need it, you know. I can't go anywhere and I swear to you I won't try to escape.'

She felt rather than saw his fingers twitch, then tighten further around it. She counted to ten in her head, then slowly, so slowly that he could see her every move, she lifted her fingers towards his face. He let out a snarl and his right hand whipped up and grabbed her wrist, forcing it down onto the bedspread, twisting the skin savagely as he did so. She registered the pain, but also the fact that the hammer had been left behind.

'Bitch,' he hissed under his breath. 'Bitch.'

'You're hurting me,' she said between clenched teeth as the burn worsened. 'You're hurting me. Let me go.'

He was breathing hard now, too hard to speak.

'Please,' she said, and they both heard the way the word came out, as much a quiet command as a plea. His response was to squeeze even tighter, his hand shaking with the force of the grip. She let out a small yelp of pain, though she didn't take her eyes away from his face. The burn made her want to cry, then just at the point where she couldn't hold out any longer she felt the pressure reduce, until gradually his fist relaxed and her hand was almost free. It took all her courage not to snatch it back, but instead she let it lie limply in his, resting there for a moment, both of them registering the touch without the violence.

This time as she moved her hand up to his face the air between them was alive with anticipation. And this time he let the touch connect. Her fingers fluttered over his cheekbone. She held them there till they were steady then slowly traced the line of his cheek down towards his mouth, and, after a beat of hesitation, played across his lips. His mouth fell slightly open. She took a breath, then with her forefinger she pulled down his bottom lip, feeling the moistness, exposing the fleshy bit inside. He made a sound, halfway between a moan and a growl, and bit backwards. At first she thought he would take her fingers with him, crush and break them between his teeth, but it was more by reflex than design, like someone recoiling from a flame.

Relax, she thought. Relax. Maybe she said it out loud. It was meant for both of them.

She waited, then began again, now pushing her finger inside. She encountered the edge of his bottom teeth, uneven and jumbled, as if they had grown crooked and never been properly corrected, then her finger slipped underneath his tongue. The flesh was alive with muscle, rough and quivering, almost like the feel of her own vagina. It sent a shudder through her and she had to steel herself not to pull out. No time for the faint-hearted now. She lifted herself up from where she was sitting on the bed and moved towards him. Their joint breaths sounded huge in the night. As if neither of them could get enough air in their lungs. She felt his hand clutch at his side again, searching instinctively for the hammer, his fingers closing over it.

'It's OK,' she said. 'You don't need it. You don't have to hurt me. That's not how it has to be.'

She waited, counting off her heart beats. At ten she moved again.

Where she had first used her fingers, now she used her tongue. His lips trembled then parted to let her in. Slipping in through the portcullis of his teeth, she made herself think of all the lovers she had known who could turn a kiss into making love; teasing and catching at your lips, pulling them into theirs, until the greedy probe of their tongue makes you want to take off your clothes and guide their prick into you. Making you ache for them ... All from a kiss.

Remember it now, she thought. Because your life depends on it. She pushed her tongue further in. His mouth was limp. 'Kiss me back,' she whispered. 'Use your tongue.'

She could almost hear his heart thumping. The tongue fluttered, then whipped out, like a lizard. She could feel the tension in him, like some uncontrollable seismic build-up, and she felt the hammer hand move nearer across the coverlet. The kiss continued, his tongue darting, still lost, but still trying. God help me, she thought, God help me here to know what to do.

She brought her hands up to cup his face. 'That's good,' she murmured. 'Again.'

This time he did as she said and the kiss connected. They both felt it. As it went deeper, she slid her hands over his neck, then slowly down his back. The wool of the jumper he was wearing was coarse and prickly and damp to the touch. Under his clothes he would be sweating. She pulled up at the sweater, to discover a shirt underneath, and some kind of vest. Too many clothes. He was dressed as she had been, smothering the desire, hoping it might go away. As her hands finally reached his bare skin he let out another noisy breath. She stopped, waiting, reading the signs, then slowly continued the caress. Again he relaxed. She let her hands linger, then slid one of them down over the edge of his trousers onto the bed and towards his right hand. At her touch his fist clenched. She kept her hand cupped over it, waiting, then slowly it opened itself, the hammer slipping onto the bedspread. She slid it as far away as she could without risking the noise of its falling on the floor. She took his hand in hers, entwining their fingers, using her thumb to play with the inside of his palm. The skin was surprisingly soft, almost like a girl's, soft and wet with sweat. She felt a sudden shaft of power.

This time when she moved away from his lips, he came towards her, his mouth messy, greedy. For a second the taste of him repulsed her, the saliva and the smell making her want to puke. She punched away the thought and sucked his tongue back into her.

She had released the rest of the clothing from his trousers and was exploring his chest. The skin underneath was rough and dry, with wiry little curls around small nipples. Lost flesh. Not cared for. Not loved. How does it happen to some people? she thought. How do they miss out? If you've never been touched, how do you know how to touch? So unfair. So dangerous. She brought up his hand and guided it slowly up under her T-shirt to her body, cupping it over her breast.

The first contact made him shudder. Before he could pull away she moved her body into his hand, pushed the weight of her flesh against his palm and heard him groan, a dark painful sound dragged out from a long way down. To her astonishment the noise delighted her, causing a sweet corkscrew twist in her stomach. And she knew in that second that somewhere inside her fear there could even be pleasure, the pleasure of her own control. Don't show it, she thought. Whatever you do don't let him know.

She was about to help him further when his fingers found her nipples, swollen from the cold and the fear and a sudden, muddied, confused kind of desire. The first squeeze was too tight, it made her draw breath too quickly. 'Gently,' she said in a whisper. This time he heard her and his touch turned her hard. Slowly they toppled from sitting to lying on the bed. And as they did so she brought up her right leg and used the bottom of her foot to locate the hammer on the coverlet and push it gently towards the edge.

It hit the floor with a thud.

The sound, or maybe it was the weight of him pinning her down onto the bed, brought back a flash of fear. They both felt it, both sensing the change and tensing themselves away from the other. She recovered first, reaching up to kiss him again, manoeuvring herself half out from under him, at the same time moving her hand to the top of his trousers, fumbling to free the button. She used the ball of her palm to push down the zip, then slid her hand inside, slipping under the frayed elastic of the underpants until she found his penis, limp and curled. You're not ready, she thought, with a sudden panic. Is that your problem? Or is that what you need the hammer for, to get a hard-on?

Maybe he heard the thought. At her touch he pulled back violently, and for a moment she thought she had lost it, could feel him thrashing around in search of some way back into control. In search of a weapon that would give it to him.

'It's all right,' she said quickly. 'It's all right.'

She kept her hand over his softness, holding it there almost tenderly, while with her other hand she pulled her T-shirt up off her body and over her head, rubbing herself against him, letting him feel her nakedness connect with his. Instinctively his hands went out to her again, moving down from the breasts to her stomach, clumsy urgent caresses, until his fingers slid into the tangle of pubic hair. And as they did so she heard herself moan.

The sound had not been deliberate. In fact if anything it was probably more a release of fear than anything to do with pleasure. But somehow it helped. Both of them.

He hesitated, and she knew that he was frightened to go further. Knew that at that moment he was more frightened of her than she was of him.

I am here, she said to herself, although the thought didn't make sense. This is me doing this. Here. Now. It's not someone else.

'I'm here,' she said, this time out loud. 'And I'm not pretending. Anything you want to do to me is OK.'

And as she said it, his penis took a jerky leap in her hand, and he let out a sharp groan of pain and desire. At the same time his fingers found their way inside her, less clumsy now, though pushy and over-eager, a sudden haste to everything, the onslaught of a frenetic kind of lust. To her amazement she realised she was wet. The discovery sent its own shock wave through the pit of her stomach. She ran her hand gently up and down his prick, her own breath coming quicker now, teasing them both into further erection. Then, registering the urgency of his need, she slid herself underneath so she could guide him into her. It wasn't that easy as he was still only half erect, but as he moved inside the mouth of her he stiffened further, then slid in all the way, letting out another shattering groan. She heard her own voice join his. And so, almost without giving her time to move, she felt him rise up and with two or three thrusts come inside her, a juddering, jerky orgasm that was too hurried and crude to bring any lasting pleasure.

AIDS, she thought, in a sudden blind moment of panic, AIDS, and the clap and a million other diseases that will rot me slowly for my sins. But even as she recited the litany, those thoughts were overwhelmed by another. The realisation that he was crying.

He had fallen heavily onto her body after the orgasm. Now he tried to pull himself off, the sobs clutched and angry, searching frantically around him, groping for something she knew would be a weapon. But this time rather than his violence all she could feel was his pain.

'It's OK. You're all right,' she said fiercely, pulling herself up with him and putting both her arms around him, hugging him hard to her and holding on, despite his attempts to wrench her off. 'It's all right,' she said again. 'Really. You don't have to do anything more. It's done. You did it. It was fine.'

And slowly as she clung to him, reading the battle in his body between the rage and the release, she felt the fury in him quieten and the crying win out.

So it was that she sat there in the winter night, her body shivering with cold and adrenaline, holding on to a man who was sobbing his heart out for the fact that the rape he had planned had turned into an act of love-making.

Time passed. And eventually the sobbing subsided so that now, when he started to pull away, she knew to let him go. She stood up and took a robe from the door to cover herself, as she did so feeling the cold trickle of his semen running down the inside of her thigh. Cold, she thought. Why is it always cold when it has just erupted from such hot depths? She used the inside of the robe to wipe it away and then, as she tied the belt around her, she felt about the floor with her feet until she located the cold edge of the hammer and slid it further under the bed.

He was pulling up his trousers, fumbling with the button. They always look so lost getting back into their clothes, she thought, suddenly remembering Malcolm and a dozen other men down through the years, all returning to little boys once the act was complete. No wonder women need to be mothers as well as lovers.

Then, after what seemed like an age, he finally looked up at her and in the gloom she knew that whatever he might feel or become in the future, as of that moment she had triumphed and she could do what she liked.

And this time her voice was her own, no longer clotted up with demands of seduction or fear.

'It's over now,' she said flatly, staring straight at him. 'Do you understand? You and I are over. Whatever it was that you thought was between us is finished. I won't say anything, won't tell anyone. And neither will you. But if you ever come near me again I swear I'll go straight to the police. I want you to go now. Leave by the front door and when you get home throw away the CDs and the papers from the book. The kitchen doors are locked now. You can't get in there any more. This obsession is over.'

He didn't reply, didn't even look at her, but instead he got up from the bed, sniffing loudly and looking around the room as if searching for something that couldn't be forgotten. But he had heard her. They both knew that.

'It's gone,' she said firmly. 'It's gone and you don't need it any more. Maybe you never did. Now I want you to leave. Go.'

At last he turned to her. She moved out of the line of his path to the door. They stared at each other and in the gloom she saw the spark of something in his eyes, but couldn't read it. And she knew she was taking a risk, showing him so clearly that she had won, but right now there was no more pretence left in her and she suddenly needed to be alone so badly that it hurt. He gave a kind of sneer, and brought up a hand in what seemed to be a gesture of mock aggression, but it never connected. Instead, after holding it there for a second, he dropped his arm and, turning on his heel, he walked out.

She waited, rooted to the spot, until she heard his steps go down the stairs and out through the front door. As she heard it slam behind him, she raced out of the door to the landing window in time to see him turn and look up at the house, then move off quickly down the road.

She was downstairs in seconds, through the kitchen door and standing in the darkness by the French windows looking out over the night garden. The silence was total.

Now it was over she discovered she was trembling, her legs shaking so violently she could hardly stand, but still she wouldn't let herself rest, still she stayed there watching, waiting. And eventually she was rewarded. Across the expanse of the night to the left of centre of the semi-circle of houses, she saw a first-floor light go on, a white hole burnt into the blackness. And as the position of it imprinted into her brain the trembling won out and she slumped onto the floor, allowing herself to feel it all again, the touch of his hands on her flesh, the stickiness of his come inside her, and the river of his saliva in her mouth.

She spat the taste of him onto the floor and in that moment of revulsion she had a clear knowledge that there was a choice to be made. That she could either allow this night to become the rest of her life, to warp and corrupt everything that came after, or she could let it go and find its natural place.

If she was going to get him now would be the time. She imagined picking up the phone and dialling the police. She saw her plump young constable sitting across the table, notebook in hand, scribbling frantically, eyes as big as saucers in wonder at her tale. Except it wouldn't be him. No. They would send a woman instead, female sensitivity to comfort her in her distress. She saw the trained sympathy in the woman's eyes and tried to imagine how she would tell it to her. And she knew then that she couldn't do it. That in some unfathomable way what had passed between them was more intimate than violence, and that she would never be able to tell it. Certainly not to the police.

Did he know that also? Did he know that she would keep his secret? His and theirs. What was he doing now? Washing her off him in preparation for starting a new life or staring at those shiny CDs on his windowsill, remembering, reliving? Had he thrown them in the bin yet?

Listen to what you told him, she thought. Believe that. You did it and now it's over. You looked into the eye of the nightmare and survived. And having done it, this should indeed be the end of it and both of them would be forgiven and redeemed, even if that redemption may have had to grow out of a landscape of humiliation and fear.

And so she got up and very slowly started to get on with the rest of her life.

fourteen

She took the hours till dawn deliberately quietly. She went upstairs and showered, but didn't try to wash him out of her, because it was too late for that and because she didn't want to give in to that kind of frenzy of disgust. She brushed her teeth and stripped the bedclothes, replacing them with a crisp new sheet and duvet cover which Sally had given her six months ago for her birthday but she had never bothered to open. It pleased her how it made the room different, less like her own.

As she folded back the cover she came across the length of twine caught in its folds. The hammer she located halfway under the bed. She had intended to throw it away but when she put out her hand she found she couldn't touch it. In the end she used a Safeway bag, scooping it up into the white plastic, turning the bag inside out so she couldn't see it any more. She even got as far as taking it out to the rubbish bins by the front gate, but once there she kept thinking about who'd been going through her garbage and instead brought it back in and hid it at the bottom of a cupboard.

Outside the kitchen doors the world was a black

hole again, with no starburst of electricity to mark out his presence. She turned on the radio. People who couldn't sleep were calling a chat-show host, regaling him with stories of real-life nightmares. He listened impatiently, butting in with inane comments until they had bored or annoyed him sufficiently – at which point he cut them off with the sound effect of a scream and a body hitting the floor.

Maybe this was the way she should exorcise it, anonymous and public at the same time, delivering thrills to some loser night-jock with a taste for the macabre. Who knows, a certain thin-lipped man with pasty skin might even now be listening, staring out at her from a first-floor darkened window. She looked back over the gardens. What if he had turned out his light deliberately, realising that if he could see her then she too could see him? The thought moved her away from the window. The host took a call from a woman called Fanny in Hendon who had reversed out of the garage and run over her dog. 'Oh, Fanny. To each their terriers, eh!' In the studio you could hear him trying not to crack up.

She hit the Off button, then turned down the overhead light. She wouldn't need it much longer anyway. The dawn was starting to come in, the sky already fading from translucent mauve to a dull winter grey. The garden took gradual shape in the light. The only thing moving was the cat. She watched Millie jump down from the back wall and pad swiftly across the lawn. For once the black tom was nowhere to be seen. Maybe Millie had triumphed too, had spent the night fucking him stupid then left him for dead in the bushes.

She emptied a whole tin of cat food into her bowl. Hungry work, confronting your demons. Then she washed up her mug, put it back on the shelf, and made her way upstairs to the attic.

From under the eaves she pulled out a set of boxes that had come from her mother's house, a collection of things that had proved too personal to sell, too old or strange to ever be of use. It didn't take her long to find what she was looking for. The pair of old-fashioned binoculars that had once belonged to her grandfather. She unwrapped them carefully from a length of black felt, the cloth giving off a smell of London as she imagined it during the war; a hint of cordite and danger in musty darkness. As she held them she remembered their heaviness and how big they had once felt in smaller hands.

She had watched her own father using them when she was a child. He would stand for hours at the end of their garden at the edge of the marshland, the glasses trained on what always seemed to her to be an empty sky, she waiting next to him, wanting to be included, trying to be still, but always becoming bored and noisy, so that in the end he sent her inside. The birds, it seemed, only came out when she wasn't there. Now she understood why. To catch something unawares you had to wait, be patient. Then and only then would it give itself up to you. She had never had enough time before, was always too busy pushing to grow up. Not like now. Now there was satisfaction to be had in surveillance.

Her bedroom gave the best view. His window, as far as she could relocate it in the light, was like all the others in that house, blank and dark, with a half-curtain across the bottom of it, like someone's old-fashioned parlour. Was it his kitchen or his bedroom? Kitchen, surely. A door to the left, half glass, half wood, led out onto an iron balustrade and some steps spiralling down into the garden. If she focused properly she could make out the peeling wood on the shed nearby. Was this the pleasure that had so transfixed her father, pulling distance closer, seeing what was not meant to be seen? The garden was unkempt, long tatty grass and overgrown shrubs, with a crazy paving path down one side of it. The wall at the end was small. Easy to get over, and from there you would only need to slip across the bottom of another garden and over another wall to reach hers. She practised the run through the glasses, jumping each stage of the journey into sharp focus, crossing fences, sliding along boundaries, dodging the path of security light triggers, before at last moving across her lawn to the cat-flap. Easy in darkness.

Prowling. A winter pursuit. She thought of all the layers of clothes on his body, the sweat on his skin and his clammy weight on top of her. Her mouth filled with saliva. Let it go, she thought, let it rest. But the taste persisted. She imagined it being sperm, saw herself crouched over the limp little cock, sucking it into a fountain of aggression. She ground her teeth together and heard a different kind of groan. Don't come back, she thought. Don't even think about it. She let the saliva mingle with the fear and swallowed them both together.

Once she could see him – or rather the absence of him – she set about making sure that he could no longer see her. Again the attic helped. Among the boxes left unopened since her mother's death, she found one filled with linen, and dug out a set of lace curtains that had once graced their living-room windows. They reminded her of years of teenage imprisonment and her mother's relentless obsession with privacy. Nets, she used to call them: 'So we can see out but they can't see in.' 'They.' She had made them sound like the enemy. How ironic that her refusal to follow her mother's rules had made her the object of a stranger's obsession. If she ever had children would they too find themselves in flight from her conventions, furnishing a house with lace curtains and strict moral codes?

The feel of the material in her hands brought back memories of springtime cleaning. 'You have to wrap them in pillow cases, darling, then they don't shred in the machine.' How was it that everything her mother had taught her had been of so little use? Were they the wrong things or had she simply not listened to the right ones?

Sometimes she thought that her mother had died simply to get away from her sense of disappointment in her daughter. Would she have been able to help her now? 'You see, Mother, I had no option but to take the hammer out of his hand and stick his prick into me. Except now I can't be sure if I'm soiled or healed.'

Maybe it wouldn't be a question of words. Maybe what she really needed was a pair of arms to hold her and let her cry it out. Forget it, Elizabeth. She's dead and you're raped. Use her curtains for comfort.

She closed the chest and took her spoils downstairs. One of the sets fitted the bedroom window perfectly. She had no rail or rod so she nailed them up instead, apologising to her mother for the brutal little holes created by the hammer (hers, not his, though it still felt strange in her hand).

The kitchen proved more problematic, the remaining lace strips too narrow for the large expanse of the French windows. Here she resorted to a sheet instead, hammering it securely along the wooden frame above so that the glass was completely covered, with a train on the floor. Millie would have to learn to negotiate her way under it to the cat-flap.

She was halfway through when the phone on the wall rang, quivering with the noise, like some neurasthenic little animal clinging to a tree. Whoever it was she didn't want to talk to them. The machine took the call. From the hall she heard a mumble of voices, hers followed by another. She couldn't make out whose. She returned to the window. In a house across the back gardens something caught her eye, a flash of movement from what might have been a first floor. She grabbed the binoculars and focused fast. The lenses located the movement and it jumped into view; the three-D vision of a woman pulling back a curtain with a small child clinging to her hip. Right direction, wrong house. She swept the glasses slowly to the left, to a set of first-floor windows that were still closed eyes. She checked above and below. Still no sign of life. From anywhere. But someone must be up, surely? He wouldn't have the whole house to himself, he wasn't the sort. She couldn't imagine him in so much space, saw him more as a man crammed in, head bowed under the weight of life's ceilings.

She put the binoculars down. Why was she bothering? It was not his style to be out in the day – not enough darkness to hide his inadequacies. Anyway, he had been up all night too. Probably longer. No, if she was going to keep him in her sights then she would have to follow his pattern; sleep when he slept, wake when he did. Cat rhythm. Why not? Her only responsibility was to the translation of a dozen chapters of Czech, and like the princess with her heaps of straw she might find the night hours more conducive to spinning them into gold.

She checked the gardens one last time and went upstairs. The bedroom felt good, the lace curtains filtering the winter light, making the room softer, more contained. She took off her robe and slid naked under the covers. She closed her eyes. In her mind the house remained empty. Benign. She didn't remember falling asleep.

She woke with a start. It was dark and there was wet between her legs, a slow dripping from thigh to sheet. The panic made it hard for her to breathe. She fumbled for the light as she slipped a hand down to her legs.

Her fingers came out red and sticky. She pulled back the covers. There was blood everywhere, caught in her pubic hair, smeared over her thighs and a fat stain of it soaking into the sheets. The panic turned to jubilation. She was bleeding, early, her body joining in the victory, sluicing out all final remains of him, even down to the lining of her womb. There would be no need for doctors or morning-after pills now. She was doing her own healing. She got up and made her way to the bathroom, enjoying the bright threads of blood that ran down the inside of her leg onto the carpet, comforted by her own warmth after the coldness of his sperm.

As she washed and slid the Tampax in she found

herself thinking properly of work for the first time in days. She imagined Mirka marooned in her basement cell. How would she cope if the stump of her little finger wasn't the only blood she had to worry about? You keep a woman kidnapped for long enough and it has to happen. It made her think about how rarely periods featured in books. Could it be that fictional women menstruate less often than real ones? Clarissa, Anna Karenina, Scarlett O'Hara – not a soiled sanitary napkin between them. The few books in which she could remember the heroines bleeding were ones set in convent schools: studies in hot-house guilt where the only acceptable blood was the miraculous kind, transubstantiating from alcohol to plasma in the communion cups.

She stripped the sheets again and scrubbed at the dark spot where the blood had seeped through to the mattress. It reminded her of a smart hotel in Glasgow where she and Tom had been staying once when her period had come early and she had been too embarrassed to leave the sheet to the chambermaid. Don't be so uptight, Tom had told her. That's what they're paid for – to clear up stains on the beds.

Not this kind of stain, she'd replied, unless of course you want them to think of it as a memento of deflower-ment. He had laughed. But it had been an unfair jibe. Among the many men she had in her bed Tom was one of the few who genuinely had no problem being smeared with blood as well as semen.

It wouldn't have been the same for *him*, she thought. What would he have done if he had pulled his prick out of her only to find it bleeding? Would the fear of one kind of blood have led him to another? Hammers and nails. Rape and crucifixion: maybe Catholic girls have learnt more about life than they realise. The thought of him took her to the window, but she had slept through the day and the semi-circle of houses was lit up with a different rhythm; a dozen households eating evening meals and watching flickering TV screens; no telling one window from the next. When she found what she thought must be his it was like all the rest. Lit but impenetrable.

She slid her finger up inside herself, feeling the wad of compressed cotton and the moistness already gathering at its edge. She ran her finger down the glass leaving a smear on the pane.

'See that,' she said softly into the glass. 'My blood's stronger that your sperm.'

But whether she really believed it or simply needed to hear the sound of her own voice in the night was hard to know.

fifteen

S he lowered the printer onto the kitchen table, feeling her back give slightly under the weight. It took her a while to reconnect all the cables, input to output, the right male to the right female, but eventually she cracked it and the computer hummed into life. The smell of fresh coffee was everywhere. Midnight Thursday and she was ready to start work.

It had taken some time to reach this point. The first night had been taken up with the pain and the blood – such a river of it that she began to wonder what exactly it was that her body was rejecting. With one threat gone it allowed her the space to contemplate another. But the twenty-four-hour AIDS helpline only told her what she already knew. If she was infected it would take two months for it to show and then she would need to come in for a test. What were the chances? Well that, of course, depended on who he was and where he had been before. Which in turn led her to wonder where he was now. The rest of the night had passed in an orchestration of surveillance; checking the windows, prowling the staircase, alert to every whisper of the floorboards.

So it was that inch by inch, hour by hour, the house became new again, and because even fear dulls when there is nothing to fuel it, and there is a limit to how long one can live on one's nerves, she began to relax. By the second night, she could discern a rhythm to the hours of darkness: the way the world fell gradually asleep around midnight or one a.m., leaving only the hum of occasional night traffic until even that died away in the dead hours between two and four. At that time you could almost believe that you were alone in the world, that your isolation made you unique, special, and that there was something to be learnt from inhabiting the still dark centre, a kind of wisdom or calm.

As the familiarity brought comfort she began to feel almost privileged. She checked his window less often and each time she did it was dark. Maybe she had helped him to sleep at night after all.

But not her. She was getting used to it. So it was that on the third evening she climbed the stairs to the attic. And this time it was not the ketchup stains that brought her down again but the more practical fact that the night was colder than the day and the central heating didn't work so well at the top of the house. So she decided to move. Besides, she thought as she dismantled the plugs and wrapped up the cables, she was not the only woman being persecuted in this house and it had begun to feel almost unsisterly leaving Mirka alone and captive while she was doing so much to make herself free.

The room was damp and small, no more than six feet by four, no window or skylight, only a grimy overhead bulb that was kept burning constantly. There was a bucket in one corner and a makeshift iron bed with a thin mattress and a few threadbare blankets.

The woman lay still, the naked light harsh and unflattering to her features. But the fat man wasn't looking at her face. He had pulled back the cover and was studying the way that sleep had dragged her skirt up over her thighs. He grunted with appreciation. He liked the way women slept when they were drugged; careless, abandoned, as if they were too shagged out to move. Like after sex.

He checked the damaged hand which she was cradling by her side. The dressing was holding and the blood was stanched. No worries there. He was good at his job. Both the hurting and the tending. It was always a surprise to him how the better you do one, the more they need the other. Nobody screams for ever. Even in his dreams.

'Keep your hands off her, Christophe.' The voice came from behind the grille high up in the door. 'You heard what they said. She's not like the other one.'

The fat man lifted his head towards the peep-hole and grimaced. 'Not yet, you mean. But what happens when her American husband comes to find her, eh? Then I bet we get to play with both of them.'

He grinned and ran a finger up her thigh towards her crotch. The woman didn't stir.

Nothing like anticipation, she thought as she refilled her coffee cup. The perfect mechanism of fear; never letting you rest, always threatening something worse. Except the fat man was enough of a caricature for the reader to understand that whatever goes around comes around, and that there would be a time when the bad guys had better keep their hands on their balls too. Simple rules of the genre. One good cut deserves another. Not that Mirka would be the one to do the cutting. That was man's work, of course. How many adjectives could a translator come up with to describe a scream? She'd find out soon enough.

She flicked back the sheet and checked outside. The binoculars tracked over a landscape of darkness. Was he really asleep? Three nights on and no sign. He had listened to what she had said. Or maybe he had recognised the change in her. If fear has a smell, then presumably one also notices the lack of it. She topped up the coffee with a hit of whisky and went back to the screen. Back in the capital Jake was waiting, impatient for revenge. Well, she thought, let him wait a while longer. Now was the season for the women to be awake in the night, and find their own voices to put against the men's. All it needed was a little imagination. Chances are, in the hands of a good translator, you probably wouldn't even notice the joins.

In a country of rationing the jailers were scarcely more comfortable than the jailed. On his camp bed in the corridor the fat man was snoring, his jacket wrapped around him, making up for what the blanket couldn't cover. His companion stepped over him, peering into the cell through the grille before putting down the tray and unbolting the locks.

She was lying in exactly the same position, back to the door, the damaged hand cradled up by her side.

That made five hours without moving. He knew because he checked her regularly. Poor bint. He'd warned Christophe not to give her more than two pills. Christ, they'd be in real trouble if she died on them. No payment then. Better try and wake her up. She'd be pretty hungry by now.

Mirka registered the sound of the key in the door and closed her eyes. In her head the ache of her finger throbbed in time to her pulse. She used her good hand to push the knock-out tablets, which she had retrieved from her cheek after the fat man had left her, further under the pillow.

The first few hours had been the worst. Then the temptation to take them had been almost unbearable. She couldn't think straight with the pain. But she was more scared of sleep than agony. Of what they might do to her when she was unconscious. In the end she had found that if she held her hand upwards in a certain position against her stomach then the pain lessened, and she could cope with it. So she had lain like that, immobile, face to the wall, willing herself to look at the blood-soaked gauze until the sight of it became almost normal. She was a woman with nine fingers and a stump. And nothing she could do would ever change that fact.

Little fingers. As a child she remembered tales her grandmother had told about how some women were born with the beginnings of a sixth digit on their hands; how it was known as the Devil's teat, the suckling of evil, a mark of a witch in the making, and how, in certain country areas, they were still superstitious enough to have it hacked off at birth.

For years after she had checked the edges of her

hands to see if there was any scar to mark her out as one of them. Even then she knew she was no witch in the making. Or that if she was, her witchcraft would take on a different physical manifestation.

She had been lovely even as a child, delicate, with honey-coloured hair and good bones, but at puberty her beauty had ripened into a voluptuousness so immediate and exotic that it disturbed the peace of the family and brought the local boys, like a pack of dogs, sniffing around the front door.

She knew she could have had whichever she wanted, and so, of course, she wanted none of them. It wasn't that she was cruel, simply that she didn't know what else to do. All she knew was that she yearned for something better. Even then she had an idea as to how to get it. While her friends contented themselves with shop jobs or secretarial posts in local government, she slaved away over inadequate English books, turning down dates in favour of extra study and evenings spent in the company of short-wave American and British radio; the language of cultural propaganda, but still more subtle than the type she was used to.

Finally, in her early twenties, she used her uncle's connections as a Party member and a bureaucrat in the Foreign Office to get herself a visa for a holiday to America. If she'd given it a few more years history would have done it for her, but she was not to know that and anyway, had she waited, she and Jake would never have found themselves on the same express subway train heading downtown from 87th Street.

He had been off duty at the time, sitting reading a newspaper when some punk had started bothering her, picking up on her funny accent, offering to show her the sights and not taking no for an answer. Jake stepped in and sorted him out.

He was different right from the start; older, colder, his control marking him out as a professional in a man's world. He was so at odds with the notion of chivalry that once he had saved her he seemed not to notice her further. It was this apparent indifference, of course, that made him so irresistible.

In the end it was she who had told *him* that she needed a drink, allowing herself to take hold of his arm as he propelled her out of the carriage and up through steamy subway steps. During that first date he reminded her of a dozen clean-cut American movie stars she had seen on flickering screens; traditional tough guys who didn't whinge or pout when they didn't get what they wanted, but simply went out and took it. It was such a recognisable fantasy that she immediately took his dislocation for strength. It was only later that she realised it was based on other things; fear, repressed anger and the seeing of too many unseeable things. But by then she was already in love, as much with the idea of being his saviour as with the man himself (another myth from another movie), and she had thrown up everything to stand by her man.

'They'll say I trapped you into it to get a green card,' she had teased him the night before their marriage as they lay together in a sweat made up from sex and a lack of air conditioning in his small Brooklyn apartment, traffic and neon providing an urban *son et lumière*.

'Well, at least they can't accuse you of doing it for my money,' he had replied, already reaching for her again.

Strange how you could fall out of love as easily as you fall into it. How long had it taken for her to realise her mistake? That not only could she not soothe his pain, but neither could she satisfy him. American men. They were not supposed to be so complicated. Hadn't the free market and rock'n'roll given them everything they wanted? Freedom of choice ought to have left no time for neurosis. His painful emotional complexity was her first indication that capitalism was not, after all, the panacea it had been cracked up to be.

Even the sex was confusing. His need for her was almost pathological, as if he somehow believed that the possession of her body was the same as her soul, and that to make sure he hadn't lost one he had to have the other all the time. Within the first year sex turned from a revelation into a habit and from a habit into a nightmare. Desire. Need. Jealousy. And performance fucking. She came across the term later in a novel and laughed out loud at its accuracy. It struck her later that this too probably came from watching too many movies, too long spent watching Michael Douglas's bare ass heaving up and down to the music of money, while the women writhed and groaned happily underneath. She had tried to talk about it with him once, but he would have none of it. Sex isn't for talking about, he would say angrily. It wrecks the spontaneity. But he already knew by then that it was over and that he was in danger of losing her.

Still, at least now he would have a part of her for always: the Devil's teat gift wrapped in a red-spotted handkerchief and delivered to his door. How would he feel? His horror would probably be less than his rage.

Jake's rages. The other side of the pain. What a joy

it was not to have to put up with them any more. Leaving him had been wonderful. She had felt like an adult for the first time in her life. This was her American dream come true. Independence. She had liked being in the city alone. She had got herself a job in a fancy art gallery specialising in the flood of new Eastern treasures that was hitting the market, where her looks and her languages had earned her enough to rent a small apartment in the Village. Before long she found herself wooed by a Brazilian diplomat, an older, softer man, with olive skin and long tapered fingers. Someone who looked after her, took her out to restaurants, treating her with care, in and out of bed. There was an elegance to their love-making that spoke as much about her pleasure as his own, and did not expect ownership in return. Nor reassurance nor congratulation every time he did it. If there was less passion, then there was also less pain. For her, by then, it was the right trade-off.

And so she had been happy. Until the day the phone rang and she heard her own language on the other end of the line. What supreme bad luck, she thought. To find herself a prisoner back in the country she had done so much to escape from, a pawn in some unknown game of revenge for an angry unsaveable man whom she no longer loved. And who, if only he could realise it, no longer loved her either. No. There was no white knight in this story. If Jake did come to save her it would only be to imprison her again. Waiting for him would be signing another kind of death warrant.

The door closed and she heard the man put down the tray on the metal table. She steeled herself not to flinch at his touch.

He put a hand on her shoulder and shook her. 'Wake up.'

A different voice. Native but not city. Not the one with the chopper. Under the pillow she checked the pills. Then she opened her eyes and turned. The pain in her hand roared up like a flame and brought involuntary tears to her eyes. She looked up into his face and thought she caught a flicker of feeling.

'Does it still hurt?'

No. This man wasn't like the other. This man seemed almost embarrassed by the thought of the pain they had caused. She nodded, not trusting herself to speak.

'Sit up. You'll feel better if you eat something.'

The dialect was more pronounced now. In the lilt of his voice she felt the heat of the cooking range in her grandmother's kitchen, and saw a host of sallow teenage boys with transistors to their ears, dying of boredom as they loitered in the local square. I know you, she thought. I've met you a hundred times: a village boy with village hunger. I know exactly what you want.

She felt a quiet ache in her womb. Hunger or fear? She would find out. 'I don't think I can get up. Could you ...' she said, and she used the familiar pronoun, 'could you please—'

Someone was ringing the doorbell. Back in an English kitchen she registered the sound with her heartbeat. Someone ringing her doorbell in the middle of the night. Someone? Surely not. He wouldn't dare.

She looked at her watch. The darkness was deceptive; in fact the night was already ending. It was

7.21: the edge of a winter solstice dawn. She hadn't realised how long she had been working. She would have liked to read it all back now, see just how different it felt. Never mind. If it was too obvious she could always doctor it later.

Another ring, this time more insistent. On the way to the front door she caught sight of a woman in the hall mirror: hollow eyes, pale face, hair all over the place. Unkempt. Unruly. Inside as well as out. So that's what happens when you stop taking any notice, she thought. She must remember to give Mirka a different kind of beauty.

She peered through the peep-hole in the door. On the pavement a distorted figure in a suit with a big face was staring up into the fish-eye lens. It took her a while to recognise him. But then it had been a long time ago. Or so it felt now.

She opened the door, but left the chain on, like a pensioner checking the gasman's identity card. He peered at her through the crack. He looked bulkier than she remembered. She had a flash of his torso above her, stomach muscles on the edge of fat. Or was that just in comparison to the body which had followed?

His first view of her seemed to leave him equally startled. She tried to imagine what he saw. Well, he already had experience of her as a mad woman.

'Good morning.'

'Hello, Malcolm.'

'I didn't wake you?'

'No.'

'I wasn't sure if you'd be up this early.'

'I haven't been to bed.'

If he was surprised he kept it to himself. He stood for a second, waiting for her to open the door.

'But you got my message, right?' he said when it was clear she wasn't going to. 'I mean when you didn't call back I assumed ...' He hesitated, reading the blankness in her eyes. 'I've come for my watch.' She kept staring. 'My watch, remember? I left it here. You haven't posted it already, have you?'

His watch. Of course. Watches, hammers. How careless these men were with their possessions. 'I – yes, I mean no. I – I've been busy.'

He nodded. 'I guessed as much. That's why I said I'd pick it up this morning before my trip. But you obviously didn't get the message.'

'No.' The answering machine was in the hall. Asleep during the day she never heard it, and somehow in the night it never occurred to her to check.

'You'd better come in,' she said begrudgingly. She glanced behind him. The street was empty. She closed the door and slipped the chain off the lock, then opened it again. He stepped into the hall. 'Where did you say you left it?'

'Um ... by the bed.'

'Stay here,' she ordered, turning on her heel and taking the stairs two at a time.

It didn't take her long to discover that it wasn't there. Not by the bed, nor behind nor under it. Nor on the mantelpiece nor in the bathroom. But when she got back down to tell him that, he wasn't there either. Then she heard the noise from the kitchen.

He was standing at the window, his hand cupped around the glass, peering into the darkness. 'What are you doing in here?' she said angrily.

He turned quickly, but without any sense of guilt. 'I thought I heard something knocking down here. You didn't hear it?'

'No.' But the only thing she could hear now was the sound of her own pulse inside her head. She pushed past him, grabbing the binoculars from the side and snapping on the patio light. The garden was empty. But his light was on.

She stared at it for a while, then turned back into the room. She had to take a few deep breaths before she trusted herself to speak. He had been watching her. Now he gave a little shrug and turned towards the computer screen. She barged past him again and pushed the close-down button. 'Do you want to save the changes?' the screen asked her. She pressed Y and watched the words count up with dizzying speed, then disappear.

'Looked interesting,' he said over her shoulder.

Jesus, the guy had a nerve. What rights did he think one night had bought him? 'It's work,' she growled, switching off the machine.

'You've been up all night doing it?'

'Yes. Look, I can't find your watch anywhere,' she said in an attempt to stop the conversation, her mind still racing around the garden. 'You're sure you left it here?'

'Well, I only ever take it off to sleep. And it's not at my house,' he said evenly.

'Maybe you left it at somebody else's?'

'I'll take that as a compliment,' he murmured dryly. 'But I think I know who I've been with.'

You're lucky, she almost added, but caught herself in time. Careful, she thought. It's the end of a long night and you're not used to company. Watch what you tell him.

'It feels different in here.' He was looking round the room, evidently curious.

'I've got a deadline,' she said abruptly. 'It's easier to work where the food is.'

He gestured to the window. 'And the sheet?'

'Keeps the glare out. Means I'm not distracted by the view.'

'Except for when you're bird watching,' he said quietly.

She chose not to hear him. There was a shiny silence. She remembered the last time they had stood in this kitchen, his hands sliding up her legs, the feel of his tongue in her ear. The thought started the flow of saliva in her mouth. Wrong tongue, she thought, wrong hands. Don't get the two muddled now.

She looked at his face. At least he had lips. It struck her that in another world she might find him attractive again. But not this one. Not now. Not yet. My God, what would he think of her if she told him? It would scare the hell out of him. Out of anybody really. It even scared her if she let herself think about it. Would it help her sense of recovery to make love to someone who hadn't got a hammer? Maybe. But not this man. This man was obviously someone on his way to work. The thought of it made her want to laugh. It's OK, she thought. He'll go soon. Then she could start searching the garden. 'Do you want a coffee?' she said, the words getting out before she had given them permission.

He appeared to think about it. 'Well, if you're making . . .'

'Ah, no, actually, sorry, I forgot. I don't have any coffee.'

He held her look, letting his amusement show. 'I drink tea.'

She scowled. 'I don't have any milk. Or at least not any that hasn't gone off.'

'You think you can manage hot water?'

She didn't remember him as someone with such a sense of humour. Tom used to be like this, she thought. Before he became so goddamn threatened. She had found it very attractive in the old days. What was that aphorism she and Sally had been so fond of quoting? A guy who could make you laugh could usually make you come. But that was a long time ago, when men in your bed were more important than men in your life. Maybe she had returned to that state without realising it.

'All right,' she heard herself say. 'But I've got a deadline.'

'And I've got a ten o'clock shuttle to catch. Do you think I'll make it without a watch?'

He sat himself down at the edge of the table, careful not to disturb any of the papers lying there, and watched as she boiled the kettle and got the mugs out. What does he think of me? she wondered. Can he tell? Can he tell just by looking at me?

'Is it the same one?'

'What?'

'The same book you were working on before?'

'Yes.'

'When do you have to finish it by?'

'Early January.'

'Will you do it?'

'Probably. If I work through Christmas.'

'Lucky you.'

'You don't like Christmas?'

He made a face. 'Do you know anybody over the age of fifteen who does?'

'Do you go home?' Strange how people still called it that, long after they had a home of their own.

'I'm lucky. Father in County Cork, mother in Australia. I'm fair to both and see neither.'

'So what do you do?'

'Get drunk, smoke dope, watch videos.'

'Really?' She laughed despite herself because she hadn't taken him as someone into drugs. One-night stands. Amazing how little they can tell you about someone.

'Why the surprise? Don't I look the type?'

'I don't know.'

'You should see me without the suit.'

'I have,' she said quietly, putting his tea down on the table in front of him.

'Sounds like you disapprove.'

'Of dope?' She shrugged. 'No. It's not that. It's just . . . well, it's been a long time. I feel like somebody else now.'

'Don't tell me, you're more of a suffering-to-gain-redemption kind of woman?'

'What makes you say that?' she said sharply.

'Oh, I don't know. Something to do with your intensity.' And again he held her gaze. 'It's all right. I meant it more as a compliment than an insult.'

They sat for a while drinking the tea and not talking, a distance of maybe four or five feet between them. It struck her that she should check the window again, but she didn't know how to do it with him there.

'I'm sorry about the watch,' she said at last.

He shrugged. 'Well, just as long as you haven't given it to anyone else.' She shot a fast glance at him, but he smiled it away. He paused. 'I've ... er ... I've been thinking about our night.'

'Have you?'

'Yeah. I didn't expect to.'

'Thanks.'

He laughed. 'I mean at the time I thought you were a bit crazy for me.'

'You're right,' she said. 'I am.'

'But then I realised I quite liked it.'

'My craziness, you mean?'

'Yes ... and other things.' A longer pause this time. 'I enjoyed going to bed with you.'

'Did you?' she said. 'I didn't think it was all that hot myself.'

He stared at her for a moment, then burst out laughing. 'Maybe that's why.'

'Why what?'

'Why I've been thinking about you. Because you don't say what's expected. Is that your final word on the subject, or do you think we might improve with practice?'

Depends on who I compare us with, she thought. But the thought didn't warm her. Instead it made her shake. I can't get into this, she thought. She shook her head. 'It's not you. I'm ... I'm committed elsewhere.'

'Aaaah,' and she could feel him backing off. 'Well, you should have said before. Sorry. My mistake.'

'It's not – I mean, it's sort of unfinished business.'

'You and your guy?'

'Er ... no. No. Someone else.'

'OK. Well, good luck with it.' He finished the tea and

stood up. 'Some other time maybe.'

Yeah, she thought, some other time. She watched him go. At the door he turned. 'Can I say something to you anyway?'

'Yeah.'

'Sally and Patrick are worried about you. Sally in particular. She thinks you're in trouble.'

'Oh really. How about you?'

'Me?' He sounded surprised. 'I'm no judge. I've always had this thing for weird women.'

'Well, tell Sally not to worry,' she said fiercely. 'It's work. I'm busy. That's all.'

'OK. OK. Just passing on the message. Listen, I hope the book and your . . . er – other business go well. And if you find the watch – you've got my address.'

She didn't see him out, just sat there until she heard the slam of the front door behind him. Then she picked up his tea mug and flung it against the wall.

sixteen

In the daylight the garden was still empty and his window was blank. He would, of course, have had ample time to get away. If indeed he had ever been there. She spent so long with the binoculars trained on his path that her eyes hurt. A knocking at 7.20 in the morning? It didn't make sense. It must have been a mistake. Or even a lie. How about if Malcolm had made it up as a way of getting himself into the kitchen? She hadn't seen herself as someone with that much appeal. 'Sorry. I'm already committed.' Well, it wasn't a complete lie.

But half-lies, she discovered, can become whole. Twenty minutes later, when she set out to make herself the coffee she'd said she didn't have, she found there weren't enough beans to fill the machine and no more in the freezer. No coffee and no milk. No orange juice either. Nor any butter for the remaining stale heel of bread. In the days since siege conditions had taken over she had stopped thinking about such things. When had she done the last shop? Seven, eight days ago? Even then the exoticism of her purchases had left no room for the mundane.

She looked at the clock. 8.40. If she went now she could make it back before the crowds. She thought about leaving the house. Even assuming it had been him at the window he surely wouldn't dare try anything in broad daylight. Anyway, now there was no way he could get in. She went back to the window and checked the locks. Why hadn't she seen him in his room? He must have been there at some point. Unless she'd got it wrong and that wasn't his flat after all? Maybe it was simply a monstrous coincidence, that one light going on at that particular moment. What if it had been someone up in the night needing a glass of water? What if all these precautions, all this surveillance, had been for the wrong person?

Too many questions. To get perspective she needed space. It was time to leave the house.

While she had been dancing with darkness the world had moved on. The High Street was tacky with Christmas cheer; the banner over the department store announced that there were now just six shopping days to go. It was a fact that the rest of the world was taking seriously. The weekday street was Saturday-full, people with heads down and cheque books open, committed to spending money they didn't have on people they didn't like that much.

She had never enjoyed it as a season; even when she was small she had mistrusted the magic, sniffing out death and deceit amid the aromas of fir-tree rosin and stock-cube gravy. Doing it for the children. Or rather in her case the child. No wonder everything had had to be so perfect. To be an only child born ten years into a marriage may have seemed like a miracle to them, but it was more of a burden on her. Would it have been different if they had had another? At least it would have taken the pressure of fulfilling the fantasies off her. She had had to go on 'believing' in Father Christmas long after she knew the truth just to keep her parents happy, extend their illusions. It was such a relief to get away from it all. The best years with Tom had been about defying the occasion; taking last-minute planes to Morocco or Scandinavia, spending the day drunk in some hotel room or on a beach.

She thought of Malcolm, rolling spliffs against reruns of *The Big Sleep*. Was she interested? That depended on what her other suitor might be doing. Christmas Eve. Maybe this year she should block up the chimneys. Or light a fire. At least this time around there would be an excuse for her alienation.

Inside the supermarket, things got worse. Like him she had become a night creature, unused to bright lights or crowds. The place was vibrating with people and trolleys, an army of crazed shoppers marching to an accompaniment of a choral version of 'My Little Donkey', which was seeping out through what seemed like gas vents in the ceiling. There was a feeling of muted panic to the scene, like the beginning of a horror movie. How amazing, she thought: I can handle an intruder in my bedroom but I can't make it through Waitrose at Christmas.

She put her head down and concentrated on the list. She got through the fruit and vegetables without a problem, then started on the long-life stuff, tins and frozen foods.

She left the trolley by the side of the freezer compartment and made a careful procession down the ready-to-eat section, picking her meals by the country: Lamb korma, Thai chicken, paella, Chinese sweet and sour prawns. If she shopped well now she wouldn't need to go out again until the book was finished. It would be better food than Mirka was getting anyway. Maybe she could help by giving her a culinary imagination. Where men fantasise about sex she could play with images of cream sauce and ginger stir-fry. She returned to her trolley and put them in – but something caught her eye. Surely this wasn't her shopping. She had only fresh foods and a few staples, she hadn't got to the tins yet. Yet there were four of them, thrown in on top of the potatoes. Cat food. Someone must have mistaken her trolley for their own. Someone? She picked up one of the tins. A picture of a handsome, well-fed kitty stared out at her, its colouring like Millie's. Like Millie's. She felt her throat get smaller, as if a layer of fear had furred up her windpipe. She looked up.

He was at the end of the aisle less than twenty feet away, no trolley, no shopping, just standing there next to the cereal counter, his hands stuffed in his jacket pockets, watching her. He looked almost haunted.

She had never seen him in daylight, knew him more by feel than by sight. Yet she recognised him immediately; not so much from the body or the face – though the slash of mouth made her heart beat faster – but from the tension that he generated; the way it lit up the air like a laser beam cutting between them.

The paralysis was equal. She stood transfixed, gut twisting, heart pounding, the tin of cat food burning a hole in her hand, his eyes burning a hole into her brain.

Then he smiled, a tight nervous little sneer which bared his teeth and seemed to speak as much of pain as pleasure. Hers or his? It broke the spell. The taste of him was like vomit in her mouth. She lifted up her hand and before she knew what she was doing hurled the cat food tin at him. Its weight gave it an added velocity. It would have hurt if it had hit him. It missed by inches, instead doing serious damage to a shelf display of cereals on special offer. The boxes scattered like skittles across the floor. An elderly woman who was walking past let out a shriek as they crashed all around her. At the top of the aisle more people turned. It didn't wipe off the smile.

Her hand fumbled in the trolley, connecting with a ketchup bottle, the replacement for his wall decorations, but she was already too late. By the time she had it in her hand he was gone. She sprinted to the end of the aisle only to see him hurtle past a woman with a small child, sending the kid crashing into a stacked display of biscuit boxes. The mother yelled as the kid exploded into tears. By the time she got past them both he was halfway through the wide aisle check-out heading for the exit.

Now he had half the store watching as he tried to shove his way through the line. A man in a donkey jacket turned on him and shoved him back, the English sense of fair play enraged by the idea of someone trying to jump the queue, but he was through and past him already, racing towards the automatic doors. She stood watching on the other side of the divide, the bottle still grasped in her hand, her breath coming in big gushing gulps. Around her there was a soundtrack of outrage and excitement.

'You all right, love?'

'What did he do?'

'He snatched her purse.'

'I thought he had something in his hand. In broad daylight. Damn cheek.'

'Bloody yob.'

She didn't hear it. What would she have done if she had caught him? she was thinking. How much damage could you wreak with a ketchup bottle?

The security officer, when he arrived, looked too young for the job. His sense of relief was palpable when she told him it was nothing, that she had simply panicked when she felt the man brush against her but now she had checked her purse was secure.

'Good for you, my girl,' said a wizened old man as she walked self-consciously back to her trolley. 'These men have got to know they can't shove you around. My daughter's like you. Doesn't take shit from anybody.' She was so distracted she wasn't sure if he was referring to the man or the security officer.

She gazed down at the pile of provisions at the bottom of the trolley. Where would he be now? Dancing his way across back garden walls to try and poke his metal coat hanger into her cat-flap? Which was preferable? Dying of fear or starvation? She took a few deep breaths and dug her list back out. Next time she went out she would wire the kitchen lock to the main cable. Give him the shock of his life.

Yet even as she thought it she saw his face in front of her, found herself trying to read the grim little smile, differentiate between nerves and triumph.

It took her almost half an hour to finish the shop. At the smallest check-out queue the woman in front of her had two stuffed trolleys. She stood behind, impatient and resigned at the same time, staring down at the bank of magazines designed to tempt you into last-minute purchases. She read their covers without thinking: 'A million ways to make your Christmas a Joyous Occasion' over a picture of a little girl dressed to match the Christmas tree she was sitting next to. Could there really be people out there who spent their lives making table decorations?

Below the glossies the local paper boasted a different headline. She looked at it with only half her brain, registering the words and not the meaning. She must have read it three times before she actually took it in. When she did it knocked everything else off the rack:

HAMMER RAPIST STRIKES AGAIN.

She picked up the paper but had to put it down again because her hand was shaking so much she couldn't read the small print. But she got there eventually; strange how, by most standards, it was not that shocking really, just an everyday tale of inner-city violence and unsolved crime.

The streets of North London once again became unsafe for local women after a young woman was attacked early on Wednesday morning. The victim, who has not been named, was a student nurse returning home to her digs after a night shift at the Whittington Hospital when the assault took place.

Her attacker, whom she later described as a white man of medium height and slim build, was wearing a mask and carrying a hammer. He

pulled her into an alleyway off the Holloway
Road leading to Whittington Park where he
sexually assaulted her. A police spokesman said
it marked the eighth such attack in this area over
the last seven months by the man whom the
authorities have dubbed The Holloway Hammer.

This latest attack differs from earlier incidents
which took place in the victims' homes. Police
today cautioned all young women living in the
area to make sure any doors and windows are
securely locked and to take extra precautions
when travelling home from Christmas parties and
where possible to walk with a friend or take a taxi.
The victim's condition is described as comfortable.

Comfortable. It was not the word that she would
have used. Early morning Wednesday. Yesterday. No
wonder there had been no sign of life. He had been too
busy. The eighth attack in seven months. Or should
that read the ninth? The only question was who would
be the tenth? So much for the power of redemption.

seventeen

The station was down a side street next to the library; another vicious architectural mismatch of Sixties brutalism and nineteenth-century civic pride. Presumably when the library had been built they wouldn't have needed the police, or at least not a whole station full of them. This would have marked the edge of the city then, England's green and pleasant land only a short bike ride away.

The date on the library foundation stone was 1875, before Jack the Ripper, when London would have had a different – more Artful Dodger – kind of crime. Now the only pockets the boys wanted to pick were the ones inside girls' bodies. But that still didn't mean you should invite them in.

She stood by the railings, listening to herself trying to tell it.

'I was too scared to do anything else. He said he'd hurt me if I didn't.' She might not have the bruises to show, but wrapped safely away in Safeway plastic she had the weapon to prove it. Of course they would believe her. It was, after all, the truth.

And yet not the whole truth. No. The whole truth

was something wilder. Something even she didn't want to understand. She saw again the tight little face, registered the electricity streaming through his body, felt it earth itself inside her. She already knew that there were some things that could not be told. It's not over till the thin man smiles. And sometimes not even then.

So tell them what you can, she said to herself fiercely. Tell them and get at least some of the monkey off your back.

A blue Ford Fiesta screeched to an unnecessarily fast stop on the double yellow line across from the building and two men in suits got out. Plain clothes. Aptly named. As they crossed the road one of them caught her eye; thirty-something, with a touch of flab to the face. Her only experience of the police was reporting two stolen bikes to claim the insurance and the young Mr Plod from the other week. But these guys didn't feel so benign.

'Three days, eh? What made you wait so long?'

'I only just read the report in the newspaper.'

'But you must have known he might try it again. Why didn't you come to us straight away?'

'I was scared.'

'Of what?'

'I don't know. Him. Myself.'

She saw him glance at his companion, then back at her. 'I gather you called the police a couple of weeks ago, Miss Skovorecky. Some trouble with a stack of CDs, wasn't it?'

'Yes.'

'Same man, do you think? He didn't by any chance mention his taste in music, did he?'

The station doors slammed shut behind them. She stood there for a few minutes longer, then walked away.

In retrospect she didn't have much choice as to where to go next, though as far as she remembered she made no conscious decision, just found herself driving home that way. The vicarage door remained closed after the third ring. But this was the third week of December, the time all good dog collars would be caught up in annual jubilation.

She had made a nice job of the church already. The main glass doors had two enormous holly wreaths attached, rich shiny leaves and fat blood-red berries, with white stencil snow above them reading: 'UNTO US A CHILD IS BORN'. It looked good, she thought. Tasteful. The equivalent of a spiritual glossy. She peered through the window and saw the main altar with more holly and a stunning display of ferns and berries.

But it was not all such successful interior design. To the side, in an alcove which had obviously housed the Nativity, a figure (the Reverend?) was on her hands and knees picking up something from the steps, while above her, like some newly apprenticed angel, a man in white overalls was precariously balanced on the top of a ladder, arms up to the sky, desperately trying to scrub out a set of giant red letters scrawled on the wall. 'MARY SUCKS AND JESUS FUC . . .' The plaster around the missing two letters was already a messy lurid pink. From the look of the stain this was more than ketchup.

She pushed the door open quietly and walked in. They were so busy at their job they didn't notice her.

'This is impossible, Catherine.' The angel was gasping for breath. 'I can't even reach them properly. It'll take me hours.'

From the ground the Reverend glanced up. 'I'm not cancelling the school service, Jim. And that's that. If necessary we'll go ahead with it still up there.'

'Why don't you paint it over?' she said as her footsteps on the wooden floor gave her presence away.

Up the ladder the angel flapped his wings frantically. 'Hey, what are you doing here?' You don't get to fly that way, she thought. 'The church is closed. Didn't you read the sign?'

'No. Some vandals must have ripped it up. Hello, Reverend Baker.'

'Hello, Elizabeth. How are you?'

The voice was good, but as she straightened up it was clear that the serene Catherine was no longer quite so at peace. All that lively crinkly hair was looking a little less Famous Five now. There were tufts of it sticking out at all angles, as if more than one morning service had been overlooked that day. Had she noticed? Maybe, among its many blessings, belief precluded vanity. She thought of her own face in the front hall mirror. It could be they had something in common after all. She shrugged. 'I was just passing.'

The woman gave her a little smile as if to acknowledge the lie but let it go anyway. She looked up.

'What do you think, Jim? Would paint do the trick? It would certainly be a lot faster.'

'Hmmn. I still don't think I could reach it all from here. How on earth did they get up this high?'

'How would it be if you used a roller? Or we could tie a brush to the end of a broom handle? There's a couple in the vestry.'

'Hmmn,' he said again begrudgingly. 'That might do it.'

Elizabeth bent down to help pick up some of the debris, now revealed as bright ceramic fragments of shepherds and wise kings lying amid scattered straw and ferns. 'What time is the service?'

'One o'clock,' the Reverend said quietly and this time her voice definitely sounded a little tired.

She handed her the bottom half of the infant Jesus, plump little flesh-coloured legs in a tasteful white nappy. 'What will you do without the crib?'

She made a face. 'I expect I'll have to do something with the power of words.'

It seemed for a moment that she might give in to self-pity, but instead she took a deep breath and straightened up, rubbing her hands down her skirt. 'This is a waste of time. We'll never be able to repair it by one. Listen, Jim, why don't we try the paint? Go out and buy a can and a roller. There's money in the petty cash box.'

'You hope there is,' he said as he came thumping down the ladder. 'What if they've taken that too?'

'Oh dear, I didn't think of that.'

'Oh, it's all right. I don't think there was much there anyway. Not after we paid for the Christmas flowers. I've got enough on me.'

He stomped out of the church, flat feet echoing on parquet flooring. They both watched him go.

'So, Elizabeth,' she said, brushing back the unruly hair from her eyes. 'What can I do for you?'

'Look, I'll ... I'll come back another time. You're obviously busy.'

'No. Not at all. They've already done enough damage to my day. I'm not going to let them wreck my parishioners' time too—' Parishioner. It sounded so comforting. Or stifling. It was hard to know which. 'Only perhaps if you wouldn't mind we could talk here in the church. I don't feel entirely comfortable about leaving it empty right at the moment.'

'D'you think they'll come back?'

'No. I just don't like to feel the place uncared for,' she said, then gave an almost apologetic smile as if she realised how precious the remark must have sounded. But it was not the time to worry about other people's embarrassment. They sat themselves in the second row of the pews, the Reverend facing the Nativity damage. She sighed. 'Apparently this kind of thing often happens at Christmas.'

'Vandalism?'

'Yes.'

'You mean it's like suicide? More people feel alienated then?' she said, thinking of herself.

She shrugged. 'Well, I suppose celebrating the birth of a child is so much about family and belonging. If you feel you don't, the temptation must be to try and destroy it all.'

'That's very charitable of you,' she said.

'You should have been here half an hour ago. I wasn't quite so charitable then.'

'What did people do before religion?'

She glanced at her. 'How big a question is that?'

'I mean at Christmas.'

'They celebrated the winter solstice in the hope that

spring would come again. Darkness and light. It's not so dissimilar really. You should come to our Christmas Eve service. The whole church is lit by candles. It looks wonderful.'

'Is that a sop to paganism?'

The vicar laughed. 'Probably. Though it wouldn't be wise to admit to it. Anyway, what can I do for you? How is your particular vandal behaving these days?'

She looked at her and gave another little shrug. When it came to it, just as outside the police station, she somehow didn't have the words. 'At least mine only uses ketchup,' she said quietly. 'Easier to wipe off.'

'Ketchup.' Catherine frowned. 'Why don't you tell me about it?'

'Because I'm not sure I know what to say.'

'Try it.'

She sighed. Where to start? 'Do you believe in forgiveness?'

The woman studied her for a moment. 'Yes, I do.'

'Isn't that the party line?'

She smiled. 'Absolutely. But that's not why I believe in it.'

'What about redemption?'

'Um ... I would say the same answer. Only I think that's less to do with me and more to do with God.'

'You mean the sinner has to find it out for themselves?'

'In a manner of speaking, yes.'

Elizabeth looked down at her hands and realised she was still holding a piece of the Nativity, a half torso of a king carrying a golden box. Was it gold or myrrh? It was all so long ago she couldn't remember. She looked up. 'What did you do before you were a priest?'

'Me? I was a school teacher. In a comprehensive in East London.'

'Was it rough?'

'It was . . . a challenge, yes.'

'So you've met these kinds of kids before?' she said, gesturing at the wall.

'Maybe. I'd like to think not.'

'What happened? Did you lose your faith in education?'

She laughed. 'I'd put it another way. I'd see it more as having greater faith in something else.' She paused. 'You know I used to say to myself that if God ever let women priests be ordained I would make him a promise that in return I would never sound self-righteous. But it's not as easy as it sounds.'

Sweet, thought Elizabeth, but something of an occupational hazard. 'I wouldn't worry. From what I remember you're better than most.'

Their voices echoed up into the cold chasm of air above the altar. She looked around her. It was not an impressive church: too young to have much atmosphere and not enough secluded places for the spirit to linger. But it felt OK, considering. Maybe it wasn't so much the place as the people who made the difference, generations of spirituality layering down through the ages, seeping into the brickwork, colouring the air. How many disturbed souls had sat here before her, seeking comfort and truth?

'Have you ever had to forgive someone who didn't deserve it? Someone who had done something serious?'

'Elizabeth, I—'

'I mean in the confessional sense. Somebody comes

and tells you something, something you really ought to tell the police about, but you can't divulge it because it's confidential.'

She thought about it for a moment. 'Montgomery Clift,' she answered firmly.

'What?'

'Montgomery Clift. In *I Confess*. It's a Hitchcock film. Clift plays a Catholic priest whom a murderer confesses to. I used to watch it all the time as a young girl. I think I had something of a schoolgirl crush on him.'

'But he was gay, wasn't he?'

'Yes. Though I didn't know that at the time. But I grant you it does give it a bit of a subtext, doesn't it?'

This time when the silence came the woman decided not to break it. She sat patiently watching, waiting, giving her the space, making it as comfortable as she could.

'I called you, but you were away,' Elizabeth said at last. 'It isn't a poltergeist.'

'So what is it?'

She sighed. 'It's a bit like this.'

'You mean some kind of burglar or vandal?'

But when she opened her mouth to say more she found the intake of breath was needed more to control the tears, not the jagged pushy sobs from the night with Malcolm, but a softer more insistent rain. It continued for a while. She wondered if it might somehow wash it all away.

The woman put a hand over hers and held it there. Eventually she said, with great gentleness, 'You know, Elizabeth, you only have to ask for help and it will be given.'

'Yours or God's?'

'Both. I promise you.'

She sniffed fiercely. 'I'm not anybody's victim.'

'No. I doubt very much that you are.'

'And I think if somebody sets out to hurt you, you have a right to protect yourself.'

'Is that what you did?'

'I—'

'Catherine.' A man's voice cut in loudly across the church. She turned and looked up. 'Catherine, I'm sorry, but the police are here.'

She let out an impatient sigh. 'Thanks, Patrick, tell them I'll be five minutes.'

He hesitated. 'I told them that you were with someone. But they said it was important. That they need to see you straight away.'

'Five minutes, Patrick,' she said, and in those few words you could feel the school teacher rising up inside her. She turned back, immediately engaged again, but the moment had passed. At the mention of the police Elizabeth was already on her feet. 'No, please, don't go.'

'I have to. I – I've got work to do.'

'Listen, if something has happened to you, or you've done something you're frightened about, you have to tell someone. It won't just go away.' And the voice was tougher this time.

Sensible, Elizabeth thought. She's so good and sensible. What would she have done? Understood his distress and talked him into the church rather than her own vagina? Giving faith instead of taking sperm? No. You couldn't understand it unless you'd been there. And even then . . .

'Elizabeth?'

'So what did Montgomery Clift do? In the film.'

The woman stared at her for a moment, then said evenly, 'He persuaded the man to go to the police.'

She gave a little snorting laugh. 'I think that's what you call a cop-out. You'd better go. They're waiting for you.'

At the other side of the church the man was still standing, trying to look as if he wasn't there. The Reverend shot him what could only be described as an uncharitable look. She turned back. 'I'll be ten minutes. Will you promise me that you'll stay till I get back?'

There was a small silence.

'Promise.'

She nodded.

'Good. Do you want to come to the vicarage or stay here?'

'Here.'

'Thank you. Maybe you could give Jim some advice when he gets back with the paint. He isn't the world's handiest handyman.'

She watched her walk across the altar to the door at the other side. The man opened it for her and they went out together. Silence returned. She sat staring at the graffiti on the wall. It struck her that if God had wanted, he could have done something about this. Have made sure the door was harder to force, or sent a crack of lightning through the nave the instant the spray paint hit the wall. They were just boys. With a little imagination they could easily have been terrorised back into line.

And what could he have done for her? Made her thin man impotent? Even given him a good hobby to keep him out of other people's dustbins. But of course it didn't work like that. Because when push came to shove He didn't give a damn. If you read the small print you realised it had all been given up to you anyway. Free will. As a statement of care she had always found it about as convincing as the Citizen's Charter. No doubt Catherine Baker would have another spin on that one. But to accept her comfort you also had to accept His. And He had already proved negligent. 'Where were you in the still of the night when I was ripe for conversion?' she said into the empty air.

The front door of the church opened and the soiled angel tramped back in, heaving a can of paint and a plastic bag over a broom handle. He scowled at her as he passed. She waited until his back was turned, then got up and walked out.

eighteen

The street was Tavistock Crescent. That much was obvious. It met the end of her road and curled round in a graceful semi-circle till it intersected with another equally residential avenue. It was a rhythmic flow of terraced houses, late Victorian, three storeys high, like everything else around. Also like everything else they had gone through incarnations of living fashions: family homes turned into bedsits, then into more salubrious first-time buyers' flats, and now (when they could manage to sell) back into family homes again. She could almost imagine them inside, layers of lino like a *millefeuille* cake baked up from a century of tenancy.

She counted the house numbers off carefully. From her kitchen window she could see what she thought was the left-hand end of the terrace, though not the right. If she had got it correct his was eighteenth along. That made it number 36 or possibly 38.

Neither of them was in particularly good shape, but 38 was definitely the loser, its bottom window-frames peeling and the door splintered at one corner with cracked frosted glass in the panels. She crossed the road and climbed the steps to the front door. There were two bells, but no names. Neither bell looked as if it worked. She pressed the bottom one. There was a thin sound from deep inside somewhere. Silence. Then footsteps.

The door opened onto a corridor cluttered with decorators' ladders and dustsheets. A woman, young, in jeans and a sweater, stood with a baby on her arm.

She flashed back to the night she had focused on a certain lighted window in her binoculars. Wrong house. Again. 'Hi. I'm sorry. I was looking for a man who I thought lived here. Tall, thin, wiry hair? I was sure he told me number thirty-eight.'

'No. Sorry. There's only the Cranwright family here,' she said in a giveaway accent made up of the outback and surfing beaches; sunshine vowels in winter gloom. 'They just moved in a few months ago though, so maybe he was here before.'

'I see. You don't know about next door, by any chance? I mean it could have been thirty-six.'

She shrugged. 'I'm the nanny. I don't live here. But I think they're flats. I've occasionally seen folk coming in or out.'

She was nice-looking, with a no-nonsense haircut and the leftovers of a tan. Fresh off the boat. Had they told her about English cities? How dark they could be? How you had to lock the windows and check the footsteps behind you in alleyways? Maybe he wouldn't be so foolish as to crap in his own backyard. More the kind of guy who preferred crossing walls and darkened gardens. 'Thanks anyway,' she said quietly.

'No worries.'

Let's hope so. She walked back across the road and

checked out number 36. Now she knew, the house looked even more appropriate. The bottom floor had a greying lace curtain with a forest of jungly plants pushed up against the glass. It would be dark inside, though hardly tropical. The middle floor – his floor – had blinds; not thin fashionable ones, but chunky wood, a leftover from an obsession with Scandinavian furniture thirty years before. Her mother's sister had had them in her living room. As a child she remembered running her fingers along them during bored Sunday afternoons, harvesting rich layers of dust. Now they were a sure sign of furnished accommodation.

Furnished accommodation. She had only done it once, a stop-gap between a friend's flat and one of her own, and she had hated it even then: hard enough to know who you are in life without trying to find out among other people's obsessions. She couldn't wait to leave. No doubt he felt the same way. And the nights, of course, would be the worst. If you were going to feel the madness you'd feel it most then.

Hmmn, I know you quite well, she thought. Your scrawny body, your zipped lips, and your nasty little hammer and twine. She saw again that wired, nervous smile. What did he want from her? Some kind of understanding, even sympathy? Forget it. Inadequate is as inadequate does. I bet you're in there now, she thought, cutting out headlines from the local newspaper and sticking them in your scrapbook. Getting a life, it was called. Except his came from destroying other people's.

Not any more. She used the phone box at the end of the road, getting the number from directory enquiries – it seemed too risky to go through Emergency.

A man answered. When she told him what her business was he said he'd put her through to the right person and asked her what her name was. When she wouldn't give it he connected her anyway. Another voice answered. 'Detective Inspector Groves, CID, speaking.'

'Are you the officer dealing with the Holloway Hammer?'

'I am on the investigation team, yes. Who am I speaking to, please?'

A familiar grammatical mistake, the kind of thing a translator comes across all the time. She took a deep breath. 'The man you're looking for lives at number thirty-six Tavistock Crescent. N19. Middle bell.'

'Thirty-six Tavistock Crescent,' he repeated slowly. 'I see. And can I ask you how you know?'

'I just know, that's all.'

'Do you have a name for this man?'

'No.'

He paused. 'You know, if you have anything to say – anything at all with regard to this case – I can guarantee you it would be kept in strictest confidence.' His voice was careful, almost rehearsed, almost, dare one say it, a little bored.

'I've told you. He lives at thirty-six Tavistock Crescent. More than likely he's there now.'

'Yes, madam. And I assure you that we will check it out. But I have to tell you we get, on average, two or three calls like this every day, and we obviously have to prioritise some of them. Now if you felt able to give us your—'

Could they be tracing the call, she thought? They do that kind of thing, don't they? Keep you on the end of the line until they have a reading.

'He carries a hammer and sometimes string or a piece of twine, OK? He's tall and scrawny with a breathy voice. And he likes to talk before he does it, likes to see people scared. I'm sure any of your eight other women would tell you the same thing. Believe me, this is not a hoax.'

She slammed down the phone, heart thumping.

By the time she got home the frozen foods were melting. She kicked aside the mail and slammed the boxes into the freezer. In the kitchen she made herself a strong cup of coffee. No point in trying to go to bed now. The adrenaline was too strong in her system. She imagined standing on the opposite side of his road, watching while they pulled him down the stairs into a waiting police car. Now that would be a dream worth going to sleep for. The reality, of course, would take a while longer. An anonymous phone call would no doubt find itself added to a list. Maybe it would warrant some checking out. How long? One hour, maybe two. Never mind. While they worked so would she.

Back in the basement cell she went for action over elegance, writing to fit her mood. She made Mirka pathetic, then sweet, then in so much pain that she was unable even to cut up her own food. The man did it for her, sitting next to her hacking through the lump of gristly meat with a knife that was sharper than it looked. As she chewed slowly she tempted him into talk; tales of village life and how it had changed since the system had imploded, of poverty and disillusionment and the upsurge in new opportunities. She was surprised by how stupid he was, expecting the thin one to be the brains for the fat one's brawn. But it made it easier.

In return she painted pictures of bright lights, big business and sidewalks paved with gold, and watched as his eyes shone in their reflection. Expecting bribery (would that have worked better, was it really just greed?) he didn't anticipate seduction, didn't consciously register the heat of her against his leg or the way that her lips grew moist around the fork, until it was too late. And so it was that at last Mirka came to learn what it felt like to rub herself up against a country boy and find his farm fingers groping their way into the wetlands of her cunt.

The words flowed like genital juices. But still she made Mirka work at it, made her use the slap-slurp sound of sex and her own extravagant groans to cover up the scrape of the knife as she slid it up from the steel tray beside the bed. And she made her suffer too, using her damaged hand to massage his cock (she needed her good one for the knife), the pain of the grasp roaring up through her like a lava-flow and causing a yelp of breath that would have given her away if he hadn't been too far gone to notice.

The playboy pleasures of American sex. They'd both seen enough of it in the movies, but she was the one who had been there, done that. Give the boys what they think they want and for that moment they'll forget to be wary of you. She pushed him gently back onto the bed, sliding herself down his body onto her knees in front of him, using her tongue as a tourist guide, heading towards places he had read about in the brochures. He gasped, then pushed her head down further towards his groin, and she knew then that she had him, and that his lust was wrenching him out of his own control.

As her tongue went down, so her good hand came up until the two connected in a triangle of soft flesh just above his penis. No time for thought now. She rammed the knife in, then twisted it up, feeling the steel pushing through a pulpy mash of sinew and flesh. And as she did so she rose up and covered his mouth with her own, sucking the scream out of him, taking its noise into her lungs and swallowing it down.

In that split second as he flung her off him in agony she was up and out of the door, slamming it behind her and ramming the bolts into place.

The wood muffled his yells, but they would still be enough to wake the fat man. She went for what she could get. A heavy iron kettle was sitting near a gas ring on the floor. She picked it up and swung it down over his head with all the force she could muster. The blow connected, she could feel the mash of bone and metal, but in her gut she knew it wasn't hard enough. He roared up, clutching out for her at the same time as his head. She dropped the kettle and fled, up the cellar steps and out through the door. She heard him stumbling up behind her. This lock was more flimsy, it would give with the first battering ram of his shoulder, but if there was any justice in the world she wouldn't be there by then.

She peered frantically into the semi-darkness of an empty room, all shadows and flagstones in the twilight. The place reeked of damp and decay, too much weather coming in around rotting window-frames. No wonder there had been no worry about her screams. The house was a ruin.

Behind her the cellar door shook with the weight of
his body. She sprinted out into a passageway and then
into another smaller room with an old iron range
under a chimney and a door giving out onto what must
be the outside. It was locked. As she rattled the lock
desperately she heard something behind her. She
whirled around in time to see a bulky shadow leap
crouching into the doorway; no face, no body, just a
shape with arms thrust out in front of it in a gesture
that echoed back through a million movies.

'Don't sh—' she screamed, but the sound never got
out of her mouth as the room exploded into fire all
around her.

She was typing so fast the letters were coming out
mangled. When she stopped to read it back she
realised she was grinning, a silly cracked smile stapled
to her face, held on so tight that it made her muscles
ache. Stupid. Total crap all of it, knee-jerk stuff without
an ounce of finesse or originality. Except who cares as
long as it does the trick? Once you stopped talking
there was nowhere to go but action. In the cinema
you'd be starting to feel the communal adrenaline now,
little ripples of nervous approval and fun. The fact that
it wasn't good enough was somehow the point; its very
crudeness was its satisfaction.

She highlighted the new text and printed it off, then
pressed the Save button. She could always rewrite it
later.

She looked at her watch. 2.55 p.m. Almost two hours
since she had rung. God, she'd like to see his face when
he opened the door.

Well, why not? It was Christmas, after all. Everyone deserves at least one present, even if she might have to wait for it.

She decided to treat it as an outing. She pulled a loaf of bread out of one of the shopping bags and hacked off some clumsy slices, making crude sandwiches with a doorstop of cheese and a thick layer of mayonnaise, devouring half of them as she went, realising only as she tasted the food how hungry she was. She dug out a couple of packets of crisps and used the new coffee to make a thermos flask full. It looked like a builder's lunch. She grabbed the printed manuscript and shoved it all in a plastic bag, along with a handful of tapes, and headed to the car.

Outside the temperature was dropping rapidly, an icy wind whipping late leaves through the gutter and across the roads. She drove to his street and parked the car facing away from his house on the opposite side, but with the wing mirror positioned so she could see his door and the road in front of it. She turned the engine off, but within half an hour had to switch it back on again to cope with the cold. She sat, eyes on the mirror, roasted air rising up all around her, and watched while a succession of women returned home with last-minute Christmas shopping, trailing children grown grumpy with the cold. The next-door nanny bounced a pushchair carefully down the outside steps, the baby, stuffed into a padded ski-suit with connecting gloves and hood, jiggling about and yelling at the top of its lungs.

Fresh air. It could be a killer. But she was beginning to feel the need for it herself. The recycled heat from the engine was making her increasingly drowsy. If she just put her head back and closed her eyes ... But she couldn't give in to it now. There would be time enough to sleep later, safe and sound in the knowledge that this time there could be nobody to disturb her. She turned the engine off and let the cold wake her up.

By 4.30 p.m. it was dark. She watched as a man and his young son carried an oversized Christmas tree up the stairs to their house. The door opened onto a hall crammed with decorations, then closed again behind them. It looked warm in there.

What would she be doing now if Tom and she had stayed together? If things had been different? Would they be loitering round travel-shop windows checking out the last-minute Christmas bargains, or might it have gone further than that? Might she now be out braving the West End with a little Tom lookalike tucked under her coat, a scrunched-up newborn face squashed up against exploding tits? There had been a while there when it had seemed an almost attractive nightmare: playing house, creating the sense of family that the death of her mother had taken away for ever. But it was all fantasy, the feeling that you needed to reclaim Eden even when in your soul you knew you were happy to have been banished from it.

So what did she have instead? Eighty thousand words of English sleaze on a computer and semen stains on her robe from a rapist lover whom she had anonymously shopped to the police. Not exactly the kind of life story to appeal to her mother. Maybe some people die at the right time, to shield themselves from life's unacceptable outcomes.

She rubbed her hands over her eyes and poured

herself a thermos lid full of coffee. The first few sips made her feel better, but as she was pushing the cup onto the dashboard she misjudged the distance and it tipped back over onto her lap and the sheaf of pages she was holding. The liquid was hot enough to make her yelp. She flung open the door and stood in the cold pulling her trousers away from her skin, swearing softly under her breath. An elderly woman walked past, frowning at her language.

She was still standing there when the Ford Fiesta drew up on the other side of the road with the two men inside and she saw the one in the passenger seat duck his head down to the window to check out the numbers of the house. They both got out.

She scrambled back into the car, but they weren't looking at her. The driver straightened his jacket, exchanged a quick glance with his companion and together they climbed up the stairs of 36.

She sat frozen in the front seat, eyes glued to the mirror. She saw one of them push at a doorbell, then stand with his hands in his pockets while the other leaned over the side to check out the windows. Nice action. If you opened the door to them now you wouldn't have any trouble knowing what they were; too much studied nonchalance to be anything else. They waited. She waited. He rang again. From the middle window she thought she detected the blinds move a fraction. If she had spotted it they must have too. Her heart gave a little leap of joy. Would he come down? He'd probably be half asleep still, mind gummed up with dreams of dark-alley violence and fun. On the other hand they weren't going anywhere without him. She watched him ring again, this time keeping his finger on for a while. Oh, the pleasure of law enforcement.

Two minutes later the door opened a few inches, but all she could see were two suit backs and nothing of what stood in front. One of the suits shifted a little as its owner rummaged inside the jacket for a card. For a heart-stopping second nothing happened, then suddenly the door opened wider and the two of them went in. It closed behind them.

She sat quietly, trying to contain the excitement within her. How long would it take them? Half an hour? An hour? Longer? Would they search the house? No, they wouldn't have to search. They'd know just from talking to him. They'd hear it in his voice, smell the desire on his breath, see the fantasies crawling like lice through his mind. It was their job. That was what they were paid for.

She sat back in the car. The dashboard clock read 5.13 p.m. She put on the radio, skimming the dial until she found something she could listen to. Not music now. She needed words. BBC news. Radio 4. The final reassurance. These commentators, you felt, would still be there after the apocalypse.

It didn't sound far off. So near to Christmas and still no sign of peace on earth. From Bosnia a breathless reporter was telling how the latest peace plan was turning inexorably into war. She tried hard to listen, but the words kept slipping down the paintwork of his front door, sliding in through the cracks, disappearing as quickly as they came. The news came and went and five o'clock moved on to six. To be there so long they must have their suspicions: be checking dates, talking women, maybe phoning through his details into the police computer. The chances are a man like him would have some kind of record; a minor assault here, a peeping tom conviction there. All safely stored in Big Brother's brain along with personal bank records and hospital tests. Would they maybe have his HIV rating? A shudder passed through her. Don't spoil the triumph with another kind of fear.

But as she stared into the mirror what she saw spoilt it anyway. Across the other side of the street, walking quickly in her direction, was a man in a donkey jacket, thin face, wiry hair, hands dug deep in his pockets against the cold. The sight of him curdled her stomach. She dropped her head hurriedly but kept her eyes on the mirror. He came nearer. He passed number 36, and 38, then at number 40 turned and took the steps up to the door two at a time. For someone who had been awake as long as he had he was looking pretty active.

At the same moment as he put the key in the lock the door to 36 opened and the two plain-clothes policemen came out alone, tripping briskly down the steps towards their car. One of them said something to the other as they went and his companion made a face and laughed. They beeped the car door open.

From his vantage point by the door he spotted them too. He stared at them for a second, then his eyes darted quickly up and down the street. She ducked her head down. When she came up he was gone, the door firmly closed behind him. From its parking place the Ford Fiesta pulled out past her, without its indicator on.

She slammed her fist on the dashboard. How could she have been so stupid? One house. Just one house out and the whole thing evaporated like smoke around her. She adjusted the mirror to centre on number 40 and found a middle window like all the others, clean and anonymous. Not even a weasel face to give it away.

On the radio the headlines were recapping on Bosnia and the slide into war. What do you do when the best-laid plans go wrong and you find you don't even have the peace-keepers to depend on any more? She was about to find out. Because this time she was going after him.

nineteen

If he could exist on so little sleep then so could she.

She allowed herself four hours, setting an alarm for ten, but when she woke, without the aid of the bell, she was convinced she must have slept through it because the room, though dark, was so deathly quiet. It was more like the early morning, surely. In her mind day and night were becoming mashed together. Her whole body felt glutted, as if the sleep had been merely a drug which had brought unconsciousness but no peace. She flicked up the light of the digital clock and found to her surprise that it was indeed just before ten. Get up, she thought. Get up and check him out.

It was only as she looked out of the window that she understood the reason for the change of atmosphere. Outside, the world had turned white. The air was filled with swirling flakes and a thick blanket of snow covered everything in its deep silence. What just a few hours ago had been a set of raggedy suburban gardens was already a landscape of ice sculpture; enchanted, remade. It was so dazzling, so completely unexpected that it made her almost stupid with delight, reading its beauty as some kind of promise of comfort in a comfortless world. Pathetic. So God was nothing but an occasional cold front. Two degrees warmer and this would have been rain; dull, remorseless, English rain bringing a chill to your bones and drowning out your optimism. Not so much comfort as a trick of nature, a kind of trompe l'oeil of the spirit.

Across the gardens his was just one of a number of lights that were blazing. She picked up the binoculars and focused. And now, at last she spotted him. Above the half net curtain, a figure took shape in the lens. Her hand shook. It disappeared. She steadied herself, and this time an orb of a face came into view, distorted and shimmery at the edges like a three-D image.

He was standing square onto the window looking out, watching the snow fall. Safe in the darkness of her bedroom she knew he couldn't possibly see her. Now, for the first time, she became the voyeur.

He stood there for so long that it hurt her hand keeping the glasses up and still. She thought about him in the supermarket, frozen against the shelves of cereal packets, then sitting at the end of her bed, watching, waiting, with a creepy, endless patience. Yes, he was a man good at withholding himself from the world, being, but not being. But that was his whole problem; while others found it easy to join in he could only watch, then go out and grab. What was he thinking now? Did it take his breath away too? Driven snow. Pure as. Maybe he only wanted to fuck it. Disfigure it with a splattered arch of urine, watching the steam hiss up from the little track of burnt holes. Or did its fabulous sense of transformation make him ache for something similar in himself; the idea that he too could wake up one morning and find that sleep had transfigured his psychic landscape, bringing with it peace and a different image of self? She thought again of the way his voice had shaken with the violence of undigested fury. She felt the heavy sweat on his skin and the way his chest grabbed for air as the anger turned to sobs. Maybe the worst thing about evil is that the Devil always knows how far from grace he has fallen, and that's what makes him so desperate and cruel. It also means that however many times he smashes the mirror he will still be looking at his own reflection. Which is why he has to smash it again. And again.

He disappeared out of the lens and she had to dart around to try and relocate him. For a second she lost him completely, then he turned slap bang into focus holding something in his hands. A cloth? A dishrag? No, gloves, he was putting on a pair of gloves. He moved away, then back again, this time wrapping a scarf around his neck. My God, he was getting ready to go out.

She watched, caught between fear and excitement, as he rubbed his hands over his face, then up and over through his hair, as if he was tugging at his scalp, trying to see how far he could pull it. She could even make out the grimace on his face. He stayed like that for what seemed like a long time, his head pulled sharply back by the force of his hands. It looked painful, a gesture of self-punishment almost. Or preparation? Then he turned away and the light went off.

She didn't think about what happened next, just did it. It was easy. Since she had gone to sleep in her clothes it took her less than thirty seconds to pull on a pair of boots and get herself out of the house. She was met by a soft assault of snow; fat, flashy flakes everywhere. The ground crunched under her feet, the fresh fall groaning as it impacted downwards. It had to be at least two or three inches deep already. It must have been snowing for hours. Her face was wet and stinging by the time she got to the car.

She drove as fast as she dared on roads where the first tyre marks were already starting to freeze. She had her headlights full on, but when she turned into his street she dipped them, just in case. Big splashy flakes tumbled down onto the windscreen, forming perfect ice crystals until they were raked away into water by the wipers. There was snow everywhere. It was a world in slow motion. She used it to her advantage. She moved at a cautious ten miles an hour. She had just made the turn when in front of her she saw his door open and watched a figure come down the stairs, almost unrecognisable in one of those bulging great-coats that had kept the Russian army warm during half a century of communism but were now only good for army surplus stores. An army surplus boy? Uniforms and balaclavas, clothes with a history of violence. Somehow she wasn't surprised.

If he had looked back now he would certainly have spotted her car – it was the only one on the street. But this wasn't the weather for sight-seeing. There was a wind picking up now, whipping up the snow and driving it horizontal into your face, making it impossible to walk unless you kept your eyes down. At the bottom of the steps he pulled up his collar and turned right, heading in the direction where Tavistock Crescent met the main High Street.

When she was past him, not too fast, not too slow, she

kept him in her mirror. He didn't look up. The High Street ahead was an arterial road and there was still a fair amount of traffic so that when she reached it she could legitimately wait to make her turn until he had caught up, turned left, then immediately crossed the main road by the zebra crossing and headed down a side street.

She followed slowly. He was quite a way in front of her by now, and the snow was falling so thickly that visibility was becoming a problem. A car pulled out of a parking place ahead of her and skidded slightly as it took off. She waited for it to right itself, by which time his silhouette was dissolving into the white mist ahead.

The lights of the pub, when they came into view, were an image from a Dickensian thriller; warmth and the promise of a hearth and good company rising out of the bleak midwinter. Except why should he be tempted by such conviviality? This was a man who could only live and work alone.

She was about forty yards behind him when he stopped and swung open the door, stamping his feet to clear them of the snow, or maybe to get some feeling back into them. Forty yards, twenty. Ten. As the door slammed behind him she brought the car to a careful halt and parked on the other side of the road. The tyres crunched on fresh snow.

Maybe he had noticed the car and used the pub as a diversion to get away from her? No, he hadn't seen her. He hadn't been looking. She was sure of that. So, what should she do now? If she went in after him she ran the risk of being recognised, but if she stayed where she was she might find herself in premature rigor mortis by the time he came out. The fact that she had already spent too much of the day sitting in cars decided her.

She needn't have worried about anonymity. Inside, the place was so full you could hardly move, let alone talent-spot. Not only was there no space on the floor, but above there were Christmas decorations every-where, big gaudy bells and twisted loops of fringed tinsel running across the whole room, low enough in places for the taller punters to reach up and touch them. In one corner they had pulled them down and the barmaid was wearing the trophy of an over-sized tinsel coronet. The whole place was vibrating with what might have been forced bonhomie, the background music so embedded in the voices that it was impossible to tell Bing Crosby from hip hop. Or to care.

Have Yourself a Merry Little Christmas. Dante's *Inferno*, more like, but then she had never been a pub person. If I'd been better at this kind of thing would the world have been an easier place? she thought.

A couple of years after she'd finished university and come down to London she had joined a band which had a regular monthly gig in a pub in Notting Hill. She'd been playing with them for about eighteen months when she met Tom. He came to see her perform there after they'd started. Couldn't keep his eyes off her. It was the most singular erotic experience, singing to one particular person in a crowd and knowing that as soon as you got off the stage they couldn't wait to get their tongue down your throat and your clothes off your body. She began to understand what the boys must feel, the power that kind of attraction brings with it. Once she had felt it she knew she could exploit it for herself, that this was the missing ingredient from what everyone agreed was a great voice. She could have done something with that knowledge, taken her performing to another level. But it didn't work out like that. As their affair got more intense she pulled out of so many rehearsals that eventually the band gave her the push. Tom was angry rather than sympathetic, insisting that she was too good for them. But he didn't go out of his way to encourage her to join anyone else. By then their record collections had already started to mingle, his classical cuckoo in her rock'n'roll nest, and her life was so full of him that she could almost convince herself she didn't miss it, either the music or the band.

Wimp, that's what Sally had called her. You're letting him walk all over you, don't you see? He doesn't so much want you to himself as doesn't want you to be anybody else's.

She stood staring at the mass of people in front of her. So easy to see it when it's over. So hard to be wise at the time. Would she do better now? She saw herself, sitting on her bed, slipping her T-shirt up over her breasts and guiding a stranger's hands towards her nipples. Maybe Tom's selfishness had taught her something after all. Sharpened her instinct for survival. And revenge.

She looked around. If this wasn't her element, then neither, surely, was it his? Where would he go to hide that warped little soul of his? The bar maybe, huddling himself over a single pint while the crowd jostled around him, feeding his malevolence from his exaggerated sense of isolation. But when she finally forced herself to the front, he wasn't there. She wondered if she ought to buy a drink, just in case she looked out of place, but the possibility of catching the barmaid's eye seemed remote, and anyway no one was taking much notice.

The background music subsided for a second, then flooded back in even louder, a Phil Spector wall of sound. A shout of recognition went up from a group nearby and a few happily out-of-tune voices yelled 'I Saw Mummy Kissing Santa Claus' at football volume. Men in suits trying to relive their youth. She turned and started to push her way away from them.

And as she did so she saw him. He was sitting at a crowded table near one of the windows, jammed in between another guy and a girl, talking. He was a fast worker. The girl was young, probably in her late teens, heavy with puppy fat and too much make-up. She was wearing one of those dresses that chain stores sell around Christmas, all lycra and glitter, designed for women with no stomach or thighs. She had both. She looked, well, Christmas-wrapped. But whose name was on the label?

She drew back into the crowd, but there was no chance that he would spot her. He was too busy. She watched, fascinated. In animation he didn't seem nearly so creepy. Looked as if he might almost be the same as anybody else. But the longer she studied him the more tell-tale signs leaked through. For one thing he stared too much. He kept looking at the girl, nodding his head at everything she said, the same nervous smile flickering over his lips. Not that she seemed to be noticing. Her cheeks were flushed and she was giggling a lot. In front of her there was a half glass of what looked like rum and Coke and two already empty ones. What would she have said if you'd told her now to be careful? Mind your own fucking business, probably. Fair enough. Hell, everybody works hard enough for the rest of the year to be able to let go once or twice. Is that how it happened? You blunted your antennae so all the normal warning signals went down on you and at the one crucial moment you said yes when you should have said no. It was easily done. There but for the grace of God go all of us at some time or another.

She shivered. But it wasn't that simple. If the girl did say yes now there would be a dozen witnesses to the man she left the pub with. They might all have double vision but somewhere in their blurred memories there would be enough of an Identikit face for the police to go on. Was he getting careless?

To her right the girls' friend said something and she turned towards her with a laugh. Instantly his face changed. The body lost all its energy. He sat still, eyes on the table. She felt him roll back into himself, pull up the drawbridge. This time when he glanced sideways at the girl there was something else in his eyes.

She couldn't bear to look at him any more. Whatever she did she couldn't challenge him here, not amidst all these people. She turned and pushed her way towards the door. As she went the first last orders bell reverberated round the bar. Nobody took any notice of it.

Outside the snow had almost stopped, but the wind was vicious. She turned the car heating on full blast and sat with her eyes on the clock. 10.56. 10.57. 10.58. The minutes passed agonisingly slowly.

By 11.10 people were beginning to swarm out onto the streets. She had the door in full view, but the crush

of bodies was such that she couldn't be sure she could
see everyone. She felt her heart beating faster. Then
about 11.15 she spotted the girl. She had on a big grey
coat, still open in the front so you could see the
sparkle of her dress. For a second she thought it might
be *his* coat, but as the girl hit the outside air she
flinched and yanked it shut with a long tie belt, pulling
up an obviously girlie collar against the wind.
Immediately after her came her friend, equally full of
Christmas spirits, and together they staggered off
down the street, grabbing hold of each other and
giggling helplessly as the icy pavements made them
skid. Two young women on their way home to another
Christmas with Mum and Dad and the rest of their
lives. How many times does fate come that close;
picking out the person two or three down the line and
never letting you know how nearly it could have been
you?

She turned her attention back to the door. The
stream continued, but with no sign of her prey. Maybe
he was still inside. He and a lot of others. In this weather
you could hardly blame them for wanting to carry on
drinking, and so close to Christmas the police would no
doubt turn a blind eye to an odd ten or fifteen minutes
of illegality with regular customers. So was he a
regular? A usual friendly face on a Friday and
Saturday night?

Why not? It wouldn't be the first time that the
monster turned out to be just one of the lads. Wasn't
that what they said when Peter Sutcliffe and the
Yorkshire Ripper were revealed as the same person?
Our Peter. A regular sort of chap. Bit quiet maybe, but
likeable enough. Good for a few drinks with the boys, a

man who liked to play with kids. Polite. Except for the night of his own full moon when he drove out with a claw hammer and spent his seed up the back passages of prostitutes. Other than that just a regular sort of chap.

The thoughts took her mind off the job and she nearly missed him. He came out quickly, head down, intent on where he was going. But where? Not home, that was for sure. He turned the opposite way and strode off into the snow. She waited thirty seconds then, with him still in view, started the car. Two hundred yards further down the street he hit Hornsey High Road. He turned left and walked up to a bus stop heading north. Already there was a line of people waiting, stamping their feet and blowing into their gloves, or – in the case of a rather drunken couple – clasped in each other's arms. He didn't join the queue, but slipped instead into the doorway of a shop window nearby where he was neatly swallowed up by the shadows. It made sense. If he was heading further afield he wouldn't want to be remembered by his fellow passengers, would he?

She drove past and parked fifty yards further along. She was becoming an expert at mirror watching. Except this time she didn't dare risk keeping the engine running. This time they would be cold together. The clock read 11.35.

At 11.50 the bus finally came, greeted by a little roar of celebration from the queue which by this time had swelled to about fifteen. They all tried to crowd on at the same time, desperate to get out of the wind, the couple still glued together. It took a while to collect their tickets and settle them all down. From down the street another man was running towards the bus stop, waving frantically to make sure the driver had seen him.

The bus waited, let him on, then pulled away. But still without one passenger. In the doorway he hadn't moved.

twenty

Time passed. The snow started again, a moving lace curtain filtering through the yellow light of the streetlamps, falling silently onto the coated pavements below. He must be so cold standing there. But still he stayed, stuck in the camouflage of darkness like an insect upon a leaf.

A man and a woman came up to the stop and stood peering anxiously at the writing on its side. Miraculously, a taxi's yellow vacant sign glowed out from halfway down the road. They hailed it wildly and it stopped. You could almost see the relief in their body language as they piled in. The clock read 12.10. It was firmly into night-bus territory now.

By 12.20 the car was so cold she had to stuff her hands up into her armpits to keep them from freezing. When she looked up again she saw the figure of a young woman coming up to the bus stop. She was not exactly dressed for the weather; a bum-length half coat over jeans, and heeled boots, with no hat and a less than serious scarf. She ran a gloved finger down the bus information panel, trying to sort out the words through the snow. In the doorway behind her he moved slightly. She must have registered him out of the corner of her eye because she turned abruptly, then said something, as if in reply. No doubt she was wondering whether he knew if the last bus had gone.

'Fraid not,' he would say. 'I've only just got here myself.'

'What about the night buses?'

'No idea. Half an hour, an hour maybe.'

She shrugged, rubbing her hands energetically to keep warm. 'How about this weather, eh? Maybe it's going to be a white Christmas.'

'Yeah, maybe.'

She hesitated, a definite hint of nerves in her body language, then turned back to the bus stop.

What had he really said to her? Maybe he'd invited her in to join him in the darkness. She was evidently more sensible than her clothes.

A little while later a couple of taxis went by. They were both occupied, but in the snow the girl wouldn't be able to see that. She hailed the first one, dropping her hands despairingly as she spotted a passenger in the back, then watching forlornly as the second drove by.

By now the pavements were deserted and the snow was getting thicker by the minute. You could see she was worried. If she waited there much longer she might turn into an ice maiden. Another five or ten minutes passed. Not only were there no people any more, there were hardly any cars. The world was closing down, leaving her and him alone in a winter wonderland. Suddenly she made a decision and with one last look into the night, turned on her heel and headed off down the road, walking as fast as the weather would allow.

In the car she felt her whole body tense up. She kept

her eyes glued to the shop window. Ten seconds, fifteen, twenty. The snow had almost swallowed the girl up when he made his move, eyes down, chin in his collar, following silently, placing each foot carefully in the footsteps she had left in the virgin snow.

As she watched him her heart went ballistic. She felt that same wedge of terror forcing its way up into her throat like vomit, and for that second she was back in her bedroom in the middle of the night, wide awake, nerve ends screaming as she registered the sound of someone else's breathing next to her.

She turned on the ignition and the engine spluttered into life. In the intense silence of the snow the sound was enormous. This time he heard it. This time he turned and looked. Would he recognise the car? He must have passed it enough times outside her house. Well, it was too late for such niceties now.

She pulled out and drove past him. The girl was fifty yards ahead. In the mirror she saw him watching. As she drew parallel with her he stopped and slipped into another doorway.

If the girl heard the car she didn't do anything to show it. She rolled down the driver's window to attract her attention. A flurry of snow rushed in.

'Excuse me?'

Registering it was a woman's voice the girl now stopped and turned, but didn't come any closer.

In the car she took a deep breath. 'I – I couldn't help noticing. I mean I just came out from a party back there and saw you standing at the bus stop. You've obviously missed the last bus.'

'Yeah,' she said with about as much friendliness as a Rottweiler.

'Well, I'm on my way north too. I mean that's where I live and I wondered if I could give you a lift home. You won't get a taxi now in this weather and it's going to get worse before it gets better.'

The girl stared at her. She was not unattractive, dark hair framing a heart-shaped face with a cute little nose going raw with the cold. She put her head to one side, almost as if she was trying to smell out any possible trouble. A splash of snowflake hit one eye and she blinked it away. 'Er, thanks, but I'm fine. I only live a few blocks away.'

Now it was clear they were both lying. Obviously the girl had detected something. In the car she tried frantically to think of something to say that might reassure her, but her mind went blank. The young woman had turned away and was already moving off down the street again.

Shit. She tried to put herself in her place. A deserted street late at night and a woman offering you a lift. There would have been a time when you wouldn't have questioned it. But that was before the sexual appetite of Rosemary West had been splattered all over the front pages, reminding one in turn of Myra Hindley and how much the world had changed. Now women in cars could mean men in the back seats. Now the world was so fucked up that girls could die from being too careful.

In the mirror she thought she detected a move from his doorway. Oh no you don't. She pulled out again and caught up with the girl twenty yards on.

'No, please, listen, don't go.' Her voice was louder now. In his doorway he would be able to hear every word carried through snow silence. So be it. 'I mean I don't want to scare you, but you must have heard that there have been attacks on young women in this area recently. Apparently there's some nutter going round with a hammer, pulling girls off the streets, raping and battering them. It was in the local paper this week. The police have put out a warning about young women walking home alone.'

'Oh, Christ.' The girl hesitated. Clearly her life was too full to bother with the local paper. But somebody must have said something about it, you could tell from the flicker that crossed her face. She rammed the point home. 'I know you're probably nervous of accepting a lift, but I honestly think you should take it. I mean I couldn't help noticing that guy by the bus stop. He . . . well, I thought I saw him start to follow you down the road.'

This time the panic showed on her face as she darted her eyes back to the street behind her.

'Oh, Christ,' she said again, but this time she came closer to the driver's window to check her out more closely. What did she see? A woman who had got straight out of bed and into the car without so much as a glance in the mirror. She probably looked worse than he did. She could feel her wavering. I should have brushed my hair, she thought. What had those young girls who accepted a lift in the Wests' car been thinking at this moment? Nice couple, no doubt. Her mumsy face and figure making up for any hint of wildness in his eyes. She kept her gaze steadily on the young woman's face. Believe your instincts, she wanted to say to her, that's what I did and I'm still alive now.

The girl glanced into the back of the car, trying to check behind the seat as well as on it. Smart cookie.

Then, at last, she said, 'I live just beyond Manor House, about two or three miles from here. Is that on your way?'

'Sure, no problem.' She grinned with wild relief. 'Get in.'

As the girl walked round to the passenger seat she glanced in the mirror and thought she saw a hand flick out from the doorway. How does it feel? she thought triumphantly. Having the prize snatched from right underneath your erection? May the snow freeze your prick off before you get it home, you bastard. She pulled away from the kerb while the girl was still doing up her seat-belt.

In normal weather the journey would have taken fifteen minutes, maybe less. Now it took twice as long. The roads were like skating rinks. Just before Finsbury Park they came across an accident; a van had wrapped itself round a street lamp and there were two police cars on either side with half the street cordoned off.

'Looks like he missed the turning altogether,' she said quietly.

'Yeah,' replied the girl. 'I hope he's all right.'

They crawled along Seven Sisters Road, a Local Authority salt spreader rumbling towards them out of the darkness like some mutant UFO, yellow flashing lights in swirling snow mists.

'Amazing weather,' the girl said under her breath.

'Yes,' she muttered, 'I can't remember the last time London looked like this.'

'They say it's going to be a white Christmas.'

'You think it'll last that long?'

'Don't see why not. There's only two days to go.'

Two days. No. It must be more than that. How long
had it been since that moment in the supermarket?
Two days? No more, surely. She realised she could no
longer remember; that caught between work, sleep
and fear she had lost her bearings. The girl was saying
something . . .

'Sorry?'

'I said if it is, it'll be the first in twenty-six years.'

'Really?'

'Yeah. And there wasn't nearly as much snow as this
then.'

She glanced across at her. She couldn't have been
more than twenty-six herself, probably hadn't even
been born then. 'How do you know?'

'Research. I had to do it for a programme idea I was
working on.'

Having started talking, she didn't want to stop. It
turned out she was a receptionist for a small independent television company working out of Docklands. It
was only her second job, but she was determined to
make it into production so was doing extra work on the
side. The company was just starting out and there was
hardly any work around but they were very
democratic, and the boss was really encouraging. He'd
promised to put forward any ideas she had. He'd also
promised to take her to a couple of TV festivals with
him, so she could meet the people, because in this
business it wasn't so much what you knew as who you
knew. Mind you, it took a long time to make all the
contacts. Not like the little town she came from in
Devon. You could put all the movers and shakers
together in the back room of one of the pubs in

Axminster and still have room to spare. Still, London
was much more exciting. Of course it would be better
with a car – she wouldn't have got stuck like she did
tonight if she had her own transport, but on her salary
... well, she'd just have to wait till she got her first idea
accepted. It was, she seemed to suggest, only a matter
of time. 'So,' she paused briefly for breath, 'and what
job is it that you do?'

The traffic lights before Manor House were coming
up. She extemporised something about translating for
a publishing company then steered the conversation
gently back to the bus stop.

'Yeah, he gave me quite a fright actually. I didn't see
him there at all. He told me I'd already missed the last
bus and that it would probably be at least an hour
before the night one came.'

'Was that what he was waiting for?'

'I dunno. S'pose so. I thought he was going to offer to
share a taxi home. But he didn't.'

'Would have you taken it if he had?'

She looked at her with scorn. 'I'm not that stupid.
There was something weird about him. That's what
decided me; I mean when you said you thought he was
following me.'

She had a sudden flash of a litter-strewn alleyway,
and a young woman pinned up against a wall. The
jeans wouldn't be easy to pull off, a tough enough job
when you wanted to get naked let alone when you
didn't. Maybe he wouldn't bother with the zip and
studs. Just use a knife. How would he keep her quiet?
He would need both hands to hold her down while he
got the clothes off her. Would he gag her? They hadn't
mentioned that in the papers. But then it hardly

mattered. In this weather there would be no one listening. She shivered. She was going to ask her if she would recognise him again, but she never got round to it.

'It's just here.'

'What?'

'You can drop me just here.'

They were still on the main road. She came to a halt. 'You sure?'

'Yeah. I only live three or four doors along that side street. It's fine, really. Thanks a lot.'

Was it something she'd said? Maybe not. Maybe it was only common sense not to show a stranger exactly where you lived. She decided not to argue. There was no way he could have followed them here and the chances of there being two rapists operating in the same five-mile radius of London on a night like tonight seemed slim. Even in hell there has to be some statistical rules.

She sat in the car and watched until she saw her walk down the road and turn in through one particular front gate. Then she locked the car doors from the inside and drove slowly home.

It stopped snowing somewhere on the journey back and the wind died down. With so little traffic the streets were eerily beautiful. Even the Holloway Road had a kind of majesty to it. When she got out of the car outside her house the silence was almost religious, the slam of the car door like thunder in the night.

She looked around. The road was shining with frost crystals, the parked cars like stranded sheep, coated in thick white fur four or five inches deep. Within a few hours there would be glove tracks all over them as the local kids scooped up an armoury of snowballs. Not now though, now it was pure magic, the glow of the streetlights throwing pale shadows on the unspoilt surfaces.

She looked up into the night sky. No stars. It felt heavy up there, as if there was more to come. At the top window of the house nextdoor she caught sight of a face, like a small white moon, pressed against the glass. Her neighbours had a six-year-old son whom she occasionally saw on his way to or from school. Sweet kid. A little over-protected for his age, she sometimes thought, but then what did she know? Not only would this be his first white Christmas, but he would never in his whole life have seen so much snow. No wonder it was too exciting for sleep.

She waved up to him. He waved back, then ducked shyly out of sight. She tried to remember what that feeling was like, when your heart was ready to burst from the wonder of it all. Then you grew up and what did you get in its place? A little hard-won wisdom? If you were lucky the occasional stretch of peace? It wasn't enough. I want the wonder back, she thought fiercely. I want to feel that intense again.

What was it her mother used to say to her? Be careful what you wish for. You might find you get what you want, only to discover that it isn't what you bargained for.

The second she turned the key in the lock she knew something was wrong. But she had no idea what it was. She stood in the hall and listened. Nothing. Not a sound. She snapped on the light and went to the bottom of the stairs. From where she was standing she could see right up to the top of the house. Still nothing. Was he in here somewhere? Was that what she could feel? No. It wasn't possible. How could he possibly have got in?

Then she saw the answering machine on the hall table, its message-light blinking the number 1. There had been nothing on it before she went out, she was sure of that, because she had erased the previous messages sometime yesterday afternoon. Keeping her eyes all around her she reached out a hand and pressed the rewind button. The machine buzzed into life. The tape whirled back, stopped, then started again.

She hadn't heard his voice since that night, but there was no mistaking it; flat, sibilant, bleached of emotion, as if he had thought of what he was going to say then practised too much. Funny how it didn't quite fit with the tension of his body.

'Hello, J1009 CYR.' It took her a second to realise what the number was referring to. 'Women drivers. They're all the same. Don't have a clue about whose right of way it is. Well, I just want you to know that if you *ever* cut me up again, I'll do the same back to you.' There was a brief silence. 'Or is that what you were after?' The words made her shiver. They made him laugh. 'Snowing cats and dogs, wouldn't you say? Sleep well.'

The machine clicked off. She grabbed the phone and punched in 1471: British Telecom's answer to heavy breathers. The female computer voice told her that she had received one call at 12.45 a.m., then quoted a local number. She scribbled it down, and before she let herself think further dialled it back. The same disjointed tranquillised tones cooed into her ear: 'Sorry.

This number does not receive incoming calls.' Phone boxes. You find them on a million street corners.

She went back to the tape, replaying it, pondering every word. 'I just want you to know that if you ever cut me up again, I'll do the same to you.' If she played that to someone else now they wouldn't know what he was talking about. Of course not. That was the whole point. But what about the last bit, 'snowing cats and dogs'? What the hell did that mean? She thought about it. Then she raced down to the kitchen.

The door was locked, and when she got inside the room was dark and empty, the sheet drawn across the French windows exactly as she had left it. She rushed to the lights and switched on the patio lamp.

The first half of the garden jumped into ghostly focus, a frosted landscape, petrified, awesomely lovely. Except for one small flaw. That perfect snow was no longer virgin.

Across the centre of the lawn was a set of deep little prints; delicate, precise, paw-like indentations. And running between each of them a splattered trail of dark stains.

She knew without looking any harder that it was blood.

twenty-one

T he tracks petered out at the edge of the flowerbed, as if the animal hadn't had the stamina to make it to the cat-flap.

She crept in low through the undergrowth, aware of the huge expanse of open garden behind her, feet and knees sinking into fresh snow. Somewhere here was Millie's favourite spot, deep under the ceanothus bush and the holly, a place where in the hottest summer a cat could find shade. Now it offered total darkness, too dense even for the snow to penetrate. Darkness and cold.

'Millie . . .' she called softly. 'Millie.'

The torch beam found the body first. She was sure the cat was dead from the way it was lying; not curled up to protect its own warmth but sprawled on its side, one leg stuck awkwardly out in front. It looked like the paw was hanging half off, one ear was badly mangled and there was a sticky, matted quality to the fur behind the neck. But, when she put out a hand to touch the body, it was warm, and the head jerked upwards, as if in reflex to pain. 'Oh, God, Millie. What happened to you?' The cat opened its mouth to tell her, but all that came out was a harsh rattling breath, as if there was something in her lungs constricting the air-supply.

She scooped up the limp body as gently as she could and manoeuvred her way back onto the lawn.

The frost and the silence clung to them both. At the end of the garden she heard a sharp rustle. She whirled round, heart half out of her mouth with terror. The black tom flew towards the back wall, a streak of sable against the glowing white of the snow. In her arms Millie reared up, shaking and snarling, caught between pain and attack as the best form of defence. She held her tighter, waiting for the little body to collapse back into her arms.

Inside, she brought a towel from the airing cupboard and wrapped the animal carefully in its warm folds while she dialled an emergency number. A bleary voice answered; Mr Vet, snug as a bug next to Mrs Vet, a litter of roly-poly puppies asleep at the foot of their bed, no doubt.

She told it well; simple, clear, no cat-lover's hysteria or exaggeration. He started to take her more seriously when she described the rattle in the lungs.

'You'd better bring her in,' he said slightly breath-lessly, as if he was already out of bed, pulling on his clothes with the phone to one ear. 'Keep her warm, and don't give her anything to drink. Just in case.'

He was waiting at the surgery door, the snow still on his boots. It felt like they were the only two people awake in the world. He let her in, then locked up again behind her. The place was freezing. The heating would take a while to catch up.

They went together into the consulting room. He laid the little body out on the table and examined her carefully. As he lifted the damaged leg Millie let out a fierce yowl, flinching away from him. 'Sorry, girl, sorry, take it easy. I'll try not to hurt you again.' He used his right hand to hold her down while his left gently examined the fur behind her neck.

She studied his face; there was a crust of sleep at the corner of one eye. Did loving animals make you better with human beings? Probably not.

'Can you help keep her down while I listen to her lungs?' he said, pulling out a stethoscope. She held her gingerly, trying to judge which bits would hurt least, but on the table Millie wasn't struggling any more. 'Does she get into a lot of fights?' He was frowning.

'Er...I don't know. There's a black tom who's always around. They've had a couple of scraps. But—' She stopped.

'But what?'

She shook her head. His concentration went back to the cat. He listened to her chest, then put the stethoscope down and went again to the leg.

'Well, I can't say for sure, but I think she may have been caught in some kind of trap. These wounds round the ear and the neck are pretty certainly fight wounds. But this paw has been half severed. It looks to me as if some sort of metal clamp has been on it.'

Metal clamp ... She swallowed. 'I - I've got this neighbour ... He - well, in the past he's threatened her ... says he doesn't like cats in his garden.'

'And you think he could have done this?'

'I don't know. Yes...maybe.'

He let out an angry breath. 'Well, I suggest you get

on to the RSPCA about him first thing tomorrow morning.'

Why not? Could be they'd do a better job than the police, she thought bitterly. Just as long as they didn't send a woman officer.

'Is she . . . is she going to be all right?'

'Well, the leg is going to be a mess for a while, but I can't detect any internal damage. I don't think she's punctured the lung. I suspect what happened is she got scared, had a vomit reaction, then swallowed it back the wrong way. I'm pretty certain that's the constriction you could hear. Whatever attacked her she managed to fight off. I'll give her a sedative and sew up that leg, then keep her in tonight for observation and do a couple more X-rays in the morning. Can you phone in tomorrow afternoon to check?'

'Of course.'

He put out a hand and massaged the cat gently under her chin. I bet he does that to all the ladies, she thought. 'You're a lucky girl,' he said softly. 'You're going to be fine.'

That makes two of us, she thought.

The house felt deathly quiet without Millie. From the cellar she got out her hammer, some nails and the wooden back of an old picture frame. The noise probably woke half the neighbourhood – it was only just after five – and it wasn't exactly a professional job, but it worked. Nothing else was going to get through the cat-flap till Millie came home.

She stared out at the lawn. The snow was a mess now, a blood trail, a deep set of cat prints and her own, clumsier ones. But not, as far as she could tell, anyone else's. Whatever had been done to Millie, it hadn't been done in her garden.

A trap. It was such a viciously corny piece of revenge, more befitting a bad movie than real life. Hit the family where it hurts. Boil the rabbit. But for all its melodrama it had worked. Millie *was* her family. She was all she had, and the idea of her with a foot half chewed off by steel jaws was exactly the kind of image she couldn't handle; a combination of helplessness and pain, of being trapped in someone else's fantasy of power.

First he steals my music, then he tries to rape me, then he mutilates my cat. That's what you call attention, she thought. Or obsession. He loves me, he loves me not ... It reminded her of a joke about a woman being sexually assaulted by a gorilla. 'I wouldn't mind,' she says as she wakes up in a hospital bed, 'only he doesn't phone, doesn't send flowers ...' She had laughed at the time. If only women *did* get off on rape. Then they really would have the boys by the short and curlies.

She locked the kitchen door and took the portable phone with her into the living room. She lit some candles and a fire and poured herself a large brandy. Stop thinking about him, she thought to herself, he wants you to be obsessed too. That's part of the pleasure, part of the power. So play him at his own game and forget him.

She picked up the TV remote and started zapping channels. Two were blank, one was a sports quiz and the fourth an archive collection of Sixties rock bands; a decade when the world was black and white and there was revolution in the air. Or so the lyrics claimed. Hard to believe it now. She was too young to remember most of the bands first time around, but those Carnaby Street-style suits and mop tops were laughably reassuring. How could anyone have been threatened by those haircuts? Look at it all. Everything about the Sixties was too close to the Formica Fifties to have ever been taken seriously.

Or could it be that that was the secret of the past; that in retrospect it always seems more innocent than the present? She tried to imagine an England of the Black Death, of armies of flagellants, crusades, wars and public disembowelling. How many women got raped and beaten then? It was probably a national pastime. Would the women have thought about it differently? Presumably something so prevalent can't have been that traumatic? An unwanted prick would almost certainly have been less painful than a tooth abscess. And considerably less fatal. As a race we have gone soft on pain. When people's lives were full of it, they must have learnt to cope better. Anyway, the more suffering you notched up in this world the greater your chances were in the next. Lie back and think of heaven. More satisfying than England. Though might it not be even more satisfying to ram a red hot poker up your assailant's arse? In a world so familiar with pain they would have known a thing or two about punishment and revenge.

There you are again, she thought, back to *him*, giving him the pleasure of your obsession. Stop it. Stop it. She drained her glass and poured another. She took a long swig. The liquid warmed her more effectively than the central heating, but then the chill was more inside than out.

On the screen some pretty faces – there seemed to have been so many of them around at that time, interesting how their bodies look too skinny now, too boy-like – gave way to cringingly youthful footage of the Rolling Stones. Jagger's mouth yawned wide into the camera, a cheeky reminder of his posturing, fuck-you lust. They were playing a track she knew from a CD compilation; one of the early hits where their homage to R and B was so naked and so jubilant. 'Under My Thumb': an old-fashioned tale of boys behaving badly and assuming that the women got off on it. Maybe she should turn up the volume and let him hear it over the garden walls.

The Sixties turned into a series of adverts for shampoo and new cars, then to a re-run chat-show on substance abuse and finally *Breakfast Time*. She snapped off the remote and, pouring herself more brandy, went for her own music instead.

The living room had no CD machine (the fall-out of separation meant everything duplicated was everything halved) so she had to rely on vinyl. Even the feel of them was archaic now, clunky and clumsy compared with those silvery little space-ships of sound. But the choice was classic, a selection to match another set of TV archives dating from a world before Tom's musical contempt had set out to persuade her that growing up was really growing away from the music of one's youth into something more serious, more profound. She ran her fingers along yards of worn spines, each touch another summer, another late night, another affair. Easy come, easy go. How was it that what had once been so simple was now so hard? Maybe it was just practice after all. Practice and life-style. You don't meet men unless you get out of the house, Elizabeth. Oh, I don't know, she answered herself; if you spend enough time in your bedroom eventually they come to you ...

She went for happier times: Eddy Grant walking along a Caribbean beach but singing of Brixton. 'Electric Avenue'. She'd been in her early twenties when this album came out. There was a love song on it that had made her toes curl, the rather cute lyrics saved by the lazy sex in his voice. '*My heart does a tango with every little move you make, I love you like a mango, wish we could make it every day.*' Now it got her to her feet again, dancing her way into a new morning with an empty glass in her hand and the snow swirling outside.

By the time she turned the record over – how weird not to have all the tracks on the same side – she had finished the brandy bottle and was feeling considerably more mellow.

She lay down on the sofa and looked around the room. Since Tom left she hadn't spent much time in here. There was something forlorn about the gaps where his furniture had been and she hadn't bothered to rearrange the leftovers. Had that chaise-longue really been his? Her memory was that it had been her Barclaycard at the auction that weekend in Wales. It was a ridiculous spur-of-the-moment buy anyway. Too large to fit into the back of the car, so they'd had to travel back to London with it roped in, and the rear door open behind it. It had seemed funny at the time, the kind of thing that they were good at doing together, the kind of thing that separated them off from the rest of the world. Or maybe it just meant they'd been happy then. Such a simple feeling, happiness. More like a lack of feeling really, an ordinariness, a sense of not being in pain.

But it had definitely been her money. Ah well, not worth arguing about now. At least she still had the wooden giraffe, brought back in the hold of a charter plane from Kenya, and arriving at Heathrow with its ear broken off. They had never bothered to stick it on again. Had it been earlier in their relationship Tom would have done it for her, but by then there was a certain selfishness to their mutuality. Your giraffe, your problem. She couldn't even remember where the ear had gone now. Maybe he'd taken it with him.

A one-eared giraffe. Did that mean the room would stay like this for ever, a touch of the Miss Havishams creeping in as decay and dust settled over the years? It made her realise that she hadn't really thought in terms of the future at all.

Who would she be in five years' time? Would she be alone? It was probably better than the alternative. What would she do with another lover? Somebody else's furniture would mean somebody else's taste, somebody else's agenda, their own game-plan.

For all the pain of the split-up she wouldn't easily give up her new-found independence, she knew that now. Better to be alone. If you liked your own company enough there was no particular reason why life shouldn't be a catalogue of occasional one-night stands. As long as the sex was safe and good enough. Maybe she should invite Malcolm back after all, give him some lessons, teach him how to make sure they both got their rocks off this time. Learning how to ask; the kind of skill all women have to master.

He probably wouldn't mind that much. Wasn't it every boy's dream – a girl who knows what she wants? Sex without commitment? He didn't seem like the kind of guy who'd be up for sharing the milk bill anyway. No danger of communal fantasies there.

She was thinking Malcolm but that was not who she was seeing. She was seeing *him*, seeing his wild, taut body at the end of the bed, feeling the dry rub of his skin and the jerky power of his penis as it swelled into life under her hand. She remembered how wet she had been and how the terror and the power had connected as he came inside her.

If you didn't feel like a victim, then maybe that meant you weren't one. Perhaps it was time she acknowledged that and owned up to the other stuff; let herself tap back into the seam of control – was that the same as pleasure? – that their encounter had opened up in her.

For a shy girl she was playing with a lot of dangerous fantasies. It must be the booze. If she was sober she'd feel scared. When had she last been this drunk? She couldn't remember. But she knew she didn't want to be sober. She got off the sofa, the tension in her thoughts making it impossible to keep still any more.

This time she couldn't find the right music for the mood; all that Seventies American rock she'd grown up with was too laidback, too forgiving. Even Springsteen's urban nightmare had too much compassion in it. She went for the Clash. Although she'd been the right age for it, punk had never been her identity badge, too 'in your face' for that. But she'd liked the knowing scream behind it, liked to think that that was who she might have been if she hadn't been herself.

Maybe it was never too late. She could become that person now. She went in search of more booze. On top of the drinks cabinet she caught sight of a family portrait; her father and mother standing in a field, she young and pretty, laughing into the wind, he older, more serious, as always. What did they do together in bed, eh? They had spent the first ten years of their marriage trying for a child that didn't come. That would have meant making a lot of love. Was it all David Niven politeness and Doris Day headaches, or was it more primal? Was that where her father earthed the violence of his despair? Sex. Everyone's dark secret.

At the back of the drinks cabinet she found an unopened bottle of Glenmorangie that Tom must have missed in his clear-out. He wouldn't have approved of her pouring it into the same glass as the brandy. But then he wasn't here to complain. She could do what she liked. With whom she liked.

So what was it she wanted to do? Was this about the power of powerlessness? She knew she had a talent for that. Seven years of living with Tom had been proof enough. But in the end it had been more social than sexual. What exactly would it mean if you translated it into sex? Her mind went back to the stash of porn magazines by the bed. They had acted more as aphrodisiac than example. If she had been less scared and he had been more keen, where might they not have gone? The thought of it made her scared all over again. Is this me talking? she thought. Elizabeth Skvorecky, single white female in search of a future?

You know what your problem is? You should have more to lose, more sense of a vested interest in life.

Then you wouldn't be so cocky about taking risks. But when she looked back on herself she realised she'd never had that. Even as a child she had grown up with a sense that the world had been designed for somebody else, someone more connected, and she was simply a casual visitor who'd have to make do with the edges and the margins.

Was that what *he* felt too? That he belonged to a sense of not belonging? Who knows? Could be they were made for each other and she should exploit the feeling. Write him an invitation to dinner. Just know when to press the panic button, or keep an ice pick under the bed.

You could make a much greater mess with a hammer, though. What had he done to those other girls, the ones in the garden flats and the alleyways? It didn't take three days in hospital to get over rape. What had they not seen fit to put in the papers? Think about it. If someone's pain was your pleasure, then once you started hitting them why should there be any reason to stop? Are you ready for this, Elizabeth? Is this really what your life has brought you to?

The malt seemed rougher on the taste buds than the brandy. Sometimes you get a wolf in lamb's clothing. But you could also get it the other way around. How would it be if she discovered that all his violence was just a cover for his pain? That the sobbing was more real than the hammering?

Why was it that sex was so complicated? Why did it have to be dark to be so alive? She rubbed her hands over her eyes, then back into her hair, enjoying the stretch as it pulled back from her scalp.

Just as he had done.

There had been a time when she had first started with Tom when she couldn't get enough of him: when she wanted every bit of him inside her, all her holes filled with his smell and his maleness. She could get aroused by watching him pull a coin out of his pocket, or the way he walked back to a restaurant table from the loo. She had loved that sense of being almost out of control. Clever Tom, to have smelt that in her. Clever Tom.

Clever *him*.

If you're going to do this, you have to do it now, she thought. You won't get any drunker, and there's a danger that if you keep looking into the drop you might get vertigo.

She got up, only slightly unsteady on her feet, and, carrying the glass with her, went into the kitchen and turned on the computer.

twenty-two

'... call the desk if you need anything, anything at all. We're here to serve you.'

The manager turned to her and said something else in Czech. She nodded and murmured back, then she gave him a small smile. The door closed quietly behind him.

It was the best suite in the place, a mix of faded pre-communist history and new hopes. Its charm wouldn't last long. Trusthouse Forte would get its hands on it and turn it into an International Hotel; the fax, the minibar and the shower cap, credit-card culture, so suitable for business, so unsuitable for life.

But not now. Now it still was poignant enough to be the setting for this scene.

Jake watched the door close, then turned towards her. She was sitting on the bed. They had found her some other clothes, a shapeless cardigan which she had put round her shoulders over the torn, bloody dress, and a pair of shoes, a little clumpy, not her style at all. They had offered to dress her finger again, but she couldn't cope with the idea of the pain or the attention, so the grim little bandage remained, the wound soothed by further painkillers rather than antiseptics. That suited her fine too. She didn't want to be in her right mind. She wanted to be asleep. She also wanted to be alone.

He was staring at her. She knew that look. She had lived through nearly two years of marriage to it. It still scared her. He thinks he loves me, she thought. He thinks I am the meaning in his life and that having me is the only thing that matters. Oh God, please don't let's get into this again. Not now.

He came up to her and knelt down at her feet. He smelt of blood and death. His face was a mess, one eye almost closed under the bruising and his lip split and swollen. Not everybody consents to die without a fight. The cut would make kissing difficult. But it wouldn't be the first time. You get used to it, he once told her. She had thought then she never would. Who had been right, him or her?

He reached out and took her good hand in both of his, holding it in front of him for a minute, then moving out towards the other one. She drew it back, instinctively nursing it against her stomach. He looked up at her, kept her gaze, then reached out again. 'I won't hurt you,' he said almost in a whisper.

This time she let him take it. He was careful not to go near the finger. He held the hand gently, turning it over so it lay palm up, his fingers playing with the soft skin inside, following her life-line, caressing the creases almost to the edge of the stump. She stayed stubbornly looking down, then at last lifted her eyes to his face. He was in more pain than she was. How many times have we been here before? she thought. He lifted the hand to his mouth and softly kissed the inside of the palm.

'Oh, Christ, I thought I'd lost you,' he said, his voice fracturing under the emotion. 'When I burst into that cell and saw the blood, I really thought I'd lost you.'

She closed her eyes and replayed the scene on the blank screen of her eyelids. She saw herself rushing up the stairs, into one room, then the next, with the hammering in her heart echoed by the hammering on the door behind her. Then she turned and saw, the shadow in the doorway. She heard a hail of gunfire, and Jake's voice from somewhere, screaming, 'Get down!'

But she was on the floor already, flinching in time to the rhythm of the bullets coming from somewhere behind her and tearing into the fleshy body, jerking it every which way, making it dance like a kinetic sculpture, alive after it was dead. And every bullet-hole opened up a spray can of blood and bits. By the end there was so much blood she was covered in it. They both were.

'Are you all right?' he had shouted as soon as he got to her.

She hadn't needed to move her head, it was doing that for her, a kind of violent trembling which she couldn't control. He tried to help her up, but she pushed him off. 'The other one,' she babbled. 'Downstairs – there's another one, I—'

'It's all right. It's all right, baby,' he said, holding her tightly to him, making sure the words got through. 'He's dead too.'

She felt the knife slide in again, in and up through the lining of the stomach. She heard his groan opening up into her own mouth. 'Did I . . . Did I kill him?'

'No.' And this time he grinned. 'But I did.'

She opened her eyes onto the fading lilac wallpaper

pattern. No more deserted farmhouse, no more bodies. It was over, it was over. It wouldn't happen again.

'I'd thought I'd lost you,' he murmured again.

The memory of it brought them closer. He laid his head on her knee. She put out her good hand and stroked his hair. Her fingers came across little particles of stuff; somebody else's brain or body fluids. She hadn't seen what had happened in the cell downstairs, but she knew that her kidnapper must have fought back. Even with his stomach opened up and his trousers halfway down his legs.

Someone always has to win. Someone always has to be the victor. Is this the way they prove their manhood? Maybe, but they still need a woman to convince them, to welcome them home. This was the bit where he turned from man to boy, then back to man again. The head between the breasts leading to the head between the legs.

Just one more time, she thought. Just one more time, then you can go to sleep . . .

No, no, no, Elizabeth.

She leant back from the computer, shaking her head impatiently, running the cursor over the last three paragraphs, highlighting the text.

Cross it out, she said to herself. You give Mirka the upper hand now and it won't work. Who cares about her wisdom? It's women's wisdom that freaks men out. Stop her thinking. Give her a body, but no brain. Remember whom you're writing for.

She hit the erase key. The words tumbled over into space and Mirka reformed herself as someone else;

someone more angry, more fuckable – with a little persuasion.

She opened her eyes onto the fading lilac wallpaper pattern. No more deserted farmhouse, no more bodies. It was over, it was over. It wouldn't happen again.

'I thought I'd lost you,' he murmured again, pulling her back to the present.

'No,' she shook her head, and her voice was loose with exhaustion. 'You can't lose me, Jake. There's nowhere I could go where you wouldn't find me.'

Sensing the resistance under her words he glanced up at her. 'That's right. That's absolutely right, babe.'

They sat looking at each other. It was still a contest. Always had been, always would be. This he understood. This he was good at. He got up from his knees. 'D'you want a drink?'

She shook her head.

'Well, I do.'

In the corner they had an ersatz version of a minibar. The lock was stiff. He pulled at it a couple of times, then kicked it. It opened. He dug out the three miniatures of bourbon and poured them all into a tooth mug. He took a slug, then turned to her.

'Are we gonna talk about it?'

Again she shook her head.

He looked at her for a moment. 'Well, I want to talk.'

She gave a little laugh. 'So now *you* want to talk. You don't think it's a little late for us to be speaking each other's lines?'

He sighed, his anger barely in check. He used to be proud of her English, how fast she picked it up, how charming it sounded. Now all he could hear was her sarcasm and her lip. 'I'm your husband, Mirka. I love you. I want to know what they did to you.'

There was a pause. She said in a cold, deliberate, matter-of-fact voice, 'They cut my finger off.'

He looked at her. 'Is that all?'

'Why?' she said angrily. 'What else would you like them to have done, Jake?'

He frowned, then turned abruptly away from her and threw himself into a chair across from the bed. He took another slug from the tooth mug, then ran his hand over his face. He wasn't looking at her.

'You know after you left I dreamed about you every night. Every *fucking* night ... I'd close my eyes and there you'd be, standing in front of me, in that green dress of yours. Remember? The one where your nipples used to show through. I used to watch you and think about sucking those nipples, just pulling the strap off the shoulder and feeling your breast fall into my hands, heavy, warm.'

She sat completely still. This was nothing to do with her. He was talking to himself. She felt more like his confessor than his wife. But then that had long been a problem between them.

'You think I played hard to get, don't you? That day we met, that day on the subway. You think I could have walked away from you? You don't know shit, Mirka. And you never did.

'I knew you were the one from the first moment I laid eyes on you. You were in a café on Broadway, between Eighty-sixth and Eighty-seventh. I was having lunch when you came in. You sat in a window seat and ordered from the breakfast menu. You didn't understand that it only went up till eleven a.m. The guy was nice to you. Probably wanted to fuck you. Or maybe he still remembered what it was like not to speak the language so well. You had a BLT with fries. He recommended it. Said it was very American. You said you liked it. Then you paid the check and walked ten blocks down to the museum, remember?

'You were a bit bored by that. I could tell. I thought you would be. All that natural history. Dead stuff. I knew you were more physical than that. Not enough going on for you there. You don't remember this, do you? You don't remember that I was there too? Well, welcome to law enforcement, baby. That's what cops are good at, tailing people so they don't know they're being tailed.

'You don't even remember me on the subway platform. How romantic it was that we got on at the same stop.

'I'm not sure what I would've done if that jerk hadn't started to hit up on you. Could be I would have had to cause an incident. I got it ready-made, though. And you liked it. Oh, yeah, I know you may think you were scared but I saw it in your eyes. This is what you'd come to America for. To be frightened, to be fought over. To be wanted. Course you didn't know that. For you it was all stars in your eyes and neon flashing. Like a kid with a paintbox. You didn't see the horror, or the fuck-ups, didn't feel the violence in the graffiti. You just liked the colours. America. Capital-letter place. Where women don't have to pretend. Where a hard man is good to find.

'We were looking for each other, Mirka. Don't you realise that? I only played it cool so you'd feel you'd won me. To give you the pleasure of getting your own way. Or thinking you had.'

The room was silent. She felt her pulse through the throb in her hand. The painkillers were wearing off.

He let his head fall back against the chair. 'You can't leave me now, Mirka. It isn't possible. Where would you go? What would you do? They'll never be enough for you, all those soft-fingered old men with their accents and cheque cards and old-fashioned diamond bracelet courtship.'

She took a sharp intake of breath. He looked up.

'What, you think I didn't know?' he laughed. 'It's me, baby, Jake. Remember? You can't take a shit without me being there. Oh, sorry. Not the kind of language you like, eh? What words would *he* use? Don't tell me, "the ladies' room"?'

But it wasn't any fun without her talking. He let the silence hang.

She took a deep breath. 'I'm not going back with you, Jake,' she said gently. 'I've decided to stay here.'

'Here?'

'Yes, here. I'm going home.'

'Home.' And this time it was a big laugh. 'Well, that's a good joke. What happened? Did playing around with a country boy make you homesick?'

'I—'

'Jesus, Mirka, it's about time you grew up,' he cut across her. 'Stay here? This place is falling apart, or haven't you noticed? I'll tell you about here. They don't have the money or the vision to hold it together. Capitalism hurts too much when you're this far behind. And these guys have already had too much pain. So people are going to get dissatisfied and then it's all going to come bubbling up from below. You can export crime like you can export everything else. And we're not even talking future here. They've already arrived. Who do you think was paying your hay boys to keep you captive? The locusts have come, Mirka. The plague is upon you.

'You don't have a clue how fucking powerful these guys are. We're talking sophistication here. They half-run America already. What price a poxy little country like this one? They'll buy anyone they want and the ones that aren't for sale they'll kill. You think I'm a big boy, Mirka? I'm shit compared with these guys.' He laughed. 'Though I can still kick their ass when I want.'

He took another swig. 'You're not going to stay here. You're coming back with me.'

She waited till he was listening. 'No, I'm not, Jake.'

He slammed the glass down on the arm of the chair. 'So, tell me, was it just him or was it the fat one too?'

She left a beat of a pause. 'What are you talking about?' she said quietly, though they both knew.

'You know what I'm fucking talking about, Mirka. He had his trousers around his ankles. I got a real good impression he'd been persuaded that way.'

'Jake.' She got up from the bed, and for the first time there was a kind of energy in her eyes. 'Jake, listen to me. They cut my finger off, do you understand? If you hadn't come they would have killed me.'

'But I was coming, Mirka. You knew that, fuck you.'

'No, fuck *you*. Fuck you, Jake, and all your Superman fantasy. You want me to sit around and wait till you burst in like something from an action movie? Well, I didn't want to be saved by you. You understand? I wanted to save myself.'

He was listening. But then he had needed to get her talking, back in the race. 'So, tell me about it,' he said lightly, as if it didn't matter to him.

She sighed. 'He was a farm boy. He didn't know what had hit him. He just wanted to be rich, that's all.'

There was a pause. 'And now he's dead.'

'Yes, well, that's the way you like them. Did you kill Luis too? You'd better be careful. In America diplomats have got more power than cops. Even a cop as good as you.'

This time it was his turn to be silent.

'You're wrong about me, Jake. Maybe I was like that once. Maybe there were stars and neon. But I've changed. You've contaminated me. Now I have this disease too, this American thing. But I'm not going to die of it. I'm going to get well. And without you.'

He stared at the carpet for a long time, his teeth playing over his bruised lip. Then he sighed. 'I love you, Mirka,' he said so quietly she almost didn't hear it. 'That's the beginning and the end of it.'

'No, you don't, Jake. You love the *idea* of me. Not me any more. Me you have to let go.'

He left a pause. Like all good cops, timing was one of his talents. 'So, did he come?'

'What!'

He looked up at her. 'I would have asked *him* only by the time I got to him he was having trouble talking. But he still wanted you. You could tell from the way he went for me.'

'Jake,' she said slowly, as if she were talking to a child and it was suddenly very important that he understand. 'Jake, I stuck a knife into his stomach.'

'Yeah, I know you did. And I know how it feels.

Because you've done it to me too, babe. Only I didn't have a hard-on at the time.'

She walked over to him, took the glass out of his hand and slung it at the wall. It smashed into a fountain of slivers. 'Is that it? Is that what you want? Well, come on then. I'll shove my finger stump up your ass.'

He let out a large laugh. 'Oh, listen to you. What a mouth the lady has.'

'And where do you think she learnt it, Jake? You don't get stuff like that from English phrase books.'

She stared at him then turned on her heel and went back to the bed. He didn't move. For a while neither of them said anything. She sighed, shaking her head as if to clear it, then, eventually, she looked up at him. 'So, what now?'

He gave a shrug. They held each other's gaze. She opened her mouth a fraction, a half-frown on her face. He got up from the chair and crossed the room until he was standing right in front of her, his body suddenly very close to hers. 'Why shouldn't I be jealous, Mirka?' he said without moving. 'I love you more than anyone else could. Is that so bad?'

She closed her eyes for a second, then opened them back into his gaze. He put out a slow hand, hooking his index finger under the rim of the cardigan and pushing it slowly down her arm, taking the strap of her dress with it. As it reached the elbow her breast came free. She didn't move. Neither did he.

'So why don't you tell me how much you hate this. Tell me to take my fucking hand away.'

She swallowed. 'Take your fucking hand away,' she said, but with no feeling in her voice.

He smiled, then slipped his palm under her breast,

lifting it up slightly. 'You must be cold.' He moved the hand to her nipple, pinching it between his fingers. 'Oh, look at that – your very own erection.' She took in a sharp breath. 'Oh, but I forgot. You don't like erections, do you? Too crude. Too "American".'

And he let his hand drop away. When he pulled the other shoulder strap down it caught. This time he tore it. She flinched. He bent over slowly and took the other nipple in his mouth. When it was ready he pushed it out with his tongue, like a grape pip. It stood there quivering.

'Do you know what I'm going to do now?' he said as he stood above her.

She shook her head.

'I'm going to fuck you. Or should I maybe use another word? What do you think, Mirka? Would you like it better if I said I was going to "make love" to you?'

No, fuck would do. He was sure he could feel it in her body. But that wasn't what her voice said. 'You don't know the meaning of the word, Jake.'

He snapped a hand back as if he was going to hit her. She didn't flinch. But then she wasn't the one who had been hurt. 'No? You really think so. Well, let me tell you something, Mirka. It's you who don't know the meaning of it. You think you do but you don't.' And now his voice was shaking with the anger. 'You wash it out of us, do you know that? Drip by drip you wash it out of us, drown out the love, till all that's left is the fuck. We bring you feelings and you walk all over them. Do you know what it's like to be rejected? Do you? Do you know what it's like to want to love someone and to hear them say that they're not interested in you tonight? That you're too up ... or too down ... or too caught up in

yourself. Too crazy. . . . Do you know what that's like? Oh
baby, if we did that to you, you'd hate us. Fucking hate
us. You'd feel worthless and ignored. But it doesn't
matter to us. We're guys after all. Sex is just sex. Go and
have a quick wank in the bathroom, Jake. Get the
tension out that way, give it to the pan rather than your
wife.'

It was the conversation they had never had. How
cruel to be having it now, when it was too late.

'That's not true, Jake,' she said fiercely. 'That's not
true. I did make love to you. I made love to you for a
whole year. But it was never enough. That's why we
started fucking.'

'No. That's why *you* started fucking. Or should I say
faking?'

'Oh!' It was her turn to laugh. 'Oh, that was what hurt,
was it?'

'Did you fake it with him too?'

She tossed the question away with an angry wave of
her hand.

'I said did you fake it with him too?'

'No,' she said after a while, her voice as quiet as his
shout. 'With him it was for real.'

'So what was his trick? Did he ask your permission?'

'He didn't have to. He just wanted me. As opposed to
needing me all the time.'

This time he hit her. Not hard – he was a pro in such
things – but enough to knock her backwards onto the
bed. He climbed on top of her, pinning her hips down.
She stared up at him, then tried to move her pelvis. He
slammed his weight back down into her. This time she
froze. Something passed between them. They both felt
it: heat as a kind of physical shock, desire and fear

flooding into one another and fusing like a chemical reaction.

'So?' he said at last, almost under his breath. 'Want rather than need? And how do I do that, eh?'

She shook her hair back onto the bedspread and lifted her hands up above her head; a deliberately provocative gesture of surrender. 'Why don't you use your imagination?' She paused. 'And watch what you do with my hand.'

She kept her eyes on his face as he moved his way down her body, pulling away the clothes until she was naked apart from her pants. He used his tongue to massage her nipples then ran slow fingers down over her stomach, tracing the arrow line of dark hair which ran from her navel until it disappeared under the edge of the elastic. He pushed a finger underneath. She shivered slightly. He removed it again. Then, moving the heel of his palm slowly over her pants, his hand reached her crotch, playing and probing, until he located what he was looking for. He rubbed his forefinger over the material into the point of her clitoris. She started to move into his touch. He got into the rhythm, his gaze still hard on her face. She became moist through the silk. She let out a slow gasp and closed her eyes. He stopped. She opened them again, a question on her lips.

'You like that,' he said, the voice almost cold, a statement rather than a question. She nodded, a little unsure of this other Jake. 'Then keep your eyes open, lady. I don't want you fantasising about somebody else here.'

His fingers started again, the material wet now beneath his touch. She felt the slow tension of orgasm building inside her. She made a move to reach up and kiss him, but he pushed her down again.

'You want me yet?' he said, watching her lips open and hearing her pull in an uneven breath. She laughed, then shook her head, starting to move herself up against him. 'Then stay still.'

She let out a small moan. He played with her more, then as he felt her excitement accelerate he pulled at the top of her pants, yanking the material hard up into her slit. She gasped. He cupped a hand under her ass and lifted her buttocks off the bed, one hand holding her up, the other probing and rubbing. He watched her as she came, his face impassive, enjoying the power as much as her pleasure. Then he moved his head down and pushed the material of the crotch to one side, using his tongue.

This time when she climaxed the sensation was almost too intense to stay with. She broke free to get her breath back, curling up away from him onto her stomach, her damaged hand hitting the blanket as she did so. She let out a yelp of pain.

He reached up and pulled down a pillow. 'Here,' he whispered gently. 'Lay it on here.' She did as she was told. 'And keep your mouth shut. I told you, I don't want to hear your groans.' They both knew he was talking pleasure and not pain.

He slid his knee high up under her thigh, pulling her towards him until she was lying half across his lap, her hips off the ground, ass in the air. He slipped his fingers back into her from behind, in and out and over. In, out, over. She was so wet now they could both hear it. 'Now that's what I call an erection,' he said softly, as she pushed her clitoris hard against his fingers. 'Come on, baby. Let's do it again.' This time when she came her whole body was shaking. When it was past she tried to slide herself round to face him.

'Uh uh,' he said coldly. 'Not unless you're ready for me.'

She gave a little moan.

He slapped her lightly on the ass. 'Does that mean yes?'

'Yes.' The word coming out breathless as she began twisting her body towards him again.

But as she moved he held her back down. This time he stroked her before he hit her, once, twice, then again, sharp rhythmic slaps, hard enough to hurt. She gasped, but made no move to pull away.

'So tell me. I want to hear you say it.'

The slap that followed was harder still.

'I want you,' she whispered, and this time they both felt her arch her buttocks off his legs towards his hand. He laughed as he caressed her ass. 'Me or this?' And the next slap was loud enough to make her groan.

'Oh my God.' Her voice was hoarse with desire. He slapped her again, then slipped his fingers into her and shoved her up onto her knees until he straddled her doggie-fashion. And as his cock pushed inside her he felt a long shudder go through them both.

'Oh Christ.' Hard to know which one of their voices it was. It was over so fast it had them both gasping for breath. 'Shit,' he said. 'Shit. Sorry. Sorry.'

She threw her head back into his shoulder. 'No. No, it's fine. It's fine.' And she laughed.

They lost their balance and fell sideways together onto the bed. He let out a huge gasp, then curled himself around her, hugging her tightly into him. She put out her good hand awkwardly behind her and tried to hold him. 'See,' she said. 'See. You don't have to be old and wrinkled to do it properly.'

Outside the clock chimed one. The beginning of a new day. Christmas. As good a time for a new start as any other. 'So,' he said after a while. 'Do you think I should try for a job in the diplomatic service? We could always live in Prague.'

She smiled. The locks were off now, on the doors of her heart as well as her body. 'Let's talk about it in the morning.'

He turned her over. 'What? You think we're going to sleep now?' As he slid his hand down towards her.

twenty-three

Someone threw a snowball against the window-pane.

The thud made her jump. She looked up, still dazed from their love-making, trying to separate herself from her words. From the back gardens she could hear the yells and shouts of children. She rose slowly from her seat. She felt dazed, her legs shaky, as if the moment of release had been shared and she didn't want to be the one who got up to make the tea.

Pulling aside the sheet she saw the smear of melting ice crystals on the glass. A few seconds later another thump hit nearby. They were coming from next door. She could hear them all out in the garden, Mum, Dad, little Jonny (was that his name?) and friends, snow and laughter flying everywhere. She saw the child's face again, pressed against the window. He'd be tired, having missed so much sleep. But it wouldn't matter, the excitement would see him through. The same could be said of her.

She went to the computer and scrolled back to halfway through the scene. Their joint lust rolled out in front of her. Did she really write that? She tried to imagine him reading it. Could you fuck like that? She didn't know who she was talking to. Him or herself. She read it again. It wouldn't work. Despite its flirtation with dominance the pleasure was too mutual. Erotic violence wasn't real violence. There was too much desire and not enough fear, not enough panic. She should try it again. Make it nastier. Make it hurt more. Either that or go back to the original. But that was dead prose, unthinking, traditional; the final rocks-off/I-love-you fuck for the man who had everything, including a wife turned on by his macho ways with a gun. He wouldn't be attracted by that. It was even more sentimental than love.

No, this was what she had written and this was what he was going to read. Anyway, what point was there in offering him another rape? He could get that any night of the year. What he wanted was the stuff he couldn't have. The cocktail of fear and complicity. You'd better be sure, she thought. You'd better be sure. On the twelfth day of Christmas my true love gave to me ... five gold rings, two turtle doves and a garbage bag full of discarded love-making. This present wouldn't even need a label.

She pushed the print button and watched while the screen notched up the page numbers. Seven, eight, nine ... Could sex really take that long? Her eyes picked up the odd sentence.

'– this time they both felt her arch her buttocks off his legs towards his hand. He laughed as he caressed her. "Me or this?" And the next slap was loud enough to make her groan ...'

Was this really what she had intended? Or had this been the booze talking? If she put the scene to one side now and took a nap, she would have sobered up and changed her mind when she woke.

The last page hummed its way smoothly out of the printer, the pages still warm from birth. At least the invitation was clear:

'Outside the clock chimed one. The beginning of a new day. Christmas. As good a time for a new start as any other . . . the locks were off now, on the doors of her heart as well as her body . . .'

No, after a nap it would feel like the composition of a mad woman, demented courage and no brains. All the more reason for doing it now.

Across the back gardens his window was dark. Sleeping like a baby, no doubt, secure in the knowledge of the pain he had caused. She picked up the papers and stuffed them into a used brown envelope. Then on the front she wrote in big scrawled letters: *Jake and Mirka. Last scene, first draft.* Just another method of filing text. When you got to the final revisions you threw the first drafts away. How were you to know what kind of perverts go through your rubbish bins?

She did it immediately, afraid that her courage would desert her if she hesitated. Outside, daylight and a hundred dirty footmarks had taken the shine off the snow. A middle-aged woman was casting salt like biblical seed along the pavements while the road had become a sledging path for half a dozen children old enough to be let out without fear of abduction. She opened a black bag that was already full and laid the envelope along with some loose pages of script casually on the top.

She kept up a surveillance point from the front window. An hour or so went by. She was beginning to feel the need for sleep. A couple walked by with a baby in a pushchair, then a man in a raincoat and a gaggle of teenagers. Nobody stopped, nobody looked at the garbage. Why should they? If he walked by now, would it be the first thing he saw? Or would it, perhaps, look too contrived? She imagined him standing by the gate, eyes darting into the bins, spotting it there so tidy and inviting. Would he read it on the street, or wait till he got home? Would he know it was for him?

Of course he would. Phone messages, visits, pet mutilation. They were having a relationship, why pretend otherwise? In which case why bother with the dustbin? If she wanted him to read a letter, she should deliver it to his front door. How else could she be sure he'd get it in time?

She threw on a jacket and walked quickly out, head down into her collar, lest anyone should later be able to recognise her. She needn't have bothered. She passed few enough people on the street and those she did were more interested in staying on their feet than checking out the traffic around them.

The steps up to his house showed the faint imprint of his boots, overlaid with a fresh covering of early morning snow. He hadn't gone out since his return. She placed her own feet in the existing prints, sliding her soles about to blur the patterns. Amazing what you think of when you have the time. Is this what policemen do – find themselves playing the game even when there's no game to play? She held the envelope up, and was just about to push it in when she realised that it didn't have his name on it. Of course he would know it was for him, but what would happen if someone else got there first? She hesitated. Was this caution or cowardice? If you want this guy to visit you, you have to invite him in. Only make it too obvious and he mightn't come. The letter stuck to her fingers, refusing to make its way through the box. She turned on her heel, her shoes making careless new marks on the snow, and headed for home.

Her heart was still thumping when she turned the corner into her street and saw the figure outside her front door.

She was standing with her finger on the bell and she looked great. The coat was obviously this season's; thick black wool with a generous swirl of cloth and a black and white striped scarf that on anyone else would have betrayed football leanings, but on Sally just made you think of fashion pages. Clothes. One of her great talents.

If only she had had Sally's dress sense what limits would there have been to her achievements? Patrick excepted, of course. Had they really been best friends? It seemed so long ago.

She slipped the envelope casually onto the top of the open rubbish bag as she came in the gate. 'Hello, Sally.'

She watched her jump at the sound of the voice. It seemed everyone was nervy these days. Had she read about the local rapist too? 'God, Eliza, you gave me the fright of my life. I expected you to be inside.'

'I've been for a walk.'

'Yes,' she said, betraying only mild disbelief at her inadequate clothing. 'Well, the lady in person, eh? I've won my bet.'

'With whom?'

'Patrick. He said you wouldn't open the door.'

'I haven't.'

She grinned. 'Ah yes, but he doesn't know that.' She grinned again and held out her arms.

She wanted to come closer, to walk into the hug and feel someone's arms around her, but she found she couldn't do it. 'What are you doing here anyway?' she said in what she thought might be a light tone. 'I thought Christmas was your busiest time of the year.'

'Absolutely. We're up to our ears in parties. But I learned my lesson from last year. I do the menus, the extra staff do the rest. So?' She took a nervous breath, so unlike Sally that it was clear the small talk hadn't fooled her at all. 'So. How are you, darling?'

Why bother? 'I don't know. How do I look?'

The hesitation was its own answer. 'When did you last check a mirror?'

She sighed. 'It's been a hard day's night, Sally. I'm tired, that's all.'

There was an awkward pause. A slab of soggy snow slid from an upper windowsill and hit the ground in front of them. Sally brushed a lump of it off her coat. 'Listen, I know this is some ghastly book you're translating, but unless you want more bodies on your hands you'd better invite me in. We're both going to die of cold out here.'

She sighed. 'Sally, I don't—'

'I'm not leaving without talking to you, Eliza,' she cut in firmly. 'So why don't you just get your key out.'

It reminded her so much of the old Sally, the slender, bolshy blonde – for blonde red hennaed, streaked and finally, now, her own chestnut brown – who had knocked on her door that second week of term and asked if she wanted to share a joint. They had got so stoned they hadn't made it to bed, just crashed out in her room, then reeled out next morning to a nine a.m. lecture where Sally had promptly fallen asleep. As their friendship progressed over the years they smoked less and drank more but some things remained constant. Sally refusing to take no for an answer was one of them. She had liked it once, had taken it as a sign of affection. Now she was not so sure.

She took her into the living room rather than the kitchen. That way she wouldn't see the sheets across the window or the computer with its final pages of triumphant fucking. As it was, Sally's visual inventory was immediate. 'I don't remember Tom taking the chaise-longue. It wasn't his, was it?' Sally's father had been an estate agent. Her brother was already a partner in his accountancy firm. Some things were in the DNA.

She shrugged. 'Disputed custody.'

'You mean his taste, your money. Well, at least what you buy from now on remains your own. Why don't you move that wicker lounge from the spare room in here? It would go perfectly.'

'Do you want tea or coffee?'

'Oh ... whichever you're making.' And she made a move to follow her.

'No, no. You stay here. I'll bring it to you. Maybe you could give me some other ideas on the decor.'

In the kitchen she flicked back the sheet. No movement. Maybe she should have put her finger on his doorbell; why should he get more sleep than her? The quicker he woke, the quicker he might get the message. Get up, you lucky boy. In a street next to you the garbage bags are overflowing. Adrenaline flushed through her like a hot wave. To steady herself she made an effort with the tea tray; sugar bowl, milk, even a plate of biscuits. She didn't want Sally thinking her more crazy than she was.

In the living room Sally had moved from furniture to music, her eyes going round and round as she tried to read the label still turning on the player. 'My God, darling, you have been going back in time. I didn't even know you had this. You used to despise punk. "Rough sound and fake fury" – wasn't that your line? You're not going retro, are you? You know Patrick's got Malcolm McLaren's brother or someone as one of his clients. You should hear the stories. Oh, biscuits, eh? Don't tell me you've started eating again?'

It had always been one of the more comforting things about Sally, the way she didn't really need anyone else in a conversation. Like listening to water flow. She poured her out a black tea and put a couple of pieces of shortbread on her plate. Why do I feel so aggressive towards you? she thought. Has there always been this potential for dislike between us, or has one of us changed? If she looked under the bed now would she find the remains of a skin sloughed off; the outer coating of the old Elizabeth, so needy, so desperate for a friend that she didn't mind who it was? Of course snakes shed their skin because they're growing bigger. But was this about growth or fuck-up?

'So,' said Sally, watching her carefully from her place on the sofa, 'do I ask or do you tell?'

She took a breath. 'Sally, I'm not at my best this morning. To be honest I'm a little drunk.'

'Well, at least you've noticed. I was beginning to

think you'd mistaken brandy for milk over your muesli. When did you start?'

'Oh, about two weeks after Tom left.' She saw the flash of concern and smiled. 'It's all right, it's a joke. I'm not quite a morning alkie yet. This one's leftover from last night. I haven't been to bed.'

'Ah yes, I've been hearing about your nocturnal habits.'

She frowned. 'Tell me, Sally, exactly how well do you know Malcolm?'

'Malcolm who?' She grinned. 'Sorry. I'm not making this any easier, am I?'

'No.'

'OK. I'll make you a deal. No more smart talk from me, no more evasion from you. Agreed?'

She gave a little shrug. To be fair, Sally didn't need to have persevered, either now or then. She had been good to her when no one else gave a toss. That had to count for something. 'Agreed.'

'So, tell me how you really are.'

'I'm fine.'

'Well, you don't look fine. You look bloody awful. If Tom has got—'

'Tom has got nothing to do with it. He's completely irrelevant. I hardly ever think about him. This is all me. I've just got myself into something ... It's to do with work, and I can't seem to get out of it. It's a weird book, this ... I mean that's why I haven't been in touch. It's sort of taken me over. All I do is write, sleep and write more.'

'How come? I mean I thought you had until the spring to finish it. Isn't that what Charles said?'

'He changed his mind. They've rushed the release

date of the film. They need the text sooner.'

'So tell him to get another translator. Jesus, Eliza—'

'I can't. And anyway – I don't want to. I know this may sound crazy, but I'm quite enjoying it.'

'The book or the pressure?'

'Oh, I don't know – both, maybe. It's . . . it's a licence for behaving badly, I suppose. I don't have to see anyone, or be nice to anyone, pretend anything any more. I can be as anti-social as I like.'

There was a pause. Sally stared at her, as if trying to assess the damage. 'Sounds like some Doris Lessing kind of madness to me. So how crazy are you? Are you having visions?' And she meant it seriously.

If only . . . she thought. She smiled. 'No. No visions. I've got it all strictly under control.'

'I rather doubt that.' Sally shook her head. 'It's strange, you know. For all my apparent bad behaviour you were always the seriously wacky one. I'm sure that's why we became friends in the first place. I might do stuff you didn't think you ought, but you could dream things I wouldn't even dare.'

'Well, you wouldn't want to be in this particular fantasy,' she muttered.

'I thought you said you were enjoying it.'

She shrugged. 'It comes and it goes.'

'Well, you just be careful you don't go with it.' She stopped. 'How was it with Malcolm, by the way? Or shouldn't I ask?'

'I thought you already knew.'

'Darling, I'm not that much of a snoop. All I know is that according to him you're weird and he likes it. But then he's a romantic, our Malcolm. Patrick says he'll never make it in business. Too interested in the idea of falling to want to climb.' She sighed. 'You know, I don't think you have any idea how much you've been scaring people these past few months. I've been thinking that maybe you were losing it.'

Losing it. Was that what was happening here? From across the room she saw Sally, as if at the wrong end of a telescope, too tiny to be taken seriously. Careful where you step, she thought. You could crush her underfoot. She watched her grow until she was the right size again. Say something. She's waiting. 'Sorry, Sally. I didn't mean to freak you. Don't worry. I'm going to be OK.'

She looked at her. 'But you won't tell me any more than that?'

She tried to imagine unfolding it in front of her like some gothic folk-tale; poltergeists, priests, intruders, rape, revenge. Doing what other people wouldn't even dare to dream. Is that how she'd got here? By not noticing every time she crossed the point of no return? 'Sally, I can't. Maybe later.'

'OK.' She put down her tea cup. 'So, do I gather from this that you're not coming to us tomorrow?'

'Tomorrow?'

'Yes, Christmas, remember? You know, babies without fucking, birth without pain. That one. I did ask, you know. Left four, maybe five messages on the machine.'

'Sorry, Sal.' She wondered, should she lie? Tell her some story about being already committed; going to the country to spend it with friends of her mother? Jake and Mirka. Foreign couple, but lovely. Lively. Always up for a good time. 'Sorry.'

'Not even for a drink tonight?'

She shook her head.

She paused. 'Patrick was thinking of inviting Tom.'

'Well, now he can.'

'Yes. Should I give him any message?'

'Tell him I'm pleased he's got a lover. It's all right, you don't have to look surprised. I heard her in the background when I called a couple of weeks ago. Is she nice?'

Sally paused. 'She's all right.'

'What does she do?'

'Er – she's a post-graduate student, I think.'

Of course. Why travel when you can harvest them in your back garden? So, Sally and Patrick had been seeing them. Would they become his friends after all? It happened. Couple split, couples reform, not so much about loyalty as convenience and shared life-styles. Anyway, Sally had always had the hots for Tom, in the friendliest possible way. So had a number of women. He was that kind of man, inviting from the sidelines. A shabby thought struck her.

'How long has it been going on between them, Sally?'

She gave a shrug. For all her apparent flamboyance Sally had never been good at lying.

'I see. That long.'

'Listen, Eliza—'

'It's all right. You don't have to feel disloyal. It's over. I've let him go. Chaise-longue and all. Anyway, I can't really blame him. I was pretty horrible to live with those last few months. Give him my regards when you see him. And wish him bon voyage.'

'And what should I tell him if he asks about you?'

'Tell him I'm in great shape.'

Sally looked at her for a moment, then shook her head. 'No. If it's all right with you I'll tell him the truth. Which is that I have no idea how you are, but you're certainly different. And maybe that's as good as . . .'

She picked up her bag. 'Oh, I almost forgot. Here—' She dug something out. 'Your Christmas present.' She made a face. 'I knew somehow you wouldn't be coming to us.'

It was long and thin and soft, tastefully wrapped in bronze paper with a bright yellow label. Sally didn't need to read women's magazines. She did it all naturally. 'It has magic properties. All you have to do is wear it with the right person.' She got up and pulled on her coat. The material swooped around her, luxurious in its intense blackness.

This time when Sally put out her arms she came into them. They stood for a moment, hugging each other.

'Thank you, Sal,' she said as she broke free. 'I'll call you.'

'You better. Or you'll find yourself opening the door to a couple of policemen.'

Little do you know, she thought. Little do you know.

She didn't notice it until she had closed the door. Yet it must have been there when she and Sally came in or whoever it was would have rung. Or would they? It was a square white envelope with her name on it. Handwritten. When she picked it up she saw that her hand was shaking. She checked the writing: small, but fluid, a pen – not a biro. She ripped it open as she went to the dustbin to check. Is that how he would write? So tidy, so sane? What could he possibly want to say in reply? No, it couldn't be a reply. Her envelope was still there.

A Christmas card dropped from the envelope onto the snow; a black and white ink drawing of a church with a radiant coloured star above it. She picked it up. The Messiah comes to Holloway. When you can't have sex, there is always religion. Inside, the message was followed by Catherine Baker's pretty little script:

'We light the candles tonight. The service starts at midnight, and tomorrow we do a family service at ten with a glass of mulled wine at the vicarage afterwards. Do come. All spirits welcome. Hope things are better. Call if you need help. Any time, remember.'

Christmas. The time of goodwill to all men. All except one, that is.

twenty-four

The trouble with visitors is they play havoc with your schedule. Nevertheless it felt invigorating, suddenly having so much to do. She walked through the house seeing it all afresh through Sally's eyes; the cup stains, the unhoovered carpets, the neglect and the dirt. It wouldn't do to give the wrong impression.

It took her the best part of two hours to turn the place around. There was something in the physical effort – the scrubbing, the hoovering and the polishing – that made her feel better. The sweat of housework; in a world where everything else was breaking down the pleasure of imposed domestic order seemed all the sweeter.

There was no time to enjoy it, though. Having left Christmas so late there were a million things that had to be done. With the weather this cruel it would probably be as quick to walk as to take the car, but if she did that she wouldn't have enough hands to carry it all. She made a list, then divided it into two.

She concentrated on the hardware and electrical stuff first: two sets of fairy-lights, a packet of wood stain and one of filler. Back home in the cellar, in what had once been Tom's workshop, she found a couple of hefty screwdrivers and a wrench or two. Not enough to build anything, but sufficient to destroy.

The lock man had been thorough. She could explain away the second lock being open by saying she had mislaid the key, but the extra bolts were well screwed in and she ended up having to gouge a number of ugly crevasses in the wood to get them out. She filled the holes as best she could. They looked awful, but presumably the wood stain would help. How long would the filler take to dry? A couple of hours? She had time. She turned her attention to unnailing the cat-flap. His window was dark. Just as well. It wouldn't do for him to arrive too early.

The next trip was more festive. In the market the best trees had already gone, leaving only the over-sized or straggly ones tied to the railings. She gave it some thought – it was like picking the runt of the litter, offering it a good home; a dog is forever but a tree is only for Christmas so make sure it's a happy one. She went for the tallest one she could carry and bargained him down so she still had enough money for flowers and a holly wreath. 'And a very merry Christmas to you, darling,' he said as he pocketed her thirty quid.

She propped the tree against the phone booth while she made the call. Her number rang three times, then the answering machine clicked on. Quietly she replaced the receiver. Better to be safe than sorry.

At home she set up the tree in the living room next to the window, ramming it into a bucket and sup-porting it with a set of broken bricks. The central heating loosed the sap and the sweet smell of death brought in a memory rush; hot-house family stuff, forced gaiety and too many glasses of sherry. But this was not an occasion for self-pity. It had been so long since she had dressed a tree she hadn't been sure of how many decorations to buy, but the lights and the shredded strings of silver looked good and if you favoured the side that was facing the window it would seem generous enough from the street. She fixed the wreath to the front door using the garden twine (nice touch, she thought), then stood back to admire the view. Very festive. Welcoming, even. She checked the dustbin. It was still there, the edges of the black bag folded back around it like fat, misshapen petals. He would come, like a bee to the pollen. How could he not? When the rest of the world was curled up in the bosom of their families he would be on the look-out for the lonely ones to pick off. Someone to share the misery. And he already knew how much she cared.

In the kitchen the wood filler was still tacky. She sanded it down as best she could, then applied the stain. She thought of taking down the sheet and opening up the kitchen doors to help it dry, another signal of welcome in a frozen world, but timing was everything and she still had things to do. She started to unplug the computer.

It was just after four when she phoned the police. Her plump young sergeant was out on a call, but she made it sound urgent, giving the desk sergeant enough information to tickle his taste buds and make sure the right person got to hear of it. He took a number and told her that someone would contact her later. They called back in less than fifteen minutes.

As far as she could tell it was not the man she had

talked to before, but she doctored her voice anyway, just to be on the safe side. He certainly listened hard enough, though that could have been less because of what she was telling him.

'—and you say there was someone standing at your window?'

'Yes.'

'Can you describe him?'

'Not really. I mean it was dark when I came into the kitchen and as soon as I spotted him I was so scared I turned on the light and he immediately ran away.'

'Where did he go?'

'I don't know. He disappeared into the darkness at the end of the garden. The wall isn't that high and from there, well, from there he could have gone anywhere.'

'But you don't know where?'

'Well, actually I did see a couple of lights go on across the way a few moments later, but I can't tell you exactly which windows. And they might not have been him. I mean it could have been coincidence.'

He paused and she heard a scraping of paper. 'And you live in . . . Dalmead Road, yes?'

'Yes.'

'So what would be the street that backs on to yours?'

'Er . . . Gosh . . . I don't know. Well, wait a minute . . . I suppose it must be the Crescent. Yes, Tavistock Crescent.'

'Right. And you say this was when?'

'Day before yesterday.'

'So before the snow?'

'Yes.' No footprints. Well, you can't have everything.

'And you've not reported this till now, is that right?'

'No. I mean, I did tell the other man – the other officer

- when I called about the things that I thought had been happening in my kitchen. But I hadn't seen anyone then and, well, to be honest I don't think he was all that impressed by what I said.'

'And now you think they're connected?'

'Yes,' she said, quietly but firmly. 'Yes I do.'

'Well, we do get a lot of calls. But I'm certain the officer you spoke to would have treated the matter seriously. I'll make sure I see his report.'

There was a pause. How tasty did she have to make it before they bit? They weren't there yet, obviously. I'm getting good at tempting men, she thought. Just flash them a little more flesh. 'Er - there is one other thing.'

'Yes?'

'I mean it's what made me decide to call you. When I woke up this morning I discovered there was a message on my answering machine. I think it's from him.'

'What makes you think that?'

'Well, it's sort of threatening.'

'What does it say?'

'That's the point. I didn't really understand it. But it's something about cutting me up . . .'

There was a fraction of a pause. 'You've still got the tape?'

'Oh yes, yes. It's still on the machine.'

You could almost see the saliva drooling from his chin. 'OK. We'll be over to see you within the hour, Miss . . . er . . . Skvorecky. Just sit tight and don't worry.'

'Thank you, officer. I'm very grateful.'

With the house ready she started putting herself in

order. She showered, washed and conditioned her hair
and chose some clean clothes; nothing fancy, but nice,
a pair of good trousers and a polo-neck sweater. She
played around with a little jewellery, but in the end
decided to go plain. She mascaraed her eyes (they
looked wider that way), and applied a small amount of
lipstick, most of which she sucked off again because it
looked too bright. She studied the final product in the
mirror. The wild woman had reformed, though there
were still signs if you knew where to look. The eyes
were too glittery and the hair was a mess, but after so
long in solitary it needed more than a comb to set it to
rights. She did the best she could. She tried a little smile.
It could have been worse. The woman who grinned
back at her from the mirror was attractive enough to
be targeted, while plain enough not to have provoked.
This must be like dressing for a rape case, she thought;
working out whether you were going to be treated like
the victim or the accused.

In the kitchen she had just had time to stick the
flowers in a vase when the doorbell rang. She gave the
place one last look. With the exception of the sheet
across the window it looked good. Homely, without
being flashy. She shoved one of Tom's leftover CDs in
the machine and turned it on. The first famous bars of a
mournful cello concerto seeped into the room. It must
have been a substandard performance for Tom to have
left it, but then a substandard ear like her own wouldn't
be able to tell.

Neither of them remarked on it either. They were
probably the same two guys she had seen at his house,
but close up she couldn't be sure. Her powers of
observation had been concentrated for too long on one

man: all the rest were fading and smudging at the edges. She tried to read their faces. One appeared tough, the other just tired. Too many late nights. The fraud squad must be easier on the sleep patterns. They took it all in, though; the clothes, the music, the flowers, the lack of dust, and the sheet nailed across the kitchen window.

They accepted tea, but she got the impression that was done more because they wanted to watch her than to drink it. As she was doing her domestic stuff one made small talk while the other stood across from him, prodding about with his eyes. With one hand he flicked the curtain aside and looked out, then appeared to spend some time studying the state of the door. As he turned back she spotted, too late, the tube of wood filler still sitting on the shelf above the CDs.

They didn't get to it for a while, though. They sat with the tea cups in front of them listening while she built up the story for them; step by step, fact by fact, using the perfect stack of CDs that had once graced the kitchen table as a model. How innocent that all felt now, not worth getting excited about really. But since that was where it had all started they were keen to get it right.

'So what you were saying is that you thought someone had been in here.'

'Well, that's what it looked like, yes.'

'But just in here. Not anywhere else?'

'No.' She left a pause. 'But then if I'm out of the house, or at night, I lock the inner kitchen door, for extra protection. So if someone *had* got in here, they wouldn't have been able to get out into the rest of the house. Not without breaking through the lock. And, of course, if I were upstairs I'd hear that.'

'And did you tell the sergeant that?'

'Er ... To be honest I don't quite remember. I don't think our meeting went that well. As I said on the phone, I got the impression he didn't really believe me.' She smiled. 'But then I'm not surprised. I don't think I quite believed myself. After he left and I came down the next morning to find the table laid and cat pellets all over the floor I got so paranoid I even thought it might be some kind of poltergeist. Which is when I went to my local vicar.'

Well, if she didn't tell them, they might find out some other way.

'The vicar. And what's her name?' Just for the record, of course.

'Catherine Baker. I have a phone number if you want. She was very nice, but of course she couldn't help. I mean she couldn't explain it any more than I could.'

'But now you think you can explain it better.'

She looked up at them. 'Yes,' she said. 'I think I can.'

And she took them over to the French windows.

First she told them, then, when she saw the disbelief on their faces, she showed them, slipping out into the freezing night and getting them to lock the door behind her, while she hooked a coat hanger in and up through the cat-flap and fiddled with the lock until, at last, the handle lifted. It was a tricky moment. Not at all the kind of thing she wanted her admirer to see, at least not quite yet. But nobody gets anywhere in this life unless they are willing to take chances. She understood that now.

She opened the door and came in shivering. You

could see that, while on one level they were impressed, on another they couldn't get their attention away from the bodged wood stains and the tube of filler on the shelf.

'I only worked it out this morning,' she said quickly. 'I got so scared when I realised how he'd done it that I put up the sheet and went out and bought some bolts to try and bolt the door and the cat-flap up, but I couldn't get them in properly.' She gave a wry smile. 'I'm afraid I made a right mess of it.'

The tired one gave her a sympathetic nod back. Girls who don't know what to do with boys' tools. Their world must be full of them. 'And you think that's what he was doing, when you saw him outside?'

'I don't know. But he did seem to have something in his hand. Although . . .' She hesitated.

'Yes?'

'Although it looked heavier than a piece of wire or pipe. It looked more like . . . well, more like a hammer,' she said, and this time she allowed herself to sound frightened.

The word carried its own impact. They didn't even bother to look at each other to register it, but then unlike all the TV cop partnerships she'd ever seen, they didn't seem to need to. What would Jake make of their technique? she thought.

'Let's move on to the tape,' said the tough one very gently. The tired one was wide awake.

She took them out to the hall and played it to them. She hadn't heard his voice since last night. She discovered she didn't need to fake the shiver.

'Hello, J1009 CYR. Women drivers. They're all the same. Don't have a clue about whose right of way it is.

Well, I just want you to know that if you *ever* try and cut me up again, I'll do the same back to you. Or is that what you were after? Snowing cats and dogs, wouldn't you say? Sleep well.'

They stopped, then played it back again. And again. They seemed to like hearing the sound of his voice, as if it was something they had been waiting for.

'When did you say you got this message?'

'Well, I didn't hear it until this morning. But it must have come through last night.'

'You were out?'

'Yes, but only briefly. I had finished some work that I urgently needed to get somewhere, so I took the letter to the nearest main post office to catch the early post. It was in the middle of that blizzard so, of course, I went in the car.'

'And that's your car number on the tape?'

'Yes, it is.'

'But you don't remember any incident?'

'No. Nothing at all.' She paused. 'But maybe when he heard it was a machine, he needed to be careful what he said.' She gave an apologetic little shrug, as if she had just said something particularly stupid. They didn't acknowledge it one way or the other.

'Why didn't you call us this morning, when you first heard this?'

She sighed. 'Well, I didn't know what you'd say. I mean in one way it doesn't actually sound that threatening. Not unless you put it with all the other stuff. I dunno...' She hesitated. 'I suppose there must be dozens of women who live alone and can't sleep properly at night now for imagining things. I mean you haven't caught him yet, have you?'

They didn't answer. 'We'd like to take the tape away, if that's all right with you.'

She nodded, snapping it out of the machine and handing it to them. There was a small silence. They can't leave it there, she thought. My God, what would it be like if I really was telling the truth?

'There is something else,' she said quietly.

'What?'

'He rang me again.'

'When?'

'Just before I called you this afternoon. It must have been around three, four o'clock. I don't remember the exact time. But I was here, so I didn't get a chance to put it onto the machine.'

'And what did he say?'

She swallowed, the distress now very clear on her face. 'Er ... He said three words, that's all. Just three words. "See you soon."' She paused. 'I think he was using a call box.'

They exchanged a glance and she was grateful she had been so careful. Even if they could track down the number, a call box on the Holloway Road would tell them nothing. Someone careful enough not to use his own phone would probably also be careful enough to wear gloves. Though it might still be worth checking. Thank God for the cold. It wasn't something she would have thought about otherwise.

'Can you get him?' she said.

The tired one frowned, as if he hadn't quite heard the question. He gave a sigh. 'Tell me, Elizabeth, are you going away for Christmas?'

So they were on first-name terms now. Why not? They were obviously going to get even more intimate.

'No. No. I . . . I've got nowhere to go. My parents are both
dead and I've got this work that has to be finished, so I
was going to stay and do that. I mean that's why I called
you. I suddenly realised what it was going to be like
here over the next few days. Most of the street is going
away . . .' She trailed off. There was a pause. 'I've got
friends, though. If you thought I should go to them I
could do that.'

At last they exchanged a glance. This time they
seemed to be deciding which one should finish the
race. The tough one got the job. But then don't they
always?

'Well, yes, you could do that. Though I have to say
that given what you've told us there'd be no guarantee
that something might not happen when you got back.'

'What else can I do?' And her voice sounded
decidedly shaky.

He left a beat of a pause. Maybe at the really tense
moments everything seems like TV drama anyway.
'You could stay here and let us protect you.' And he
kept on looking at her as the impact of what he had
said sank in.

She counted to sixty. When that didn't feel long
enough she counted on to one hundred. Then she said
quietly, 'If I do that, can you promise me you'll get to
him before he gets to me?'

'You have our word.' He smiled. 'That's our job.'.

Twenty minutes later she walked with them to the
front gate. It was night again and the streetlights were
throwing a dirty sodium glare on the ruined snow. In
the dustbin the black bag had crisps packets and someone's discarded hamburger wrapper littering the top.

The package was gone. She smiled to herself.

Inside the house the telephone was ringing. The text had not included an RSVP. If he had something to say, did she want to hear it? Maybe he needed more encouragement. She picked up the receiver. 'Hello?'

The man on the other end of the line was kind but efficient. But then it was after five on Christmas Eve and no one likes to be left with a dead animal on their hands over the holidays.

'I'm sorry to break it to you like this. I tried to get you earlier but your phone was engaged.'

'But I thought you said there was no—'

'I said I didn't *think* there was any internal damage. But it's always very hard to tell. As soon as we realised it was a pulmonary oedema we drained her chest and gave her steroids for the shock, but cats can react very badly to shock. In the end it was just too much for her and her heart stopped beating. I'm sorry.'

'I see.' Although she didn't. Didn't see and didn't feel. The silence grew. You have to say something to him, she thought. 'Was she in pain?'

'No. There would have been no pain. I'm sure of that. She died very peacefully.'

He made her sound like a Victorian grandmother, sliding away amidst bed silks and loving relatives. And I didn't even say goodbye, she thought.

Millie, the bird killer, the warm weight at the end of the bed, the deep-throated purr, the garden adventurer who could no longer go out for fear of the blackness in the shadows. You should have fought back, girl, I told you. You should have laid your own traps, like I've laid mine.

On the other end of the line his sympathy was

stretched by the hands of the clock.

'Listen, I'm sorry but I have to ask. What would you like us to do with the body? We could dispose of it here, or if you want we could keep it till after the holidays. I'm just about to close up the surgery now.'

Now? She couldn't possibly go now. The locks were off the doors and there were still things she had to do. Millie would forgive her. 'Er, thank you. I'll pick her up in a few days.'

'The twenty-eighth. We open again for a morning surgery. And listen, if you really think that she was hurt by someone then you ought to report him. Chances are if he's done this once he will do it again.'

In the kitchen, she picked up Millie's bowl, washed it, then filled it anew with cat pellets. Downstairs, from the box where she kept the gardening implements, she extracted a tin of weed killer. She poured a hefty slug of it into the bowl. The dried food would absorb it quickly, pumping up the little pellets till they were juicy and moist. She laid the bowl carefully next to the water on Millie's tray. Every good house offers its visitors refreshments at Christmas.

Out through the cat-flap she threw a handful of un-doctored pellets onto the frozen snow. They scattered like brown dice over a white carpet. Luck be a lady tonight.

From the cellar she brought the step ladder and carefully unnailed the sheet/curtain from the window, then switched on the patio lights. The frozen snow glowed and sparkled under its beam. She lifted up the lock and opened the doors onto the garden.

A wall of freezing air hit her; so cold it hurt to

breathe. She thought how long it had been since the summer and the music of possibilities. She exchanged Dvořák for a Bob Seger compilation bought in that first autumn raid on the New York record store. Weird things, compilations; mixing up emotional memories into a new order, disconcerting to listen to until you had learned their alternative rhythm. But she knew exactly what she was looking for. She had always had time for Bob Seger, the kind of old rock'n'roller who was not afraid to show how he felt ... or sing what he wanted. His voice cruised out into the snowy darkness, making whoopee with a badlands love song by Frankie Miller ...

> '*I'm looking for a woman*
> *About five foot six,*
> *Who ain't into glamour*
> *She's just into kicks.*
> *Just a sweet fashion lady,*
> *Stepping dynamite*
> *Who's gonna take me for granted*
> *In the heat of the night.*'

She stood in the doorway and sang along with the words, her breath sending smoke signals out into the night. Not exactly Donne or Yeats. But it said what had to be said.

> '*Come on baby, don't run away.*
> *Look here in my face,*
> *Be it night or day.*
> *I ain't got no money,*
> *But I sure got a whole load of love.*'

Across the gardens a light shone like the Christmas star from one particular first-floor window. Was it her imagination or was that his silhouette against the frame?

twenty-five

They came just before eight o'clock, and, given that it was Christmas Eve and they would have had better things to do with their time, they were impressively enthusiastic. But then to be on duty the night you caught the Holloway Hammer would be the stuff that reputations were made of.

She had been waiting for them, sitting by the front window in the glow of the tree lights, watching the street, the inner kitchen door firmly locked from the inside, the key in her pocket. She saw them drive past, then go a little further so their unmarked car wouldn't stand out on the street. As they got out they checked to see that no one was watching. This time she scored a set rather than a pair: the weary one of the two, with a woman, both dressed casually, she in jeans and a featherdown jacket, he in suit trousers with a sweater and an anorak. A man and a woman. Would they sleep in separate dorms? Would they sleep at all?

As they crossed the road the woman slipped slightly on the ice and he put out a hand to support her as she righted herself. She was younger than he was, not unattractive, though a little solidly built. Were they

lovers? Friends? Compatriots in crime? Or was it like the
movies; professional coolness masking the thinly veiled
dynamic of sexual politics, women muscling in on what
men saw as their territory? Presumably in a situation
like this there had to be a woman – no doubt there was
some regulation about it – in case they didn't get to her
in time and someone was needed to mop up the distress.

Not this time. Not this night. Tonight she could smell
victory. Promotion for all.

As social challenges go, having two police officers
staying the night on Christmas Eve was tougher than
most. Luckily, all three of them seemed cut from
similar cloth; quiet, more interested in work than
chatter. There was one thing they did want to talk
about though: him. She rationed her answers, feeling
almost jealous of their interest. Mistaking her reticence
for fear they didn't push it, but concentrated instead on
the house, checking all the windows and the locks,
anticipating his movements, planning his entry. They
had a special place in their heart for the kitchen. Aware
of the windows on the other side of the gardens, they
were careful, turning the light off before they went in
so that he couldn't see them. They checked the lock
and the cat-flap, then the man – Detective Inspector
McCormick but she could call him David – moved
upstairs, while the woman, Veronica (she had
forgotten her second name as soon as she was told it),
stayed behind to help her make the tea. The talk was so
small it hardly registered, though she did get around to
asking about the cat. She told her that Millie was a
wanderer; sometimes you saw her, sometimes you
didn't. So, did that explain the pellets scattered in the
garden?

'An incentive to find her way home. Sometimes she needs it.'

But it had been more of a cat lover's question than a professional enquiry and the chat petered out quickly afterwards.

Along with the tea she heated up some mince pies and they ate them in the living room, sitting away from the windows. She glanced around the place, trying to see it through their eyes; the gap where the chaise-longue had been, the one solitary present under the tree. It looked rather sad. But it was none of their business, her life. They were just there to save it.

Eight o'clock turned to nine. They made it clear that the best thing would be if she could act normally, do whatever she would have done at this time of night. But the word normal seemed to have gone from her vocabulary. She spent some time upstairs sorting out her study, moving bits of paper from one side of the desk to the other, but the walls throbbed with the leftover ketchup stains and the lights across the gardens burned brighter than any she could put on.

When she couldn't think of anything else to do, she went downstairs to make herself a hot drink. It was after ten and they had already taken up their positions: the man in the back room (nearest to the kitchen), the woman in the front, lights off, everything silent. Their knowledge of previous cases would no doubt have told them what time he went stalking, alerted them to any kind of pattern. She was aware of the intense irony of the situation. There they were with their theories and reports and suspicions, all obviously considered too confidential to disclose to a potential victim. There she was, not only knowing the man they were searching for, but having had him in her bed, even having written him love letters.

It made her realise that at some point she would have to tell them about the book extracts. Not yet, though. Until they found them in his flat how could she know that he'd been collecting them? No reason for her to know who was going through her rubbish.

It also meant she would have to send Charles a version of that final sex scene, to prove its authenticity. Poor Charlie. He'd think she'd gone mad, unless she braved it out and pretended that it was faithful to the original. After all, he wanted a best-seller, so why be squeamish about how he got it? Maybe she'd find herself writing bodice rippers after this, becoming rich and famous, until, at last, she wrote a book about a woman persecuted by a stalker...

She offered them more tea but they turned it down. They were working now and needed to be alone. As she cleared up the kitchen she could feel them in their separate rooms, getting ready for the night. The tension of their presence filled the bottom floor of the house, like a low mist hovering over a landscape.

She made herself a drink and went out of the kitchen, deliberately leaving the door ajar behind her. She looked back into the darkness. Come on, she thought, something for everyone: food and entertainment. Come and get it.

'I'm going to bed now.' She put her head round the back door to where the man was sitting in the shadows. 'I've left on the central heating. It makes the odd noise, creaking, that kind of thing. Just in case you think...' She trailed off.

'Thanks,' he said quietly. 'Don't worry. Everything's going to be all right.'

'Yes.'

Next door Veronica was tucked in an armchair behind the door, sitting very still, hands resting in her lap, like someone who practised yoga.

They exchanged good nights, but she couldn't quite leave it there. She sat herself on the edge of the sofa. After a while she said, 'I don't know if I'll sleep.'

The policewoman nodded sympathetically. 'Have you got anything you can take?'

She shook her head. She looked over at the tree, all bright lights and trimmings. 'It's a weird way to spend Christmas Eve, eh?'

The woman smiled. 'I can think of nicer.'

'But not as exciting, I bet.' She hesitated. 'Do you get frightened?'

'Not really. In this kind of case the waiting is more boring than frightening.'

'And what if something happens?'

'If something happens then you're too busy to be scared.'

'Yes,' she said, thinking back to a man at the bottom of her bed. 'I imagine that's true. Well, let's hope you get busy tonight.'

The woman seemed to study her in the darkness. 'Don't worry,' she said quietly. 'He won't get anywhere near you. We'll see to that.'

She sounded so determined, as if there was something personal in it for her. Had she interviewed some of the other women? Seen what he could do? She was torn between wanting to know everything and nothing. 'Just in case I miss it all, have fun.'

Upstairs she ran a hot bath, but the idea of lying there naked made her feel too vulnerable and she let the water run away without getting in. In the bedroom she looked out over the gardens and the blaze of windows lit up in the freezing night. Would this view ever be ordinary again? In next door's back garden a squat figure rose up from the middle of an icy lawn, battered hat perched on a snowball-sized head, a scarf round its thick neck and what must be a carrot for a nose; a modern snowman trying to look like an illustration from a children's book. Nobody knows how to do these things for real any more, she thought. We're always just copying something we thought we once knew, even if it never really existed.

She moved over to the door and turned on the light, leaving the curtains open, then came back into the room and started undressing. She imagined her silhouette in the window-frame seen through the lens of a peeping tom, binocular eyes greedy for snapshot lust; a glimpse of inner thigh as the stockings roll off (tights had wreaked havoc with the elegance of fantasy), the line of the breasts as the woman lifts the T-shirt over her head. It was always a good moment, when the top covers the head. Less problem with personality that way. She thought all this as she pulled off her sweater, stepped out of her trousers and undid her bra, her lack of speed the only concession to a possible voyeur. Would he be watching? If he'd read the letter he'd be undressing her anyway, in his head if not through his eyes. She shivered as she pulled on a nightgown.

When would he come? Did he need her to be asleep? Maybe it didn't work unless you caught them unawares, wrenched them out of dreams to face the nightmare. Well, tough luck. This time he wouldn't even get up the stairs.

She got into bed, the sheets cold to the touch. She remembered her blood, and the streaks of his semen running down her legs. She saw his face again as he turned and walked out, like a sullen child. What if he didn't come back? What if the very act of her wanting him made him resist? Or, even worse, made him smell a trap? Under her pillow she fingered the plastic bag, feeling the shape of the hammer through the covering. She had put it there before the police arrived, protection in case he saw her invitation as an excuse to turn up without a weapon. This way she had both weapon and fingerprints. At some point she would need to plant it downstairs or outside. But not until the coat hanger went through the cat-flap and started to scrape at the lock. Would she be able to hear so particular a noise from up here? Why not? She had heard it enough times in her head since.

Not yet though. The digital clock by her bed clicked to 22.56. Christmas Eve. She thought of Catherine Baker, standing by the altar, newly painted walls, reconstructed crib and a hundred candles flickering in homage to a more medieval festival.

On the radio she cruised through Christmas wallpaper, the Beatles and jazz to what sounded like Radio 3: a man with rounded vowels was talking in church, telling of times when carols were pagan dances, too dangerous for institutionalised religion, but too powerful to leave outside. So the early Church had set about absorbing them, prettying them up, stilling the feet, taming the spirit. But it would still have been bleak midwinter. How did you keep warm if you couldn't dance?

She imagined Catherine Baker throwing off her dog collar and gyrating over the altar to the sound of high-energy carols. Then watched as a group of men smashed down the doors outside and came rushing in, pinning her to the altar steps, forcing her cassock up above her waist: the images of exploitation, as copycat and stultifying to the imagination as the carrot for the snowman's nose.

The commentator stopped talking and the choir began, a multitude of the heavenly host praising God in the highest of keys. Choir boys; nothing like that last sweetness before the testosterone kicks in. But you can't keep them like that for ever. No juice. Not fair. Everybody needs juice.

She lay and listened in the darkness; the readings told of censers and journeys and stable midwifery. Was the birth as immaculate as the conception? Did the cows eat the placenta and lick up the blood, clean up the babe before the swaddling clothes went on, large rough tongues over slimy little limbs? It was not the kind of detail that made it into any gospel. The choir hustled in the shepherds, the Wise Men and the happy ending. The announcer wished everybody a merry Christmas.

Midnight.

You could almost feel the world sigh as the clock moved.

She turned off the radio and stayed inside the silence. This time last year she and Tom had been lying in a four-poster bed in a fancy hotel in northern France, their bodies curled as far away from each other as it was possible to get. They had come on a morning ferry, winter winds across black seas, sipping brandy to keep their stomachs level. Off the boat they had driven for two and a half hours down the valley to a picturesque little market town, recommended in all the guides, with a ruined fortress, and streets of formal shuttered houses with their echoes of Madame-Bovary-type frustration. It was too beautiful a place to be unhappy in and they had started drinking early to blot out the pain; crisp white wines to go with winter oysters, cold and briny like the North Sea, followed by a three-course dinner with selected local reds – Tom knew his wines – and, at the end, a selection of different, richer brandies. The more they drank the less they had to talk to each other. It was a method of non-communication perfected over the last months.

Upstairs he had fallen asleep almost immediately, snoring as he often did after too much booze. If the hotel hadn't been full she would have taken another room just to get away from him. As it was she had lain awake for hours trying to trace the line of how they had got to this; where it had all gone, the pleasure and the passion. She had made a vow to herself that night. Whatever happens, by this time next year she would be alone. And however bad it was, it would not be as bad as this.

Of all the many roads she had imagined leading away from Tom, this one had not been on the map. In the last year she had had two men; one she had frightened, the other had frightened her, one she had cried with, the other had made cry. Neither had really known the meaning of sexual pleasure. I want a lover, she thought. A man who isn't scared of me or of himself, someone who will put his fingers up inside me and find my heart. What was it her gay friend Maurice had once said to her? That when you were fist-fucked you could almost imagine his hand reaching up through your body and grabbing at your heart. Love and pain. Maybe they were never meant to be separated. Maybe romance was like icing on the cake, too sweet to have any real taste.

She pulled herself up against the pillows and looked out onto the empty room. She saw him again sitting at the end of the bed, his body shaking with tension. Did you really think you could just walk in here and fuck me? she thought. That I was your right, like the woman in the pub, or the one at the bus stop? Well, now it's your turn to find out how it feels to be so frightened.

She closed her eyes, tired of the sight of his wiry body and lopsided smile. She tried to think of something else. Then she tried to think of nothing. She tried to sleep. She tried to stay awake. Still no sound of entry.

It must have been sometime after three when she heard the movement from below, a sort of scraping metallic noise, over so fast that she thought she might have imagined it. Her body had heard it too, though; a flush of terror swept through her, hot and cold at the same time. She slid the plastic bag from under the pillow, got out of bed and glided silently to the top of the stairs. Nobody had given her any instructions as to what to do if it happened. But if he was there she was going to see him. She waited. Then after about a minute or so she heard something else, a series of footfalls with the crack of a floorboard underneath.

The whole house seemed to jump to attention at the sound.

She squatted down and gazed between the banisters. On the landing, at the top of the stairs which led down to the kitchen, a figure was flattened against the wall, more a shadow than a man. In the doorway to the living room Veronica was standing, frozen-frame.

The policewoman looked up and saw her on the stairs. She gave a quick flick of the hand to keep her away, but at that instant her partner went for the door and Veronica was across the hall and behind him within seconds.

Elizabeth heard the crack as the kitchen door smashed open against the wall, presumably under the force of his foot, and the light went on. She waited for the shouts. But they didn't come. Nothing. Then she heard the metallic snap of the cat-flap and a harsh little laugh. The light went off again. She stashed the plastic bag hurriedly in the bathroom at the top of the stairs and tiptoed downstairs.

They were already back up on the landing.

'What happened?'

He snapped his head up towards her, clearly pissed off to see her there.

'Nothing. Go back to bed.'

'What happened?'

Veronica shrugged slightly. 'I think your cat came home.' She paused. 'I'm afraid it didn't get a chance to eat much. We scared it out again.'

The RSPCA would give them a medal. Never mind, she thought. The tom would come back. Stomach over cock. He was easy to tempt.

She felt suddenly rather faint and in need of a drink.

She took a few steps down the stairs.

'Stay up there,' he said firmly.

'I need some water.'

'Get it from the bathroom.'

'I haven't got a glass.'

'Then use the tooth mug.'

'It'd be better if he didn't see any lights on,' Veronica said, trying to soften his edge. 'I doubt very much he'll come if he thinks you're still awake.'

In which case you two dummies just comprehensively scared him off by turning on the light in the kitchen, she thought, but didn't say. 'All right.'

The man turned on his heel and went back into his room. Interesting how even professionals can be undermined. It must be so embarrassing, using up all your adrenaline and style on empty air.

'Maybe he won't come now. Maybe it's too cold for him,' she said to Veronica.

But as she did so she saw him standing in the snow, watching the girl at the bus stop. No, he wasn't afraid of the weather. The itch he had to scratch was too powerful for that.

'There's still time,' she replied. 'Why don't you try and get some sleep?'

Upstairs, she didn't even bother to try. Three turned to four. The night grew slower and colder. Around five she heard someone climb the stairs and go into the loo. She wasn't even mildly frightened. She had known for some time by then that he wasn't coming.

What happened? she thought. Did I make it too obvious? Was Mirka's lust too much of a giveaway? Perhaps men like that can't handle women taking the initiative or showing sexual desire. She got up and went to the window. Across the way everything was black night, save for the odd set of Christmas tree fairy-lights acting as homing devices for Santa's reindeer.

God, I'm so tired of this view, she thought, again. I want it out of head. It and you. Out of my head and out of my life. I want it finished. Now.

But it wouldn't be now. She knew that.

The morning came in cold and sluggish. She waited until it was beginning to get light, then pulled on a skirt and sweater and went downstairs. This time they didn't try to send her up again. They both looked tired. Tired and subdued. She made them tea. In the kitchen the cat bowl was full, though the garden pellets had gone. She put on the light and picked out some music. Christmas Day. More a question of what you didn't want to hear. She went for Sting, early hits. Christmas morning with the Police. Would they get the reference?

She brought the tray into the living room, tea and buttered toast. Veronica played Mum. 'Did you sleep at all?' she asked her.

Elizabeth shook her head.

'Well, you can catch up today. He won't come now.'

'No.'

On the sofa the inspector said nothing. He was looking at her strangely. Was this bruised pride, or wasted time? she thought. Isn't this what police work is meant to be; slow, careful, with small rewards? Not like the movies. They ought to be used to it. Or maybe it was more serious than that. Maybe he was wondering whether they should have been there at all. What must that first report by that young sergeant have said? Unstable young woman, possibly seeking attention? Listen, she wanted to say. I didn't make up that tape.

Neither did I put those fingerprints on the hammer. But then he wouldn't know about those. Maybe she should 'discover' it in the bushes out in the garden. That would give them something to think about.

He was stirring his tea when his radio spluttered into action. He grabbed it out of his pocket and put it to his ear. He said 'yep' a couple of times, then, glancing across at Veronica, got up and went out. Her eyes followed him. He went into the back room and closed the door. For a while they sat there in silence.

'Will you have the rest of the day off?' she said, mainly because she couldn't bear the sound of the silence.

'After we've filed a report, yes.'

'What will you do?'

But she never got an answer because as McCormick came back into the room Veronica stood up immediately, reading the urgency in his face.

'I need a word,' he muttered.

'What's happened?' Elizabeth asked quietly.

He scowled, and it was clear he didn't want to tell her. Veronica raised her eyebrows slightly. They had some kind of conversation without talking.

'What's happened?' she said again.

'There's been an incident,' he said at last.

'An incident? Where?'

'In a house in St John's Way.'

St John's Way. Four streets along the other side of Holloway Road. An easy journey from Tavistock Crescent.

'Was it him?'

'I just need to talk to Inspector Peters for—'

'Was it him?' she said, this time much louder than she

intended. So loud that they all registered the panic. 'Please?'

He sighed impatiently. 'We don't know yet.'

Which meant they did.

'Is the woman all right?'

'I can't tell you any more than that.'

He turned on his heel and Veronica followed him out of the room. They were only gone for a moment or two. She had to put down her cup, her hand was shaking so much.

When they came back in he had on his coat.

'Do you have anybody you could invite to come over and be with you? A friend maybe? Or someone whose house you could go to?' She stared at him, not speaking. 'Inspector Peters could stay with you till they arrive. There's nothing to worry about. You're completely safe. But you might feel better to have someone with you.'

She spent a long time trying to get her breath right, make her voice sound in control. 'I appreciate your concern,' she said at last, 'but I don't respond well to being patronised. If something has happened which involves this . . . this madman, then I think you at least owe it to me to tell me.' There was a pause in which no one spoke. She stared at him. 'He's done it again, hasn't he? He's attacked someone else.'

Another little interchange of looks. This time it was Veronica who spoke. 'It looks like that, yes.'

'And did she describe him? Was it the same man?'

The policewoman took a breath. 'No, she didn't describe anyone. But there's a report that someone saw him leaving the house; they're checking that out now. Listen, why don't you give me a phone number,

Elizabeth? I can call whoever you want for you.'

She sat staring down at the mug of tea. Its heat could no longer warm her hands. It was too weak, really. She should have let it brew for longer. She's dead, she thought. That's why they won't tell me. He's killed someone.

'Elizabeth?'

'Er . . . it's all right. I've . . . I've actually been invited to a friend's house for lunch. I can go there.'

'Good. I'll stay with you till you—'

'No. No. I'd prefer it if you didn't. Really,' she said firmly. 'If it's all right with you. I think I need to be alone.' The man frowned slightly. She smiled at him. 'It's all right. I promise. I'm fine. I'll keep all the doors and windows locked and nail up the cat-flap. Though I doubt whether it's necessary now. I mean he's hardly likely to want dessert, is he? Not so soon after a main course.'

The man stared at her for a while. He didn't like her, that much was clear, although whether that was because she'd just marred his career prospects or something more substantial was hard to tell. 'OK. If you're sure.'

She saw them to the door. 'By the way,' he said, turning to her as he walked out, 'I think you can put away that hammer now. It wouldn't have been much use against his anyway.'

'I don't know—' She started to deny it, but the flush in her face gave her away. Like being caught lying in class, the shame rising up like vomit. If he'd seen inside the bag, chances were he'd have put his stupid mitts all over it too. Idiots. All of them, idiots.

'You'll be fine,' Veronica said quietly, but it was

definitely more the social worker than the police-woman talking. 'You know, it's all right to be scared sometimes, Elizabeth. Living alone can do that to people. But you should forget it now. Go to your friends and put it all behind you. We're going to get him this time. I promise you. We know what we're doing.'

She turned to follow her partner but the sight of her leaving was suddenly too much. Before she realised she had done it Elizabeth leant out and grabbed hold of her hand. 'Number forty Tavistock Crescent,' she said quickly. 'He lives in the middle flat of forty Tavistock Crescent.' The policewoman looked at her sharply. 'I'm not making it up, I swear to you. I've been trying to work it out all night . . . which light it was that I saw go on that evening. And I'm certain now it must have come from number forty.'

From halfway down the garden path the man let out a noisy sigh. Both women heard it and knew what it meant. 'Thank you,' said Veronica carefully. 'That's really helpful. I promise you we'll check it out.'

'Do it now. He'll be back there by now.'

The policewoman pulled her hand gently out of the grip. 'Don't worry, leave it to us.'

They turned and walked down the path. She watched them get into their car. They'd be laughing about her now. Laughing or bitching.

She slammed the door after them and burst into tears.

She was still crying when she heard the cat-flap snap open. She got herself downstairs in time to see the black tom striding across the room as if the house belonged to him. But arrogance had made him slow and this time she caught him. As she grabbed him up he swiped out at her with his claws, ripping red lines across the backs of her hand. She held him down, cuffing him hard across the head. He lashed out again, the claw raking her arm this time. The pain made her loosen her grip. He smashed his way out through the cat-flap and over the wall.

Nursing her hand, she slammed the cat pellets into the bin. She was still crying. Enough. Enough revenge. It didn't work. All it did was to make you feel more soiled than them.

The scratch marks were raising blood tramlines up her arm. She went up to the bathroom and dug around in the medicine cabinet. The antiseptic hurt more than the cuts, but she quite liked the pain. At least it gave her something to cry about.

St John's Way: big Victorian houses, most of them converted into flats but with gardens generous enough to be divided off. It was a cornucopia of opportunity; he could have helped himself from a dozen French windows or spiral staircases. Did he know who he was getting or was it just pot luck? How much had he hurt her first?

It wasn't her fault. How could anyone have predicted where he'd go next? Even if the police hadn't been with her, there was no reason for them to have been in St John's Way on the off-chance of finding someone to protect. She couldn't be held responsible for the woman's death. It wasn't her fault.

She looked at her watch. 7.49. How was she going to make it through the rest of the day? She was so tired. How long was it since she had slept? Not last night. Nor the night before. When, then? She realised she couldn't remember. Veronica was right. She needed help and she needed to get out of here.

'Remember. Call me if you need me. Any time.' On this of all days surely Catherine would take her in; hear her confession and absolve her of the sins she was afraid she might have committed. Of all people she'd understand how it was possible to feel guilty for one's innocence. She wouldn't judge her. It was either her or Sally.

She decided to call as soon as she had stopped the bleeding. She cut off a length of gauze and started tying it around her lower arm. She was digging around in the cabinet looking for the pair of surgical scissors she kept there when the doorbell rang.

The sound of it stopped her in her tracks. It was Christmas Day, for Christ's sake. Nobody visits anybody this early on Christmas Day. Especially not her. Everyone knew that she and Tom usually went away. Unless it was the family next door taking pity on her single status?

She waited. But whoever they were didn't ring again. She realised she was shivering slightly. It couldn't be him. He wouldn't dare. She went down the stairs and peered through the peep-hole. No, the pavement in front of the house was empty.

She went into the front room, sneaking a look from behind the muslin curtains. Sometimes, if people stood right on the step, the fish-eye lens couldn't catch them. But the step was deserted too. She thought about opening the door to check, but decided against it.

By the telephone in the hall she had written Catherine Baker's number on a pad. She dialled and it connected. As she stood waiting for someone to answer she felt her arm throb from the claw marks and it was then that she remembered where she had left the surgical scissors. They were in the kitchen by the stove: she'd used them to try and prise out the French window bolts, the bolts that once gone left the kitchen vulnerable again to the determined visitor. Suddenly, in that instant, she understood it all.

She smashed the phone back onto the receiver and threw herself down the stairs as the opening chords of Van Morrison's 'Enlightenment' hit the air.

twenty-six

The door to the kitchen was wide open. She made a grab for the handle, but he jumped her from the side before she was barely in the room, slamming his body weight straight into hers, so that she smashed first against the wood then headlong onto the floor. She was back on her feet straight away, hurling herself across the room towards the French windows, one of which had to be open, and from where someone was bound to hear her screams over the music. She never got there. Once again he used his body like a battering ram, tackling her from behind and catapulting her forwards. This time she struck a chair on her way down, the corner of it cutting into her chest underneath her ribs. As she hit the floor he was on top of her. But it didn't stop her fighting. Oblivious of the pain she flailed underneath him, yelling at the top of her lungs, lashing out wildly in all directions. It took all his weight to pin her down.

The second her hands were immobilised he had the twine out of his pocket and was wrapping it round one of her wrists. As he bound one hand she pummelled him with the other, but the rope had been prepared in

advance and with the noose over her hand he only had
to pull to tighten it savagely. The skin burn caused her
to yelp in pain. Like the cat, she got in one final claw
attack, collecting blood and skin under her nails, but
once he had both hands bound he could pull her wher-
ever he wanted. She was still screaming as he
wrenched her across the floor.

'Shut up. Shut up,' he hissed under his breath, the
words coming out like a rush of wind. He went for the
first place he could find, lashing the other end of the
twine around the door to the oven set high up in the
wall pillar, then yanking her towards it until her arms
and half her upper body were slammed against the
metal and glass door. Still she struggled, trying to prise
herself away, half opening the door with the force of
the pull. But this time as he slammed it closed he
rammed his other hand into her stomach and the hurt
was so great that for the moment she couldn't breathe,
let alone fight back. She collapsed, her legs giving out
beneath her, her body shaking with pain and terror.
Don't pass out, she thought. Whatever you do, don't
pass out.

'Don't fucking move,' he yelled, standing over her,
his own breath coming in great wild gulps. 'What did
you take me for, eh? Did you think I was stupid? Did
you? Did you think I'd be fooled by that piece of
pornography? Think I wouldn't know it was a trap?'

Somebody's got to be hearing this, she thought.
Eight o'clock on Christmas Day. Nobody puts on Van
Morrison this early in the morning then yells over the
top of it. This has to register as more than marital
discord. All you've got is your voice now, girl. Use it.
Use it.

'Let me go!' she screamed, 'let me go!', the saliva behind the words meeting his face as missile spittle.

His answer came by wrapping his hands round her neck and pushing his thumbs into her windpipe.

The pain and the panic were instantaneous, followed by a terrible, useless clutching for breath. The crushing of the windpipe; a thing so fragile you could almost feel it break. No air, no life. I don't want to die... Please don't let me die.

'Please ...' She felt herself choking on the word, knowing that her face was swelling up, feeling the pressure building up behind her eyes until she was sure she was going to black out. How easy it is to kill someone. How quick. No room for words, even the thoughts were getting fainter, like a light bulb dimming into blackness.

Suddenly the pressure was released. She took huge desperate gulps of air, but it hurt so much she thought for a moment she was still dying. Then came the coughing. He stood back from her, watching, waiting, moving nervily from foot to foot, as if his violence had surprised even him.

'You shout one more time and I'll shove a petrol rag in your mouth and light it. OK?'

She tried to nod, but still didn't seem to be breathing properly. He growled at her, as if her weakness was making him even madder, but he moved over to the sink and poured her a cup of water. When he brought it back he had to hold it to her mouth. She took small sips, felt a waterfall of it pouring down her chin onto her clothes. Like a baby. How quickly you can take it all away from someone, make them slobber, make them scream. But I'm not going to thank you, she thought.

And the force of her defiance made her feel alive again.

She made herself look at him. His face up close was red and blotchy, as if in throttling her he had half throttled himself, with the marks of her nails running a crossword grid across one cheek. This is the man I'm going to have to fuck again before I die, she thought. Before I die. But how? More choking, or the hammer? No one had mentioned strangulation. But she couldn't see the hammer. Where would he hide it? In his jacket pocket? In the back of his jeans? Cracking skulls like egg shells. Where had she heard that phrase? Jake, Jake and his cop poetry. Except the imagery didn't leave any room for the blood. She was crying. But it didn't seem to matter now. Nothing mattered as long as she could breathe again.

'You should see yourself.' He snorted. 'You need a handkerchief. You've got snot coming out of your nose. Now you know how it feels, eh? Eh? You lied to me, you know. You said it was over. You said you wouldn't tell anyone. But you didn't keep your word, did you? So why should I have kept mine?'

She opened her mouth to speak, but he smashed his hand over it again. 'You got something to say? Or do you just want to stop breathing again?' She shook her head. He kept his hand there and the mucus from her nose trickled over his fingers. The humiliation of it made her feel like a child. 'You shouldn't have done it. Stupid bint.' He pulled his hand away and wiped it on his trousers. 'Your word, you know, "bint". I never use it. But you've made me get to like it. It's not what you usually call ladies. But then you're not one anyway. Maybe that's why I chose you in the first place, eh?'

He paused and his silence timed itself into the music: Van at his most content, a voice like a caress, making your heart bleed at its beauty.

> '*This must be what paradise is like.*
> *So quiet in here. So peaceful in here.*'

Music to die to. A love song. Third track of the album. Had it really been playing for so little time? It felt as if they had been locked into this for hours. He laughed, a tight, guttural little sound. 'You like him, eh? Me too. It's yours, remember. I've brought it back for you. Thought you might want to hear him again.'

And all the time that he spoke, he kept jiggling around on the balls of his feet, a man unable to stay still, not knowing what to do with his own body. He was like some peripheral fuck-up character from a Tarantino movie, jerky both in mind and soul, his violence almost too capricious for anyone to take much notice of it.

Nerves, she thought. Everything about you is nerves. An overload of adrenaline. No wonder he had liked Jake so much. Both of them were dying to lose it. All they needed was to be pushed hard enough. But he was the one who'd done it. Twice in one night. What had happened to the first to make him still so hungry? Had she died before he got his rocks off properly? She felt herself start to shake again.

'You scared then?'

She tried to shake her head but the movement didn't entirely work.

'Yeah. Well, you've got something to be scared of. Because you're on your own now. They've gone. And they're not coming back. Did you really think it would work? Eh? You should never have given them the wrong house. What? You think I didn't recognise your car outside? Your car, your house, your book. I've seen it all. That's what I've been doing. Getting to know you. Getting to like you. Getting to hope you like me.'

He sang the last sentence in a tuneless high voice, as if laughing at himself. 'Not as good as you eh? But then we haven't all got your talent. Was it their idea you send me that filth? No, too much of you in there, I'd say. You liked it, didn't you? Just like you liked standing up there last night taking off your clothes like some cheap stripper. I bet they didn't know about that bit. Too busy chasing cats through cat flaps in the middle of the night. None of you slept much after that, eh? Me neither. But then I was too excited by what was to come.'

There was something in what he said that didn't make sense, but she couldn't work out what it was. She was crying so hard now she couldn't see through her own tears. He stared at her for a moment, then dug something out of his pocket. She flinched, expecting a gag, but instead he wiped a piece of cloth across the end of her nose. It smelt foul. Petrol.

'Thanks,' she murmured. 'I—'

But he clamped a hand back over her mouth. 'Shhhh. Don't spoil it. You'll only lie, and then I'll want to hurt you again.'

She stood still, trying to find a way to make her eyes convince where her tongue couldn't. He seemed to hesitate, as if he wasn't sure of the next move. He growled, as much at himself as at her, then quickly pushed his hand up under her skirt, fumbling for the rim of her pants.

I should have worn jeans, she thought. It would have given me more time. Except then he'd have had to cut them off me. And you can't do that with a hammer. She glanced round the room. The knife block was on the other side, near to the washing-up bowl. Too far for either of them. The scissors would be closer, somewhere near the stove.

'I promise . . .' she said quietly as he took his hand off her mouth, her voice thin, pushing up through the bruising in her throat. 'I promise you, it wasn't all lies. I really did want to see you again.'

He gave a groan, as if the words hurt him, but at least he didn't hit her, just kept prodding about, as if he didn't know what he was looking for. Then he found it, and slammed two fingers up into her. This time there was no moisture to welcome him. This time it hurt. And not just in her cunt.

Inside her head a voice was talking. Is this what you wanted? it was saying. Pleasure like this. You wrote it, babe, you better live it.

You already know this man, she thought, as if in answer to herself. What can be so bad about it second time around? Even if you're not ready for it. Fuck me, but don't kill me, please. I don't want to die. Please. Don't make me have come through all this, all the pain and the crap of Tom and me, the learning to be alone, all of this just to become some murder statistic. Somebody they'll talk about. Worse, somebody they'll forget. The tenth victim. The one after he started killing. Oh God, I don't want to die. The thoughts rolled in like heavy surf, she felt herself tumbling over in them, taking in water, unable to think straight.

He brought his face near to hers and pushed his tongue inside her mouth. She wanted to throw up over him. But if she did that she might end up choking on her own vomit.

The sound smashed through the pain. It cut into both the music and the fear. They both froze. The door-bell, long and loud. Somebody was at the door. Somebody had come to save her.

He yanked his tongue out of her mouth but kept his face close to hers, forcing her head backwards.

'Who?' he hissed.

But his hand was so tight she couldn't talk. He loosened his grip. 'The police,' she said quickly. 'They told me they'd come back to check.' The bell rang again, someone was keeping their finger on it this time. Whoever it was they really expected her to be there to answer it. 'They won't go until they see that I'm all right.'

He almost believed her, you could see that from the way he looked wildly round. But he wasn't stupid. That much she already knew. And if the police had been coming back she would have played it as a trump card sooner.

She didn't have much time. She had a sudden flash of Malcolm standing on the doorstep, a bottle of vodka in Christmas wrapping and a couple of spliffs in his jacket pocket. I'm here, she shouted in her head. But whoever it was wouldn't stand outside for ever. Could they hear the music? Maybe not – it was such a quiet track. But it was also ending. Don't go, yet, oh please God, don't go yet. In the silence between songs they would certainly be able to hear a scream.

She never got to deliver it. As the music faded and she opened her mouth he saw the scream coming and slammed his hand into her face, smashing her head back into the glass door. This time his body came with it and she felt the thrust of his prick against her stomach.

The silence came and went and the music started again, Van still in meditative mood, no thumping rock'n'roll chords to boom their way out through wood and glass.

Whoever it was stopped ringing and went away. By the oven door he went to work immediately. The rag came back out of his pocket and this time went straight into her mouth. The fumes were unbearable. They would make her sick. But they wouldn't kill her.

He's taken your voice, so start using your brain. But to do what? Whatever it was, she was going to need her hands. She pushed herself upwards a fraction, to take the strain off her wrists, using the fingers of her right hand to push between the twine and the wrist of her left. If she could free one she could then loosen the other. She had to be careful, though – too much movement in her hands and the oven door would pull open and he would spot it, and read it as an attempt to escape. What she needed was time. And now he was in a hurry.

The bell had made him angry. He was pulling at her pants, impatient, ripping away at the material. His face was sweating now, contorted with something that seemed like pain as much as lust. No, not pain. A kind of fear. Just as on that first night, he was scared. Of her, but also of himself. And it was the fear that would make him kill her.

He moved away from her and fumbled with his trousers, ripping at the stud, pushing down at the waistband to free himself. This was the bit you never saw in the movies. Even the most violent of rape scenes stopped short of showing the engorged cock. Instead you got to read the size of the erection from the

panic and trauma in the woman's face. Her fear working as the trigger of fantasy. The perfect censorship for
voyeurism.

He let out a grunt as the trousers came free and slid
down onto his knees, pushing himself towards her. And
as he did so she suddenly knew what it was that hadn't
made sense to her earlier. If he had spent so long
watching them watching him, when could he possibly
have had time for St John's Way?

There was no space to think of it now. Pinning her
shoulders to the door he tried to slam himself into her.
But this bit wasn't like the movies. With her body half
slumped on the ground he couldn't penetrate properly,
couldn't negotiate the angle of entrance. The failure
drove him wild. 'Get up,' he shouted, trying to push her
body to a standing position. 'Get up or I'll cut you in
two.'

Then came the noise. A battering, crashing wail
from the French windows. They both turned their
heads in time to witness the extraordinary sight of a
middle-aged woman in a winter coat hurling herself at
the window, her arms outstretched against the glass
like some crazed avenging angel.

Christmas morning, and if you can't go to church,
then the church will come to you. The window shook
under the impact but it didn't give. While the spirit was
willing the flesh was weak. And since it is God's will
that the contest between good and evil should be a fair
one, Catherine Baker now found herself trapped on the
outside, a helpless spectator on the dance of death
unfolding within.

In the kitchen, the sight of her drove him into a
frenzy. But it also distracted his attention for a split

second. Now she was ready for him. Using both her hands she grabbed the handle of the oven and, as he turned back to her, yanked the door open with all her might. The side of it caught him full in the face, sending him sprawling backwards into the table. She manipulated the cords on her left hand frantically. As he righted himself she saw there was blood flowing from above one eye. The twine was almost loose enough. He came towards her again. This time she used her foot, going for the exposed groin, missing it, but connecting near enough to the swelling to cause him a crippling pain.

Outside she could hear Catherine shouting, the voice rich and strong, trained on sermons and blessings, raising the alarm. She gave one last tug and her left hand came free. She picked frantically at the right, but the noose was still too tight. With her good hand she could now reach the work top. She grabbed the scissors and started hacking at the twine between her wrist and the door handle.

He was already uncurling himself from the floor and coming towards her, his right eye completely obscured by blood. The twine gave way just as he reached her and she turned, the scissors clasped in front of her.

He rammed so hard into her that it sent the handle digging deep into her stomach. His groan was like the one she remembered from his orgasm, rising up from somewhere dark inside him. He stood rigid against her, his eyes staring into hers, as if trying to work out how it was that she could have hurt him so much, then he fell heavily against her. She had to put her arms around him to stop him crashing to the ground. They stood there clinging to each other, the sticky wetness growing between them like the first wild flow of menstrual blood.

Suddenly, it was as if someone had turned out all the other lights in the world; they were alone together, no avenging angels, no disturbance, not even any voices through the glass. Just a man and a woman squeezed into the stillness between the hands of the clock, all their energy focused on his pain, and the greedy gushing blood.

When she couldn't hold him any longer she slumped down onto the floor, grasping his body and pulling it half across her legs in a bloody pietà. There was so much blood now; it was gulping out over him, soaking his shirt, running down onto her bare legs, the scissors jutting awkwardly from the wound. She was too scared to touch them. He was too bound up inside the pain to care. The one time in her life when she had really hurt herself, had burned a layer of skin off the palm of her hand, the agony had been so intense that the world around had ceased to exist; there had been just her and it, locked in total combat. She saw the same thing in him now.

'It's OK,' she said hoarsely, her voice raw from all kinds of damage. 'It's OK. You're going to be OK. Hang on.'

But even as she said it she knew it was a lie. He tried to say something in response, but the words came out as a vomit of blood, oozing down his chin and onto her hand supporting his head. The feel of it was warm and generous. One more appalling intimacy between them.

He shivered and she pulled her arms tighter around his shoulders, bending her body over him until her head was cradled next to his. It was like the end of their love-making, when she had hugged him and he had started to cry. She should have known then that he wasn't a killer. That the hammer was just a piece of copycat bravura, and that underneath all that fury and frustration there was only pain.

He was having trouble breathing now, the air in his lungs mingling with the blood and sending a gurgling sound up through his throat. It reminded her of Millie when she had found her under the bushes. Another part of their story. They had so much history between them. A relationship really. But then that was what it had been. She knew that now. Soon she would be the only one to know it. To know exactly what it was he had done. And what he hadn't.

She stared down at his face. His skin was going grey, you could actually watch it happen, see the blood and the life draining away. They had been through so much together. Why be embarrassed by difficult questions now? She put her lips next to his ear. 'Can you hear me?' she whispered.

He made a small noise. How familiar they are to me, she thought, all your little grunts and moans.

'It was only me, wasn't it? That's what you meant about choosing me. You never did anything to anybody else, did you? It was always only me.'

A frown flickered over his face, but if he had anything to say, the time for saying it had already passed. Even the blood was ebbing slowly now, the trickle from his mouth already drying on her fingers, crusting on his chin. Instead there was only the pressure of her arms around him and the long wait for the help which was never going to arrive in time. As it hadn't in his life, so it wouldn't in his death.

At some point – she would never know when – the world began again and she found herself back within it. From the commotion going on behind her, she understood that the French windows were being forced open, then the sound of someone in the room.

'We need help here,' she said loudly, her back to the figure, and as she did so she realised she was crying. 'We need an ambulance.'

'It's on its way, Elizabeth,' the voice replied gently, but it didn't come any nearer, didn't try to interfere. Clever Catherine; a woman who knew how to get a number from an unanswered call, a woman who would climb walls when she couldn't get in through front doors. But most of all a woman who recognised a spiritual need as well as a physical one.

She looked down at him, but he didn't seem aware of her any longer. There was nothing else she could give him. It was finished between them. When the end came it was scarcely noticeable. No great Victorian death rattle, not even a last wild sigh, just a stopping, a ceasing, a breath that didn't come after the last one. An absence almost, and a sense of release.

One of his arms had fallen at a strange angle to his body. She picked it up carefully and laid it on his chest. It was then, for the first time, that she noticed the wrist watch. Surprising that she hadn't recognised it before. So easily done; pick it up from a bedside table and slip it onto your own wrist. Of course he would have known where it had been. Two lovers. One watch. Had it given him a sense of ownership or just a sense of time? He didn't need it now. She slipped it over his hand and onto her own.

Behind her she became aware of Catherine's voice, low and rhythmic, speaking intently, with a sense of purpose. But not to her. Given the circumstances of this particular leaving someone would need to have a word with God. And who better to do the interceding?

Sometime after dark it started snowing again, tentatively this time, more like an afterthought, watery little flakes caught in flurries of wind. She stood by the glass and watched them fall.

The room was cold, the boarded up window adequate for security but not for draughts. If she was going to stay up longer she'd need to put on the central heating again. She ought to sleep now, but she wasn't ready to leave the room. It wasn't that she was scared – from the moment she had held him in her arms all the fear had somehow been washed out of her – more that she needed to get used to being on her own again. After twelve hours of policemen, doctors and forensic gatherers, crawling like lice over the kitchen, their absence was almost as disconcerting as their presence.

The first thing she did was to take a scrubbing brush to the floor. In the movies the stain always remains, the blood soaking through the cracks into the very fabric of the world, black instead of red. But here, in her kitchen, she found that it washed away too easily. She looked around her. Clean the surfaces, put the hinge back on the oven, take off the boards and reglaze the windows and there would be nothing left. Nothing, that is, but her memory. Somehow it didn't seem enough. She left a corner of the stain untouched. Maybe given time it would seep its way into the wood. A wound in the floor. It was the most and the least she could offer him.

Police files would supply the rest of his immortality, though he would always be a footnote rather than a headline. Mad stalker as opposed to serial killer. That was what the army of fluid and fibre collectors were there to verify; there was only one scene to his crime, and only one victim.

They hadn't needed much convincing.

From what they had told her it sounded almost routine. Like many before him, the real Holloway Hammer had turned out to be an otherwise respect-able fellow: a freelance car mechanic, married with two kids, living in Hendon and working on a break-down contract for the AA in the Islington, Holloway area. The kind of job that took him all places at all hours. Especially in the winter. But in St John's Way at four that Christmas morning his luck had run out when a woman across the road had spotted a suspicious-looking man coming out of a basement flat and walk-ing to the end of the road to where an AA truck was parked. Sometimes, somewhere, even the cleverest of them get careless.

He'd been playing with his kids when they got to him, setting up a Christmas model garage for his youngest boy, his wife in the kitchen peeling the sprouts for lunch. Just a regular sort of bloke. Hard to imagine his family visiting him in prison.

She had listened quietly while Veronica related it –

the two of them sitting together in the living room as
they had the night before. When she got to the capture
the policewoman had barely been able to conceal her
excitement. Maybe this was a first time for her too.

As for the others, they had been kindness itself. The
police doctor they wheeled in had offered pain killers
and sedatives. She took the first and refused the
second, even so her throat was too swollen to do much
talking. They didn't seem to mind. Most of what they
needed to know was there for them to see. She added
only what was necessary. The rest she kept private,
between him and her. Like the end of any relationship
it was not for public consumption.

Later, Catherine Baker had called to offer her a bed
for the night. But there would be time enough for the
two of them to talk if the guilt didn't wash away with
the bloodstains and for this of all nights she needed to
be alone.

She went upstairs and ran herself a bath. She
stripped off her trousers (her other clothes – the blood-
soaked skirt and the top were long gone, preserved in
plastic and carefully labelled for the forensic labs) and
as she did so something fell out of her pocket. The wrist
watch from his hand. She had slipped it in there during
the interrogation and then forgotten all about it.
Strictly speaking it was evidence now. But not unless
she told them. She picked it up and let it lie in the palm
of her hand. To whom did it belong now? Caught
between the two men, maybe it would be OK to keep it
herself. Or maybe not.

She looked at the time. 11.10 p.m. Christmas Day. A
lot of dope and videos would have gone down by now.
In another incarnation she might have felt like phoning

him. But not now. There would be time enough for such things another day, if she so decided.

She laid the watch on the edge of the bath, near to her head, and soaked in the hot foam, eyes closed, listening as it ticked away the seconds till midnight.

Afterwards she put on her robe and returned to the kitchen.

She stood in the doorway and took it all in: the smashed window, the scrubbed floor, the leftovers of a violent history. What did she feel? Sorrow? Pity? An echo of fear? The words of the Morrison song came back to her. '*So quiet in here. So peaceful.*'

The snow had stopped now and the garden was dark. She moved over to the work top. She turned on the stereo, her fingers picking up the dust of finger-print powder. She blew them clean, then pushed the eject button. The CD compartment slid open, but the disc had gone. Police business, no doubt. It seemed almost fitting, the whole thing ending as it had begun. 'Enlightenment'. She had another copy of it some-where, but it was too early to be that brave. She would play it again though. She knew that now. Because although she didn't quite understand why, it was clear that in some way the healing had begun. She turned the phrase over in her mind. It found its own cadence. 'The Healing Has Begun': track eight from the album, 'Into the Music', blue cover, 1979. Van the Man in love and in recovery.

She ran her fingers along the spines until she found it, then slipped it into the machine, cueing it into the track and watching the seconds tick by as it played . . .

'*We're going to make music underneath the stars.*
We're going to play violin and the two guitars.

*And we're going sit there for hours an' hours an'
hours.
When the healing has begun ...'*

Like all great albums this one renewed itself with
each era. She had once made love to this song with a
man who had turned out to be less important than she
had at first thought. But the track itself had grown and
grown inside her, until she knew every flow and note of
it; the way the piano came in like shafts of sunshine, the
way the arrangement got looser and looser, like two
bodies who couldn't get enough of each other, the
sense of their intoxication growing through each long
musical phrase.

Maybe that was the point about love. You never
knew where you were going to find it. Which one was
going to last or which one fade away. That was why
you had to keep on trying. Until then, all you could do
was to keep on listening.

She turned the music up and looked out over the
back gardens. Christmas night and the world was a
safer place than it had been twenty-four hours before.
Safer and emptier. She found herself looking for the
one light that she knew would not be on. How much
was she going to miss him? Or the him in her. It wasn't a
question she could answer yet. Maybe she never
would.

*'I want you to put on your red summer dress.
Wear your Easter bonnet and all the rest.
And I want to make love to you, yes yes.
When the healing has begun.'*

Roll on the spring when she could open the windows
and let the world in again.

Go to bed, Lizzie, she thought. You have a book to

finish and in the real world the night is for sleeping.

As the track finished she turned and went upstairs to bed, leaving the CD playing, and the door to the rest of the house unlocked behind her.

acknowledgements

This book, like my life, is made much richer by the music in it. A special thanks to Van Morrison and Exile Publishing Ltd/Polygram Music Ltd who gave permission for me to use lyrics from 'So Quiet Here' and 'The Healing Has Begun'.

'The Music of Love' words and music by k. d. lang and Ben Mink © copyright 1992 Bumstead Productions (US) Incorporated/Polygram International Publishing Incorporated/Zavion Enterprises Incorporated/Rondor Music International Incorporated, USA. Polygram Music Publishing Ltd, 47 British Grove, London W4/ Rondor Music (London) Ltd, 10a Parson's Green, London SW6. Used by permission of Music Sales Ltd. All rights reserved. International Copyright Secured. 'Ain't Got No Money' words and music by Frankie Miller © copyright 1976 Chrysalis Music Limited, The Chrysalis Building, Bramley Road, London W10. Used by permission of Music Sales Ltd. All rights reserved. International Copyright Secured. 'Drop Baby Drop' words and music by Eddie Grant by permission of International Music Publications Ltd.

Warner Books now offers an exciting range of quality titles by both established and new authors. All of the books in this series are available from:

Little, Brown and Company (UK),
P.O. Box 11,
Falmouth,
Cornwall TR10 9EN.

Fax No: 01326 317444.
Telephone No: 01326 372400
E-mail: books@barni.avel.co.uk

Payments can be made as follows: cheque, postal order (payable to Little, Brown and Company) or by credit cards, Visa/Access. Do not send cash or currency. UK customers and B.F.P.O. please allow £1.00 for postage and packing for the first book, plus 50p for the second book, plus 30p for each additional book up to a maximum charge of £3.00 (7 books plus).

Overseas customers including Ireland, please allow £2.00 for the first book plus £1.00 for the second book, plus 50p for each additional book.

NAME (Block Letters) ....

....

ADDRESS ....

....

....

☐ I enclose my remittance for ....

☐ I wish to pay by Access/Visa Card

Number ⬚⬚⬚⬚⬚⬚⬚⬚⬚⬚⬚⬚⬚⬚⬚⬚⬚⬚

Card Expiry Date ⬚⬚⬚⬚